Discover the Golden Treasure
of Timeless Romance

Don't Miss These Other Timeless
Romances From Avon Books

GENTLE ROGUE
by Johanna Lindsey

WHEN LOVE COMMANDS
by Jennifer Wilde

GYPSY LADY
by Shirlee Busbee

SWEET SAVAGE LOVE
by Rosemary Rogers

DEVIL'S DESIRE
by Laurie McBain

THE FULFILLMENT
by LaVyrle Spencer

SO WORTHY MY LOVE
by Kathleen E. Woodiwiss

Other Avon Books by
Bertrice Small

LOVE WILD AND FAIR

BERTRICE SMALL

THE KADIN

AVON BOOKS

An Imprint of HarperCollins*Publishers*

To my dearest husband, George, who, having lived all these years with Cyra, Firousi, Zuleika, Sarina, and me, can tell you that having a harem isn't what it's cracked up to be.

This is a work of fiction. Names, characters, places, and incidents either are the products of the author's imagination or are used fictitiously. Any resemblance to actual events, locales, organizations, or persons, living or dead, is entirely coincidental.

AVON BOOKS
An Imprint of HarperCollins*Publishers*
10 East 53rd Street
New York, New York 10022-5299

Copyright © 1978 by Bertrice Small
Library of Congress Catalog Card Number: 77-99226
ISBN: 0-380-01699-0
www.avonromance.com

First Avon Books printing: February 1978

Avon Trademark Reg. U.S. Pat. Off. and in Other Countries, Marca Registrada, Hecho en U.S.A.
HarperCollins® is a trademark of HarperCollins Publishers Inc.

Printed in the U.S.A.

30 29 28

CONTENTS

Prologue   1

PART I   7
The Ambassador's
Daughter
1490–1493

PART II   63
Cyra
1493–1494

PART III   167
The Kadin
1501–1520

PART IV   305
Hafise
1520–1533

PART V   365
Janet
1533–1542

Epilogue   440

CONTENTS

Prologue
April, 1484

GLENKIRK CASTLE stood dark against the gray sky, its drawbridge down. Along the walls, men-at-arms paced slowly, always on guard. There was peace in the land, but yesterday's friend could easily became today's foe.

From within the castle courtyard came the sudden sound of hooves. A large black horse ridden by a man wearing a cape clattered across the drawbridge and onto the road. The rider, his cape fluttering wildly in the wind, pushed the animal into a gallop.

Behind him, Patrick Leslie, lord of Glenkirk, left a group of wailing women, his newborn son, and his dead wife, Agnes.

As he rode on, his mind slipped back to the weeks and months just past.

He had waited eagerly for the birth of his heir. Agnes had had an easy confinement, managing to keep her sunny disposition even in the beginning when she had been so sick in the mornings. Patrick Leslie was twenty-four and, having been orphaned at ten, had grown up guided by an old uncle and the men-at-arms who inhabited his home. He had married late, and in a time when most men his age had sired several sons, he had sired none. Then his eye had lit upon the petite, golden-haired daughter of the Cummings clan. He had married her quickly, and with what some said was almost indecent haste.

The day they both awaited had finally come. Anxiously he had paced the anteroom outside his wife's bedchamber, his cousin, Ian, keeping him company. There had come a loud and lusty wail; and a few moments later his wife's lady-in-waiting appeared in the doorway, a small bundle in her arms.

1

"Your son, my lord. The lady Agnes wishes to know what ye would name him."

Patrick grinned broadly and stared down at the tiny, wrinkled creature. "Adam. Tell her he is to be called Adam, for he is but the first."

The lady-in-waiting curtsied and returned through the door with the infant. Ian Leslie cocked his head.

"The first, cousin? What of little Janet?"

"Adam is my first son, my legitimate heir, you clod!"

Ian chuckled and ducked the friendly blow aimed at him.

"You'd best send a messenger to Agnes's family, or Lady Cummings will be on your neck, and what's worse, she'll be moving in for a long stay unless you reassure her quickly."

Patrick nodded. As they turned to leave the room, the door to Agnes's bedroom opened, and a little maid flew out. "The lady Agnes . . . the lady Agnes . . ."

Patrick grabbed her and shook her sharply. "In God's name, girl, what is wrong?"

"Blood," wailed the servant, "blood! Oh, Holy Mother have mercy on her!" Sobbing, she rushed from the room.

Patrick Leslie crossed the room in two strides, but the open door to his wife's bedchamber was barred by the midwife. "She is dying, my lord. There is nothing I can do."

"What," he asked, "in God's name has happened?"

"She is bleeding, and we canna stop it, my lord. Ye hae best go in now. She dinna hae much time." The midwife's face registered her genuine distress. She liked the lord of Glenkirk and thought that his lady was a brave and bonnie lass.

Pushing past her, he strode quickly to his wife's bedside. Agnes Leslie lay quietly on the large bed, her blond hair spread about her pillow. Her fair skin was drained of all its color, her closed eyelids translucent and blue-veined. He bent and kissed her brow.

"You have given me a magnificent son, madam."

Her gray eyes opened, and she smiled weakly at him. "You must ask Mary MacKay to come and look after the bairn. She is not too old."

"You'll ask her yourself, sweetheart."

"Patrick, I am dying."

He groaned and turned his head away.

Her fingers gently caressed his face. "My poor Patrick," she whispered. "Never able to face that which displeases him."

He turned back to her. "Love," he pleaded, "you must not talk this way. You'll get well. You must!"

"Patrick," her voice was urgent now. "You'll keep your promise to me?"

He looked at her blankly.

"When I told you I should give you a child, I asked that when it was born, you bring Janet to Glenkirk. You promised to legitimize her and let me raise her with our own child. She is your true daughter, Patrick. She is a Leslie."

"How can I manage without you?" he pleaded.

"Swear to me, Patrick. Swear on the Holy Virgin's name!"

"I cannot."

"Patrick!" Her voice sank low. "This is my dying wish. Swear!"

"I swear it! I swear it on the Holy Virgin's name. I'll bring my daughter, Janet, to Glenkirk, legitimize her, and raise her with our son, Adam."

"Thank you, Patrick. God will bless you for it," said Agnes Leslie, and then she died.

The lord of Glenkirk was brought back to reality as his horse, out of habit, slowed his gait and turned off the high road into a tree-lined lane. At the end of the lane stood a neat thatched cottage. At the sound of the horse's hooves, a small apple-cheeked woman appeared in the doorway and called out.

"Patrick, ye dinna tell me ye were coming. How is Agnes?"

"Agnes is dead," he said bitterly.

"The bairn?"

"A lad. Healthy and strong." Dismounting, he followed her into the cottage.

"Do ye want to tell me about it, Patrick?"

"I don't understand it, Mary. Everything was fine. Then the midwife told me she was bleeding and they could not stop it. It was over so quickly."

"Och, my poor boy! I am so sorry."

"Before she died, she asked two things of me. One

was that you return to Glenkirk and look after the bairn.
Will you, Mary?"

"Yes, Patrick. I was your nurse, and I'll be nurse to
your son. What was her other dying wish?"

"That I legitimize Janet and raise her with our son at
Glenkirk. She asked it when she first knew she was with
child. It was her last request of me, and I swore on the
Virgin's name I would."

"God bless her and rest her sweet soul," whispered
Mary MacKay. "Many a wife would have held my lass
against you, even though it happened before ye were wed.
Agnes Cummings was a good woman."

He nodded.

"But if ye wed again, Patrick, how would another wife
feel about Janet?"

"I have killed two women with the bearing of my
bairns, Mary. First your own daughter, Meg, who was just
sixteen. Now Agnes, and she but seventeen. I'll never wed
again."

"Bad luck, my lad. Plain bad luck, but the porridge is
burned now. If one day ye decide to make another pot, I
suppose we can cope then. Tell me, what will ye call the
babe?"

"Adam."

" 'Tis a good name."

For a moment they sat in silence before the hearth fire,
and then he asked, "Where is Janet? I want to take her
back to Glenkirk tonight."

"In the shed looking at the new lambs." She went to
the door and called, "Janet, your father is here."

A little girl of four, her unruly, reddish-gold hair flying,
ran to the cottage.

"Father, you never said you were coming! What have
you brought me?"

"She is surely your daughter, Patrick Leslie," sighed
Mary.

"A pocketful of kisses and a bag of hugs, you greedy
minx," he laughed, snatching her up. She giggled and
snuggled into his arms. "Janet, how would you like to go
back to Glenkirk with me tonight?"

"To live, father?"

"Yes."

"For always?"

"As long as you want, my little sweetheart."

"Can grandmother come, too?"

"Yes, Janet. Your grandmother is going to come and take care of your new brother, Adam."

"And may I call the lady Agnes mother?"

Mary MacKay turned white.

"Lady Agnes is dead, Janet," said Patrick Leslie. "She has gone to Heaven like your own sweet mother."

Janet sighed. "Then you have only grandmother, Adam, and me, father?"

"Yes, Janet."

The child shifted in her father's arms and thought for a moment. Finally she looked up at him with her strangely adult green-gold eyes and said, "Then I'll go to Glenkirk with you, father."

Patrick turned to Mary MacKay. "Get her cloak. I'll send a cart for you and your things tomorrow."

Mary bundled the child into a woolen cloak and took her outside where her father, already mounted on his horse, waited. Handing the child up, she said, "Dinna grieve, Patrick. Ye must think of the children now."

"I know, Mary, I know." And, wheeling his horse around, he rode back through the fast-darkening day toward Glenkirk Castle, his small daughter seated before him on his saddle.

PART I

The Ambassador's
Daughter

1490–1493

1

Wiping his hands on his shirt, James IV, king of Scotland and the Isles, leaned back in his chair and surveyed the scene before him. On his left sat Patrick Leslie, lord of Glenkirk, who at the moment was engaged in conversation with James's lovely mistress.

James's eyes swept the room. A minstrel sang a sad song of the Borders, and the unusually warm March day made the hall reek of the long, unaired winter. The king noted from beneath hooded eyelids that many eyes were darting back and forth between himself and Patrick Leslie. Good, he thought. Let the scheming bastards wonder! Dear God! Why are there so few I can trust? But he already knew the answer to that question.

On his right sat the Hepburn of Hailes, newly created earl of Bothwell, who, James saw, had an ardent admirer in the person of a young red-headed girl who was sneaking a look at Bothwell from beneath her lashes.

"They say you seek to wed with a Gordon, my lord."

"At court only two days, Mistress Leslie, and already up on the gossip?" the earl replied, looking down at his little admirer.

"Choose Lady Mary, my lord. She is bonnie and sweet of temper."

"And Lady Jane?" said Bothwell.

"She has cat's eyes and the Devil's own temper—so I am told," she added demurely.

Lady Jane Gordon, who was sitting on the other side of the earl, glowered at the child. "Since when does my cousin Jamie allow young brats at his table?" she demanded.

"I am not a brat, my lady."

Lady Jane Gordon rose from her seat. "I have half a mind to box your impudent ears," she snapped.

The little girl stood, legs apart, facing her beautiful antagonist. " 'Stand Fast' is my family's motto. Yours is something about 'cunning,' isn't it, Lady Jane?"

The room became deathly quiet as Lady Jane Gordon, hands raised, advanced on Janet Leslie. But Janet didn't wait for the regal hands of Lady Jane to smack her. Instead, fists flying, nails raking, Janet flew at her.

Caught off guard, Lady Jane Gordon screamed in surprise and tried to protect herself. Laughing, the earl of Bothwell stood up and, prying the child loose, swung her up in his arms.

"Put me down," shrieked Janet, beating at his chest with her hands.

"Hold, lassie, the battle is over, and you've won. Hush now," murmured the earl, setting her down.

Janet looked up at him with her green eyes.

"Give us a smile now, lass."

The corners of the little girl's mouth curled up, and she said, "You smell of heather and the moors, my lord."

Bothwell grinned delightedly, and the king snapped, "Will someone send that flirtatious minx to her bed before she starts a feud between the Leslies and my Gordon cousins?"

Patrick Leslie rose and walked over to claim his wayward daughter.

Janet's face darkened. "I'll not go," she shouted, "unless Bothwell takes me!"

The hall erupted with the loud guffaws of the men mingled with the embarrassed titters of the women, all of whom knew too well the earl's reputation with the ladies.

"God's nightgown," roared James. "How old is that wench of yours, Leslie?"

"Ten, sire."

"God help us all when she's fourteen! She'll turn this court upside down. Very well, my lady Janet. Lord Bothwell will escort you to your apartments. Leslie, you come with me." James faced the hall. "The rest of you, get out and go back to your schemes and intrigues! The feast is over."

The king moved swiftly to his own quarters with Glenkirk following. Settling himself in a chair, he looked up at the Highland chief standing before him.

"So, my lord of Glenkirk, it takes a royal summons to get you to court," said James Stuart.

"Aye, Your Majesty."

"Yet you were one of the few Highland chiefs who supported me against my late father. Why is that?"

"I felt Your Majesty had the right on his side. In his day your father was a great king, but he grew old and foolish, and Scotland needed a young man to rule her. So I supported Your Majesty. I have kept from court because my estates need me and, as Your Majesty well knows, I am not a man of intrigue. Intrigue is necessary to survival here in Edinburgh."

"Perhaps not a man of intrigue, Patrick Leslie, but certainly one of great diplomacy. That is why I have summoned you." The lord of Glenkirk looked puzzled, but James continued. "I am the first king of the Scots to send ambassadors to represent me in other countries. I want you to serve as my ambassador to the duchy of San Lorenzo."

"Your Majesty will forgive my ignorance," said Patrick, "but where *is* San Lorenzo?"

James Stuart laughed. "I didn't know of it myself until several months ago. It's a tiny country on the Mediterranean, but it is vital to our merchant trade with Venice and the East. Our dear cousin Henry of England has been trying to get a toehold there for several years, but his emissaries are as dour and as pinchpenny as Henry himself. They annoy the duke, who is a man of culture and generosity. He sent a delegation to me this Christmas past. I sent them back with many fine gifts and the promise that I should send an ambassador come spring."

"But Your Majesty," protested Patrick, "I am no court gallant! I am a simple Highland chief. I know only of my lands and my people. Surely there is someone more suited than I."

"Nay, my lord. I want you. For all your talk, I know you to be an educated man, a man with a silver tongue, they say. The duke of San Lorenzo is a man of elegant tastes. Those wily fools my cousin of England has sent to him have angered him to the point of turning to me simply to annoy Henry. Scotland is a poor country, Patrick. With a haven of safety in the Mediterranean where our ships can stop to replenish their water and supplies, we can

trade with the Levant, and England will pay dearly for
what we can bring back! I have asked nothing of you before, my lord, but I ask this. Do not make me command
it. I value your friendship and loyalty too much."

"But who will look after my estates and my people?"

"We shall send your cousin, Ian. He is honest and loyal.
Also, he has angered too many husbands and fathers here
at court with his winning ways. We will choose him a good
wife and send him to Glenkirk as steward over your estates."

"How long must I stay in San Lorenzo, sire?"

"I shall ask you to remain only three years, Patrick.
Then I shall send someone else, and you may return.
Take your household and family with you." James rose
and stood by the window. "You have two children?"

"Aye, Your Majesty. My son, Adam, who is six, and
Janet, my daughter."

"Ah," smiled the king. "The little redheaded wench
who bested Lady Jane Gordon tonight. What a vixen! Is
she bethrothed?"

"She is only ten, sire."

"Many a lass has been wed that young. The duke of
San Lorenzo has an heir, a boy of fourteen. We should not
be displeased if he is taken with your girl. However, that
is not a command. He could turn out to be a snaggle-
toothed dolt, and I should not like to see one of our Scots
lasses wasted on a fool."

"Thank you, Your Majesty," said Patrick wryly.

"You will be ready to leave within the month. Sir
Andrew Wood will arrange for your passage and that of
your family and servants—and, Patrick, because I wish to
do the duke honor, I am creating you earl of Glenkirk."

The interview was at an end. Patrick Leslie bowed low
and backed out of the room. His head was whirling. Earl
of Glenkirk! Ambassador to the duchy of San Lorenzo! A
possible marriage for his daughter with one of the oldest—
albeit smallest—royal houses in Europe! He should be
elated, yet he wasn't. He felt sad, as if he had lost something very dear to him. Cursing his mystical Celtic herit-
age, he shrugged and hurried off to tell his family the
news.

2

SAN LORENZO basked beneath the warm September sun. Its emerald-green hillsides, tumbling gently to the sea, flashed occasional spots of red, yellow, and orange flowers. To the south, the vineyards burst with plump purple and gold wine grapes; and in the valley beyond the coastal hills, the ripening grain eagerly awaited the harvest.

Perched precariously above the Mediterranean in wild and colorful disorder was its capital. The cobbled streets of the town ran up and down past houses of every hue, not one the same. Hence its name, Arcobaleno, meaning "rainbow" in Italian.

Overlooking the town sat the palace of Sebastian, duke of San Lorenzo. Slightly below it, facing on the sea, was the pink marble villa where his excellency, Patrick Leslie, earl of Glenkirk, ambassador of His Most Catholic Majesty, James of Scotland, had resided for two years.

Lady Janet Mary Leslie sat cross-legged upon her bed, brushing her long, red-gold hair. Her green eyes sparkled mischievously at her eight-year-old brother, Adam, who impatiently paced the room.

"For heaven's sakes, Jan, can't you hurry? You've kept Rudi waiting almost an hour now!"

She laughed. "You may go on if you wish, Adam, but I'll bet Rudi won't go without me."

"You are a vixen, Janet Leslie, just as father says," retorted the boy.

"And you, Master Saucebox, are allowed to ride with us only because 'tis more seemly now that I am of marriageable age!"

"Hah," snapped Adam. "Marriageable age, indeed! Father will not allow your bethrothal to Rudi until you are at least fourteen!"

"He never said that to me."

"One does not discuss these things with a mere female," said Adam loftily.

"You were eavesdropping! Oh Adam, tell me what father said! I'll give you one of Fiona's puppies when they're born."

"Pick of the litter?"

Janet debated. She wanted to give Rudi the best pup, but her curiosity was too great, so she nodded her consent.

Adam climbed upon the bed next to his sister and said in a conspiratorial voice, "I wasn't really eavesdropping, Jan. Father forgot I was waiting for him. I overheard him talking to Duke Sebastian last night. He said he felt even fourteen was too young, but he'd permit it provided the marriage isn't celebrated until you are sixteen or seventeen."

"You're a liar, Adam Leslie!"

"I am not! Ask him yourself!"

Janet jumped off the bed and, giving a shake of her hips to settle her long skirt, ran from the room. She was a tall girl for her age, and the recent onset of puberty had matured her slender body. Her mind raced as she traveled the corridor to her father's suite. She had hoped next Christmas would bring the announcement of her bethrothal to Rudolfo, heir to the duchy of San Lorenzo, with their marriage to follow within the year. Pushing past a startled servant, she burst into her father's rooms.

Patrick Leslie had been lying upon his bed fondling a well-endowed, golden-skinned brunette. He leaped up, smothering an oath. "You have been told not to enter my chambers without knocking, Janet!"

"You would not have heard me, my lord father." She mocked a curtsy. "I want to speak with you on a matter of great importance."

Patrick turned to the girl on the bed. "Get out!" The girl rose slowly, her mouth sulky. "But don't go far," he added. Her mouth turned up in a smile, the girl slipped out.

"And now, my lady, what is so important that you burst into my rooms unannounced?"

"Adam said he overheard you tell Duke Sebastian you would not permit my bethrothal until I was at least fourteen, and then no marriage until I'm sixteen."

"Your brother has large ears and talks too much," answered Patrick.

"Then it's true?"

"Aye, Jan."

"Why, father? Why must you do this to me? Fourteen is not too young to be wed."

"I will not have you die at fifteen in childbirth, like your mother, or Adam's!"

"God's foot!" she swore. "I'm nothing like Meg in either face or form, and as for Agnes, she was frail. Leslie women have always been good breeders, and I'm Leslie-born." The last was said proudly.

Patrick winced. He adored his daughter and always had. Why did time go so quickly? Yesterday she was but a wee lass climbing into his lap to wheedle a story out of him. Now she stood before him, no longer a child, but—dammit!—she was not yet a woman, either.

Janet continued. "Look, father." She pulled her skirt tight across her flat belly, revealing a wide span between hip bones. "Grandmother says I'm meant to bear children. So do Brother Dundas and Padre Gian."

"Goddamn your grandmother and those prattling priests to Hell!" he shouted explosively. "I'll not see you wed at fourteen! What do you know of marriage, and for God's sake, don't quote the catechism to me! You think it will be all fetes and hunting parties. Well, let me tell you, my fine lady, it won't be! You'll be expected to produce an heir posthaste, and then protect the precious succession with a gaggle of brothers and sisters. At the first sign you are with child, you'll be cloistered like a nun. As for Rudi, you'll scarce see him, except for the bed!"

"That's not so!" Janet stamped her foot at him. "Rudi is every bit the gentle knight."

"Aye, in the courting. But once the marriage is consummated and you are big with child, he'll be off with some appealing creature like the one who waits for me now."

"I'll have him get me with child," she retorted defiantly. "Then you'll have to let us wed!"

Patrick Leslie grabbed his willful daughter by her arms and stared down into her face. His fingers pressed cruelly into her soft flesh. His voice was dangerously low. "I'll not be defied, mistress. If you should dare to try to force my hand, I'll ship you back to Scotland to a convent; and, bairn or no, you'll remain there until you rot! Do you really think Rudi would wait? He'd marry some Medici or some princess from Toulouse." Releasing her, he took the heart-shaped face in his strong hand and looked down at his stubborn daughter. "Och, Jan. I've had you such a short time. Would you leave me so soon?"

"But, father, I am a woman."

"By scarce two months," he observed wryly.

"Oh, you are impossible," she shouted.

Patrick burst into laughter. "All right, you witch. I'll compromise with you, but only providing my physician says you are strong and fit. If he agrees, the betrothal will be announced next Christmas as Duke Sebastian desires."

Janet's face lit up.

"But," he continued, "the wedding will not take place until your fifteenth birthday."

Janet picked up her skirts and danced about the room. "Thank you, father! Thank you! I must go tell Grandmother Mary and Adam." Whirling by him, she planted a kiss on his cheek and danced out of the room. "You may go in now," she told the waiting brunette.

3

Janet Leslie's betrothal day dawned clear, bright and warm. It was December 6, the feast of Saint Nicholas. Lying quietly in her bed, Janet allowed herself the luxury of a few moments' peace before the day to come. She was very excited and, at the same time, frightened at the finality of the step she was taking.

At noon her father would lead her into the cathedral in Arcobaleno where she and Rudi would be formally betrothed by the bishop. On her fifteenth birthday, which was just two years and six days away, she would be wed. She shivered in happy anticipation.

Entering the room, Flora, her maid, called softly, "Mistress, it is time you were up. Your bath is waiting."

She helped the girl arise and removed her nightgown. Walking across the cool tile floor, Janet stepped into her bath. It was scented with roses. Flora, a stern older woman who had been with Janet since she was four, scrubbed the girl vigorously, then, commanding her to stand, poured clean water over Janet to rinse her creamy skin. Toweling her dry, she sat her young mistress down and pared both her finger- and toenails.

Mary MacKay entered the room, followed by two servant girls who carried Janet's betrothal gown. It was her first adult dress, and she eagerly stepped into it. Mary looked fondly at her granddaughter. There is nothing at all of my Meg in her, she thought. Janet is pure Leslie.

Gazing at her image in the mirror, young Lady Janet Leslie knew she was beautiful. Her gown was of heavy white silk with a deep-cut, square neckline and long, flowing sleeves. Beneath it she wore a low-cut bodice and a petticoat of silk. An inverted V, embroidered with gold flowers, divided the skirt into two panels. Between the

17

panels the pristine silk glistened. At the point of the V she
pinned a broach fashioned of gold, diamonds, and topazes
—her betrothal gift from Rudi.

Flora set a cape of topaz-colored velvet about her shoulders. Her grandmother gave her hair, which was unbound
to show she was a maiden, a final brush, and placed a
small cap of gold mesh upon her head. She was ready.

Patrick Leslie, equally resplendent in a suit of dark-
green velvet, felt a pang of remorse at the sight of his
daughter. Damn James Stuart, he thought. If it weren't for
him, this betrothal would not have happened. But in his
heart the earl knew that whether it be Rudolfo di San
Lorenzo or some other lad, he would have lost his daughter someday. He consoled himself with the fact that the
wedding would not take place for almost two years.

"You are most bonnie, little sweetheart," he said.

Janet smiled at him and, placing her hand in his, accompanied him to the waiting horses.

The day had become unbearably hot for December.
Even within the cathedral, with its thick stone walls, the
moist, sticky heat prevailed. The old bishop droned on
longer than usual, and Janet silently sent up a prayer of
thanks that she had forbidden a Mass on this occasion.
The High Mass should be reserved for the wedding, not a
simple betrothal ceremony, she had told them.

Then, mercifully, it was over, and she and Rudi signed
the official documents which contracted them to marriage.
As they left the cathedral, they stopped and stood a moment on the top steps of the church. The slender, red-
haired girl, and the tall, handsome, curly-headed boy
heard the joyous cries of the San Lorenzans. They were
both so young, so beautiful, and so touchingly innocent
that the people below, taking them to their hearts, cheered
louder.

Rudi's tanned face flashed a smile. "I have a present
for you," he said.

"A present? But I thought the broach was my betrothal
gift."

"It is. By tradition. This is something that I have personally picked for you."

She smiled back at him. "What is it?"

"A surprise," he answered, leading her down the steps
and setting her upon her horse. "You'll see it when we get

back to the palace, but I assure you you've never had anything like it before. You will be the envy of every woman in San Lorenzo."

They rode back up the hill to the palace to accept the congratulations of the entire ducal family, the clergy, and the other nobility of the region. Afterward, alone with their immediate family, Rudi slipped his arm about her tiny waist.

"Did I tell you I love you today, cara mia?"

"Just today?"

"Every day, my sweet," and he kissed the tip of her ear.

She blushed, and he laughed. "Being my fiancée officially has made you more demure. It is most charming."

"Rudolfo," boomed the duke, "I think this would be a good time to present Gianetta with her gifts." He clapped his hands, and a troupe of servants entered bearing trays of packages and bouquets. Much to everyone's amusement, Janet cried out in delight.

"Now you see why I am hesitant about letting her wed so young," chuckled Patrick to Duke Sebastian.

"Marriage will mature her," replied the duke.

The white-leather case Janet first reached for contained the San Lorenzo pearls—the traditional gift of the reigning duke to his future daughter-in-law. The duchess presented her with a red morocco toilette case containing two combs, a brush, and a mirror of gold; a gold box holding tortoise-shell hairpins; three Venetian crystal scent bottles, one filled with rosewater, one with lavender, and the third with rare Eastern musk; and a pale blue velvet bag containing pure white wax candles and a crystal-and-gold candlestick.

Young Adam had brought his sister a gold ring fashioned with the Leslie coat of arms and engraved inside with the words, "To my own dear sister, Janet, from Adam." She rose, walked over to him, and kissed him on the cheek.

"You are the sweetest brother any girl could have."

Adam flushed and wriggled in embarrassment.

Janet turned back to her gifts. On the last tray was a beautifully carved leather saddle.

"Oh, Rudi," she exclaimed, "it's wonderful!"

"But it is not from me, cara. It is from your father."

"But you said you had another gift for me, and there are no others left."

"Greedy wench," said Patrick.

"Oh, father," she giggled. "I'm sorry. The saddle is a marvelous gift."

"It goes with something else, little sweetheart. Come out on the terrace and see what your grandmother has for you."

The entire family adjourned to the terrace. There, standing quietly, was a beautiful white mare, and holding her bridle was a young black man wearing bright red satin pantaloons, a yellow turban with a white plume, and a gold earring in his left ear. His bare chest had been oiled, and it glistened in the bright sun.

"The mare's name is Heather," said Patrick.

"And this," said Rudi, placing a hand on the black man's shoulder, "is Mamud. He is a tamed and Christianized African, and my special gift to you. I purchased him from a trading ship that put in here last week. He is gelded, and therefore a eunuch."

Though Janet was delighted with Mamud, Mary MacKay was not. She was quite horrified. "Black as a crow, and he'll bring bad luck, too," she said. "What could Master Rudi have been thinking to give ye such a gift?"

Mamud regarded the Scotswoman warily out of liquid brown eyes and immediately summed her up as the enemy.

"Don't be silly, grandmother. Blackamoors are becoming quite the fashion."

"If he were a child, it would be one thing," persisted the older woman, "but he is not. Gelded or nae, I dinna like the looks of him."

That evening, Janet stood on her balcony overlooking the sea. The day had been a long one, and she was relieved that it was over. A jagged streak of lightning cut across the sky, followed by a rumble of thunder that echoed into the hills. Soon the rain would begin, bringing an end to this awful heat.

Janet moved from the balcony and lay down on her bed. Closing her eyes, she let her body relax and her mind wander. Something had happened to her this evening that seemed to indicate that Rudi was as eager as she to be wed.

They had been sitting in the duke's garden. Rudi, who up to this point had given her no more than an occasional kiss on the cheek, had slipped his arm around her and kissed her on the mouth. At first she had been startled, but as Rudi whispered soft endearments in her ear, she had allowed herself to be kissed again. Her innocently ardent response had encouraged his hands to begin a gentle fondling of her breasts. Janet had heard herself murmuring in soft contentment as her body grew warm and strangely weak. But the sudden loud sounds of her brother and Rudi's younger brothers playing a boisterous game nearby had roused her, and she had pulled away, suddenly frightened.

Rudi had smiled slowly at her. "It is a long time until our wedding day, Gianetta."

"I know," she had sighed, "but father is firm."

Reliving that moment in the privacy of her bedchamber, Janet began to wonder if her father weren't right. She loved Rudi terribly, but he had awakened feelings in her she wasn't sure she was equipped to handle at this moment. Perhaps she *was* too young.

Maybe, she thought, I shall ask father to move the wedding date, and maybe not. I have plenty of time to decide.

The rain came in a rush and began to beat fiercely on the red-tile roof of the villa. Flopping over on her stomach, Janet allowed the sound of the rain to lull her, and promptly fell asleep.

4

CHRISTMAS WAS OVER, and the new year of Our Lord, one thousand four hundred and ninety-three, had begun. The holidays, with all their feasting and merriment, had been happy ones. No longer considered a child, but not yet quite a woman, Janet had been expected to take up some of the duties of a future duchess of San Lorenzo. She had appeared with Rudi at all official and church functions, and on Christmas Day had distributed alms to the poor of Arcobaleno. She was feeling very grown up.

Under her grandmother's guidance, she gradually began to take over the task of running her father's house. When she became the reigning duchess of San Lorenzo, it would be her duty to oversee the housekeeping and provisioning of the castle. She would become responsible for seeing that the servants did their work well and for the feeding of the entire household—family, retainers, servants, and soldiers. She must learn how to order the provisions, which meant studying many recipes, and she must learn the difference between ordinary wines and those fit for the palates of the nobility.

However, the matter of servant discipline was the hardest lesson of all. By nature Janet was softhearted, and the servants knew it. One day Janet overheard two young kitchenmaids discussing the desire of one of them to go to the carnival with a butcher's apprentice.

"Just tell her," said the first, "that you want to go home to visit your sick mother. She will be all sympathy and will not question you."

Janet seethed. She did not like being made a fool, but her anger quickly died, and her good Scots common sense took over. When the kitchenmaid requested leave to visit her ailing mother, Janet was all sympathy. Of course

22

she must go and, continued Janet, she herself would accompany the girl with a basket of delicacies to speed the poor invalid's recovery.

The little maid was terrified. Unable to shake her mistress's good intentions, she finally burst into tears and confessed the deception. Janet sent for the other kitchenmaid and then pronounced punishment.

"You," she said to the weeping girl, "will receive five lashes for lying to me. It is little punishment, but the soreness of your guilt will be greater than the soreness of your back. I know you will not lie to me again. Had you asked to go to the carnival, I should have allowed it provided your work was done."

The girl fell to her knees and kissed the hem of her mistress's dress.

Janet turned to the instigator of the plot. "Your crime is far worse," she said sternly. "You encouraged your friend to deceive me. You will receive ten lashes at the end of this day's work. Then you will spend the night in the chapel praying to Our Blessed Lady Mary to help you mend your ways. I will pray with you so you will not be tempted to sleep. If any servant should lie to me again, I will dismiss him or her immediately."

The servants learned their lesson well, but so did Janet. She never again indulged them. Only the blackamoor, Mamud, was spoiled.

He had turned out to be a wonderful gift. His command of Italian increased daily. He kept Adam amused by the hour, telling him stories of his native land, showing him how to track and trap small animals, and even teaching him a smattering of Arabic. Janet joined him in these lessons, for she loved the study of languages and was quite adept at it.

Mamud was also an excellent sailor, and one sunny afternoon in early February, Janet, unable to sleep during the customary siesta, called to him to go sailing. Passing Adam's room, she looked in and observed the boy sprawled sleeping across his bed. Kissing his russet head, she walked on. She stopped a servant on the terrace steps and told him, "Tell my grandmother that I have gone sailing with Mamud and will return by sunset." The servant nodded, and Janet walked down to the beach where Mamud waited ready to push the small craft into the surf.

The afternoon was balmy and breezy. The sea, a clear

azure green capped with white foam, sparkled and danced in the sunlight. Janet noted that Mamud had set a basket with white bread, a small yellow cheese, some fruit, and a flask of wine in a corner of the boat. She complimented him on his thoughtfulness, and he flashed her a smile, his teeth blindingly white against his black face.

Sailing into her favorite cove, Janet motioned to Mamud to lower the sail, and the little boat scudded up onto the sand. Taking the basket, she leaped out and walked up the beach.

"Do you wish to swim, my lady?"

"Aye. Do you, Mamud?"

"Yes, mistress. I love the sea."

Janet pointed to a strip of secluded beach a short distance away. "Very well, go along."

"But, mistress, I should watch you lest you drown."

"I am a strong swimmer, and you need have no fears, my good Mamud. Go."

Reluctantly he left her, and, now alone, Janet divested herself of the simple peasant skirt and bodice she wore. The sea was cool and tingling, and she swam slowly, letting the gentle current waft her along. Turning, she returned to the shore and flopped down on the warm sand. Loosening her hair, she shook the water out of it and braided it up, then slipped her skirt and bodice back on over her dry skin.

Down the beach Mamud cavorted in the waves like a porpoise, and when he returned she motioned him to sit. Delving into the hamper, she spread the simple meal on a napkin.

The late-afternoon sun was warm, and the wine from the hamper sweet. Janet lazily studied the young black man who sat slightly apart from her. She was normally an outgoing, inquisitive girl, and by this time should have known everything about Mamud's history right down to his great-grandparents, but her recent elevation as the future duchess of San Lorenzo had completely occupied her time. Mamud actually spent more time with her brother. Adam, she was sure, knew all about him. Suddenly she could no longer contain her curiosity.

"Mamud," she said, "I wish to know of your past life. Were you born a slave?"

"No, mistress. I am the son of a chief in my own land.

One day Muslim slavers raided our village. I was captured while seeing to the safety of my wife and son. My only consolation is that they are safe."

"You are married? Then you cannot be a eunuch."

"The slaver told that to my lord Rudolfo so he would buy me."

"Oh," she said in a small voice.

The slave laughed. "My lady need not be afraid. By the standards of my tribe, my lady is quite ugly."

Janet stared at him for a moment, wondering if she should be offended. Then she chuckled. "This will be our secret, Mamud. As soon as I can find a way, you shall have your freedom."

"Thank you, mistress. I would do anything for my freedom."

Picking up the basket, Mamud helped his young mistress into their small boat and pushed it back into the sea. Raising the sail, he turned the craft to catch the wind. The sun was just beginning its nightly trip into the Mediterranean. Staying close to the coast, he guided the boat toward Arcobaleno.

As they rounded a small point, they saw a ship within the cove, apparently taking on water. Mamud made for it.

"What are you doing, Mamud? We have not time to visit that ship, and besides, it doesn't look like a merchantman to me. Turn the boat."

The slave stared straight ahead and gripped the tiller.

"I order you to turn this boat at once, Mamud. The sun will soon be gone. We must reach home before dark."

"You will not be going home, mistress. I told you I would do anything for my freedom, and delivering you to a slaver for gold will gain me that freedom."

Flinging herself at him, she grappled with him for the tiller. She fought desperately, but Mamud raised his arm and shoved her away. Tumbling back, she struck her head against the side of the boat. She struggled to maintain consciousness, but the blow was hard, and she spiraled downward into the blackness. Somewhere in that darkness she felt a thud, then hands upon her body, followed by the feeling of floating freely, and then the hands again.

Upon regaining her senses, she became aware of a rocking motion and realized she was aboard the ship. Hearing voices nearby, she cautiously opened her eyes and looked about her. She was lying on a divan in a moderate-sized cabin. Beside her a little window looked out on the sea. There was the coast of San Lorenzo. The ship was still at anchor.

Turning her head slightly, she saw Mamud and another man who was white but was dressed like her slave. They were talking. She cocked her head to hear.

"How will you explain the girl's disappearance to her father?" the white man asked.

"I will tell him we were attacked by pirates. I fought valiantly to save my mistress but was overcome and thrown into the sea for dead. Your men must strike me several times so I look beaten. I shall swim to shore and walk back. Capsize the boat."

"Your plan is sound, but what will it gain you except the money we've paid you for the girl?"

"The earl is a sentimental man. He will not want me around to remind him of the girl. Since he really doesn't believe in slavery, he will free me rather than be reminded of his precious daughter. I am sure of it! With papers of manumission from him and the money you've paid me, I can safely return to my home."

Janet had heard enough. Leaping from the divan, she dashed through the cabin door to the ship's rail, but before she could leap overboard, two arms grasped her tightly and hauled her, kicking, back to the cabin. "You pig," she shrieked, flying at Mamud's face with her nails. He leaped back, startled at the gentle girl's sudden rage.

"You have sold me a tigress, Mamud," laughed the slaver captain, catching hold of Janet. "Calm down, little lady. No one will harm you."

Janet faced the captain. "What ransom are you asking? Whatever it is, my father will pay it. Do you know who I am? This sly slave has misled you. I am no pretty peasant girl. I am the Lady Janet Mary Leslie, daughter of Lord Patrick Leslie, the earl of Glenkirk. My father is the ambassor of His Most Catholic Majesty, James of Scotland, to the court of San Lorenzo. I am betrothed to Rudolfo, heir to Duke Sebastian."

"Your pedigree is most impressive, my lady. However, there will be no ransom. You will be taken to Crete, where you will be sold to the highest bidder at auction.

No ransom can possibly match what you will bring on the block."

Janet turned to Mamud. "How could you?" she asked.

"I am truly sorry, mistress, but I told you I would do anything to gain my freedom. I was a gift from your betrothed. How could you free me without offending him? It would have taken a miracle, and I do not believe in miracles."

"I hope my father finds out what you've done, Mamud, and when he does, may God help you."

The slave grinned at her, and Janet hit him so hard that Adam's ring opened a cut near his eye. The captain shouted for his servant, who dashed through the door and pinioned the girl's arms. Janet opened her mouth and began to scream. Quickly the captain motioned Mamud out of the cabin and, dropping something into a goblet of water, forced her to drink. Unconsciousness came quickly and mercifully.

Her first realization of returning consciousness was the cradlelike rocking of the ship. She lay quietly for a moment, lulled by the false sense of security. Then, remembering where she was, she rose quietly from the divan and inspected her prison.

The cabin was spacious and furnished in the Eastern manner, with a thick carpet on the floor, a large, pillowed divan, a low, round, inlaid table, more pillows, and several hanging brass lamps. Looking out the little window, she saw the moonlight sprinkling itself across the now-dark sea.

Turning back to the cabin, she noticed wine and a goblet on the table. Suddenly she realized how thirsty she was and, pouring herself a full measure, drank it down. Its fire restored the warmth to her chilled body. The sound of a bolt being drawn on the door sent her spinning around, and as it opened, she hurled the goblet at the man who stood there.

"Your aim is no less impressive than your beauty, my little lady. And now, if you have vented your anger, let us talk. I am Captain Gian-Carlo Venutti, at your service."

"You are a pig and a bandit, Captain Venutti! If you are truly at my service, you will return me to San Lorenzo at once! I will personally guarantee your safety and a large reward."

Captain Venutti ignored her words. "Lady Janet," he began, "I sail under the protection of Venice. We are now on our way to Candia on the island of Crete. You will be sold at auction to the highest bidder, and a substantial portion of this profit will go into the Venetian treasury."

"But the duke of San Lorenzo will pay a large ransom for my safe return."

"We are businessmen, not kidnappers. My dear young lady, is it possible you do not realize how beautiful you are? All the money in San Lorenzo could not purchase your freedom. You are worth a king's ransom, and now the matter is closed. Please do not distress yourself by trying to escape. Your every move will be watched. I hope you will be comfortable here. If you desire anything, simply ask the slave at the door." Then he left her, locking the door behind him.

For the next six days the ship sailed smoothly across the waters of the Mediterranean. Captain Venutti allowed Janet a small measure of freedom and gave her a portion of the upper deck for exercise and air. In order to take her mind off her predicament, he pointed out the different islands and their characteristics.

Corfu, second largest of the Ionian isles, and very, very fertile. Mount Aenos, towering over mountainous little Cephalonia. Tiny Zante, which not only raised sheep and goats but somehow managed to grow grapes, olives, wheat, and a variety of fruits. And, of course, the Peloponnesus of southern Greece, also called Morea, and now under Turkish rule. Here, aside from the usual grapes and olives, tobacco was also raised, a small silk industry flourished, and there was an enormous fishing fleet.

On the evening of the sixth day, the ship reached Candia. The pleasant cruise was at an end, and Janet faced the frightening reality of her situation, and the fact that she might never see her family again.

5

LORD PATRICK LESLIE had gone wild on learning of his daughter's disappearance. The slave Mamud, coming from a world where women counted for less than animals, had read his lord wrong. The noble Scot did not reward him with gold and his freedom for his alleged valor in defense of his young mistress. Instead, the enraged father had him clapped in irons and thrown into the duke's dungeons pending a thorough investigation of his story. Mamud had been right about one thing—Patrick Leslie wanted the slave out of his sight!

Duke Sebastian's executioners questioned Mamud carefully and with great skill. Their first discovery was that the eunuch was not a eunuch after all—a situation they quickly remedied.

Then he was tortured, and throughout the process, one nonparticipant watched. Standing stoically in her dark silk gown and starched coif, clutching a plaid shawl about her shoulders to keep out the dampness of the dungeons, Mary MacKay's blue eyes never left Mamud's face. The slave was, and always had been, deathly afraid of the old woman's light-colored eyes. He felt they saw things that mortal eyes did not. She knew what he had done, he thought. She waited only for his verbal confirmation and the details.

Slowly, with care, his toenails were removed with red-hot pincers. Mamud shrieked prayers to his tribal gods as this new pain ripped up his legs, through his thighs, and slammed into his chest, almost suffocating him. Rivers of sweat poured down his body.

He closed his eyes to blot out the pain. When he opened them again, he found that woman standing at his side. Her eyes bored into his, and he felt his little strength ebb away.

"What hae ye done with my granddaughter? Who has her?"

He did not want to answer. He wanted to confound and curse the old witch, but he couldn't. Those terrible blue eyes were the strongest magic he had ever encountered.

"Who has my granddaughter?" she repeated.

"Captain Venutti," he heard his own voice croak. "Captain Gian-Carlo Venutti of the Venetian Levant!"

She touched his chest, and he shivered violently.

"Go, laddie," she said, and he died.

Mamud's confession was substantiated when a ship's captain putting in from Crete spoke in a tavern of a young, red-haired Christian slave girl to be auctioned within a month. Brought before the duke and the Scots ambassador, the captain repeated his story.

It was common knowledge in the Mediterranean community, said the seaman. An old trick to excite interest and bring in the top connoisseurs. Yes, Captain Venutti of the Venetian Levant was the slave girl's current owner. She was booty from a raid, it was said, and rumored to be quite a beauty. Curse Venutti! He had all the luck.

Patrick Leslie ground his teeth in rage. He would have outfitted a warship and stormed Candia to rescue his daughter, but Duke Sebastian prevailed. Mediterranean-born, he was used to these situations and knew how to handle them. He would send his cousin, Pietro di San Lorenzo, to the auction to buy the girl back.

In that way, if the girl were saved, he would stand high in the Scots king's favor; if she were lost, no one could blame him, and the sticky diplomatic situation that would ensue between his country and Scotland would quickly blow over.

Perhaps his clever cousin *could* pull it off and regain the little maiden, but privately he doubted it.

In any case, there could no longer be any possibility of young Lady Janet's marrying his heir. God only knew what had happened to the girl during her captivity. He was a liberal man, but a duchess of San Lorenzo must be above suspicion. Already there had been a tentative overture concerning a match from Toulouse, and he had made secret inquiries of his own archbishop about annuling the betrothal between his son and the Scots girl; but these thoughts Duke Sebastian kept to himself.

He turned to his companion. "Come, my friend," he said to Patrick Leslie. "All will work out well, and as God wills it."

The earl of Glenkirk, suspecting the wily duke's thoughts, glowered at him in impotent fury but said nothing.

6

SEVERAL WEEKS LATER, Janet sat quietly in an alcove off a private auction room. She sat quietly, not because she had suddenly become docile, but because she was still partly in shock. The betrayal of Mamud was more than her young mind could grasp, and the swift trip from San Lorenzo to the auction block in Candia had left her numb.

She had not been treated unkindly at any time since her abduction. Indeed, every effort had been made to provide for her health and comfort. Captain Venutti had brought her from his ship to the house of Abdul ben Abdul, a purveyor of the best merchandise in the world—as Abdul himself had told her. She had been pampered and cosseted for over a month while word swept the Mediterranean of the virgin with the red-gold hair who would be sold at the next full moon.

During this period she had been kept secluded from the sun while her body was bathed in perfumed waters and bleached with lemons to restore its true whiteness. She had been massaged with sweet-smelling creams until her skin was like silk to the touch. Her tan, under this treatment, had gradually given way to its natural Celtic white.

This night, the slaves had clothed her in a strange garment. A diaphanous fabric of a pale gold color, it was long, pleated, and covered her from her collarbone to her ankles. It was belted at the waist with a green ribbon and tied at each shoulder with matching green ribbons. A long veil of the same color as her dress covered her hair, which had been gathered in one piece, secured with a pearl clasp, and hung down her back. Another veil covered her face, leaving only her green-gold eyes, highlighted with kohl, visible.

She was not afraid, however, for the visit of Pietro di

San Lorenzo, Duke Sebastian's cousin, who had been sent
to buy her freedom, had given hope. He had arrived on a
swift ship from Arcobaleno and, by bribing the head eunuch in Abdul ben Abdul's house, had been allowed to
visit her for a few minutes. He carried a great deal of gold,
which he assured Janet would buy her freedom. His only
regret was that a lady of her high station would have to
submit to public auction, but there was no other way.

Secretly, Pietro di San Lorenzo was worried. Word was
spreading quickly about Janet Leslie, and already several
important buyers had arrived from the East. There was
even a rumor that Hadji Bey, chief of the Turkish sultan's
eunuchs, was coming. Pietro put this down to Abdul ben
Abdul's desire to get as large a price as possible. Nevertheless, Pietro prayed fervently that he could rescue his
cousin's daughter-in-law-to-be. If he did, the reward would
be great, but if he lost the girl—well, the wrath not only of
Lord Patrick Leslie but of the king of Scotland would fall
upon his country. The whole situation was disastrous.

Janet looked up as a black eunuch touched her arm.
"Come, little lady. It is almost time for the sale. I will pull
the curtain aside a crack so that you may see the illustrious
company you have attracted."

Fascinated in spite of herself, Janet followed him and
peeked through the curtain. She saw a room, neither large
nor small, a little platform in its center, the walls covered
with frescos of men, women, and animals whose activities
left nothing to the imagination. There were only about
twelve men in the room, one of them Pietro di San Lorenzo.

"Why are there so few buyers?" she asked the eunuch.

The eunuch smiled broadly. "My master, Abdul ben
Abdul, blessings be upon him, has set an opening bid on
you of five thousand pieces of gold. You are not merchandise for a camel driver!"

Janet had the ridiculous urge to laugh at the prissy attitude of the eunuch, but then Abdul ben Abdul entered
the room, and the eunuch quickly led her out onto the platform. The buyers turned eager eyes upward to the platform
where she stood. The beginnings of fear lightly touched
Janet Leslie.

Abdul ben Abdul slipped his hand beneath her elbow

and drew her toward the center of the stage. "French," he said softly, "is the language of trade. You will understand all."

"You are wasting your time and shaming me with this foolish charade," she said. "Pietro di San Lorenzo will purchase me, and I shall be returned to my father."

"Allah forbid," returned the slave merchant, and he turned to his clientele. "My friends, we come now to the most important sale of this year. This high-born virgin with hair like a golden-red sunrise, skin as smooth and white as polished bone, and eyes the color of the rarest emeralds. Behold, gentlemen!" Quickly he removed the veil that covered her head. "The opening bid is five thousand gold pieces. Who will bid?"

"Five thousand," came a voice.

Abdul ben Abdul smiled. "The agent of the sultan of Egypt bids five thousand."

The bidding came thick and fast—six thousand, seven, eight, nine, ten thousand pieces of gold.

"Gentlemen," said Abdul ben Abdul in a voice filled with hurt, "you insult my house by offering a mere ten thousand gold pieces. This is a rare and priceless jewel, a houri that would grace the harem of the Prophet himself. This maiden has never known a man." He brushed a soft, flabby hand lightly across Janet's belly. Instinctively, she recoiled. "She will bear many strong sons."

"You have proof of her virginity?" said a voice.

"I have," said Abdul. "I will give the purchaser three certificates of proof signed by three different doctors. If they have lied to me, I will refund the buyer triple his money, and he may keep the girl, besides."

An excited buzz ran around the room. Abdul ben Abdul was considered an honest merchant, but not one to part lightly with a dinar. It was proof enough. The bidding began again.

Janet's eyes swept the faces of the bidders for the first time. The agent of the sultan of Egypt stared back at her coldly, and she quickly looked away. There was something sinister about the man, and her stomach turned uneasily. The representative of the caliph of Baghdad reminded her of a small worried black owl, but her urge to laugh was quickly stifled when she glanced toward the man her prissy eunuch had identified as the prince of Samarkand. His cruel Mongol eyes swept her body lustfully, with an open passion that revolted her. Swiftly she turned her gaze to the kindly face of Pietro di San Lorenzo who nodded at her reassuringly. But he had yet to offer a bid.

At a nod from Abdul, the eunuch loosened the ribbons at her shoulder, and the tunic fell, baring her to the waist. Sudden silence filled the room as a dozen pair of eyes greedily feasted upon the girl's perfectly formed, rose-tipped breasts.

With the wisdom of his Semitic ancestors Abdul ben Abdul gave them a minute to look, then said, "The bidding stands at fifteen thousand six hundred pieces of gold for this exquisite but as yet unopened flower." Sixteen thousand, seventeen thousand, seventeen thousand five hundred.

Abdul motioned to the eunuch, who now untied the ribbons at Janet's waist. The tunic slipped with a whisper to her feet, and a sigh ran through the bidders. Janet was completely naked.

At this point, Janet felt as if her mind and her body were two separate entities, and wondered why she hadn't fainted at this new shame to her body. But all the while, a voice pounded in her ears: "A Leslie never shows fear. A Leslie never shows fear." Stiffening her backbone, she stood still—cold and scarcely breathing.

Eighteen thousand. Eighteen thousand nine hundred. Like a dog sensing the kill the slave merchant reached out and with one hand removed the pearl clasp holding Janet's hair. It spread over her shoulders and back like a fan. With the other hand he whisked the veil from her face.

"By the teats of Fatima," came another faceless voice, "a face that rivals the body."

"The caliph of Baghdad bids twenty thousand gold pieces!"

Oh, holy Mary, thought Janet, there isn't that much money in all of Scotland, let alone San Lorenzo. I am lost!

"And the duke of San Lorenzo bids twenty-five thousand gold pieces to ransom his son's beloved betrothed."

Inwardly, Janet whispered gratefully, "I apologize, gentle Mary. I will give you a finely wrought enamel-and-silver statue with real sapphire eyes in thanks for my deliverance."

"Twenty-five thousand," taunted the voice of Abdul ben

Abdul. "Who will bid more?" He looked hopefully about the room. It was a good price. Janet heaved a sigh of relief in the deep silence of the room. Abdul had raised his gavel to finalize the sale when a voice called out, "The sultan of Turkey bids thirty thousand gold pieces." A tall, slender, elegantly garbed man made his way to the platform. "I am Hadji Bey, chief of the sultan's black eunuchs." He flung the happy Abdul a purse. "You may count it," he said.

Janet glanced at him from beneath her lowered eyelashes. His height dwarfed all in the room, and though his features were Negroid, he was, she was sure, of mixed blood. His skin, unlike that of other dark men she had seen, was neither black nor brown, but rather a rich, deep, golden color. His eyes were somewhat elongated in shape and shone velvety black beneath their heavy-lashed, hooded lids. His forehead was high, the smooth brow running into a shaved round skull that showed from beneath a small green turban. His nose had a slim bridge that widened as it descended to broad, flaring nostrils, and his lips were thick and sensual. His body had none of the flabbiness associated with eunuchs, lacking the sagging breasts Janet found so obscene in these castrated men. This was probably due in part to his height. He was a large man, but definitely not fat.

His clothing was magnificent. He wore a long-sleeved, open pelisse, spring-green in color and banded from neck to hem and also at the midarm and wrists with dark, glossy sable. It was lined, she saw when he moved, in gold cloth. Beneath it shone a flowered red silk brocade underrobe belted with a broad gold sash which was sewn with a fortune in tiny pearls and emeralds. His turban sported a cabochon emerald from which sprouted a white egret feather, and his feet were encased in very soft, heelless dark brown leather boots. Rings adorned his long, supple fingers, and about his neck he wore a heavy round gold medallion in which was carved a lion's head.

Pietro di San Lorenzo leaped upon the platform. "I protest! You raised your gavel to finalize the sale," he shouted at Abdul ben Abdul. "The girl is mine!"

"But I did not knock with it. If you wish to bid again, I will permit it."

Hadji Bey smiled gently. "Yes, good knight. If you desire to raise my bid, feel free to do so."

Pietro turned to the other men in the room. "By your own religious laws, this auction is illegal. This girl is betrothed to the heir of the duke of San Lorenzo. The contracts were formally signed last December in the cathedral of Arcobaleno. Your religion forbids the taking of a living man's wife, and by the signing of the contract, she is as good as his wife. She was abducted from her home and brought here by force."

"Our laws do not apply to infidels any more than your Christian laws apply to us," said Hadji Bey. "Raise my bid or let me depart with my merchandise."

"He buys her for a man old enough to be her grandfather," pleaded Pietro di San Lorenzo. "You all have gold with you. Lend it to me, and I will repay you double. Let me return my cousin's bride to him."

Stony silence greeted his words. What Pietro said about the Turkish sultan was true, but no man among the bidders would defy Bajazet's agent.

"Count the gold," commanded Hadji Bey to the merchant.

"No, no, my lord agha," said Abdul ben Abdul, mentally weighing it in one hand. "There is no need."

Hadji Bey turned to a now very frightened, shivering Janet. Removing his pelisse, he wrapped it about her. "Come, my child," he said kindly.

"We shall come to Turkey, my lady. We will ransom you!" shouted Pietro di San Lorenzo.

Hadji Bey turned on him. "Do not lie to the girl and fill her with useless hope. There is no ransom from the seraglio of my master. Tell her the truth so that she may face her new life honestly and without fear."

The knight looked up at Janet with sorrowing eyes. Her heart went out to him. "Do not grieve, my lord," she said, "but promise me you will go to my father and tell him of all that has transpired. The slave Mamud betrayed me." She felt the gentle pressure of a hand upon her shoulder. "And, my lord, tell him I will return to Glenkirk one day. Promise me!"

The knight nodded, and as she walked bravely off the platform, he felt a tear roll down his cheek.

7

BUNDLING JANET into one of the two waiting litters, Hadji Bey stepped into the other. Quickly the bearers hurried their passengers through the warm, moonlit night, finally stopping before a large house. Slaves rushed to help the girl out, leading her through the building's open atrium into a small, pleasantly furnished, cheerfully lit room. Clapping his hands, Hadji Bey gave instructions in a strange tongue to the slave who answered his summons. Then he turned to Janet.

"I have ordered the slave to bring you more suitable garments, but before she returns, please remove the cloak."

Janet stared at him.

"The cloak, my child," he repeated gently. "The light at the merchant Abdul's was poor. I did not get a proper look at you."

"Then why did you buy me?"

"Your hair and face alone were well worth the price. Now, the cloak," he said, holding out his hand.

Not quite understanding her compliance, Janet let the cloak slip from her shoulders to the floor. She stood quietly in her young nakedness while the eunuch gravely studied her.

Janet was too young and inexperienced to comprehend how truly lovely she was. Having attained her growth in the last year, she seemed tall for her age, though actually she was of medium height. She had long, slim legs. Her narrow waist flowed into softly rounded hips. Her chest was broad, the bones well hidden, and her breasts high and full. Her smooth, flawless skin glowed with good health. Hadji Bey noticed with pleasure that her green-gold eyes were clear, good evidence that she had not wept a great deal and was, therefore, of strong character.

"Turn, please," he said.

She did so gracefully, which again brought pleasure to the eunuch, and further corroboration of his wisdom in spending such an outrageous sum.

The slave returned and helped Janet into lime-green Turkish trousers, a matching bodice, and an amber-colored silk caftan. The slave then silently stole out.

"Now, my child," said Hadji Bey, "I think it is time to introduce you to your two companions."

Taking Janet's small hand in his, he led her from the little chamber to a large, airy suite facing on the sea. The first thing Janet saw upon entering were two young women of approximately her own age. One was petite, faintly plump, and silvery-blond; the other was quite tall, dark-haired, and had an oval face containing two bright, almond-shaped eyes of jet black. They rose as Hadji Bey came toward them. Drawing the blond to him, he said to Janet, "This is Firousi, so called because her eyes are the shade of the turquoise, or firousi in our tongue. She is from the Caucasus."

Firousi smiled at Janet. "How wonderful that you are to join us. We are now a beautiful trio." She spoke in perfect but accented French.

"And," continued Hadji Bey, "this is Zuleika."

"I've never seen anyone like her before," whispered Janet.

"Of course you haven't. I am from Cathay." She, too, spoke in French, though she was harder to understand than Firousi.

"You are from Marco Polo's Cathay?"

"Yes."

"What is her name, Hadji Bey?" asked Firousi.

"She will be called Cyra."

"My name is Janet Mary Leslie," snapped Janet with a flash of her old spirit.

"Hardly a suitable name for a Turkish sultan's gediklis," smiled Hadji Bey. "In my own ancient tongue, Cyra means 'Flame.' It is most suitable. Now, my children, I shall leave you to get acquainted. You will have tomorrow to rest and gather your strength. We leave on tomorrow

night's tide for Constantinople." Bowing slightly, he
turned and departed.

Janet stood gazing out over the silvery, moonlit harbor
of Candia. It was packed with ships whose tiny lights
twinkled at her in a friendly fashion. Among them was a
ship from San Lorenzo—from Rudi.

"Go ahead," said Firousi, reading her thoughts. "Try
it."

Janet stepped over the threshold into the garden. Two
turbaned black slaves, each holding a curved scimitar,
stepped to her side. Quickly she stepped back.

"There is no escape, Cyra," said the blond girl. "The
sooner you accept that fact, the happier you will be."

Janet began to sob.

"Why do you cry?" asked Firousi.

"In that harbor lies a ship which waits to carry me back
to my father, my little brother, and my betrothed—if I
could but reach it."

"Well, you can't," said Firousi bluntly. "You're lucky.
At least you have a family living. My entire family, including my husband, are all dead, killed by Tartar slaves."

"You were married?"

Firousi nodded and, clapping her hands, summoned a
slave to bring food, for she sensed Janet might now be hungry.

"I will tell you my story, Cyra." Her lovely eyes grew
misty in remembrance as she began her tale.

On her wedding day, she had awakened just before
dawn and slipped quietly out of bed. Pushing back the
wooden shutters of the window, she saw the cobwebby
mists rising above the newly green meadows. Her wedding
day would be fair and warm.

My wedding day, she thought. My wedding day! It has
all come about because my brother saved the life of our
enemy's youngest child. Now I will marry his oldest son,
and our villages will live in peace forever. I don't even
know what this Pyotr looks like or if he is a kind man, and
when I ask papa, he just chuckles.

She turned as the curtain that separated her tiny bedchamber from the main room of the house was pulled
back, and her family, laughing and singing, spilled inside.
Her great, bearlike father, her small, plump mother, her

sisters—Katya, the eldest, with her husband, and Tanya, the youngest. Here were her brothers Paul, Gregor, Boris, and Ivan, all her aunts, uncles, and cousins with their arms full of spring flowers.

"So," boomed her father, "the bride cannot sleep."

"And she'll get no sleep tonight," laughed Gregor.

"You," said his mother sternly, but her eyes were laughing, "put down your flowers, and then out! All of you! Katya and Tanya, remain."

They left her with her cheeks wet with their kisses and her arms full of flowers.

"Now, Marya," said Sonya Rostov, "first you must eat." She placed the plate and cup she was carrying on a small table. "Poppy rolls, jam, and tea with sugar."

Katya raised an eyebrow. Her wedding breakfast had been brown bread, honey, and goat's milk. Mama would deny, of course, any favoritism toward her daughters, but Marya had always been her pet. Look at the wedding gown, for instance. When the old peddler had visited them last winter, he had had a length of creamy white silk in his pack, and nothing would do but that silk have that silk for Marya's gown. And gold thread for the embroidery, and little white Turkish slippers embroidered with gold thread and little seed pearls. Papa had growled that he wasn't the Grand Turk marrying off his daughter, just a simple Caucasian mountain farmer; but when the peddler had left, Mama had had the silk, the gold thread, and the slippers—at the cost of two fine goats.

Katya smiled wryly as she watched her sister eat the soft white rolls. My wedding gown was wool, and hers is silk. But silk becomes Marya, with her fair, creamy skin, her silvery-blond hair, and her turquoise eyes. A smack from her mother brought Katya back to the present.

"Get the water heating over the fire for Marya's bath, daydreamer. Tanya, take your sister's dishes and wash them."

The morning flew by, and the noon hour approached. The entire village was decked in festive finery for the wedding of its headman's daughter. Tables had been set up in a field by the church for the feasting. Suddenly a boy posted at the edge of the village cried out, "They come!"

Marya flew to the window and peeped out. A tall youth on a white pony led the procession. He laughed merrily,

his dark eyes sparkling as the children who scampered by
his side shouted, "The bridegroom comes! Make way!"

Marya felt her mother's arm about her shoulders. "That
is your husband, daughter."

"He is so handsome," she whispered.

"Pah," snapped Sonya. "His looks are a bonus and
would mean nothing if he were not a good man, which he
is. Do you think that papa and I would give you to just any
man?"

The people of both villages murmured appreciatively
as Marya Rostov was led past them to the church by her
parents. Her gold-embroidered white silk skirt and blouse
lay over several petticoats of sheer white wool, two of
which were ruffled in silk. A wreath of yellow and white
flowers crowned her head.

"What a little beauty!" exclaimed Pyotr Tumanov to his
father. "When you would not let me see her, I had visions
of a goat-faced horror. If she is as sweet as she looks, I will
be a happy man."

"Then you will be happy," replied his father. "If I had
let you see her before today, she would be no virgin. This
marriage is to settle a feud, not to start another."

The couple met at the altar, and Father Georgi Rostov,
Marya's uncle, joined them in wedlock. Shyly Marya
looked up at her new husband, who, perceiving her genuine innocence, kissed her tenderly and said, "How do you
do, Madam Tumanova. I do believe I love you."

Blushing, but with her eyes twinkling, she returned,
"And I also, husband."

Nikolai Rostov had spared no expense for his daughter's
wedding feast. Whole goats and lambs turned slowly over
the fires on their spits. The wine flowed endlessly. The
tables were piled high with fruits, breads, and cakes. By
late afternoon almost everyone was pleasantly drunk, and
the bride and groom became the targets of broader and
broader jests. So it was with befuddled amazement that the
revelers turned at the cry of "Fire!" The village was
ablaze, and Marya watched in horror as the Tartar raiders,
white teeth gleaming in their yellow faces, swept down on
the celebration.

It was a slaughter. Neither the Rostovs nor the
Tumanovs had come armed to the wedding. There were
screams and shouts. People began running. Marya grabbed

her two younger brothers, Boris and Ivan, and her little sister Tanya.

"Quick, hide in the woods!"

Twelve-year-old Boris struggled in her grasp. "I want to fight them!"

Marya slapped him hard. "Father, Paul, and Gregor are dead," she hissed at him. "You are now head of the family. Take Ivan and Tanya to safety! In God's name, Boris, run!"

He hesitated a moment, then, taking his brother and sister by the hand, sped toward the trees. In less than a minute—though it seemed an eternity—the children disappeared into the forest. A terrifying scream rent the air near her, and Marya turned to see Katya writhing in a bloodied patch of grass miscarrying her baby while the three men who had just raped her stood nearby, encouraging those who now assaulted her mother. Feeling an arm tighten about her waist, she shrieked, only to hear her bridegroom say, "Quick, Marya, the forest! Hide before they take you, too!"

She looked up at him. His wedding garments were torn and grimy, and a purple bruise was visible on his cheek. He held a bloody meat spit in his hand.

"I will not leave you. Come with me, Pyotr."

He shook his head.

"Then I will die with you, my husband."

"They will not kill you, my dove. They are Tartar slavers. Run, my bride, before—" His words were cut short as he fell forward. Behind him a huge Tartar withdrew his lance.

"Pyotr!" Her cry tore the firelit twilight. She fell to her knees and tried to raise him. He was dead. Stealthily she reached for the meat spit. Grasping it firmly, she leaped to her feet and attacked. The Tartar, surprised, received a small wound before disarming her.

"Murderer!"

Grabbing her, he ground his mouth on hers in a wet, disgusting kiss; and then, with his foot, he knocked her legs from beneath her while he pulled up her skirts. They fell to the ground. Straddling her, the Tartar fumbled with his breeches while his other hand held her down by the throat.

Struggling to escape him, she felt herself choking.

Suddenly a voice cried, "Hold!" As his grip relaxed, she gasped great gulps of air to clear her head. Her assailant was pulled off her, and she was dragged to her feet before a tall Tartar on a horse.

"Yesukai, you great fool! Can you not see that this girl is the cause of our good fortune? Behold, the bride!"

"But Batu, why may I not have her?"

The hetman dismounted. "Are you a virgin, girl?" She did not answer.

Grabbing her by the hair, he cruelly twisted her face to his. "Are you a virgin?"

"Yes!"

"No little games in the mountain before the wedding?"

"We met for the first time today."

"Bring a torch," shouted the chief.

It was handed to him. He thrust it toward Marya.

"By the gods, a real beauty!" Turning to his men, he roared, "Hear me, all of you sons of the Devil. Any man who so much as glances at this girl is dead. She will bring us a fortune in Damascus. What a beauty! And a virgin to boot. Gather up the women and children, you idlers, and pen them in for the night. We leave at dawn!"

The church was the only building left in the village. Marya and the other survivors were herded into it, but not before all the little boys were separated from them.

"Why have they taken the boys?" Marya asked her aunt.

"They will castrate the prettier ones to be sold and trained as eunuchs," said the woman numbly.

Shortly afterward, most of the boys reappeared—frightened but unharmed. Three were missing, and their mothers cried out in anguish and tore at their hair as horrifying screams came from outside the church. Moments later, three Tartars entered, carrying the unconscious, disfigured boys to be cared for by the women.

At dawn, they began the trek to Damascus. The Tartars rode while their captives walked. One of the castrated boys had died in the night.

Marya, now numb with shock, plodded along, speaking to no one. At first her fellow unfortunates had looked to her—their chief's daughter—as their leader, but now they left her alone. Marya's aunt walked at her side, glowering fiercely at any Tartar who came too near, bringing her food which she scarcely touched, and warming her with her own body at night.

As Marya's plumpness dissolved, Batu became frantic. He saw a fortune slipping through his greedy fingers if the girl died. Appropriating a donkey from a farmer, he let her ride so that he might save her strength. Desperately he sought the choicest delicacies—newly ripe peaches, crisply browned doves, wine, and fresh breads —to tempt her. Finally he threatened her aunt with instant death if Marya did not eat. She ate, but her young body remained thin and stark. Her lovely hair and bright eyes became dull and lackluster.

Upon reaching Damascus, Marya showed emotion for the first time since her wedding day, when Batu removed her from the rest of the captives. Sobbing, she had to be forcibly separated from her aunt, who along with the rest was sent to one of the city's open slave markets.

Leading his prize, Batu headed for a bathhouse, where on his orders Marya was scrubbed, plucked, massaged, creamed, and her hair braided. Dressed in new clothes, she followed the Tartar chief to one of the better private slave merchants. But even a scrubbing and fresh clothes could not hide her dismal appearance.

"No," said the merchant. "Virgin or not, I will not buy her."

"Listen," replied Batu, "you should have seen her when we captured her. A plump, silvery-blond pigeon! And look at those eyes! When did you ever see eyes like that? Pure turquoise!"

"Batu, my friend," retorted the merchant patiently, "she may have been all you say, but now—no. She is an emaciated bag of bones. She is pining away of a broken heart. I've seen many like her. She will not live a month. I cannot embarrass either myself or my discerning clients by offering such a shoddy piece of merchandise. Take her to the open market with the rest of your cargo. You can get a few dinars for her there."

Gnashing his teeth, Batu dragged Marya from the house to the marketplace. She arrived in time to see her aunt sold to a rich, kindly-looking farmer who wanted a housekeeper for his motherless brood. Marya smiled to herself. If she knew her aunt, the hapless farmer would find himself a bridegroom before the year was out.

Gradually Batu's stock of captives dwindled until only Marya remained. The auctioneer did his best, but no one wanted the sad, stark girl. Furious, Batu was ready to beat her, when a stern, deep voice ordered, "Hold!"

They turned to see a very tall, elegantly dressed man striding to the platform.

"What do you want for the girl?"

Batu gaped.

"Well, my Tartar friend, surely you have put a price on her?"

"A hundred gold dinars?" ventured Batu.

The crowd hooted, but the tall man began emptying coins from a very fat purse.

"I will give you a hundred and fifty because I see her true worth." He placed the coins in the amazed Tartar's hands and stepped up onto the platform. Taking Marya's icy little hand in his large, warm one, he spoke softly to her. "My name is Hadji Bey, my child. If you will trust me, I will help you to live again."

"My family is dead. I have no wish to live."

"I know, little Firousi. Your pain is great, but if you choose, your future can be bright. Come now. We will go to my lodgings, and I will tell you all."

Leading Marya from the platform, he placed her in a large palanquin and, joining her, ordered the bearers homeward. Installing her in his house, Hadji Bey ordered a soothing drink for the distraught girl. Convinced that she was now at least physically comfortable, he gently pressed her to unburden herself. At first she was hesitant, but gradually the drug that Hadji Bey had ordered put in her drink took effect, and, relaxed, Marya poured forth her woes.

He listened sympathetically, and when at last the exhausted girl finished, he nodded. "Yes, my child, it is all very tragic, but what you have told me has happened many times to many others. It is over and cannot be taken back." He fixed her eyes with his and went on softly. "You are tired, little Firousi. You have suffered much. Now you will sleep, and when you awake, the pain of the past will be gone. You will begin your life again. You will not forget what has gone before, but you will no longer hurt."

Her eyes were drooping, but she spoke. "Only if I am avenged. Batu and seven of his men for each member of my family killed. The one called Yesukai for my bridegroom."

"It is done, Firousi."

"What do you call me?" she asked sleepily.

"Firousi. It means 'turquoise,' the color of your eyes. Now sleep, my child."

Unable to keep her eyes open any longer, she obeyed.

"When I awoke I felt marvelous! And that, dear Cyra, is how I came to be here," said Firousi.

"But what of Batu?" asked the Scots girl. "Did Hadji Bey have him and seven of his men killed?"

"Oh, yes. When we heard of you and left Damascus to come to Crete, I saw their heads rotting on pikes as we passed through the main gate. I never spoke of it, nor did he."

"You heard about me?"

"Oh, yes. Everyone from Damascus to Alexandria knew of the high-born virgin with the red hair to be sold by Abdul ben Abdul. What a price Hadji Bey paid for you! Zuleika and I together didn't bring a tenth of your price."

"I hardly consider that an honor."

"You should," snapped Zuleika.

Janet looked startled at the almond-eyed girl's tone of voice.

"Pay no attention to her," laughed Firousi. "She is Princess Plum Jade, a daughter of the emperor of Cathay, and only camel drivers and dirty, barbaric herdsmen bid on her. She would be slaving for some primitive tent dweller if Hadji Bey hadn't seen her and bought her. In the weeks we have been together I have learned that pride is very important to these people of Cathay. It still rankles that she was betrayed by—"

"If you don't mind, Firousi, I'll tell my own story." Zuleika rose from her distant divan and plumped herself down amid the pillows next to Cyra and Firousi. Unlike her blond companions, who had wept remembering the past, Zuleika's voice grew hard.

* * *

She would never forget the afternoon that decided her fate. It was spring, and she sat beside the marble fishpond in her mother's garden watching the large fantail goldfish snap and chase at the falling blossoms that ruffled the serenity of the pond's surface. The soft voice of her slave girl, Mai Tze, disturbed her, and she looked up questioningly.

"Mistress, your noble mother requests your presence."

"I will come at once."

"No, no," cried the slave girl. "First you must change your robe. *He* is with her."

"My brother, the emperor?"

"Yes, mistress."

Quickly she returned to her room and, with her slave's help, changed into a white silk robe embroidered with pink plum blossoms. Mai Tze brushed her long, glossy black hair, braided it, and wound a braid about each side of her head, fastening them with small pearl ornaments.

Waving the slave away, she stood for a moment and gazed at her reflection in the glass. A tall, slender girl with ivory-gold skin, perfectly shaped black almond eyes, a flawless face with high cheekbones, a slim nose, and a small, haughty red mouth gazed back at her. She was well aware that she was beautiful. She turned and walked slowly and with dignity into her mother's chambers.

"The Princess Plum Jade," intoned the eunuch.

Gracefully she knelt, bowing her head to the floor.

"Rise, younger sister."

She stood up, carefully keeping her eyes lowered and averted from the emperor's gaze.

"I have arranged for you to be married," he said.

She glanced toward her mother, whose face betrayed no emotion, but whose eyes warned her to be silent.

"You will," continued the emperor, "be wed to the shah of Persia. In three months' time you will leave your home for Persia. You will travel with a full retinue of servants and imperial soldiers as befits a Ming princess and a daughter of our late father, the honorable Ch'eng Hua. When you reach Persia, our people will leave you in the hands of the shah's servants and soldiers. You may retain only your slave girl, Mai Tze."

"Thank you, my honored lord."

"I have made you queen of Persia, sister. You! The daughter of a concubine. Is 'thank you' all you can say to me?"

"You, too, are the offspring of a concubine, and one not half so noble as my mother."

Hung Chih laughed. "You are too proud, sister. You will make the shah an excellent queen, and bind his kingdom closer to China."

"I am grateful for this opportunity to serve my lord and my homeland."

"Hah," chuckled the emperor. "Your subtle mind is beginning to calculate the advantages of being a queen, little peacock. Do not change, my sister. I like your pride. Never lose it. Now"—he turned to Plum Jade's mother—"let us have tea."

Three months later, the great caravan of the imperial Ming princess Plum Jade left the Forbidden City in Peking and turned westward toward Persia. It was now midsummer, and as they passed through the many villages of China the peasants crowded out to press gifts of melons and other newly harvested fruits and vegetables upon the princess. She accepted everything with gracious aloofness. She felt nothing for the people who wished her well.

And toward the shah, her intended husband, she also felt nothing. No anticipation. No hopes. He was considerably older than his sixteen-year-old bride. He had had no previous wives, only a concubine, Shannez, from whom he would not be parted. Unfortunately the woman was barren, and the shah eagerly desired an heir. He also desired to remove the threat of China from his borders, and Princess Plum Jade was the answer to both his wishes.

Her mother had told her all these things and had advised her to insinuate herself into her husband's affections or she would never truly be queen. It was not necessary to be a man's first love to be his last.

The imperial caravan traveled the width of China and across the barbarian mountains to the border of Persia. They were ahead of schedule, as the captain of the imperial guard had hurried the caravan to avoid any early snows in the mountains. Their encampment was large, and Plum Jade was grateful for the chance to rest and prepare herself to meet the shah.

Three days later the Persians were sighted, and the princess's women hurried to prepare their mistress, dressing her in silk robes of imperial yellow embroidered with white peonies. The Persians thundered into the Chinese encampment, and Plum Jade, watching from the door of her tent, saw that riding with the leader was a woman. It did not take a great deal of intelligence to know who she was.

"Shannez," hissed the princess angrily through gritted teeth. "He has brought that woman with him! Mai Tze, slip out and find out which one is the shah."

The slave girl did as bidden, returning a few moments later to say that the shah himself had not come, but would instead greet his bride in his capital city.

Plum Jade was furious, and her fury was heightened by the sudden intrusion into her tent of Shannez and the Persian captain.

"Get that woman out of my quarters!" she screamed. Her servants hurried to obey but were brushed aside by Shannez. "I see her imperial high and mightiness has heard of me," laughed Shannez to the captain. "By Allah, she is beautiful! If she had looked like a goat, like so many of these royal daughters, I might have pitied her and been her friend."

"Even a goat would not befriend so ill-mannered a bitch as you," raged the princess. "How dare you invade my quarters without being announced or invited? On your knees, woman! I am your queen!"

Shannez was astounded. "You speak our tongue?"

"On your knees!"

The captain nudged the shah's concubine, and she grudgingly knelt before the princess.

"I beg Your Imperial Highness's forgiveness, but so great was my desire to welcome you to Persia—"

Plum Jade stopped her with an imperious wave of her hand.

"I am 'Your Majesty,' insolent slave!"

"Not until you have wed with my lord," snapped Shannez.

Plum Jade slapped her. "Do you think the shah

can return the merchandise if it displeases him, which, I guarantee, it will not?"

"Your Majesty, I have acted hastily in my enthusiasm. I have been highhanded and rude. Forgive me, my queen, and let us be friends. I can help you."

Mollified, but not fooled by the woman's words, Princess Plum Jade spoke. "I doubt, Lady Shannez, that we can ever be friends, but perhaps we do not have to be enemies. Leave me now. I would rest."

The Persian withdrew, and once out of hearing, Shannez spoke.

"That bitch must never be our queen. She is too proud of her race and will be more loyal to China than to Persia. When she bears the shah a son, she will turn him and our country into vassals of China." She turned to the captain of the shah's guard. "Hassan, you must help me."

Hassan was not taken in by the concubine's patriotic speech, but her words had made some sense. "You cannot kill her, Lady Shannez. The truth would reach the imperial court of China, and we would have a war on our hands."

"I do not intend to kill her. Princess Plum Jade will marry the shah—but not the real princess. None of our people has seen Plum Jade, and they will not until we are ready to leave. Tomorrow the Chinese return home. You will insist on resting the horses another day, and I alone will wait on the princess. When evening comes I will drug her, and two of your men will carry her to Baghdad to be sold as a slave. I will substitute the princess's slave girl, Mai Tze, for the princess."

"But will the slave girl cooperate with you?"

"If she wishes to live a long life, she will," smiled Shannez. "And, Hassan, tell your men I want the princess sold unharmed. They are not to use her. Virgins bring a better price, and the higher the price, the greater their share. Have them sell her in the open market. I will grind her pride to dust!

"The shah will wonder why the princess has no slave girl of her own. It was part of the agreement that she be allowed to keep her. I will tell him that the princess became angry with the girl's insolence and, not wishing to trouble the shah, sold her."

At dawn the Chinese departed for their own country, and Princess Plum Jade and Mai Tze were left alone with the Persians. Shannez gently insisted that they spend a quiet day in preparation for the long trip ahead. To facilitate this, the concubine played soft songs on a lute and even brought the princess's meals with her own hands.

Night fell, and the shah's mistress suggested that Plum Jade try a cup of warmed goat's milk. It would help her to sleep, and the shah frequently enjoyed it, she said. The princess thought the goat's milk revolting, but drank it all and soon fell into a deep sleep. Mai Tze, who had also been allowed to partake of the liquid, slept, too.

Several weeks later, Hadji Bey passed an open slave market in the city of Baghdad. This was the furthest afield he had come in his search, and he was becoming discouraged. He had visited every good slave merchant in the city but had not found what he was looking for. There had been many lovely maidens, but none had the qualities of spirit, beauty, and intelligence which he sought.

Now something caught his eye on the raised platform. A girl—naked and dirty—crouched in a corner attempting to cover herself with her long hair. He stopped and stared. Aware of his close scrutiny, she shot him a look of defiance.

Hadji Bey signaled the slave master and pointed. "That girl. How much?"

The slaver forced Plum Jade up. "A rare flower from the ancient land of Cathay, my noble lord." His hand cupped a firm, pear-shaped breast. "A virgin. Fresh and nubile."

"Stop fondling the girl and tell me the price you have put on her," said Hadji Bey.

"Fifty dinars—gold. I bought her months ago from a caravan and paid a pretty penny. Fifty gold dinars, my lord."

"He bought me three days ago from two soldiers who kidnapped me, and he paid them twenty dinars," spoke the girl.

The slave master shot her a furious look.

"Thirty dinars," said Hadji Bey, counting the coins out and dropping them into the man's outstretched hand.

Pocketing his gain, the merchant shoved Plum Jade at Hadji Bey. "Go to your master, girl."

She turned on him and raked him with her nails. "Do not touch me again, you foul vermin!"

Hadji Bey put an arm around the girl. "Gently, my daughter. Your ordeal is over." Then, to the merchant, "Give me her clothes. She has been shamed enough and must not walk through the streets naked."

The slave master reached into a trunk on the platform and drew out some shoddy rags.

"Thief," screamed Plum Jade. "Where is my silk robe?"

Hadji Bey firmly pushed the man aside and, reachng into the trunk, withdrew the yellow-and-white silk robe. The girl snatched it and put it on.

As he led her away, he said, "Tell me your name, my child."

"I am Princess Plum Jade of China."

"I shall call you Zuleika."

She looked at him.

"Zuleika," he said quietly, "was a great warrior princess."

"And so," said Zuleika, "we returned to Damascus to fetch Firousi, heard about you, and hurried here to Crete."

Janet stared at her two companions. "Are you sure there is no escape?" she asked.

"None," answered Firousi, "and why would you want to escape? Where would you go? You couldn't go home. No one would ever believe you had escaped still innocent from the sultan of Turkey. People would point at you in the streets, and no good father would permit his son to wed with you. You would grow old, never knowing love, pensioned off, perhaps, to help raise your brother's children. Neither a servant nor a respectable member of the family. At least as members of Sultan Bajazet's household we will know luxury, perhaps love, and even children of our own. Do you still want to return?"

Janet shook her head. "No," she said, "you are right. There is no turning back for any of us. I have heard that the women of the sultan's harem intrigue against one another to keep his favor. We three have all been torn from our families, we have known misfortune. In union there is strength. If we must be slaves, let us be powerful ones. Let us agree that, no matter what happens, each of us will support the other two. In this way we may someday rule not only the harem but the sultan as well."

Zuleika and Firousi smiled at Janet.

"The child in you flees with the dawn, Cyra," said Firousi.

"Yes," she answered. "Gone are the Princess Plum Jade of Cathay, Marya Rostov of the Caucasus, and Lady Janet Leslie of Scotland. They were little girls. In their places stand three women, members of Sultan Bajazet's household—Zuleika, Firousi, and Cyra. Will you agree to my pact?"

"Yes," said Firousi, placing her hand on Janet's.

"And I, too," answered Zuleika, putting her hand on theirs.

Dawn began to break over the island of Crete. The three girls, comforted by each other's presence, changed into night garments and lay down to sleep.

Janet, taking one last look at Candia's harbor, sighed at the sight of the ship that was now making its way out to the open sea. At its mast flew the golden falcon of San Lorenzo. Slowly she turned to her couch and lay down.

Across the room a small panel slipped noiselessly into place on the wall, and behind that wall Hadji Bey spoke quietly to himself. "I have chosen well. May Allah be blessed. Now the empire will be safe."

8

THE VOYAGE FROM CRETE to Constantinople was a pleasant one. Cyra, Firousi, and Zuleika were permitted to lounge under an awning that was set up for them on the broad deck. Hadji Bey had insisted they be heavily veiled and had forbidden them to wander about lest the sight of them arouse the galley slaves, many of whom were European captives.

The ship traveled swiftly through the pleasant waters and charming islands of the Aegean, and Hadji Bey pointed out several sites of historical interest that Cyra found much more engrossing than the agricultural islands shown her by Captain Venutti. There were Naxos, where Theseus had left Ariadne; Chios, reputed to be Homer's birthplace; and Lesbos, home of the poetess Sappho, which had been the center of civilization in the seventh century before Christ.

They slipped through the Dardanelles, which had in ancient times been called the Hellespont. Forty miles long and one to four miles wide, the strait was lined with the watchtowers of the Ottoman army and was essential to the defense of Constantinople. The towers were used as advance warning posts should anyone attempt to attack the capital by sea. Shortly, the Dardanelles gave way to the Sea of Marmara. Their journey was almost over.

The night before they reached their destination, Hadji Bey called them to his vast cabin in the stern of the ship. Entering, they noticed he had placed his fierce mute guards at the door. He motioned the girls to pillows set about a round table, and after allowing a slave to place refreshments on it and depart, he sat down beside his charges.

"Now, my lovely children, I have a matter of vast importance to discuss with you. As you already know, I am the agha kislar, the head of Sultan Bajazet's black eunuchs. In this capacity I am a man of vast power. I have chosen to use this power to right a terrible wrong, and I will need your help to do it.

"Many years ago, my master took as his first wife, or kadin as we say, a beautiful Circassian girl called Kiusem. After a year she bore him a fine, healthy son, who was named Mustafa. However, while she carried her child, the sultan's attention wandered, and he took a second kadin, a Syrian girl named Besma. Eighteen months after Kiusem's son was born, Besma also gave birth to a son, Prince Ahmed.

"Several months after the birth of her son, Besma invited the two-year-old heir, Prince Mustafa, to visit his baby brother. Although Kiusem was wary, she allowed him to go. The child returned after several hours full of happy chatter and with a fistful of sweetmeats, which he offered to his mother. She accepted one to please him. Shortly afterward, the little prince became violently ill, and the lady Kiusem, too, though less so. The physician diagnosed poison. Prince Mustafa died at dawn, but his mother recovered.

"Tearfully, Kiusem accused Besma of the foul deed, but the sultan, who was then only Prince Bajazet, refused to condemn the mother of an imperial heir. Kiusem's heart was crushed, and try as Bajazet might, he could not cheer her. She grew peaked and wan, and finally he left her in peace.

"Now allow me to deviate from my story a moment to tell you why I am so loyal to the lady Kiusem. When I came to the harem, I was a frightened child. Kiusem, who was then but a child herself, cared for me and saw that I got the proper training so that I might advance myself. When she became the sultan's first wife, or bas-kadin, I was made her head eunuch. When Prince Mustafa was born, the sultan honored her by giving me the post of agha kislar, replacing the old agha, who had just died.

"I loved the lady Kiusem, not as a man, for I am not a man, but as a dear and good friend. Secretly I nursed her back to health, not only in body but in mind, too. It took many months, for her grief was great.

"Then one day she came to me privately and asked this question: 'If I bore the sultan another son, Hadji Bey, would you help me gain the throne for him?' 'What makes you think the sultan will take you again to his bed?' I countered. 'He has made my twin sister, Refet, his new favorite,' she replied. 'I think he still yearns for me.' So I agreed to help Kiusem, and when the sultan next held a reception for his women, she appeared before him for the first time in over a year.

"She was dazzlingly beautiful that evening, and Bajazet, once again under her spell, sent for her that very night. Nine months later, she bore him a second son, named Selim." Hadji Bey paused to help himself to a sherbet. Refreshing himself, he continued.

"Kiusem was clever, for during the months she carried Selim in her womb and could not go to her lord, her sister, Refet, went in her place. Besma was furious, for as fascinated by Kiusem as the sultan was, he was equally fascinated by Refet. In addition, Besma was very much out of favor because the sultan's third kadin, Safiye, had given birth to a son two years after Ahmed was born, while Besma, unfortunately, had given birth to a stillborn son.

"After Selim's birth, great precautions were taken to protect him so he might grow to manhood. Kiusem, pretending the birth of Selim so soon after the tragic death of Mustafa had addled her wits slightly, withdrew again from court life. She lived and dressed simply, as did Selim. Before all but a few trusted friends she appeared half-mad, and, because of this, the sultan out of his great love for her permitted her a great measure of freedom.

"Now I must explain that in our country all male heirs of a sultan are taken from their mothers at age six and given their own courts. Under these conditions Kiusem could not be sure that Selim would be safe, so, using her illness as an excuse, she managed to keep him with her until he was fourteen. At that time my master had become sultan, and Selim was sent to the city of Magnesia to learn the art of government. Prior to that,

he had been educated by the finest scholars our empire
had to offer.

"Last year my lady became ill, and the physicians
were forced to tell the sultan she would not recover.
Before she died she gained Bajazet's promise to return
Selim from Magnesia and give him a province nearer to
Constantinople to govern. She suggested he go to the
Moonlight Serai, which had been a gift to her from the
sultan, and that to show his love of Selim, the sultan
declare this on the prince's twenty-fifth birthday, which
is in four months.

"At that time the sultan will celebrate his son's birthday with much pomp and ceremony. Kiusem's dying wish
was that Prince Selim be given his choice of six maidens
from his father's harem as a gift. Before she died, my
lady instructed me to find three special maidens with
both beauty and intelligence to help him toward his goal
as his father's heir replacing Prince Ahmed.

"I have picked you three to fill this role. Prince Selim
is a gentle, handsome young man of great charm and
learning. You should be very happy with him. One day
he will be sultan, and the women who are his kadins,
the mothers of his sons, will hold positions of great
power and wealth."

"You take your life in your hands, do you not, Hadji
Bey? What if we do not wish to go along with your
plans? We could betray you and gain our freedom," said
Cyra.

"I rely on your intelligence, my dears. I do not think
you will choose death over power and riches, for if you
betrayed me, death would be your only freedom. If the
freedom of death intrigues you, throw yourself from
the ship's rail and be done with it; but do not, I beg you,
interfere with my plans. Your fate, or kismet, as we
say, has brought you to me. How you accept your
allotted portion is up to you. If you are as wise as I
believe you to be, I already know your answers."

Again Cyra questioned him. "How can you keep us
hidden from the sultan? If he should see us and favor
us, we would be lost to the prince."

The eunuch smiled. "The seraglio is not, as many
outsiders think, a place of unchecked lust and depravity.

It is a well-ordered household, guided by rules, regulations, and many customs.

"The women of the house fall into several categories. Some are simple servants. Some are attendants on the sultan, or in the baths, or for his women. The maidens who make up the harem are also ranked according to their status. The majority are called gediklis, the privileged ones. Next are the guzdehs, girls who have caught Bajazet's eye but have not yet gone to his bed. Then come ikbals, those girls who have been to the sultan's couch and managed to keep his favor. Finally we have the kadins, who have given the sultan a son or sons. A sultan may have only four kadins, with the bas-kadin—the mother of the heir—being highest-ranked. Though Besma's son is the heir, the sultan never took the rank of baskadin away from Lady Kiusem.

"The highest positions in the harem are those of the sultan's daughters and the sultan valideh, who is the sultan's mother. Our sultan has no mother living, so we have no valideh at present. This is the highest position to which a woman in the Ottoman household can climb. Her word is law in the palace and among the women of our empire. Only the sultan himself can countermand her orders, and many times he does not dare.

"Guzdehs, ikbals, and kadins have their own apartments and attendants to wait upon them, but the gediklis live in dormitorylike odas, each of which is presided over by an older woman. It is the duty of this woman to train her girls in our ways and develop their individual talents.

"I am placing you in a small, unobtrusive oda. Its mistress is the lady Refet."

"The sultan's favorite?"

"She is no longer a favorite, Firousi. She never became a kadin, having had the misfortune to bear Bajazet twin daughters. They are now grown and married to government officials. Rather than retire to the Pavilion of Older Damsels, she became mistress of an oda. It is not a particularly distinguished one, for since Kiusem's death, Besma has regained some of her power over the sultan. You will, however, be safe there, and out of Bajazet's way if you obey me and the lady Refet. She is a kind

woman and has been apprised of our plans since the
beginning.

"The next four months will be a period of intensive
study for you. Not only must you learn our language in
that time, but you must learn our customs, some of our
music, our dances, and, most important of all, the physical ways to please your master. It will not be easy for
you, but I believe you are each extraordinary in your
own special way. I know you can do it.

"Will you help me, Cyra?" She nodded.

"Firousi?"

"Yes, Hadji Bey."

"Zuleika?"

"Yes."

"Good! This is a dangerous task I have set you, and
your silence is the key to its success. Discuss it with
no one, not even among yourselves. I cannot stress that
enough. The seraglio is filled with slaves whose only
task is to listen and report all that is said among the
maidens. The merest hint of my plans, and you could
easily end up in a weighted sack tossed into the sea.

"Go to your cabin now and rest, for tomorrow evening
we reach Constantinople. From this moment on, I am
the agha kislar, not your special friend, but fear not, my
daughters, I will be watching you and guarding your
lives."

They left him, and for a moment he stood quietly.
Then, going to a chest by his couch, he lifted up a black
velvet bag. Slipping out a shallow, seamless crystal bowl,
he set it on the table and poured some fresh water into
it. He sat down and gazed deeply into the still water.
For several minutes he contemplated the visions that
came to him in the water. A smile played across his
lips.

"It will go well," he whispered softly to himself. "Praise
Allah! It will go well!"

At the moment Hadji Bey was gazing into his crystal
bowl, Pietro di San Lorenzo was landing at Arcobaleno.
Delayed by a fierce storm, he had not thought to see land
again. He went directly to the pink villa of the earl of
Glenkirk. The earl was devastated by his news.

"Was there nothing you could do?" he asked.

"My lord, I thought I had her safe. I jumped the caliph of Baghdad's bid by five thousand pieces of gold. Abdul ben Abdul was raising his gavel to finalize the sale when that devil Hadji Bey bid thirty thousand. I protested his bid. I even tried to raise the money from among the other buyers, but there was none who would dare defy the sultan of the Ottoman Empire. All sales must be cash."

"Perhaps the sultan would ransom her," suggested the earl.

"There is no chance, my lord. It was not just any eunuch who bought your daughter. It was Hadji Bey, the agha kislar himself. He is the most powerful man, aside from the sultan, in Bajazet's household.

"This man rarely leaves Constantinople. He is not a buyer of slave girls, yet the gossip is that he has been out of Constantinople for several months. He is reported to have bought a maid of Cathay in Baghdad and an exquisite blond in Damascus. He almost killed himself to get to the sale in Candia. Your daughter and these other girls are obviously meant for something special. There is simply no hope of ransom."

Six weeks later, a heartbroken Patrick Leslie, his son, Adam, and Mary MacKay returned to Scotland. When the king had the temerity to suggest another diplomatic post, the earl exploded.

"I have given you three years of my life, and lost my only daughter in your service, James Stuart! You'll not get more from me! I return to Glenkirk and never will you see my face again!"

Rudolfo di San Lorenzo mourned his loss but three months. Then, the negotiations being settled, he married Princess Marie-Hélène of Toulouse.

PART II

Cyra

1493-1494

9

SULTAN BAJAZET'S THIRD SON, Selim, was a tall and slender young man with his mother's fair skin and gray eyes. His hair was dark and slightly wavy. His face, which generally wore a grave expression, was smooth-shaven, with high cheekbones, a slim but prominent nose, and thin, yet full, lips.

Because it was expected that he would never inherit the throne of his father, little attention had been paid to him since his birth. This suited his mother who, remembering the murder of her first son, desired that she and her child be as inconspicuous as possible.

With the permission of Selim's grandfather, Sultan Mohammed, Kiusem and her child lived in the most remote section of the Eski Serai—outside the women's quarters—in the Tulip Court. They were discreetly but fiercely protected by a troop of the agha kislar's militant and trusted mute eunuchs, and attended by a dozen fanatically loyal slaves. They rarely left their court, and the young Selim grew up in an atmosphere of cautious watchfulness.

This life had its effect on the young child. He rarely smiled and was never given to outbursts of boisterous play or laughter as other children were. By the time he was three, he had matured so rapidly in mind that he spoke not like an infant barely out of leading strings but like a boy of seven or eight. He was wary of strangers, though few ever visited the Tulip Court.

Although neither his mother nor his nurses were aware of it, he frequently slipped out of his quarters to visit his father's stables or to play quietly alone in the sultan's gardens. He was always careful not to be

noticed, for although no one had told him, he instinctively
understood that his life depended on his discretion.

One day when he was six, he sat amid the branches
of a tree in the imperial gardens and discovered to his
surprise that he had two half-brothers. He had never
seen another boy in his whole life and was very tempted
to climb down and join them, but a small voice in his
head warned him not to, so he remained where he was.
He later learned the other boys' identities from his
half-sisters, Leila and Aiyshe, his aunt Refet's twin
daughters. They were the only children who came to play
within his mother's house.

The older boy was ten-year-old Prince Ahmed, his
father's assumed heir. He was no taller than Selim, and
fat, with olive skin, dark eyes, and black hair. His round,
petulant face was marked with acne, and his manner
was arrogant. He never hesitated to beat any member of
his retinue who did not immediately respond to his commands, and Selim did not regret his decision to remain
hidden.

The younger boy was taller, with wavy, dark-brown
hair and large blue eyes. He was solemn of manner
and gravely courteous to all who served him. This was
eight-year-old Prince Korkut. He was so royal a young
boy that even Prince Ahmed was polite when they met—
which was as infrequently as Prince Korkut could manage without seeming rude.

For over a year Selim sat in his tree and observed
his brothers—each playing separately within his own
retinue—for imperial princes had their own households.
Why, Selim wondered, are they allowed the freedom of
my grandfather's garden, but I am not? If he spoke to
his mother on this matter, she would learn of his ventures
into the main part of the palace, and he would be
guarded more closely than ever. Then one day as he sat
in his tree, he heard a voice.

"Why do you always hide within the branches of this
tree?"

Startled, Selim answered, "I do not want to be seen."

"Why not?"

"Because my mother wishes it."

"Who is your mother?"

"Kiusem Kadin."

"Ah! You are my brother Selim!"

Selim peered between the branches, and a smile lit his face. "And you are my brother Korkut, son of Safiye Kadin."

The boy beneath the tree laughed. "You are correct, little brother, and since you cannot come down, I shall come up."

So began the friendship between the two princes. Selim, confessing his adventures to his horrified mother, finally won her consent to allow Korkut within the Tulip Court.

To Kiusem's delight, Prince Korkut was an excellent influence on Selim. The older boy, like his father, was a scholar, and encouraged his younger half-brother, an indifferent student, to pursue his studies more diligently. The finest minds in the Ottoman Empire were discreetly brought to the Eski Serai to teach the boys. Selim, once he applied himself, discovered he enjoyed his studies. He was not brilliant, like his father and Korkut, but he was quite intelligent.

When Selim was twelve, his grandfather, Sultan Mohammed the Conqueror, died, and his father put on the sword of Ayub and ascended the throne. When Selim was fourteen, Sultan Bajazet sent the boy and his mother to the city of Magnesia. There Selim learned the arts of ruling, and governed the city and its surrounding province for his father.

Kiusem's archenemy, Besma, had attempted to prevent the sultan from giving Selim this responsibility, claiming that Bajazet's youngest son was an idiot and Magnesia would suffer. The Ottoman ruler thought that his second wife was merely being vicious. He did not realize that the few occasions Besma had seen Selim had been carefully staged by Hadji Bey to make Selim appear a dunce. This was all part of the wily agha's plan to make Kiusem's son appear harmless and ineffectual.

In Magnesia Selim was free to be himself, for Besma was so convinced he was useless that she sent no spies to watch him. Here the sultan's youngest son grew from hesitant and shy adolescence to strong and sure manhood. The scholars had taught him well, and he governed fairly, with scrupulous respect for the laws of the empire and the Muslim faith.

Hadji Bey had taught him well, also. Slowly and

carefully he gathered underground support for himself
and his cause. A piece of luck brought him loyalty from
the Crimean Tartars when he saved the life of a visiting
high chieftain. The grateful man returned home full of
praise for Selim and sent him as a gift two troops of
Tartar horsemen to be his personal bodyguard.

He was now a man, and although he had been kept
free of romantic entanglements longer than most Turkish
princes, Hadji Bey and Kiusem decided the time had
come for their serious young charge to learn the ways
of women. Selim was seventeen and so well aware of his
position that he did not think it odd when his mother
and the agha explained to him that there must be no
children as yet.

"Women and children at this time will make you
vulnerable to Besma's treachery. When we have strength-
ened your position with the sultan and chosen the right
maidens, then Selim—and only then—may you have sons,"
said the agha. "In the meantime, should you desire a
woman, you have but to ask, and the most beautiful and
skilled of maidens will be brought to you. They are sterile,
of course, so you need not fear."

The prince trusted both his mother and Hadji Bey
implicitly, and so he obeyed. And in the capital, Besma,
at first terrified by Selim's appetite for women, chuckled
with satisfaction as the time went by and no children appeared. Unaware that the maidens Selim bedded were
sterile, she rejoiced to her own son, Ahmed, "Your brother's seed is like sea water. Nothing grows in it!"

The years passed, and shortly before Selim reached his
twenty-fourth birthday, Kiusem fell ill. The agha was informed and hurried to Magnesia from Constantinople.

Seeing Kiusem shocked the agha. She was clearly dying,
and she did not deny it.

"I know, old friend. My time grows short."

Tears sprang to his eyes, and he took her small white
hand in his own slender brown one. Faintly she squeezed
it. "We must act now, Hadji Bey. You must obtain the
sultan's promise that Selim will be honored on his twenty-
fifth birthday with the governorship of the Crimean province nearest Constantinople. And the girls, Hadji Bey.
Bajazet must allow my son the pick of the maidens. No
Ottoman has ever honored a son so. It will impress the

people and secure my son's future and safety. Besma will not dare to harm him if he stands high in the sultan's esteem."

"It will be as you wish, my dearest lady. I will not fail you."

"The special ones—have you obtained them yet? They must be ready."

"I have not found them, my lady. I must go myself."

She looked worried. "There will be questions. You are the agha, not a buyer of slaves."

"It is because I am the agha that no one will question my actions. They may think—I cannot stop that—but no one except the sultan himself may question me, and he will not, as he trusts me above all men."

"Selim must be told everything now," she said.

"I will do it myself, my lady. The prince must comprehend the seriousness of our undertaking. He is sometimes inclined to rashness, but from now on, he must act with extra caution and extreme self-discipline."

The prince was called into the agha's presence and greeted his old friend warmly. When steaming cups of coffee had been brought and the servants dismissed, the agha spoke. Selim listened quietly, his handsome face grave, as the agha outlined the plan that he and Kiusem had conceived even before the prince's birth.

Ahmed must not succeed his father. He was, unfortunately, too influenced by his mother, poorly educated, and depraved. Turkey could not support such a sultan.

As for Prince Korkut, he was a good man but more a scholarly recluse than a future sultan. He was not a soldier and had no interest in women. Should he, Allah forbid, succeed his father, he would not last a month. Fortunately Prince Korkut had informed the agha that he did not wish to be sultan. He would, he said meaningfully, support the "right" man.

Now the field was clear for Selim, said the agha. The first part of the plan was to keep him isolated and safe during his youth, to see that he was superbly educated and then given the governorship of Magnesia—the same province his father had ruled in his youth.

Step two of the plan called for Selim's governorship to be transferred to the Crimean province nearest Constantinople. Using Bajazet's love for Kiusem, this had already

been accomplished. Selim would leave Magnesia shortly
before his twenty-fifth birthday to visit his father in the
capital, and depart the day after for his new post.

In case of emergency he would be a day's hard ride
from the city, and, more important, the sultan would
have easy access to his son.

This brought Hadji Bey to step three. Kiusem's arch-
rival, Besma, had never stopped her campaign to discredit
Bajazet's youngest son in order to advance the cause
of her own offspring. She dared not compare the two
princes' morals, for Ahmed's degenerate behavior was an
open scandal. His mother, in hopes of ruling through her
son one day, had, in order to keep him under her thumb,
directed his sexual appetites in twisted directions.

She could not compare Ahmed and Selim in the field
of governorship, for the province of Magnesia was peaceful, fruitful, and well-run. Ahmed's domain in the east on
the Persian border was a constant source of trouble.

. Her only hope had been to keep Selim from his father,
to fill the sultan's ear with what poison she could, and
hope for Bajazet's death and Ahmed's succession before
the sultan learned the truth.

Besma's desires had suited Kiusem and the agha, for
the result was that Selim enjoyed unprecedented freedom.
Now, however, the time had come for the sultan to know
what kind of a man his younger son had become. Moving
him nearer to the capital would help to accomplish this.
Setting him up with a bevy of lovely maidens from his
father's own harem would impress upon the people Bajazet's regard for him.

Later, when sons were born, Selim's position would be
solidified—especially since Hadji Bey was quite certain
that Prince Ahmed's preference for young boys negated
his chances for having sons. The agha was sure that once
the sultan realized what a fine and capable man Selim
was, the succession would be changed.

Selim absorbed the agha's words carefully. He did not
tell his friend that from the time he was old enough to
understand, it had been his intention to replace his dead
brother on the throne of their father one day. He knew
his brothers much better than they knew themselves, and
he was neither a hedonistic seeker of personal pleasures
like Ahmed, nor a monkish lover of learning like Korkut.

There had been only one man he had admired in his life, and that man had been his grandfather.

He had been almost thirteen when the conqueror had died, and he remembered the old man vividly. Mohammed had lived in the Yeni Serai, where he could keep an eye on the construction going on about his new palace. One day he had ordered his grandsons to be brought to him. Both Ahmed and Korkut arrived with retinues befitting their imperial state, but the seven-year-old Selim came with just one attendant.

Mohammed raised an eyebrow, but said nothing. There had been wrestlers for entertainment, and Ahmed boasted that he could beat any of them. The old sultan said nothing but eyed the overweight braggart with intense dislike. After that, only Selim was invited to the Yeni Serai. When Selim asked his grandfather why, the old man replied with an honesty that surprised even himself.

"Only you, Selim, are worthy to learn what I have to teach."

"What is that, grandfather?"

"I will teach you to be a warrior—the greatest warrior ever known. From now on, you will be taught the art of fighting by my own chosen men. Twice each week we will meet secretly, for I do not wish Besma to know of this, and you will show me what you have learned. I myself will teach you the tactics that won me so many battles —and the greatest prize of all, this jewel of a city. When I die, Turkey need not fear for her future, for you will help to protect it."

Six years later, Selim attended Mohammed on his deathbed. The last words spoken by Mohammed had been spoken harshly, and only Selim had heard them.

"You—you must follow my successor!"

Selim remembered those words. They burned in his mind like hot coals and reaffirmed his secret desire to rule. The agha's words today pleased him, though he showed no emotion other than agreement to his plans. It was a dangerous and painfully patient game he was being asked to play, but he would enjoy it. The logic and skill of tactics had always intrigued him.

"You smile, my son," said the agha.

"I am thinking of the image I must create." He laughed. "Good Prince Selim! The perfect son, the perfect brother, the perfect husband and father. Allah, Hadji Bey! You ask a great deal of a rough soldier. What happens if I do not like the maidens I choose from my father's harem? A pretty face is not a guarantee of a man's happiness."

The agha smiled. "When you choose, I promise you that at least three of the maidens will be to your taste. I go to seek them myself."

"So you think you know my tastes?"

"Beauty, intelligence, warmth, independence, and perhaps a touch of mystery."

"Find me one woman with all those traits, Hadji Bey, and I shall be a happy man."

"I shall, my prince, and you shall."

On Selim's twenty-fifth birthday, and at the sultan's order, the entire empire from the Balkans to the borders of Persia, celebrated. Selim had arrived in Constantinople just a week before, and at his father's order been housed in an apartment in the Yeni Serai.

Most of his time was spent alone, for the Ottoman court, unlike its counterparts in Western Europe, had no nobility from among which its princes could draw friends. Coupled with his lonely upbringing, his position made him shy and wary. He was more at ease among his Tartars, for among them he had proved himself in the arts of war and therefore won their admiration and respect. He could outride any man, throw a lance farther than any other, and no one was his equal with either knife or scimitar.

He saw his father three times. Bajazet had, as Kiusem hoped, been favorably impressed with Selim. At their first meeting, both had been hesitant. Neither father nor son really knew the other. Then, in a supreme effort to make conversation, Selim mentioned that he wrote poetry. Immediately Bajazet grew enthusiastic. He, too, wrote poetry. In that moment the floodgates opened, and though neither could erase the twenty-five years of neglect, a friendship was born between them.

Selim also saw his elder brother, who had been summoned to the celebration. Mellowed by forbidden wine but primed by his mother's constant carping, Ahmed eyed his handsome brother suspiciously as Selim bowed deeply.

"Our father does you great honor."

"It is not me he honors but my mother's dying wish."

"I am the heir."

"Our father's wish is mine also, brother."

"My mother says you seek to steal my throne, but I told her she was wrong." He raised his cup and drained it.

Selim smiled. "I will not steal your throne, brother," he said, but he was thinking, *Fat fool! You have no throne and never will!*

One day Selim was taken secretly by the agha to a hidden room overlooking the women's baths in the Eski Serai. Never had he seen so many females in one spot at one time—especially naked females.

"How many women does my father have?" he asked, never taking his eyes from the scene below him.

"At this moment, about three hundred," replied Hadji Bey, "but there are only about a hundred and ten gediklis. There are three kadins, five ikbals, and about a dozen guzdehs. The rest are servants."

The prince did not answer, and the agha chuckled. Though he had never functioned as a man, he was an appreciative connoisseur of the female body. Under his watchful eye, only the most exquisite beauties were trained as gediklis. Sitting back for a moment, Hadji Bey and Selim viewed the living picture below them.

The baths were constructed of a pale pink marble with a domed roof of rose-colored glass panes. Spaced at various intervals along the walls were dark-blue and beige tiled panels from which sprang deep, shell-shaped rose marble basins with hot and cold gold waterspouts in the form of flowers. Several large rectangles of pink marble filled the center of the room. These were used for seating, resting, and massages. It was a beautiful foil for the various maidens who composed the sultan's harem—dusky Spaniards and Moors, golden Provençals and Italians, coffee-colored Egyptians, cloud-white Grecians and Circassians, coal-black slave girls from Nubia.

Gradually the room emptied until only about a dozen maidens remained. Selim started as a woman accompanied by several young girls entered the room.

"Ah," said the agha, "the lady Refet."

The prince was slightly discomfited at seeing his aunt. "I had forgotten how identical in looks she is to my late mother," he said.

"Not quite," observed Hadji Bey. "Your mother had a rather charming mole, but it is not your aunt I have brought you to see. She guards the three special ones. Can you tell me which they are?"

Selim's eyes moved to the little group. A tall, golden-skinned girl with almond-shaped eyes unbraided her long ebony hair.

"That one," he said.

The agha nodded.

"And if you have not chosen that rosy-buttocked silver-blond, I shall." He pointed toward Firousi.

"Correct, my son. And the third?"

But he did not speak, and the agha, following the prince's gaze, smiled with satisfaction, for Selim was staring at Cyra. She reclined on one of the marble sofas, three slave girls attending her. One manicured a slim foot, another a slender hand, while the third rubbed a strand of her lovely red-gold hair with a silk cloth to give it more luster.

"That is Cyra," said Hadji Bey. "Is she not lovely?" He did not wait for the prince to answer. "She is in many ways wise beyond her years. Your aunt tells me she speaks several languages fluently and has become a perfectly accomplished maiden in the Turkish fashion. It is fitting that she be the mother of your sons. Your father's indiscriminate breeding produced Ahmed. However, my son, you must be gentle with her, for though she has been schooled by our women in the arts of pleasing her lord, she is still a virgin. In her land, whence she is newly come, men and women are fairly equal in many things. She retains her independence, and we have taken great care not to break her spirit. You have never known a woman for more than one or two nights. They were women skilled only in the arts of love. Cyra will be shy at first, but treat her with candor, Selim, and she will love you to the death."

During the next few days, Selim thought of Hadji Bey's words, and he thought of Cyra. The agha had puzzled him. Allah had created woman for man's pleasure, and certainly the women he had possessed had given him pleasure, but nothing more. Suddenly he wondered if he had given them pleasure, too. And if a man were to spend a lifetime with a woman, there must be more than a simple physical act between them. Animals mated, too, but had not Allah given man dominion over the animals? If man was the superior being, then it must be love that made him so.

He was twenty-five years old, and he did not know what love was. Would Cyra teach him? What was she really like? He longed to hear the sound of her voice, to speak to her. Suddenly he was frightened. Would she like him? Hadji Bey could deliver her slim, white body to him, but no one could make her love him. The panic subsided. He knew her not, but tomorrow night he would sit on the dais with his father and choose her—and she *would* love him! He would make her love him. He had seen her only once, but he knew he could not live his life without her.

The muezzin's call rang from the Great Mosque, the former Christian church of Hagia Sophia. Selim fell to his knees and prayed.

10

FOR MONTHS the gediklis of Sultan Bajazet's harem had prepared for Prince Selim's birthday. It wasn't every day such an opportunity presented itself, and each girl secretly hoped that she would be one of the fortunate six to be chosen.

The sultan had three living kadins, and their constant intrigues to keep their lord and master's favor was an open scandal. Although he was growing old, many girls were still summoned down the Golden Road to the sultan's bed. Those who managed to please him and avoid the wrath of his three wives counted themselves lucky. The less fortunate were relegated under guard to the Pavilion of Forgotten Women.

Therefore the prospect of possibly being chosen for the harem of a young and handsome prince was a very attractive opportunity. Never had the girls worked so hard on their personal appearance. Never had they studied so diligently, and never had they spent their slipper money so freely on jewelry, perfume, or spies to discover the prince's preferences.

Cyra, Firousi, and Zuleika had been quietly introduced into the household of Sultan Bajazet. The entries made by the keeper of records showed nothing unusual, merely stating the girls' ages, origins, places of purchase, and prices. Knowing that the enormous sum he had paid for Cyra would attract unwelcome attention, Hadji Bey had used his own wealth to purchase the girl, and had listed her price as five hundred dinars, which would not be considered an outrageous price for a beautiful virgin.

The girls were then assigned to the oda of Lady Refet. Hadji Bey could not have made a wiser choice than entrusting them to Prince Selim's aunt. She was a slender

woman with lovely dark hair which she wore elegantly
braided upon her head. Her beautiful face, with its high,
sculptured cheekbones, was gentle and kindly. Her soft
brown eyes at once discerned that the facade of bravery
worn by each girl covered anxious uncertainty, and perhaps even fear.

Warned of their approach by her eunuch, she was
ready as they entered her salon with the agha. Coming
forward, her arms outstretched, she warmly hugged each
girl and said in her low, cultured voice, "Welcome, my
dears. I am so glad you have arrived safely."

"I leave them in your kindly charge, Lady Refet," said
Hadji Bey. "Farewell, my daughters. May good fortune
attend you."

Lady Refet did not allow them time for tears. "It is the
hour of the baths," she said. "Since we are alone, let us
have a cool drink, and while we are waiting, I will show
you the oda."

She signaled a slave for the refreshment and then
ushered her charges to their quarters. "This," she said,
waving her hand, "is where you and the other young ladies
in my charge live and sleep."

Cyra looked about the room. She saw three round,
low, inlaid tables, several piles of colorful cushions, and
a chair.

"Where are the beds?" she asked.

Lady Refet pointed to the paneling along the bottom
half of two of the walls. "Behind the paneling are cup-
boards. Each girl is assigned one, and it contains her
sleeping mattress, bedding, outdoor clothing, and other
personal possessions. Each morning after prayers, we air
our bedding. It is then put away until night."

"Very practical," noted the young Cyra, much to Lady
Refet's amazement. "Do we also eat in this room?"

"Yes, my dear."

"Are we ever allowed to leave our quarters?"

"Gracious, my child, of course! You are not a prisoner.
Naturally, your movements are limited to a certain degree,
but is that not so even in your own country?"

"No," replied Cyra. "I was free to go where I chose
in my own land."

Lady Refet placed an arm around the girl's shoulders.
"Then, my dear, perhaps your adjustment to our ways

will be a bit more difficult, but we will try to make it as
easy for you as we can. There is so much for you to learn
that you should not have time to chafe against your fate.
We speak French now, but you must quickly learn Turkish. You have no knowledge of our customs, and if you
are to be presented to the sultan and his son in five
months' time, you must be proficient in many things. And
all this must be accomplished within the daily harem routine.

"I hope you do not think that all we do is sit about
painting our toenails, eating comfits, and waiting for a
summons from the sultan. Oh, no! Each girl is assigned a
light household task that must be performed daily. And
then there are the baths, and exercise periods, and, of
course, your studies. You will find your life very full."

The next few months sped by. Lady Refet had been
correct. There was no time for looking back. The three
new arrivals quickly learned Turkish, though it was Cyra
who was most proficient. Languages were her forte, and
she enjoyed them. They absorbed the history of the Ottoman Empire because Hadji Bey believed that in order to
understand the present and anticipate the future, they
must be familiar with the past.

The manners and morals of the Turks kept them busy
for hours on end. They studied music and dancing—an
important part of Turkish life. Zuleika shone in music, for
Eastern music was not unfamiliar to her ear. Firousi was
the dancer and very adept at singing her native songs to
her own accompaniment on the guitar. Cyra was neither
musician nor dancer, but she studied hard and became
adept enough to be considered accomplished. She found
the wailing of the reedy instruments not unlike that of
her native bagpipes.

Each girl was expected to embroider—which all three
could do—and to read and write. In their own languages
Cyra and Zuleika could do both. A scholarly old woman
named Fatima was assigned to teach them to write Turkish. Cyra helped Firousi, who at first found writing difficult—and reading worse—but Cyra was patient, and
Firousi eventually succeeded, to her pride and delight.

As the weeks went by, each made her own adjustment
to the situation. For Zuleika it was easiest. She was accus-

tomed to the cloistered existence of the imperial Ming
court, and only the burning memory of her true identity
and the betrayal of the shah's concubine still rankled in
her memory. Gradually she pushed these thoughts to the
back of her mind—although never forgotten, they did not
intrude on her everyday consciousness.

Used to the openness of her mountain home, Firousi
might have found the transition difficult had she not been
enchanted, amazed, and overwhelmed with all the sights,
sounds, and luxuries of her new existence. Though she had
lost everything—her home, her family, and her bridegroom—she was sensible enough to know that nothing
she could do would bring them back, and when she
thought of what her fate might have been, she thanked
God and accepted the situation. Her own ebullient spirits
did the rest.

For Cyra it was the hardest. Raised in freedom-loving
Scotland and used to coming and going as she pleased, she
chafed at the restrictions of the harem. Her world now
consisted of her oda, the baths, the women's mosque, and
the gardens. She would have given anything for a horse
and a long gallop across an open field. Like Firousi, she
accepted her situation, but there were times when she
thought she might go mad.

Lady Refet noted this and tried to ease the young girl's
restlessness. She assigned a eunuch to Cyra with orders
that, when the girl wished, she be allowed long walks in
the gardens provided she was suitably clothed.

This meant that Cyra must wear a loose-sleeved cloak-
like garment of pale mauve silk called a feridje. It covered her from neck to ankles and had attached at her
shoulders a large, square cape that hung nearly to the
ground. With it she also wore the yasmak, a veil consisting of two pieces. The first was placed across the bridge
of her nose and fell to her bosom; the second lay on her
head and extended as far as her eyebrows. The rest of it
fell behind her. In this costume no one could have told
whether she was young or old, fair or ugly.

This was proved one day—much to the terror of Cyra's
eunuch. They were walking in the gardens when around
the hedge came the sultan and his retinue. The eunuch
went gray and almost fainted, having been warned by the
agha that Cyra's presence in the harem must remain

secret; but Cyra reacted quickly. She bowed low, and the sultan, who might have stopped had he caught a glimpse of this muffled creature's fabulous green-gold eyes, passed her by without so much as a glance.

Cyra gave a great deal of thought to the incident. Until now, the sultan's power had not seemed real to her, but one look at the terrified eunuch's face had changed all that. I must spend the rest of my life in this strange world, she thought. I can be either a frightened slave like my poor eunuch, or I can be the willing and loving wife of a future sultan. Under Prince Selim's protection I need never be afraid, and I shall have power. Perhaps I shall even love this prince. From that moment on, her periods of restlessness became fewer, and her attitude genuinely cooperative.

"What can have caused this change?" Lady Refet asked Hadji Bey.

"I do not know," he replied, "but our young Cyra is a thinker. It is obvious that some incident has given her pause for thought. I could not be more delighted. Her cooperation is vital to our plans, for it is she whom I have chosen to be Prince Selim's first ikbal and, Allah willing, his bas-kadin."

"My nephew will not be told whom he must love, my lord agha."

Hadji Bey smiled. "I shall not have to tell him. He will choose to mate with her first. Selim has become very astute where women are concerned. Both Zuleika and Firousi are beautiful, but the girl from Cathay is proud, and deep within her heart she is bitter. She will be fiercely loyal to Selim, but he will never be able to get truly close to her. And behind the little Caucasian's smile is a deep sadness. She, too, will be loyal, but she will always carry with her the memory of the boy to whom she was wed on the day of her abduction, and who died in her defense. Selim will sense these flaws, and though he may love them and beget sons with them, he will never feel completely at ease with either of them."

"But does not Cyra have her memories? She has told me that she was betrothed when she was abducted."

"Cyra is younger than either Firousi or Zuleika. She was in love with love, not with her young fiancé. Besides, she is—whether she realizes it yet or not—far too realistic. She has been with us now for several months, and during that time her mind has been busily absorbing all we can offer. Her senses have been awakened and stimulated. She is ripe for love, and once that love is returned, she will mature, using not only her body to please her lord, but her mind as well. There is not another maiden in the harem to compare with her. Selim is already besotted by her beauty."

"He has seen her?" Lady Refet was incredulous. "By Allah, Hadji Bey, you risk our very lives!"

"No, my lady, I do not. Overlooking the baths is a small hidden room I had installed by my mutes when I became agha. No one knows of it—not even the sultan. From it I can observe the girls without embarrassing them. It allows me the opportunity to cull the wheat from the chaff—for the most beautiful face can have an unfortunate bodily imperfection. No girl of this sort may go to the sultan. I took Selim there several days ago to see your charges in order that he might identify them at his birthday fete."

"How I long for that occasion to come," said Lady Refet. "This secrecy is beginning to get on my nerves."

Finally the great day dawned, and pandemonium reigned throughout the palace. The crowded baths hummed with excited chatter. The hairdressers, in constant demand, rushed from one girl to another. The mistress of the wardrobe mediated so many quarrels over clothing between screaming and crying gediklis that she finally retired to her bed vowing to ask for a transfer to the Pavilion of Older Women.

In her unimportant little oda, Lady Refet closely inspected her three prize pupils. It amazed even her to think that for six months she and Hadji Bey had managed to keep these girls from the sultan's eyes. There would be questions tonight about that, but Lady Refet trusted Hadji Bey to handle the situation.

"You are exquisite," she said to Cyra. "You will outshine every other female at the reception."

"You're sure the colors are right?" asked the girl. "We spent hours yesterday choosing them."

Lady Refet nodded approvingly. She knew who had bribed the mistress of the wardrobe to allow her girls to

choose their costumes a day early. That lady owed her
position to Hadji Bey and was completely loyal to him.
"Look at yourselves, my little birds. You are all lovely."

They gazed at each other again. Cyra wore sheer,
pale-green silk pantaloons with a matching bodice that
was shot through with golden threads and fringed with
small pieces of jade; a wide gold girdle encrusted with
jade rested upon her hips. Her red-gold hair had been
brushed until it glistened. Held back by a simple gold
clasp with a pearl tassel, it fell straight down her back.
On her feet were green-and-gold brocade slippers. Lady
Refet slipped a matching green pelisse lined with gold-
colored satin about her shoulders.

Zuleika wore lavender silk pantaloons and a matching
bodice trimmed in purple velvet. A beautifully worked
girdle of gold and amethysts, brocade slippers, and a purple silk pelisse lined with lavender velvet completed her
costume. Her blue-black hair, pulled severely back from
her face to best show off her delicate Oriental features,
was braided with lilac-colored ribbons and pearls.

Firousi's pantaloons and matching silver-threaded bodice were turquoise, to match her eyes. Her girdle was
heavy silver set with rare Persian lapis. On her feet
she wore turned-up brocade slippers, and about her
shoulders a turquoise-blue pelisse lined with creamy
satin. Her silvery-blond hair fell in luscious curls about
her plump pink shoulders.

Lady Refet handed each girl a little tassled cap—
cloth of gold for Cyra and Zuleika, cloth of silver for
Firousi. "Hadji Bey will be very pleased," she said, smiling. "Now sit quietly while I inspect my other girls." She
moved among the others, bestowing a word of praise on
a costume here, the suggestion of a bit more red on the
cheeks there, a comforting pat to a frightened girl.

A eunuch came to call them. It was time for the reception. The gediklis formed two straight lines.

"Now, remember," said Lady Refet, speaking softly
to her special charges, "separate as soon as you reach
the Great Hall. Do not be seen together. Firousi, when
the maidens begin to approach the sultan and the prince,
be among the first. You, Zuleika, wait until half the girls
have passed, and you, Cyra, be in the last group."

Bajazet's royal residence had been the former home of

the Byzantine emperors, and the Turks called it the Eski Serai, or "Old Palace," to distinguish it from the Yeni Serai, or "New Palace," which had been begun by the sultan's father, Mohammed the Conqueror. The Yeni Serai was used by the Ottoman ruler for state functions, and also for privacy when he wished to escape his household. No women were allowed to live there.

Entering the Great Hall, Cyra caught her breath at its loveliness. It was domed in gold leaf; its walls shone with blue-and-gold mosaic tile; the floor was made of great blocks of pure, cream-colored marble. Although it was autumn, large jewel-studded porcelain pots containing small palms, roses, azaleas, and tulips filled the room. Decorative cages of canaries and nightingales hung everywhere. Musicians, carefully hidden behind carved screens, played softly. Moving discreetly through the crowd, slaves passed small cakes, sherbets, candied fruits, and nuts.

Then, suddenly, the great gilded door was flung open, and there came a cry: "Behold our great sultan, Bajazet, a loyal defender of Allah upon this earth." The sultan and his retinue, consisting of his three veiled kadins, their attendants, and Prince Selim, entered. The sultan and the prince settled themselves on the raised dais. The kadins were placed nearby.

Bajazet lifted his hand and spoke. "Because of the love I bore my late bas-kadin, Kiusem, the 'Peerless One,' I have recalled our son, Selim, from Magnesia. His new duties will be to govern a nearby Crimean province, and in honor of his twenty-fifth birthday, I have given him leave to choose six maidens from among my gediklis. These are my gift to him. Those who are chosen will be his own forever. Let the virgins pass before my son."

The ceremony began, and slowly, one by one, each girl paraded before the sultan and his son, her arms folded across her chest in the traditional pose. Some were aloof, some frightened, some giggled, and some smiled knowingly. The women of Bajazet's harem had been culled from the four corners of the world and their reputation for beauty was well earned. As she stopped before the sultan, each was divested of her pelisse by a slave, who draped it again over her shoulders after her presentation. Cyra watched all of this from a quiet corner of the hall.

Gazing at Prince Selim, she got her first good look at the
man who would be her master. He was tall and slender,
with his mother's fair skin and light eyes. His hair, dark
and slightly curling, was visible beneath his small white
turban. His face, which was smooth-shaven, wore a grave
look, but his lips occasionally twitched in a half smile of
amusement at the carefully staged pageant going on before him. Next to him stood a slave holding a silver tray
upon which rested six embroidered white silk handkerchiefs.

When Firousi, who was the third girl presented, stopped
before the throne, Prince Selim motioned to the slave,
who stepped from the dais and presented her with one of
the silks. A murmur of approval hummed through the
hall.

The second girl chosen was a Spaniard with warm
olive skin, topaz-colored eyes, and tumbling chestnut hair.
Her name was Sarina. She took her place at the foot of
the dais, casting a sulky look at Firousi.

Selim's third choice was a tiny maiden from the plains
of India, Amara. Her dark-brown eyes lowered shyly as
she was handed the silken square. A rosy blush suffused
her creamy brown cheek as the prince smiled at her.

Zuleika was the fourth choice. The sultan motioned to
Hadji Bey.

"I have not seen that girl before," he said. "Nor that
glorious silver-blond my son chose first."

"They are new, my lord. You know the harem is constantly being restocked. This is the first time in several
months you have had a reception and the opportunity to
see all your maidens."

More girls passed the dais, but two silk squares remained on the tray. Then Cyra appeared before the potentate and his son. Gracefully she glided to the foot of
the throne, her proud head held high. The slave removed
the pelisse. The sultan leaned forward, his tongue passing
quickly over his sensuous lips. The chatter among the
kadins ceased, their eyes narrowing at this potential rival.

For the fifth time Selim nodded at the tray-bearing
slave, and a moment later Cyra pressed the silk to her
forehead and to her lips as she took her place with the
others.

"Another new girl, Hadji Bey?" inquired the sultan.

"Yes, my lord."

"How long has she been in my harem?"

"Four months, my lord."

"And why have I not seen her before?"

"She resisted us strongly, my lord. We could not properly train her until recently."

"I see," said Bajazet, a slightly petulant tone entering his voice. "So I must sit here and watch my son skim off the cream of my harem. Perhaps I have been too hasty."

"Surely not hasty, my lord; but, rather, generous. Believe me, these girls are but semiprecious stones compared to the jewels I have hidden for you—maidens who are not here this night." He smiled knowingly at the sultan.

The sultan chuckled. "You have always looked after my interests, Hadji Bey. Forgive your ruler for doubting you."

The agha nodded graciously as the remaining silk handkerchief was given to a lovely golden-blond from northern Greece with deep sapphire eyes and marble-white skin. Her name was Iris.

"You have chosen well, my son," said Bajazet in a tone implying that perhaps Selim had chosen too well. The loss of the red-haired girl still rankled slightly. "Let the foreign and local representatives present their gifts to my son."

Hadji Bey motioned to Selim's new harem to sit by him on the dais. Fussily he arranged them so that when he finally stepped back and clapped his hands to signal, Cyra, Zuleika, and Firousi were seated closest to the prince.

Once again the slaves swung wide the great doors to the hall, admitting a large and colorful procession. First came the gifts from foreign nations. Egypt sent a dinner service for twelve—hammered gold plates with matching jewel-studded goblets. From the Mongol khan a marvelous coal-black stallion and two beautiful mares. One Indian ruler sent a gold belt two inches wide, studded with sapphires, rubies, emeralds, and diamonds. Another prince of India sent two pygmy elephants. From Persia came several bolts of various-colored silks, the finest in the world. The Venetian Levant sent a flawless crystal vase, four feet in height, filled with pale pink pearls, each one perfect and identical in size.

Next came gifts from every part of the vast Ottoman

Empire. One by one they were laid before the dais—beautifully woven rugs, silken bags containing rare tulip bulbs, cages of exotic birds, half a dozen Pygmy eunuchs, a choir of castrated Christian boys prized for their singing voices, the newest telescope, carved from a piece of ivory and banded in silver. This last gift, from Magnesia, the prince's former province, particularly pleased Selim, who was an avid student of astronomy.

As the pile of gifts grew higher and wider, Cyra watched the kadin Besma, mother of Prince Ahmed. Though she sat quietly, her face expressionless, her eyes flashed pure hatred at Selim and envy of the vast honor being paid this younger son of her lord and master.

Cyra debated with herself for a moment, and then, when the ceremony of the gifts was over and attention was diverted by the dancing girls, she reached up unobtrusively and touched the prince's hand. Startled, he looked down.

"Forgive the liberty taken by this humble slave, my lord. May I speak?"

He nodded.

"Please notice the lady Besma. The surface of the pond is smooth, but beneath, the currents are deadly. Would it not be wise to oil those troubled waters?"

"My slave is as wise as she is lovely," replied Selim. "It shall be done."

When the entertainment was over and Bajazet started to signal an end to the evening, Selim rose and prostrated himself before his father.

"Yes, my son?"

"My lord father, I can never repay your kindness to me nor your great nobility in honoring your word to my mother, but I can try." Reaching into a satin bag, he withdrew a sapphire the size of a hen's egg, a gift from the caliph of Baghdad. "Please accept this trifle, my lord, although it cannot possibly repay you for your generosity to me."

Pleased with the gesture, the sultan took the jewel.

"And," continued the prince, "for the pearls of my father's harem . . ." He reached into the Venetian vase and, removing two handfuls of the pink pearls, presented them to the third and fourth of his father's wives. He then turned to face Besma. "And, for the rarest jewel in

all the seraglio, an opal from the mines of Solomon. Its
fire and beauty cannot begin to match yours, and its size"
—which was that of a plum—"is surely smaller than
your heart. For your son, my beloved brother Ahmed,
my choirboys to sooth and entertain him."

From behind her thin veil Besma looked as if she had
swallowed a small hedgehog. "For myself, my son, and
my husband's kadins, I thank Prince Selim," she said
sourly.

"Well done, my son," said the sultan. "Well done!"
Raising his jeweled hand, he signaled the end of the evening and departed the Great Hall, followed by his kadins
and their attendants. The gediklis, forming into two lines,
then filed out.

The Great Hall stood empty save for Prince Selim, his
new harem, and Hadji Bey, who bustled forward, a broad
smile upon his face.

"Come, my lord Selim. I have arranged your apartments for this night. Tomorrow after morning prayers,
you and your household will depart the Eski Serai."

"Where am I to go? No word has been given to me
save that I will govern the Crimean province within two
days' ride of the city."

"Years ago, my prince, your father gave your mother
a small palace overlooking the Black Sea. It is now
yours. The lady Refet will accompany you as chaperone to
your harem."

"May Allah bless you, old friend," replied the prince.
"My aunt will be safe now. My father's kadins hate her
because of her loyalty to me."

"I know," said the agha gravely. "Already there have
been two attempts on her life."

"What?"

"Do not be angered, my lord. I tell you this but to
warn you to be constantly vigilant. But come, the walls
have ears. We will talk later." He turned to the waiting
girls. "Follow me, my ladies. The hour is late."

Leaving the blue-and-gold hall, they trailed Hadji Bey
through the winding corridors to a large apartment where
they were greeted by Lady Refet. The few possessions
they owned had been packed and transferred to their
temporary quarters, and their nightclothes had already
been laid out.

"I suggest, ladies, that you retire now. We leave early," said Lady Refet.

"But what if the prince should want one of us tonight?" asked Sarina.

"He will not," replied Lady Refet.

"How can you know that?" persisted the girl.

"Sarina, it is obvious to me that in your excitement at being chosen by Prince Selim, you have forgotten your manners. Your status in this world has not changed. You are still a slave—a mere gediklis—and so you shall remain unless one day you manage to please my nephew. I find that highly unlikely unless your behavior improves. Turkish gentlemen deplore rude women and usually end up bowstringing them."

Sarina had the good grace to flush at this well-deserved rebuke. Mumbling an apology, she made ready for bed. Lady Refet stopped by each girl's couch to chat a minute and make her feel at ease. Then, seeing that all was well, she signaled a slave to dim the lamps, and left the room.

"Allow no one except the agha or myself to enter here," she instructed the guards at the door. "Your lives will be forfeit should you disobey."

She entered the apartment next to the one housing the girls. Prince Selim and Hadji Bey greeted her.

"It is safe to talk here," said the eunuch.

"Praise Allah!" replied the good lady. "I shall be glad to leave the Eski Serai." Turning to her nephew, she said, "Dearest boy, how can I thank you?"

"I am ashamed to say it is Hadji Bey's doing, aunt. I never even thought of it."

"I merely arranged that which I knew Your Highness would want were he not so involved with other matters."

"I become more amazed each day by your ability to 'arrange' matters," replied the prince wryly. "Now, what of the girls you chose for me? Why those three?"

"Each is suited to be a kadin, my lord. At your mother's request I left Constantinople late last year to seek three exceptional wives for you. We wanted girls uninvolved with the harem system, who, knowing their future ahead of time, would give you their complete loyalty. Firousi is from the Caucasus. I purchased her in Damascus. Zuleika is from Cathay. I found her in Baghdad.

Cyra comes from a country called Scotland. It is north of England. I bought her in Candia. It is for *her* that our hopes are highest. She is endowed with that rare combination of intelligence and beauty, and has a budding wisdom, which, guided properly, will one day make her invaluable. Still, she remains completely feminine. I can only hope she will please you."

"I was treated to some of that wisdom this night. It was she who suggested I present gifts to Besma."

Hadji Bey and Lady Refet smiled at each other. "The small bird learns to fly quickly," observed the chief eunuch.

"She also has magnificent eyes," said the prince. "Green eyes like hers are rare. They are so clear, and there are small flecks of black and gold in them. Something like leaves in a pond."

"Then you are pleased with my choices, my lord?"

"Yes, but I think my father was not. I hope you have something equally lovely for him, lest he take my harem back. Firousi is magnificent, and Zuleika exquisite. You must truly be blessed by the stars to have succeeded with this coup. What do you think of my choices?"

"The Greek and Indian girls are lovely. They are simple and placid and will be a comfort to you. However, I would rather you had chosen someone other than the Spanish girl. She is quick-tempered and sharp-tongued. She may have a tendency toward troublemaking."

"Alas, that is true," said Lady Refet. "She attempted to question my authority this evening."

"We shall keep a close watch on her," replied Hadji Bey. "Now, to the business at hand. You already know that your mother planned for you to succeed your father. Finding you perfect wives to help you and moving you closer to the capital were merely *part* of her plan."

"Yes, I know the plan, Hadji Bey. But you know that the succession goes to the eldest living male in our family. Ahmed is my father's heir."

"Your father's heir was your older brother."

"Mustafa died at two of a chill."

"He became violently ill after visiting Besma one afternoon. The sweets he returned with and offered your mother were suspect. The child suffered horribly and by morning was dead. Your mother was ill for several days. However, when she recovered, she was quite prostrate with grief. I was newly agha then, but I suspected poison from the start. I took the remaining candies and fed them to a dog. He died. When I told your mother, her grief became hatred toward Besma, who was now mother of the heir."

"Why did my mother not expose Besma?"

"She did, but your father would not listen. After some months of solitude to recover from her agony, she appeared before your father again and, still being his favorite, was welcomed back. You were born of that reunion. Fortunately for Besma, your father now had two sons— one by his third kadin, Safiye—and the witch knew her Ahmed would be safe since your mother couldn't discreetly dispose of two children. However, your mother had determined from before your conception that you would take Mustafa's place.

"*That* is why you have been educated so carefully, and that is why, when she knew she was dying, your mother begged your return from Magnesia. You have been so carefully guarded all your life that even your father does not know you well. She wanted him to see and know you so that he might possibly alter the succession.

"She knew you must be more in the public eye so the people might get to know you, and the Janissaries might see the great difference between you and your brothers. You are a good man, an excellent soldier, and a devout Muslim. Add to this several sons, and you are the perfect candidate for sultan.

"When the time comes for Bajazet to join his ancestors in Paradise, you must act swiftly. Before the sultan's last breath, your brothers, their mothers, and all loyal to them must die. You will then be sultan, and your mother and brother will be avenged!"

Silence engulfed the room as Hadji Bey finished speaking. Lady Refet anxiously watched her nephew for a reaction. Walking out on the balcony, Selim gazed over the slumbering city of Constantinople, its lights dimmed, its quiet broken only by the occasional barking of stray dogs baying at the full moon. Below him the waters of the Golden Horn flowed swiftly.

"They will all be strangled, placed in weighted sacks,

and thrown into the straits," he said grimly. "All except
Besma. I will personally toss the bitch to the dogs."

Hadji Bey smiled slowly. "It will take many years, my
lord. Like the Prophet's cat, you must cultivate great patience. If our plans become known, you are a dead man."

"I will not fail my mother, Hadji Bey—nor you, my
old friend. I understand that many lives are involved."

"The hour is late," said Lady Refet. "I think we had
best get some sleep. We have a three-day journey ahead
of us."

They rose, and the agha, bidding them goodnight,
slipped out through a secret door behind the tapestries.

"Sleep well, dearest nephew," said Lady Refet. "I will
return to guard your doves."

"And you, dear aunt, sleep well, also." He escorted
her to the door and watched as the eunuch guarding his
harem passed her through into the next apartment.

Closing the doors to his own rooms, Selim clapped
his hands for his body servant. The slave divested him
of his finery, and then, placing a soft wool garment over
his master's shoulders, slipped out.

Standing once again on the balcony, the prince studied
the night sky. It was clear and filled to overflowing with
bright stars. Breathing slowly, he allowed peace to fill his
soul. He was now firmly aware where his destiny would
take him, and he knew what role he must play to fulfill
that destiny. He would be good Prince Selim, devoted to
his father, his half-brother Ahmed, and his family. He
would be unobtrusive but always known, and he would
appear to be content with his portion. And then, when
the right moment came, he would strike and take it all.
The empire would be his. The others were not fit to rule!

Iron had entered his soul. Turning from the night, he
reentered his room, lay down upon his couch, and fell
into a deep, healthy sleep.

11

THE MORNING brought a clear blue sky and bright sun. A fresh, clean breeze wafted across the city, bringing with it the scent of early autumn flowers and ripe fruit. The crowded streets were in a holiday mood, for all Constantinople knew of yesterday's events within the Eski Serai. Today Prince Selim and his household would depart the palace for their own province.

The more enterprising householders along the route of exit had sold seats in their windows and on their balconies and roofs. Those fortunate enough to have bought the places would have a fine view of the procession.

A murmur of excitement rippled through the crowds as the Main Gate of the Eski Serai slowly began to swing open. Necks stretched, vying for the first look at what was to come. It was a company of Janissaries in their red-and-green clothing, astride glossy brown horses and brandishing metal-tipped whips at the crowds to keep them back.

Next came Ali Hamid, the sultan's crier, resplendent in orange silk pantaloons and vest, his silver-and-orange-striped cloak spread over the shining bay flanks of his mount, and an orange plumed turban upon his head. He advanced his horse several paces out from the gate, stopped, and held up a hand. A hush fell over the spectators.

"Behold," he intoned in a deep, strong voice, "behold, o people of Constantinople, behold the loving kindness of our great sultan, Bajazet, the loyal servant of Allah upon this earth—may he live forever. Today his son Prince Selim, child of the sultan's beloved late wife, Kiusem, leaves his father's house in great honor. Look upon him, o people of Constantinople, and see the greatness of a parent's love. Learn from the example of our great sultan, Bajazet.

"Behold, Constantinople, the six virgin damsels, each one more lovely than the dawn, that our prince takes with him. A gift from his sire, selected from the very harem of his father. His own free choice. Who among you has ever heard or known of such true generosity?"

A hum of approval ran through the vast gathering.

"See, o people of Constantinople, the many gifts sent from those who fear and respect our power and greatness. These gifts are to honor our lord's youngest son. Look upon this spectacle well, and in the winter of your years tell your grandchildren of the greatness of our mighty sultan, Bajazet, beloved son of Mohammed the Conqueror of Constantinople."

The sultan's crier moved his horse onward, stopping every few minutes to repeat his words. Behind him came the caravan bearing the fabled gifts. Flanking it were the prince's household slaves.

A figure mounted upon a night-black stallion appeared framed in the vast gate. The crowds surged forward for a better look at its rider. The Janissaries forced them back.

"It's the prince," shouted a voice in the mass. The crowd took up the cry. "Selim! Selim! Selim!" they chanted.

Urging his stallion forward, the prince rode into their midst. He sat well upon his mount, a smile turning up the corners of his mouth. He was dressed in white and gold. Jewels sparkled upon his hands, and an enormous blood-red ruby glittered in his turban. The people crowded about him, defying the Janissaries' whips, touching his soft, golden-leather boots, drinking in his youth and charm.

The captain of the Janissaries pushed his horse to the prince's side. "Sir, you will be injured. Let my men disperse this vermin."

"I have a better way than whips, captain." Selim reached into a pouch on his saddle and drew out a fistful of coins, which he flung to the excited mob. It parted, and he rode on, occasionally reaching again into the pouch and tossing more coins, to the delight of the scrambling men and women.

Selim was followed by the Pygmy eunuchs, dressed in their new uniforms of yellow and green. Behind them

came Lady Refet in a silver-and-gold palanquin carried
by four oiled black slaves. She was followed by six camels,
all white, which carried upon their backs gold-colored
howdahs hung with violet silks. Within each rested a member of Selim's harem. The crowds murmured, their imagi-
nations taking flight at their glimpse of the heavily veiled
figures.

The procession slowly wended its way through the narrow streets, down the hill into the main city, and along the
broad avenues. The day was growing warm, and Cyra,
swathed in all her veils, began to wish with impatience
that this Oriental pageant, of which she was such a small
part, would end. Two hours after passing through the
Main Gate of the Eski Serai, they went through the
eastern gates of the city. Almost at once, the procession
picked up momentum.

In late afternoon they stopped, and an encampment
was set up on a small hill overlooking the sea. The following morning the camp was dismantled, and they moved on.
In late afternoon of the third day, they reached their destination.

Set like a fine jewel amid the soft green hills above the
Black Sea, the Moonlight Serai nestled shining and white.
At first glance, Cyra was enchanted, but as her camel
trotted down the dusty drive, she noticed the neglect surrounding her. Tall poplars lined the roadway, but the
land surrounding them was thickly overgrown. As they
arrived at the palace itself, she was doubly shocked to
find buildings so lovely from a distance in a sad state of
disrepair. Clearly, the Moonlight Serai had neither been
used nor cared for in many years. Her camel knelt, and
the Pygmy eunuch assigned to her helped her out of the
howdah. She ran to Lady Refet.

"Are we expected to live here?" she asked.

"The sultan's generosity has obviously not extended
beyond Constantinople," the older woman said dryly.

"It is appalling. We cannot possibly live here," cried
Cyra. "Something must be done at once!"

"Indeed we cannot," said a masculine voice.

They turned to face the prince.

"Your temper matches your hair," he laughed.

Cyra flushed. "Forgive your humble slave this outburst,
my lord and master," she began.

"You are neither humble nor slavish, Cyra."

She paled.

"But," he continued, "I prefer it that way. In the future, I expect all of you to address me as a man, not some court demigod. However, your respect for me as your master should not diminish. I will never be ruled by a woman." He turned to his aunt. "I know nothing of these household matters. What must be done here to make my palace habitable? Will you take charge for me?"

"Dear boy, I cannot. I know very little. You forget that your mother and I entered the harem when we were only nine years of age. We were trained from the first to be gediklis, not household servants, but Cyra has been trained in these things in her country. Let her take charge. I will oversee all she does, as my knowledge of our customs is greater."

"Very well," said Selim. "I suppose, however, that the first thing we should do is set up the tents so we may be comfortable. Cyra, send a message to Hadji Bey informing him of our plight."

"Yes, my lord." She turned and, pointing at a slave, said, "Can you ride?"

"Yes, my lady."

"Saddle one of the Moorish geldings and then come to me. I will have a note for you to take directly to Hadji Bey."

The slave ran off to do as he was bidden.

"Lady Refet, will you write for me? My written Turkish is not yet perfected."

"Of course, my dear. What shall I say?"

"Tell Hadji Bey what we have found. That we need men to repair the buildings, the water pipes, the kitchens and baths. We need gardeners for the grounds, furnishings for the palace, and many more household slaves. Tell him it must be done within the month. That we are camped here like savage nomads."

Lady Refet called to her maid to bring parchment and pens. As she wrote, Cyra walked over to the other girls.

"Well, my sisters, this is a fine mess we find ourselves in today."

"I notice you were quick to offer a solution to our lord," sneered Sarina. "Why should you be in charge?"

"It was Lady Refet who offered my services to our

master. Oh, Sarina, let us not quarrel. There is so much to be done. Have you ever run a large household? If so, I will be happy to turn over my responsibility to you. Do you want it?"

"No."

"Well, then, I must shoulder the burden. Before I came to the seraglio, I helped my grandmother to run my father's castle. Were I not here, I should now be running my own. We must all help so that when our lord returns he will be pleased."

Sarina turned away. "My father was a gardener in the house of a great lord," she said. "I know much about plants and their care."

"Wonderful! Then you must take over the rebuilding of the gardens. Turks love their gardens, and the prince is no exception. Will you do it?"

"Yes," replied the Spanish girl. "I could do it."

Cyra put an arm about Sarina's shoulders. "Then, sister, the gardens are your responsibility—and your domain."

The Spaniard gave her a little smile. "See that the palace is as beautiful inside as my gardens will be without," she said.

Cyra looked startled. Then, seeing that the girl was teasing, she grinned back. They burst into laughter.

When the note had been dispatched to the capital, there was nothing for the prince's maidens to do. Cyra asked permission of Lady Refet to explore the grounds a bit. It was granted, and she strolled off.

She quickly saw that with work the property could be magnificent. Set on the cliffs high above the Black Sea, it had both fields and wooded areas. Wandering among the trees, she heard the bubbling of a spring and, following the sound, found a clear, sandy-bottomed pool that was filled by a little waterfall at one end, flowing out and down the cliffs between two small rocky hillocks at the other end. The banks surrounding the pool were thickly carpeted with moss, and the warm sunlight filtered through the trees. Kneeling, she dipped her hand into the water. It was invitingly cool, and Cyra was hot and dusty from the journey.

I will tell the others later, she thought, but first I am going to bathe by myself. It had been so long since she

had had the privacy of her own bath. Stripping her
garments, she left them where they fell and, pinning her
long hair up, waded into the water. Before long she was
happily swimming and then leisurely floating about the
pool. The late-afternoon sunlight dappled the water, and
she felt freer and more relaxed than she had in months.
Turning to swim back to the shore, she was horrified to
see Prince Selim sitting by her clothes and regarding her
with amusement. Her feet touched the bottom, and she
stood regarding him, half-perplexed, half-angry.

"Come out, my little Ondine. You will shrivel your
lovely skin."

"I cannot, my lord."

"Why not?" His face grew worried. "Do you have a
cramp?"

"My lord." She struggled, trying to find the right
words. "My lord, I am not accustomed to appearing
naked before a man."

"I will change all that." He grinned at her.

"Please, my lord—" Her eyes pleaded with him, but
he was not to be swayed.

"If you do not come out, my little mermaid, then I
shall come in." Laughing, he removed his shirt. His broad
chest was smooth and tanned and well muscled.

Daring possessed her. "You will find the water quite
refreshing, my lord."

So, she wants to play, thought the prince, surprised.
The little vixen! He stripped his boots and pants off,
never noticing that Cyra carefully kept her eyes on his
face. Plunging in, he surfaced to discover himself alone
in the water—Cyra had scrambled ashore as he dove, and
was frantically trying to get into her clothing. Swimming
to the pool's edge, he vaulted out. He was furious, and
the look in his eyes was unmistakable.

She was naked from the waist up as he caught her to
him and loosed her hair. It tumbled about their wet
shoulders. Kissing her slowly and deliberately, he forced
her mouth open and touched her tongue with his. She
trembled violently and then went limp.

Taken aback, Selim lowered the inert girl to a mossy
carpet. Her dark lashes were like a smudge against her
pale cheeks. He could see her heart fluttering wildly between her breasts. Confused—for he had never before

been faced with a fainting woman—he wondered what to do. Her obvious helplessness had cooled his lust, and he suddenly felt strangely protective. As he reached for her cloak and covered her, her eyes opened.

"Please, my lord," she whispered, "not like this. I am not a peasant wench to be tumbled in a wood."

"Why did you faint?"

"I was afraid, my lord." A little smile touched her lips. "You looked very angry."

"I should have you beaten."

"Yes, my lord."

Her repentance was so sincere he could not help laughing. "You did invite me to come into the water."

"I was thinking only of gathering my garments and fleeing you, my lord. I did not think you would chase me without your clothes."

Her honesty perplexed him, and he heard himself say, "I have, you know, seen you naked before. You need not blush. You are quite lovely. The human body is nothing to be ashamed of. Perhaps when we know each other better you will not be so shy."

She lowered her eyes, and for a few moments they sat in silence. Then he bent and kissed her. He felt her tremble again.

"Do not fear, little virgin. I will not ravish you," he said gently.

"My lord—" Her voice was apologetic.

He stopped her mouth with his hand. "You were correct, my lovely Cyra. You are not a peasant wench to be tumbled in a wood. For you it will be a full moon and a scented chamber. The softness of a Persian love song, and a prince who at this moment is already in love with you. Put on your blouse and return to the encampment. I need not tell you to speak to no one of this interlude."

After she had left him, he sat by the pool in deep thought. The sight of her slender body had aroused him terribly. Had she not swooned, he would have raped her and ruined everything. Hadji Bey had spoken to him at length about the three girls he had purchased, but always the agha had come back to Cyra. When Selim asked him why, Hadji Bey had smiled, and said only, "You are perceptive, my son. You will soon see why this maiden touches me. I will not influence you further."

Selim had quickly discovered enough to pique his interest. Her actions at his birthday fete had aroused his admiration. Her wisdom, immediate loyalty, and intelligence pleased him. In their three days of travel he had observed that she was a natural leader, yet sweet-tempered and kind to her peers. She deferred to his aunt, and this afternoon he had discovered her modesty. It was more than enough to encourage his further investigation. He wanted to know more of his lovely slave than just her body, but right now it was her body that disturbed him.

It would take a good month to get his palace into order, and if he must remain in the constant presence of this virgin temptress, he could not be responsible for his actions. He had promised her a scented, moonlit chamber, and he did not think it would do his cause any good to break that promise.

He might, of course, take one of the other girls to his bed, but he did not want another, and it might hurt Cyra. It surprised him to find he did not want to hurt her. Swiftly he stood up, and, striding back to the camp, he sought out his aunt.

"I am going hunting," he told her. "This domestic uproar is no place for a man! It should be a month before the palace is habitable. I will return then."

Without giving her a chance to reply, he mounted his horse and, shouting to his Tartars to follow him, rode off.

12

THE SLAVE sent to Hadji Bey returned with the message that the agha kislar himself would be arriving by the following morning to survey the situation. Cyra casually tossed him a small bag of coins. "Serve me well, and you will never lack," she said softly. The slave flashed her a knowing smile.

When the agha arrived he was not alone. With him came a caravan bearing luxurious tents, food, and additional slaves. By sunset the prince's household was comfortably settled, and the fragrance of lamb kebabs drifted through the encampment.

When night fell, the residents of the small tent city settled down to sleep. Hadji Bey and Lady Refet remained talking alone in her tent.

"I would have thought my dear Bajazet would have seen to the repair of my sister's palace."

"I see Besma's fine hand in this business," replied the eunuch, "but never mind. I have already spoken to the sultan of the few minor repairs necessary, and received his permission."

"Minor repairs!"

"A small stretching of the truth, perhaps," remarked her companion. "However, it is not imperative that our lord be informed of the extent of the repairs. He is also less likely to mention such unimportant matters to Besma. She will do a great deal of speculating, and it will be very difficult for her to place spies within our ranks."

"If she has not already done so."

"Impossible! You know I personally kept the new slaves given the prince segregated from the rest of the palace people. The workmen arriving at dawn I selected myself. Nevertheless, we shall keep close watch. Nothing must be done to arouse the suspicion of that she-wolf. When the prince's household is settled, I shall allow her to place a spy or two. There will be nothing to report, and in a year or so Besma will be lulled into a false sense of security. She has enough enemies in the Eski Serai to worry about without being overly concerned with a minor prince living several days' journey from her precious Ahmed."

"Sometimes your sense of strategy amazes even me, old friend," said Lady Refet.

"I shall not rest until Lady Kiusem's son succeeds Sultan Bajazet."

Refret gazed hard at the proud black man across from her. "Did you love my sister so much, Hadji Bey?"

"I loved her as only a man who is not a man can love. She was my mother, my sister, my friend. When I came to the harem, a frightened little boy of nine, I had been torn from my family, cruelly castrated, and carried from my homeland. Most boys of my age died from castration. I was one of the fortunate ones, but at that time I did not know it. Kiusem saw my fright, though she was just a child herself. You remember how she took me under her wing. When she became the sultan's ikbal, I became her head eunuch. When her son was born and the old agha died, I was, thanks to her influence, given the post. I owe everything to her, and I have always shared her dream of Selim's succession. She saw, as I did, the degenerate, warped man that Besma has raised Ahmed to be. My lady is dead, but you, Refet, and I live. We will make Kiusem's dream become a reality."

The campfires burned low, the night waned, and slowly the new day lightened the eastern sky. The encampment came alive with activity. The workmen arrived from the city to begin their task of restoring the Moonlight Serai to its former elegance.

Cyra, with Firousi and Zuleika in attendance, explored the small palace checking for needed repairs, while the Greek girl, Iris, and the Indian maiden, Amara, jointly took over supervision of the household slaves and set them to various tasks. Sarina, well veiled, walked through what had once been the gardens. She made mental notes and without delay set a group of slaves to work

removing the heavy undergrowth and the weeds that had
so long ruled the area.

The gardens, free of weeds and brush, were tilled,
fertilized, and newly planted with thousands of spring
bulbs, flowering shrubs, and fruit trees of every kind.
Expectantly they awaited the spring. The air was fragrant
with late roses and other autumn flowers transplanted
from the sultan's greenhouses.

Within a month the Moonlight Serai was transformed
back to its past glory and sat like a fine jewel amid the
green hills. Its exterior had been scrubbed with sand to
remove the dirt. The broken columns, windows, iron-
work, and fountains had been restored. In the kitchens
the ovens grew warm again, and the pantries were full.
The roofs of the outer buildings were newly thatched,
and in the freshly cleaned and painted stalls the royal
horses neighed contentedly.

Within, furnishings brought from the storehouses of
the Eski Serai had been skillfully placed. Lamps were
hung, rugs laid. Cyra, in her first inspection of the palace,
had found a small wing overlooking both the sea and the
the hills, which she decreed would be the harem.

To gain entrance, one had to pass through large double
doors which opened into an inside waiting room. There
the local female vendors might come to show and sell
their goods to the prince's women. To the right of the
main door was a paneled door opening into a small
private anteroom which let to the rooms of the harem.
The main room was a large, square salon whose far end
looked out through a wall of leaded-pane windows into
the harem garden, which faced the sea. Here Selim's
harem could walk in complete privacy. To the left of the
salon a hall led to the harem baths. To the rear right was
an arch opening into a long corridor. On the left side of
the corridor were six small bedrooms, each with its own
separate outer chamber for a eunuch or slave. On the
right side of the corridor were Lady Refet's rooms—a
nicely proportioned private salon and bedroom, each of
which faced her own small, secluded garden.

It was now understood that Cyra, with Zuleika and
Firousi, would oversee the running of the household until
a competent slave could be trained to handle the situa-

tion. Amara and Iris continued to oversee the household slaves, and Sarina ruled the gardeners like a Tartar warlord.

One afternoon, a horseman came galloping up the newly graveled road to the palace. He was immediately brought to Lady Refet.

"Prince Selim will arrive by late afternoon," the soldier reported.

Upon hearing this, the six maidens took action. Sarina went to the gardens. Firousi hurried to the kitchens to inform the cooks that tonight's meal must be without flaw. Amara and Iris marshaled the house servants and gave instructions that the prince's rooms must be cleaned and freshened immediately. Cyra and Zuleika flew from one place to another overseeing all the preparations.

Returning to their quarters, the six girls descended to the baths. Lady Refet smiled to herself and wondered how long this era of peace and cooperation would last now that her nephew was returning.

Selim arrived and much to his delight was greeted by a beautiful home, his aunt, and six lovely girls who smiled shyly at him from behind their sheer veils.

"Well, nephew, do you approve of your house?" asked Lady Refet as she escorted him to his new quarters.

"Frankly, I am amazed. When I left I did not expect to return to such perfection. Even the gardens look as if they had been here forever. How in Allah's name did you do it?"

"I didn't."

He stared at her in disbelief.

"Do you not remember? You left Cyra in charge. She and the other women of your harem have created this miracle. If you like the gardens, thank Sarina. If the cooking pleases you, Firousi is responsible. Your slaves are being trained by Iris and Amara. Zulieka has seen to the furnishings, having twice traveled in secret to Constantinople to choose them from the seraglio storerooms. Over it all, Cyra has ruled and administered with a firm but kindly hand. You are truly blessed to own such a harem."

"Indeed they seem clever, but are they as skilled in

other matters? Or have I chosen a group of Amazons to warm my bed?"

"Bah," snapped his aunt. "Would you prefer six fat, lazy, and selfish women instead? I have lived practically my whole life in Turkey, and if you do not have enough sense to realize the treasures you have, then you are a fool beyond belief! Your girls excelled in the classess on those 'other matters.' I doubt you will suffer any disappointments! You men are all alike. Had you found your house a pigsty, no amount of skill in carnal matters would have pleased you."

Selim burst into laughter. "Oh, aunt," he gasped, wiping the tears from his eyes, "my mother always said you were the serious twin. I am but teasing you." He put an arm about her and kissed her cheek.

Lady Refet sniffed, but a little smile flickered on her lips. "You are the age of a man, but you still play tricks like a small boy."

He chuckled and, trying to make amends, asked, "Will you take supper with me this evening?"

"Ah, I had almost forgotten. Your maidens wondered —if you were not overly fatigued from your trip—if you would dine in the harem this evening. You really should, Selim. They have worked so hard to please you, and they hardly know you."

"Very well, aunt. I have been in the company of men for over a month now, and it is time I came to know my damsels. Tell them I will come."

Lady Refet bowed courteously to her nephew and departed.

That evening Selim sat cross-legged at the head of his table and stared in frank delight at the girls about him. They were like the flowers in his garden—Amara in pale sky-blue, Sarina in lime-green, Iris in peach, Zuleika in peacock-blue, Firousi in dusky rose, and Cyra in a soft wisteria color. Their unveiled faces were a pretty mixture of races and cultures. He began to feel a slight stirring of desire. It had been over a month since he had lain with a woman—unless you counted that savage little nomad girl he had surprised one day while hunting. Selim, like all Ottoman princes, was a healthy and virile man.

Firousi, smiling up at him, asked, "Might I sing for you, my lord? Songs from my homeland? Cyra has studied my native language and can translate them for you."

He nodded, and a slave brought a stringed instrument, which Firousi began to strum. Her songs were merry, and the silvery-blond played and sang well. Cyra softly spoke the words to Selim, occasionally blushing at the more ribald parts. The prince laughed heartily. Then Firousi began a soft, romantic Persian love song. Rising quietly, Sarina began to dance, her slim body moving suggestively to the music.

Selim glanced at the other girls. He was definitely beginning to feel the need for a woman that night. He had decided, the afternoon he sat by her at the pool, that Cyra would be the first of his maidens to come to his bed—Cyra, cool, competent, and infinitely desirable. What fires smoldered within that lovely white body?

Motioning to a slave, he told him to bring his aunt to his quarters when he signaled an end to the evening. The slave bowed. For a while longer he allowed his harem to entertain him, then, smiling his pleasure at them, he ended the evening.

Chattering among themselves, the six girls reviewed the evening with pride. It had gone well; Prince Selim was obviously pleased with them. They did not notice Lady Refet's absence until she reappeared among them.

"My nephew has requested a specific maiden to join him this night."

The chatter stopped, and they gazed, half-frightened, at her.

"Cyra, you have one hour to prepare yourself. Go now and do so."

13

As THE FIVE wide-eyed girls watched, Lady Refet led Cyra to the waiting litter. For months they had planned and dreamed of the moment when one of them would be chosen to go to their master's bed. Strangely they were happy for Cyra. Though each was a trifle envious that she had not been chosen, at the same time, each was glad she was not to be the first.

Picking up the litter, the slaves moved swiftly down the hallway to the prince's quarters and through the bronze doors that led to their lord's apartment. In the silence of the dimly lit corridor, even the reassuring patter of the slaves' feet on the tiled floor could not still Cyra's pounding heart. Setting the litter down before a carved wooden door, the eunuch who accompanied them whispered, "Go. Our lord awaits his pleasure."

On trembling legs, Cyra allowed herself to be handed out of the litter, and, reluctantly pushing the door open, she entered the prince's chambers.

It was a pleasant, medium-sized room, with a tiled stove in a corner, its fire glowing softly. The walls were hung with thick Kir-Shehr carpets in hues of blue, green, and red. Highly polished brass lamps cast a warm glow, and beneath her feet, which seemed to have turned to ice, she felt the softness of another rug.

The room was Spartan in its furnishings, yet rich in its accessories. To the left was a raised marble dais the color of cream, upon which rested a square bed with gold-colored velvet hangings. By the door sat a large wooden chest banded in gilded leather. In a far corner was a low, round table surrounded by multicolored silk cushions. A tall silver censer filled with fragrant burning aloes stood by the bed. Directly in front of her, the room

opened into a private garden facing the sea. His voice
came to her from the garden.

"Come here to me, Cyra."

Entering the garden, she fell to her knees, her head
touching the ground. He raised her up and gravely kissed
her on the forehead.

"Never prostrate yourself before me again. It is the
act of a menial slave, not an intelligent woman."

"Thank you, my lord."

He led her to the balustrade overlooking the sea. "The
moon on the water cannot rival your beauty, my dove."

"Thank you, my lord."

He scrutinized her closely. "By the Prophet's beard,
they have decked you in the traditional finery, have they
not?"

"Yes, my lord."

A smile on his lips, he fingered the veils, and she
shivered.

"Are you cold?"

"Yes, my lord."

"No wonder. These garments are meant to reveal,
not to warm." He laughed softly. "At the foot of the bed
is a woolen robe. Wrap yourself in it."

Reentering the bedchamber, she removed the six veils
that covered her and slipped into the soft, white wool
robe. It fastened beneath her breasts and fit as if it had
been made for her. Moving to return to the garden, she
saw the prince standing in the doorway watching her. He,
too, wore a long, loose woolen robe.

"Warmer now?"

"Yes, my lord."

"So far this evening you have said 'Yes, my lord' three
times, and 'Thank you, my lord' twice. You have been
much more articulate on other occasions."

Looking at him, she whispered, her voice close to tears,
"I am sorry, my lord."

He gazed at her a moment. A devilish look entered his
eyes, and he moved swiftly toward her. Sobbing, she ran
from him, to be stopped suddenly by the sound of his
laughter.

"I thought so," he said. "You are still frightened of me.
Rest easy, my sweet Cyra. I have yet to force a woman
—though once I was tempted."

"Oh, my lord. I am so ashamed! Please forgive me."

Moving to her side, he gently put his arm about her. "Come and sit by me, little virgin." Drawing her down on a pile of cushions, he continued. "Now listen to me. Do you know why I went away after our meeting at the pool?"

"I thought you were displeased with me."

"No, I was not angry. I was afraid. Afraid that if I stayed near you, I should forget my promise to you and possess you by force. Do you smell the aloes, my little one? And do you see through the windows a full moon? Did I not promise you these? Mine are not the actions of a man bent on rape, my precious little fool."

"I did not think, my lord."

"Which, I have noted, is very unlike you, Cyra. Could it be that you perhaps return some of that which I feel for you?"

He turned her toward him. Her head was lowered, but he could see the blush on her cheeks.

"Look at me."

Shyly she raised her face to his, and he was blinded by her shining eyes. Allah, he intoned wordlessly, Allah give me the strength not to ravish her instantly. He bent his head and lightly kissed her mouth.

"You did not faint!" he exclaimed in mock surprise. "Dare I try again?"

She giggled. "Yes, please, my lord. When you are gentle I am not afraid."

This time he drew her into his arms. Her firm young body with its soft skin delighted him. Their lips met, and what he had meant to be a short kiss lengthened and increased in sweetness. He felt her arms wrap about his neck, and then, to his amazement, her little tongue brushed his teeth. Shuddering, he loosed her.

"Little virgin," his voice was low, "little virgin, if you tempt me further, I may succumb."

"I am afraid, my lord, but I am but a woman."

"My poor child," he said. "In my delight of you I had forgotten how terrifying the first venture into love can be. Undoubtedly they had drummed into you your responsibility to please me, and the fact that, should you fail, your life would be over."

Tenderly he gathered her into his arms, his lips brush-

ing against her fragrant hair. The freshness of her scent,
the closeness of her body sent a stab of desire through
him. I must not hurry her, he thought, as his lips moved
along her cheek.

Then she turned her face up to him, and his mouth
found hers again. Their breaths mingled. Her arms went
about his neck, and she pressed against him. With a groan
he lifted her up and carried her to the bed.

She protested the loss of his lips as he placed her
against the pillows and then lay propped on one arm, gazing down at her. His hands were clenched into fists that
opened and closed violently as he restrained himself from
falling on her. He bent, and tentatively his tongue explored her mouth. Then, unable to wait any longer, he
moved his hands to her breasts. She quivered as his fingers
impatiently opened the clasp of her robe and touched the
soft flesh. His other hand now moved along the satin of
her inner leg and up to the warmth of her thigh.

"No!"

Stopping, he gazed for a long moment at her full young
breasts, flat belly, and long, slender legs. A sigh escaped
him. "Ah, Cyra! If the stars could but see you thus, they
would put out their lamps for shame of their own ugli-
ness."

She moved to draw the two halves of her robe together.

"Hold!" he commanded. "It pleases me to look at you."

She paled at the sharpness of his words, then blushed,
and he laughed. A bold hand cupped her breast. He could
feel the dainty nipple harden against his thumb, and her
heart beating wildly against his palm.

"Say my name," he demanded. "I have never heard you
speak it."

"Selim," she whispered.

"Again." Releasing her breast, his hand brushed the
curve of her hip.

"Selim."

Reaching up, he loosened her hair, and it tumbled like
a sunset over her shoulders.

"How fair you are," he murmured almost to himself.
"I have known many beautiful women, but never have I
seen one as exquisite as you. Little virgin, I want you. If I
must wait in order to win your heart, I will wait; but, by
Allah, I would take you now if I dared!"

She drew him down to her. "Yes, my lord," Cyra said softly.

He looked at her wonderingly, and she smiled softly back at him. Then she was beneath him, and he heard the word "Gently" pounding in his head as his throbbing manhood entered her. Her maidenhead blocked his passage, and, feeling her body tense, he stopped for a moment to tenderly kiss her face and stroke her silken hair. Gradually she relaxed, and in that instant he swiftly plunged through the barrier.

She did not cry out, nor did her green eyes close. Instead, they widened in surprise at the sweetness of the pain, then in wonder at the pleasure she felt racing through her body. She heard a low, animal moan and, startled, realized it came from her own throat.

At that moment Cyra felt herself plunged into a whirlpool of pain and delight. Her lithe body arched to meet him; her young breasts, their nipples hard, pressed against his chest. She felt him moving rhythmically within her, and as the pain subsided, she was drawn into a whirling vortex of dizzying warmth.

Suddenly she sobbed his name, and tears spilled onto her cheeks. He buried his lips in her hair, and then unable to control any longer the storm of passion he had contained, he released it into her throbbing body.

In the split second that their souls touched, he lost himself to her forever. He adored her. He could not get enough of her. She belonged to him completely, and yet it was he who felt enslaved.

The moon had set, and he looked over at the sleeping girl. She lay on her side facing him, one arm beneath her head. His eyes feasted on her naked body—the moist, pearly sheen of her skin, the coral-tipped nipples of her breasts, the sooty fringe of her lashes against her cheek, her hair a red-gold mass of disarray against the pillows. He shuddered with hunger for her, but, remembering how newly opened the bud of her maidenhead was, he rose instead from the bed and, going to the door, called a slave to bring a basin of warm water, linen, cool drinks, and sweet cakes.

When all he had requested had been brought and placed by the bed, he gently rolled the sleeping girl upon

her back. Dipping the soft linen into the scented water, he
tenderly sponged the dried blood from her thighs. A slave
should have done this, but he wanted no one else in the
room to break the spell their love had created.

Finished, he pushed the basin aside and after drawing
a light cover over the still form, walked out onto the terrace. Breathing deeply, he inhaled the cool air, and slowly
his mind began to clear. I am in love! The words rang
jubilantly in his head. Never before had Selim Khan had
a real relationship with a woman. There had been soft,
compliant bodies upon which he had vented his desire,
but these had lasted no more than a night or two.

She had bewitched him, his little love. Never before
had he felt the emotions that now assailed him. He felt
loving, tender, and protective. How could one innocent
little girl stir up so much confusion in a grown man's
heart and mind? He shook his head and walked back inside. He wanted to talk with her, hear her musical voice,
and know that she felt the same.

Taking a cup of fruit juice in one hand, he sat down on
the bed and playfully ran his other hand down the curve
of her body. She murmured in soft protest and then,
stretching like a newly awakened baby, opened her eyes.
He handed her the cup, and she drank greedily.

"Have I slept long, my lord? I have never felt so
rested."

"A few hours, little love."

He could not take his eyes off her, and she flushed
shyly beneath his gaze. Placing the cup on the table near
the bed, she drew his head down to her breasts.

"If you continue to stare at me so, my Selim, I shall
burst into flame and become a cinder."

She looked at the man who lay contentedly on her
breasts. "Have I pleased you, my lord?" The power of
her conquest sang in her voice.

Looking up at her, his eyes twinkling, his voice amused,
he murmured. "You are incomparable, o moon of my
delight!"

Realizing the foolishness of her question, she turned her
face from him and giggled. The prince sprang from their
couch, clutched her hand, and vowed passionately that
never had one such as she graced his bed. They both dissolved into gales of laughter, and the slaves outside the

door nodded to one another that their master's first ikbal must indeed be wise to please her young lord so much that they could laugh so happily in the midst of their love-making.

She pulled him tumbling back into the bed, and he looked down on her. "If you tell anyone of this farce, I shall strangle you," he glowered, but his eyes were laughing.

"My lord, I am well aware of your position," she answered him, and he realized their silly byplay was something she would never share with anyone, because it was theirs alone. Was it possible she loved him a little? he wondered.

Cradled in each other's arms, they talked softly until they fell asleep.

She woke at a touch of her shoulder. "My lady, it is almost dawn," said the slave.

Nodding, she rose slowly.

"Where are you going, Cyra?"

"It is almost dawn, my lord Selim. Custom demands that I return to the women's quarters."

"You will come again?" His eyes adored her.

"When my lord commands me."

"Tonight?"

Her brilliant smile assented. "My lord must officially summon me."

"You will be summoned." He stood, picked her up, and carried her to the waiting litter. The astounded slaves kept their faces impassive as they padded back down the cold, silent corridor.

Cyra thought how frightened she had been but a few hours past. Now her heart felt as if it would burst with happiness and joy.

The litter returned her to the harem, where Lady Refet waited. Cyra ran to her.

"Oh, madam, I am so happy."

"And so you should be," smiled the older woman. "Now, I have ordered the masseuse, and your bath awaits. Then to bed, my child."

Cyra allowed the bath attendant to sponge the perfumed water over her, and the masseuse to lull her overexcited body and mind into a more restful state. When they had finished, Lady Refet appeared again.

"Come, dear child. I will escort you to your new quarters."

"I am not to go to my old room, madam?"

"It would not be fitting for Prince Selim's ikbal to sleep in the quarters of an ordinary gediklis," replied the woman. "For several weeks now, my nephew has had the slaves working secretly on your apartments. They have been decorated to please just you."

"But he has been away, and returned only today."

"Yet we have had several messengers from him in that time."

"But how could he know he would choose me first?"

"He has known from the beginning, Cyra. I know that Europeans find it difficult to believe that an Oriental prince, surrounded as he is by many lovely maidens, could love honestly; but did you find your first visit to my nephew tonight a simple physical experience?"

"Oh, no," cried the blushing girl. "It was beautiful, and pure, and—" She stopped, suddenly at a loss for words.

Lady Refet smiled gently. "Say no more," she said, patting the girl's hand. "Once I, too, felt the same way." She flung open the doors at the end of the female sleeping quarters, and they entered the reception room of Cyra's new suite.

The walls were tiled in a rich blue glaze decorated with a yellow geometric pattern. Directly facing them was a small fountain of polished, dark-red stone. At each end of the room was a door.

"The eunuchs guarding you are quartered there," said Lady Refet, pointing to the left. "Your own female slaves will be here." She motioned to the right.

Beneath their feet, the floor was of the same polished red marble as the fountain. On the fountain wall were two doors. One was small, the other a large double door of carved and gilded wood which opened into a charming salon.

Cyra gazed about her in delight. The yellow walls were set with heavy wooden beams decorated with painted floral designs in reds, blues, greens, and golds. The paneled ceiling repeated the motif of the beams. The floor was a creamy marble.

In the center of the room stood a round fireplace tiled in red and yellow. Above it hung a highly polished, conically shaped copper hood. The fire, blazing merrily, warmed the salon and cast its sparkling reflection into the windows at the far end of the room. Small glass panes covered almost the entire wall and concealed a door that opened onto a colonnaded porch and out into a private walled garden that hung above the sea.

Walking into the chill of the early morning, Cyra looked about her. The garden had been perfectly laid out. Narrow paths wandered among the flower beds. There were flowering trees and shrubs, now dormant, with thickly covered buds awaiting the spring to come. There were firlike trees that reminded Cyra of her childhood Scots homeland. Moving along one of the paths, she came upon a pool with a little waterfall designed to appear as if nature had placed it there.

Suddenly the girl realized that the garden had been made to look like Glen Rae, a favorite childhood haunt of which she had often spoken to Lady Refet. Hot, silent tears splashed down her cheeks, and she quickly brushed them away.

"We thought to make you happy, my dear. If the memory is too painful, the garden will be changed." She placed a motherly arm about the young woman.

"No, madam. Change nothing. I weep with discovery of the love that surrounds me. I have no regrets. The garden is lovely."

"Very well, then come and see my nephew's crowning touch, for he had a bit of Turkey placed in your Highland glen." Leading her charge away from the pool, she pointed to the exquisite pale-pink marble kiosk at the far end of the garden. "Selim calls it the 'dawn kiosk,' because the first rays of the morning sun touch it and reflect the aurora colors on its dome. Do you like it?"

Wordlessly, Cyra nodded.

Lady Refet smiled. "There will be time to explore later, but now it is time for you to rest."

They reentered the salon, and Cyra again silently admired her new riches—the thick, colorful rugs spread about the floors, the shining brass and copper lamps, the polished woods of the furniture, the rainbow silks and velvets of the cushions and draperies.

Lady Refet moved to a wall. "Here is a secret entry and exit to your bedchamber." She gently pressed a barely visible raised carving on a beam. The wall slid open, and she stepped through, beckoning Cyra to follow her. "Tell no one of this and use it only in an emergency," she counseled.

The bedchamber was a miniature of the salon. A large sleeping couch hung with green silk curtains and set on an elevated gilded platform dominated one wall. In the corner next to it was a tiled fireplace.

At a clap of her hands, two pretty slave girls appeared before Lady Refet. "This is Fekriye, and this is Zala. They are yours," she said.

The two girls bowed and, without a word, set about divesting Cyra of her garments and replacing them with her nightclothes.

"And now, my dear, I leave you to your dreams. I am sure they will be happy ones." Kissing her nephew's new ikbal on the forehead, she left the room.

"When shall we awaken you, my lady?" asked Zala.

"At the hour before midday," replied the suddenly exhausted girl.

The two slaves bowed and left their mistress.

Cyra lay down on her couch, but she could not sleep. Restlessly, she shifted her position several times. She finally arose and, snatching a cloak from her wardrobe, walked out into the garden. The sky was awash with color, the sun just beginning to rise as she reached the kiosk. Here, alone with herself, she could try to sort out the thoughts that tumbled through her mind.

Prince Selim was in love with her. This much she was certain of, for no man other than one in love could have been so gentle with her. That she was young and inexperienced, she knew; but only a fool could have missed the hunger in his eyes. He was the master, and she the slave. Yet he had gone out of his way to please her. Would he be the same with the others? No, she decided, he would not. He would expect them to behave as they had been taught in his father's harem.

With a shock she realized the power that was potentially hers. She must tred lightly, for he was not a man to be ruled by a woman, no matter how deep his feelings. And

unless she gave him a son before one of the others. . . .
His influence was good only as long as he lived.

The others! She felt a stab of jealousy prick her. He
could send for any one of the others at any time; and even
if he did not right away, when she became pregnant he
would not wait. Selim Khan was a healthy and lusty young
man, and Cyra was a realist.

"No, no, no," she whispered fiercely, and then, remembering his kisses, his caresses, his hands gently exploring
the secret places of her body, she flushed and grew warm.
She wanted to go back to his bed and be loved, and then
afterward sit facing him and talk.

Am I in love or am I simply a shameless wanton? she
questioned herself. She did not know. Slowly she rose and
walked back into her bedchamber. I must sleep, she
thought. If I do not, I shall look like an ancient hag tonight. Oh, Allah, let the day go quickly.

14

THE SUMMONS CAME AT NOON, and, with it, Selim's gifts to his beloved in honor of their first night together—and as a token of his pleasure with her.

The little harem had gathered in Cyra's new quarters. At first they were shy, but the new favorite, though aware of her exalted position, was the same Cyra they loved, and soon her chambers hummed with lively chatter and occasional bursts of giggles. Sherbets, fresh fruit, and coffee were being served when a slave entered and whispered something to Cyra.

"He may enter." Turning to her friends, she said, "The prince's messenger is here."

The room became silent as the eunuch entered. Placing the traditional wrapped handkerchief in front of her, he said, "Most blessed and exalted of women, I bring you greeting from our lord, Prince Selim Khan. May he live a thousand years! He sends these tokens of his affection to you and asks that you join him at the tenth hour this evening."

"Tell our gracious lord that his slave thanks him for his gifts. I shall obey his commands at the tenth hour this night," she answered.

The eunuch bowed and left.

She stared at the handkerchief. She had heard talk of Sultan Bajazet's gifts in the Eski Serai. It was said that the more ornate the cloth, the higher the compliment. The square was of the palest eggshell-blue, embroidered on all four sides with a two-inch border of gold thread, small seed pearls, coral, and turquoises. She touched it reverently.

"In Allah's name," Sarina's voice cut through the quiet, "open it before we die of curiosity."

For once they all agreed with the prickly Spaniard.

Cyra loosened the intricate folds, and the silk opened to reveal an exquisite Kashmiri shawl of soft spring green, a necklace and matching earrings of turquoise set in gold, a heart-shaped ruby ring, and several charming gold bracelets, carved with flowers, that Selim had made himself. Like all of Osman's line, the prince had learned a trade. He was an extremely competent goldsmith.

Cyra was speechless at the generosity of it all, but her companions exclaimed in delight.

Sensing her friend's mood, Firousi spoke gently. "There is more, Cyra."

"More?"

"The slave who accompanied the eunuch also left this." She pointed to a large carved-ivory box at Cyra's feet.

Opened, the box revealed the traditional bag of gold coins, two bolts of cloth—the first a peacock-blue silk, the second a sheer golden gauze—and, lastly, a dark-green leather case fitted with two gold brushes, half a dozen tortoise-shell and gold combs, a crystal box holding tortoise-shell hairpins set with pearls, four crystal scent bottles, and a carved gold mirror set with real Venetian glass.

"You have obviously found favor with the prince," said Sarina archly, fingering the silk.

Lady Refet looked up from her embroidery.

"I do not know why he chose me first," said Cyra. "I thought surely it would be you. You danced so beautifully last night. Or perhaps Firousi, who sang so well."

"In Allah's name," snapped Sarina, "must you always be the diplomat? Of course I'm jealous of you, Cyra! All of us are, but you are the chosen one. I could have danced my feet off, and Firousi could have sung until she was hoarse as a crow, and still our Lord Selim would have seen no one except you. I accept that." She laughed, "However, when you ripen with child, he will see one of us, and then you'll be the jealous one!"

"I think you're hateful and spiteful to spoil Cyra's happiness," cried Firousi.

"No," replied Cyra. "She is simply reminding me of the truth. Each of you will be called to our lord's couch eventually, and then you will know the happiness I know. This is our fate, and we must not allow petty jealousy to turn our quarters into a nest of intrigue like the sultan's harem.

This is a small household, but it must always be a happy one for our lord."

Lady Refet bent again over her embroidery. Such wisdom in one so young, she thought. Praise Allah—and Hadji Bey's sharp eye!

"I hope Cyra does have a child soon. Then she will be bas-kadin," said Firousi.

"She will," said Zuleika, looking directly at Sarina. "It will be a boy."

Sarina glared at the beautiful Chinese. "What will happen is Allah's will, not yours, Zuleika."

"Nevertheless," replied Zuleika, "I tell you that Cyra will bear a son before a year has passed. He will be born under the sign of the Lion, and, like the lion, he will be a warrior. Both Europe and Asia will tremble at the mention of his name. He will be a ruler of great wisdom, much beloved by his people."

"Zuleika," chided Lady Refet, "you must not tease Sarina."

"I am not teasing her, my lady. I have seen all this. I know."

"Where have you seen it, child?"

Zuleika unhooked a thin gold chain from around her neck. Attached to the chain was a large opal in the shape of a teardrop. "My mother gave me this before I left China. She told me if I ever wished to see into the future, I should empty my mind of all thoughts and concentrate on the opal."

"Then," challenged Sarina, "why didn't you look into it and see what was to happen to you before you reached the shah?"

"I did look, and I saw myself surrounded by luxury, and a man who loved me. I had never seen the shah, and naturally assumed it was he, but it was our Prince Selim. Last night when he called Cyra to his couch, I gazed into my opal. I see much happiness for Cyra, and I see her son who will be a great sultan."

"And what do you see for the rest of us?"

"I have not looked, Sarina. My opal is not a toy to be played with lightly."

Sarina sniffed disbelievingly.

"You show much maturity, my child," said Lady Refet. "And now, my young ladies, the afternoon lengthens, and

you have not yet completed your daily tasks. Cyra will
be excused today since I wish her to rest."

Reluctantly but obediently they arose, and Cyra and
Lady Refet were left alone.

"I cannot rest."

"You must practice self-discipline, Cyra. As my
nephew's bas-kadin you will have many responsibilities.
As the mother of a sultan you will be the ruler of all our
women. You will have to do many things you don't want
to do, things that inconvenience you and seem foolish
and wasteful of your time; but you will do them because
you must. This is self-discipline, and you must cultivate
it."

"You believe Zuleika? She just said those things to annoy Sarina."

"Yes, I do believe Zuleika. There are many unseen
forces in our world that do not conform to one's sense of
logic, but nevertheless they are there. The power to see
into the future is one of those things."

"It is witchcraft!"

"It is a gift from God. You speak like an ignorant
peasant! Do not your own people have this ability? The
Celts and the Gaels are well known for their psychic
powers. You yourself, I am sure, have it. Have you
never asked yourself why you did not struggle more
against your captivity? You did not, because some inner
sense told you that this was your fate, and all would be
well. Zuleika has simply cultivated her ability. You have
not. Her people understand these things, but yours, because of their Christian religion, have been taught to
fear those things which are not within, and approved by,
your strict faith. This is ignorance of the worst sort. But
have no fear, my dear. You become more Turkish each
day, and soon these childish beliefs will fade. Now, go
and rest. I shall look in on you later."

Cyra rose and went to her bedroom. Lady Refet's
words puzzled her, and she pondered them. Absently, she
allowed her slaves to remove her clothing, sponge her
with warmed, perfumed water, and place a light robe
about her. Dismissing them, she relaxed upon her couch,
mulling the words of Selim's aunt over in her mind.

When the older woman peeked in several hours later,
Cyra lay fast asleep, a look of peace upon her face.

15

THE MONTHS PASSED, and Cyra was the only one called to Selim's couch. Touchingly in love, she and Selim could scarcely contain their eagerness to be alone. Although the prince was affectionate and courteous to the rest of his harem, they could not help feeling slighted. Only their fondness for Cyra—and the knowledge obtained from a slave girl who had it from one of Cyra's slave girls that the favorite had had no show of blood in over a month—prevented an unpleasant situation. Soon she would have to tell him, and one of them would be called.

Selim's harem would have been very surprised to know that he and Cyra did not spend all their evenings together locked in passionate embrace. The prince and Cyra certainly did not neglect the physical side of their relationship, and each night left him breathless at her increased ardor, but not all their time was spent in lovemaking. In the small hours before the dawn, they talked of many things—in the beginning about themselves, and then, feeling safe with each other, about their future. Cyra did not divulge that she knew Selim would one day be sultan. She understood that he might love her, but she was still wary. In time, when she had his full trust, she would speak. The future now consisted of the children they would have, their home, and the problems of the province which he ruled for his father.

Selim had never before had a real friend, and to his amazement he realized that Cyra had become one to him. In private, as well as before the others, Cyra treated Selim with courtesy and respect, but never did she cringe or debase herself before him. He could not help but treat her in the same manner. This would always set her apart from the others.

121

So the days passed slowly in peace and contentment, and the fire- and love-filled nights passed too quickly. The harem and their lord lived as a family. Almost every evening they ate together—a thing unheard of in Turkish society—but Selim enjoyed his aunt and his women. Often he arranged for entertainments in the evening. Once it was an Indian fakir who magically raised a rope into the air, climbed it, and disappeared from view—reappearing a few moments later bearing a bouquet of flowers which he presented to Lady Refet. Another time it was a troupe of performing animals, and once an Egyptian came with a group of dancing girls. Selim enjoyed them, but his harem did not.

The prince began to know his harem as no other man might. He quickly learned that the aloof Zuleika was in reality shy, and that Firousi's merriness hid an extremely sharp mind. Amara and Iris were exactly as they appeared—sweet and docile. The fiery, knife-tongued Sarina was actually kind and openhearted, but feared rejection. He like them all, and he felt fortunate; yet Cyra consumed him completely, and for the moment Selim was content to savor the unending variety of his flame-haired slave.

And the Scots girl was content to bask in the love of her lord, but never did she flaunt her good fortune, so peace was preserved in the harem. Then, at the beginning of February, she was forced to admit that her link with the moon had been broken, and she was with child. The knowledge at first delighted her and then sent her into hysterical tears. Lady Refet laughed gently.

"I felt the same way when I first knew I was with child," she said.

"It is all over," sobbed Cyra. "I can no longer go to him, and he has summoned me for this very night."

"You may go tonight, but you must tell my nephew, Cyra. He will be overjoyed to learn the news."

The girl stamped her foot. "These superstitions are ridiculous! Why can I not go to Selim after tonight?"

"They are not superstitions, my dear. Even in Europe an educated man does not practice intercourse with his pregnant wife. She might miscarry. Do you want to lose the child? Is your own pleasure more important to you than my nephew's son?"

Noiselessly the tears poured down the girl's face. "No!

I don't want to lose the child, but neither do I want to lose Selim. If I cannot go to him, someone else will. He will love another and forget all about me. It is this I cannot bear."

"I am surprised at you," chided the older woman. "Do you think so little of my dear nephew that you believe he would discard you?" She took the distraught girl into her arms. "There, my child. Weep. It is simply your condition. It will pass in a few weeks."

"I am so ashamed," sobbed Cyra. "You are perfectly right. I expected this. I am truly happy and proud to be bearing my dearest lord's son."

Selim's aunt raised an eyebrow. "You are sure it's a son?" Her deep-blue eyes were teasing.

"Zuleika said I would bear a son, and I feel she is right."

"Then dry your eyes, my dear, or they will be puffed and red tonight."

That evening Cyra took particular pains with her appearance. She had had the sea-green brocade Selim had sent her made into a pelisse which she wore over trousers and a bodice made from the golden silk gauze which he had also presented to her. She was still as slender as ever; only a slight swelling of her belly betrayed her condition.

Around her neck she clasped the gold-and-turquoise necklace, and she fastened the matching earrings into her earlobes. Her hair was arranged in the fashion Selim loved best—parted in the center and divided into two pieces, each held by a silver ribbon, one streaming down her back and the other falling over her right breast.

When the appointed hour arrived, she climbed into the familiar litter and was borne through the palace to Selim's apartments. As she hurried in, the slaves smiled broadly at the beautiful ikbal's impatience to be with their lord. Selim came forward to greet her.

"I have missed you, heart of my heart."

"And I you, my lord. Did you hunt, or was it another trip to Constantinople?"

"Cyra, what do you know of my trips to the city?" His fingers squeezed her hand cruelly.

"My lord, you are hurting me. It is enough that I tell you I know that one day you will be sultan."

He released her hand. "How did you come to learn this?"

"From Hadji Bey, my lord. We have all known since the beginning."

"What beginning? Who is we?"

"Zuleika, Firousi, and I. The night before we arrived in Constantinople, Hadji Bey explained the whole situation to us and told us of the plans to make you sultan one day. Did you think it was an oversight that your father never saw us among his gediklis? We were deliberately hidden from his sight so you might choose us. Your mother planned it that way. She sent Hadji Bey to find three maidens of intelligence and beauty who he felt would be of help to you as your kadins. We were the fortunate ones chosen."

"So," said Selim grimly, "you and your friends were bought with the promise of riches and power."

She turned on him, her green eyes blazing with anger. "Yes, we were bought, my lord Selim. But not by promises of any kind, just gold. And each of us has stood naked in our shame before a crowd of leering creatures who dare to call themselves men. Some even had the audacity to demand proof of our virginity! Did Firousi ask to be torn from her bridegroom at their wedding feast? And Zuleika, destined to be the wife of the shah—did she ask to be betrayed by a common concubine and sold on the block in Baghdad? And what of my betrothed, Rudolfo di San Lorenzo? Did either he or I expect I should end like this? It was our fate and the will of Allah that this should come to pass. Do you dare to question the will of Allah? And do you dare accuse us of selling ourselves? Had we not loved you on sight, my lord, we could have betrayed you at any time!"

Selim stared in amazement at the outraged girl. He knew she had a temper, but her outburst surprised him. "So, my 'Flame' is truly fiery. And how could you have betrayed me?" His tone was amused and conciliatory.

"By sending word to Lady Besma. She would pay a fortune for proof of your treachery against her son."

"And just how could that be done?" His tone was less conciliatory.

"Through one of her spies, my dear lord. Our palace has several."

"What?" His face showed his incredulity. "How do you know this? Who are they?"

"Only Hadji Bey and Lady Refet know who they are."

"I shall go to the agha tomorrow and demand the names of those who spy on me and my household. Then I shall eliminate them!"

"My lord, you are a child! If Hadji Bey did not allow Besma to place a few of her spies in our palace, she would become suspicious and wonder why. We cannot permit it. All would be lost, and you could easily lose your life." She laughed softly. "How unskilled you are in the devices of women."

He turned angrily and found himself staring into green eyes brimming with mischief. Cyra was not one to hold a grudge and had already forgiven his suspicions of a moment ago.

Her mood was infectious, and slowly a grin spread over his face. "By Allah, I am truly a fool! Can you forgive me, Cyra? How could I ever have doubted you or the other girls?"

"There is nothing to forgive, my lord. You have lived in danger for so long that you are naturally suspicious of everyone, but you need not fear me or the others. We are loyal." Resting her red-gold head on his shoulder, she nestled against him. "I have a terrible temper, my lord Selim. Will you forgive this worthless slave?" She looked up and fluttered her kohl-darkened lashes at him.

His laughter was low. "You must pay the penalty for your bad temper, my little fire-eater. Unskilled I may be in the devices of women, but not in their ways." Slipping his hand beneath her fur-lined pelisse, he fondled her familiar body. She moved so that his hand cupped her breast and rubbed teasingly against him.

His lips found the soft hollow between her neck and her shoulder, and his voice murmuring her name over and over again communicated his urgency. Turning her to face him, he found her sweet, moist lips. His lips still clinging to hers, he carried her indoors to the couch.

That night their lovemaking was sweeter than it would ever be again, and when in the split second of eternity their souls touched, Cyra wept for the joy of it.

She lay awake in the night, and in the dim light of the chamber gazed at the man beside her. In sleep, the cares and fears stripped away, he was vulnerable and seemed like a boy, though he was eleven years older than she. His fair skin was slightly darkened by the winter wind and sun. With his dark-gray eyes closed, the thick fringe of his lashes were like smudges of soot against his cheeks. His nose was straight and proud, and the lips that covered his even white teeth were generous despite their thinness. Unlike his brothers, he wore no beard, for once, when he was younger, he had grown one, and so regal was his look that his mother had made him shave it off lest he draw attention to himself. He had vowed never to wear a beard again until he was sultan. Stirring, he stretched his body to its full length, and Cyra thought he was at least as tall as her father.

His voice pierced her thoughts. "Why aren't you sleeping, my little houri?"

"I am too happy."

He buried his face in her marvelous hair.

"I cannot come to you again, Selim."

Sitting up sharply, he looked at her.

A smile played at the corners of her mouth. "I am with child, dearest lord."

Staring at her, the sleep gone from his eyes, he whispered, "You are sure?"

She nodded.

"When?"

"Late summer. As the wheat ripens, so shall I. Zuleika says it is a boy and he will be born under the sign of the Lion. She also says he will be a great sultan."

"A son," he murmured. "A son!" He crushed her in his arms and asked, "Who else knows of this?"

"Only Lady Refet."

"No one else must know until—"

"Selim!"

"Until I have provided you with a food taster and two personal bodyguards. Once it becomes known you are with child, Besma will stop at nothing. She has been known to use poison before."

Cyra whitened.

"Do not be frightened, sweetheart. No harm will come

to you or the child. I shall go into Constantinople myself in the morning and personally purchase the slaves."

"Let Hadji Bey help you, Selim. His instincts are infallible."

"If I am seen at the Eski Serai, it will arouse suspicion."

"I can send a message to Hadji Bey at dawn. He will await you in Constantinople."

"Another secret, Cyra?"

She giggled. "We have several pigeons in the dovecote. They are a gift from Hadji Bey. Loose them, and they fly straight to his dovecote at the palace."

"By the beard of the Prophet, the agha kislar is a wily old devil! Send your message." He smiled and drew her down to the couch. "Our last night, eh?"

"Until the child is born."

"Then let us make the most of it. When I return from the city, I shall have to go about the boring business of deflowering and teaching another frightened virgin."

She grabbed a handful of his dark hair and yanked. The prince roared in amused outrage. "Beast," she hissed at him. "Son of a mangy camel!"

Laughingly he wrestled her quiet, then kissed her pouting lips. Struggling loose, she hurled several additional epithets at him. His eyebrows rose. "Your command of Turkish truly astounds me, beloved, but the night grows short."

Melting into his arms, she cried softly, "Love me, love me, my lord Selim. We have so little time."

16

Lady Refet looked sternly up at her nephew. "I do not approve, Selim. I do not approve at all."

The prince smiled down at her from his saddle. "Nevertheless, aunt, it is my wish. We shall return within four days' time. Be sure you guard both my treasures well." Wheeling the horse, he called to the turbaned boy mounted next to him, "Come, lad," and galloped off toward Constantinople, his escort of Tartars following in his wake.

Once on the main road, he turned to his companion. "Well, Firousi, how do you like your adventure?"

"Very much, my lord," replied his turbaned companion, "but I don't understand."

"Cyra is with child."

Firousi gasped.

"But no one knows except my aunt, and they must not know until I have taken steps to protect her."

"Besma!"

"Yes," replied the prince. "We are to meet Hadji Bey at the house of David ben Kira in Constantinople. David deals discreetly in slaves for persons of importance. I shall purchase a bodyguard and a food taster."

"But why do you need me, my lord? You take a terrible chance. If word of this escapade should reach the wrong ears, there would be a terrible scandal."

"I want to buy Cyra a very special gift, Firousi. I need you to help me pick it out, since you, as a woman, know her tastes perhaps better than I. Dressed as a boy, you will attract little attention."

"I don't know whether I shall ever get this brown stain off my skin, my lord."

"If your slaves have no luck, my little jewel, we shall try together in a few nights' time, eh?"

Firousi was shocked. "But Cyra—" she began.

"Cyra understands that the sooner I take another ikbal, the less painful it will be for her. I do not wish to cause her pain." He eyed the girl beside him. She was well disguised. The brown stain covered her skin, her hair was hidden beneath the turban, and her generous breasts were bound flat beneath a tight layer of cloth. "You are most beautiful, my dear. I begin to anticipate the conclusion of our business." Firousi, eyeing him tremulously from beneath her lashes, did not reply.

Riding all day, they camped outside the city that night, and after the dawn prayers, they rode on into the Jewish quarter. Dismounting before the house of David ben Kira, Selim warned the girl, "Speak little, and call me master." She nodded.

They were greeted by David ben Kira himself. He bowed. "You do my poor house great honor, Prince Selim. Please come this way. The agha kislar awaits you in my private quarters."

Hadji Bey rose as they entered the room. "Selim, my son! You are looking well. Now, why this urgency to buy new slaves? Have I not provided your palace with enough servants?"

"Cyra did not tell you?"

"Her note simply stated you wished to purchase a bodyguard and a food taster and you needed my help."

"Caution again," said Selim. "I can learn much from her," he mused. "Cyra is with child, my old friend. When word reaches Besma—and Cyra assures me it will—my father's evil kadin may be tempted to act rashly. It will not please her, with Ahmed childless, to have me become a father."

"Your good fortune delights me, and your precautions show wisdom." Turning to David ben Kira, he said, "Can you provide us with such slaves?"

"Indeed, yes, my lord agha. We have an excellent selection." He clapped his hands, murmured a few words to the attending servant, and a few minutes later the door of the room opened to admit a dozen young men.

Selim looked them over carefully and found his eye drawn to an enormous dark-brown Negro with close-cropped hair and a rebellious look; but before he could speak, David ben Kira turned to his slavemaster.

"Idiot!"—he pointed at the very slave Selim had noted —"get that wild man out of here! These slaves are for the prince, not some provincial merchant."

"Hold, David. What is wrong with the man? It appears he would suit my purpose quite well."

"No, Highness. Arslan is flawed in the mind. He has almost killed two masters. I am selling him to the quarries."

"Step forward," Selim commanded. The giant stood before him. "Is this true?"

"Yes, my lord."

Selim noted the intelligent light in the man's eyes. "Why?"

"Because, my lord, they were cruel masters. I have been a slave since I was five, and I have known nothing but unkindness; but before that, I knew tenderness and compassion. I cannot bear to see innocent young girls mistreated because of their fear, or good wives beaten because they are no longer beautiful. If this is a flaw, then I am flawed."

Selim replied, "I do not mistreat my women, and I do have need of a strong, loyal man to guard with his very life the most precious of jewels—my wife. She is with child."

"If you will have me, I will watch over her, but if you are cruel, lord, I cannot be responsible for my actions."

Selim looked to Hadji Bey.

"Trust your instincts, my son."

The prince nodded, and turned to David ben Kira. "I will take this one. Do not look so fearful, my friend. I need a eunuch such as this. His loyalty will be only to my Cyra, and no one will ever be able to bribe him."

"Very well, my lord. It will be as you say." He motioned Arslan to the side of the room and waved the other slaves out. "Now, my prince. Hadji Bey and I have already chosen a food taster. He is an Egyptian with an incredible ability to ferret out poisons, even those that have no taste. He also has the ability to make you immune to any poison. He is expensive but well worth it."

"Then our business is concluded, David."

"Ah, but you must not leave without refreshments, my

lord. I have a slave girl who makes a sherbet fit for the Prophet himself." He clapped his hands, and two servant girls entered, one bearing a tray.

The female with the tray, a small, plain creature, stumbled against a low table and cried out, "Lord Lamerey! Tables where footstools should be."

"Master," whispered Firousi, "I can think of no better gift for my lady than a female slave who speaks her tongue. It would please her greatly."

"You are right, lad. David, what price on that girl?"

"That one? Five dinars, my lord, but she is useless. I have been trying to train her as a waitress, but she is as stubborn as a mule, and twice as troublesome."

"When a woman is troublesome, there is usually a man involved," remarked Hadji Bey.

"True," said David, "and in this case it is the girl's husband. A remarkable young man. He is a scholar, and not only does he speak, read, and write several European tongues, but Turkish and Persian as well. He would be an excellent secretary."

"How much for the four of them?"

"All four, my lord?"

"I have said it!"

"Let me see now. Fifty dinars for Arslan, my lord. One hundred for the Egyptian. A very special price to you, and I am losing money. One hundred for the secretary, and five for his useless wife. Two hundred and fifty-five gold dinars in all, my lord."

"One hundred for the Egyptian, David. Twenty-five for Arslan, fifty for the man and his wife. One hundred seventy-five dinars, and I am being generous."

"My lord! You will drive me into poverty! Two hundred thirty is the lowest I can go."

"Two hundred is all I will give you."

"Done!" replied David ben Kira. "I will include a cart and driver to transport them to your palace. Do you want them today, my lord?"

"Yes, but no cart, David. Lend me four horses. One of my slaves will return them to you the next time I come to the city. A cart will slow me down. As it is, I will not get back to my home until late tomorrow."

David ben Kira arose. "I shall arrange it at once. You

will be ready to leave within the half hour." He motioned
to the waiting slaves to follow him and left the room.

"Here, lad," Selim called to Firousi. "Tell the girl her
husband goes, too."

Firousi walked over to the girl, whose name was Marian, and put a hand on her arm. "Don't be frightened,"
she said kindly. "My master has bought you to serve his
wife, and he had also bought your husband to be his secretary. You will see him in a few moments. Now go along
with David ben Kira."

"Thank your master for me," replied the girl, tears rolling down her cheeks. "If I had been separated from
Alan, I should have died. If we must be slaves together,
we will serve your master well for this kindness." She left
the room.

Firousi moved back to Selim. "It is done, master. The
girl is grateful and will give no trouble."

"You make a charming boy, little turquoise," remarked
Hadji Bey.

"You knew! And I was feeling so pleased to have
fooled you!"

"So you might have, my child, had you not showed me
those wonderful eyes." He turned to Selim. "A very dangerous game, my boy. Why did you bring her disguised
thus? If Besma gains knowledge of this, she will use it,
you may be sure."

"I needed her to help me choose a special gift for Cyra,
and she did. No one knows but Lady Refet. Her absence
is concealed by the ruse of a high fever. We are safe."

"Yes, only one of the harem slaves spies for Besma."

"Who, Hadji Bey? Give me the name."

"Selim, Selim. If you know, you will never be able to
contain yourself. Believe me, the slave involved holds an
unimportant post and can hurt none of the girls."

"Very well, my friend. You have guided me successfully so far. There is no need for me to doubt your judgment now."

"Have you taken other ikbals, Selim?"

"No, but when we return to the Moonlight Serai, Firousi
will journey down my Golden Road, eh, little page?"

Firousi blushed beneath the brown stain on her cheeks.
"Yes, my lord," she whispered.

"And the others," continued the agha, "they please you?"

"It's like being offered a plate of cakes after a fast, my friend. Each is more delectable than the other. The fool gobbles them up quickly, but the wise man savors each in its turn to enjoy the full flavor."

"Well spoken, Selim, and your choices were excellent, though the Spanish girl still worries me."

"My sharp-tongued Sarina? She hides a warm heart, Hadji Bey, and Cyra found her weakness immediately. She is clever at making things grow. We have put her in charge of the gardens, which she rules like a benevolent dictator."

"Good," smiled the agha. "Ah, David ben Kira, we are ready to depart?"

"Yes, my lord. The prince's new slaves are in the courtyard, mounted and waiting."

They arose and walked to the courtyard. Selim pressed a purse into the Jew's hand. "Your price—and for you, a small token of my thanks," he said, holding up a large yellow diamond.

The merchant, gasping, took the stone. "My lord prince —such generosity—if I can ever serve you again—"

"I shall remember, David ben Kira."

"Well done, my son," whispered Hadji Bey. "And now," he said, raising his voice, "I bid you farewell." He climbed into his litter and raised his hand in salute. Commanding his bearers to go, he disappeared through the courtyard arch.

Led by Prince Selim and his page, the new slaves and the prince's Tartars quickly left the city behind. They camped that night beside some ancient ruins, and Firousi had time to catch her breath. As her original journey to the Moonlight Serai had taken three days, she was amazed at the speed with which they now traveled. Of course, on her first trip they had taken the main road and were slowed by the vast caravan of slaves, women, and household goods. Yesterday morning they had ridden out of the palace, taken the more direct and rougher road, and arrived outside the capital before sunset. On their return trip they were again on the more direct road, but their progress was slowed slightly by the presence of the female slave.

Firousi was enjoying this respite from her friends and their more civilized way of life. Raised in the Caucasus Mountains, she had camped beneath the stars many times with her father and brothers. Gazing at the sky, the subdued noise of the camp behind her, she imagined for a moment she was home again. A touch on her shoulder startled her. Turning, she looked into the face of the prince.

"What do you dream of, Firousi?"

"My homeland, my lord. I often camped with my father beneath the night sky."

"Are you restless in your captivity, my little mountain girl?"

"Perhaps a little, my lord."

"Soon you will have other interests, and your past with its sad memories will fade away." He put an arm about her shoulders.

She smiled up at him. "Yes, my lord."

"Do you love me, Firousi?"

"No, my lord. I do not know you—and perhaps, when I do, I shall still not love you—but I like you. You are a good man and a kind master. I shall, Allah willing, bear your children with pride and always be loyal to you."

He bent down and gravely kissed her on the forehead. "I can ask no more of you than that, but you *will* love me, my jewel."

"Perhaps, my lord." She laughed up at him. "However, I would suggest we return to camp lest your Tartars obtain the wrong impression about their prince and class you with your brother Ahmed, who, they say, prefers young boys to girls."

"One day I shall have you whipped for your teasing tongue. You do not show me the proper respect."

"Yes, my lord," she replied meekly, but her eyes sparkled merrily at his threat.

Selim glowered at her, then laughed. "You are an appallingly impudent maiden."

Dawn had barely shown itself the next morning when the prince and his companions were on their way. Firousi had dropped back to ride with Marian.

They arrived at their destination shortly after noon. Selim turned his new slaves over to Ali, his chief eunuch. The young English couple presented him with an unusual

problem. Married slaves were not a common event, and
normal men were not permitted in any other man's harem.
Ali was quick to point out a small cottage near the
edge of the gardens which might house the couple. The
prince gave orders that the little house be made habitable
at once.

"When you are not on duty," he told his secretary, "you
will live here. You will answer to Turkish names. Alan,
you will answer to Yussef. Marian, there will be no need
to change your name. We have a similar one, so we can
pronounce it. Yussef will teach you Turkish."

"I already speak some, my lord. My husband taught
me."

"How is this possible?"

"Alan—ah, Yussef, was coming to Turkey to be a clerk
in the merchant house of a friend. His father has a small
trading business in London and wanted him to learn about
the East. My husband's father says future trade of importance will come from the East. Yussef began teaching
me Turkish months ago, when he knew we would be coming here. My Turkish is not perfected—as you can see, my
lord—but since I shall be using it every day, it soon will
be."

"I think I have found a valuable servant in you, Marian. Take good care of my wife, and you will never want
for anything."

"I will, my lord. I shall never forget that it was your
kindness that kept my husband and me together. Had you
not rescued us, we would have been separated."

He dismissed them in a kindly fashion and turned to
Firousi. "I shall be sending for you soon, my jewel. Slip
in through the secret entrance and see that you get all that
stain off. I shall personally inspect your lovely skin myself
tonight."

She flushed and fled him. He stood for a moment, a
smile upon his sensual lips as he thought of the delight his
gifts would give his beloved Cyra and the pleasure Firousi
would give him now that Cyra could no longer share his
bed.

17

LATE THAT AFTERNOON, the women of Selim's harem gathered together in the main room of their quarters. Heavy curtains were drawn across the windows at the end of the room, and in the center of the floor a round, raised open hearth blazed merrily, taking the chill off the late winter's day.

Lady Refet quietly presided over the women while plying her needle through her ever-present embroidery. Amara and Iris were working together on a woven tapestry. Sarina, sitting cross-legged on the floor, surrounded by parchments and pens, pored over plans for their first summer garden. Cyra, Firousi, and Zuleika sat around the hearth playing a word game. Each in turn would point to an object and say its name in Turkish. The other two would have to give the same object its name in another tongue—not their own. The three friends were clever at languages, and in this way increased their knowledge.

Cyra's heart leaped at the entrance of the prince's messenger. Then, remembering her condition, she dug her fingernails into her palm. Who would it be? Which one would take her place? His eagerness to take a new ikbal seemed rather indecent to her, and she felt a twinge of anger run through her.

The messenger stood before Firousi, who flushed, then whitened. "Most fortunate of maidens, I have the honor to inform you that our master, Prince Selim, may he live a thousand years, requests your presence tonight at the ninth hour."

"I hear and obey," replied the blond girl in a shaking voice.

The messenger bowed and left the room. Their chatter

stilled, the other girls looked from Cyra to Firousi and back again. Sarina broke the silence.

"So, our lord grows tired of green eyes."

"But not eager for your yellow ones," snapped Zuleika, squeezing Cyra's hand hard. "Your tongue is no less sharp than the bee's sting."

Cyra broke the tension. "It is not seemly I go to my lord's couch now that I carry his son beneath my heart."

Breaking into an excited babble, they rushed to crowd about her.

"Stop!" laughed Cyra. "I cannot answer your questions if you all talk at once." Immediately they were silent. "My son will be born in late summer. I did not tell you before because I wanted to be sure. Then our lord had to be told, and he asked that I keep our secret until he returned from Constantinople."

Firousi began to weep softly, but Cyra placed an arm about her friend's shoulders.

"I know what you are thinking, dear sister. Don't. Have you forgotten all we have learned?"

"You do not mind?"

"Of course I mind, but it is our fate. Since our lord Selim must take another, I am happy it is you, rather than some devious stranger who would sow dissension in our household."

"Then you will forgive me my foolishness?"

"It is already forgotten. Would you like to wear my brocade pelisse tonight? It is almost the color of your eyes and will be most flattering. I will have Fekriye take up the hem for you."

Firousi nodded, and a little smile played on her lips. "I am a donkey," she said, "but suddenly I was so afraid."

Cyra took her friend by the hand and led her to a quiet corner of the room. "Let us sit and talk," she said, settling herself on some pillows. "You must not be frightened, Firousi. There is no need. Selim is the gentlest and most considerate of lords."

"But you are his wife."

"I am his ikbal," admonished Cyra gently. "If Allah wills it, I shall be his kadin in five months. Do not, I beg you, tell me you have fallen back on your European morality? There is no future in it, and it is very foolish of you. With luck, this time next year we shall both be nursing

sons, who will grow up together, the dearest of friends, as
we are. Was it not you who a year ago in Crete told me
there is no return?"

Firousi smiled. "You are right, and I should be rejoicing
now. What girl does not envy me or would not change
places with me? Come." She rose and pulled Cyra up with
her. "Help me choose what I shall wear tonight. You know
our master's taste best of all." And together they hurried
off to Firousi's small room.

"You would think she had been born in the East instead of the West," observed Zuleika softly to Lady Refet.

"Her courage is great," replied the older woman. "She
loves my nephew dearly, and this cannot be easy for her."

Selim chose that moment to visit his harem. Walking in
unannounced, he went over to his aunt and kissed her.
"Where is Cyra? I have a gift for her."

Lady Refet spoke to the attending slave. "Fetch Lady
Cyra at once. Tell her the prince is here."

Cyra came quickly, Firousi following. "My dear lord,"
she said, bowing low.

"Beloved," he murmured. His eyes caressed her gently.
Then, remembering where he was, he spoke. "I have
brought you a gift from Constantinople, my love." He
clapped his hands, and the head eunuch, Ali, ushered in a
group of four people.

Selim drew the one female in the group forward. "This
is Marian, sweetheart. She is yours. Greet your new mistress in your native tongue, Marian."

"I will try to serve you well, my lady," the girl said.

Cyra's eyes lit up. "Selim! A Borderer! How wonderful!
Where on earth did you find her?"

"A Borderer? But she said she was English"

Cyra laughed. "Forgive me, my lord. You could not
know. Of course she is English, but she comes from the
northernmost of that land, which borders my own country. Both these people, the English Borderers and the Scots
Borderers, sound very much alike. Had you brought me a
London girl, I should have been hard pressed to understand her."

"Do not the English and the Scots speak with the same
tongue?"

"The people of Magnesia speak Turkish, yet do they
sound the same as those of Constantinople?"

"I see. Then she pleases you?"

"Yes, my lord. We Scots and English have been known to fight, but so far from home a fellow islander is welcome. Is it not so, Marian?"

"Yes, my lady."

Selim next drew from the little group a man. "This is Yussef. He is Marian's husband, and although I disapprove of buying married Christian slaves, I did buy him because he is a scholar and will make an excellent secretary." Yussef bowed, and Cyra smiled back. She knew the reason Selim had bought these two—having tasted the joys of love himself, he realized the pain it would cause the young English couple to be parted. Wisely she held her tongue.

"I have arranged for them," continued the prince, "to live in the small cottage at the edge of the gardens. In this way they will not be separated, but Marian may go to the cottage only when she is not needed by you. Ptolemy!"

The old Egyptian stepped forward. "This is Ptolemy, my love. He is an expert in the art of poisons and will be your food taster. You are to eat nothing, even a sweetmeat, without checking with him first. He will both taste and drink before you. And now, your bodyguard. This is Arslan. He has almost killed two masters for cruelty to their wives. In his care you will be safe." He grinned at her. "What do you think of my gifts, sweetheart?"

"Magnificent! And overly generous, my prince. Thank you."

He gazed at her for a long moment, then caressed her cheek with his fingers. "I shall eat alone this evening," he said, and, turning on his heel, he left the harem, followed by Yussef and Ptolemy.

She gazed longingly after him, then, turning, called, "Zuleika, Firousi. Come over, and bring Marian." She seated herself beside Lady Refet as her friends and new slave joined them.

"Do you understand our language, Marian?"

"Yes, my lady."

"Then tell us about yourself. How old are you?"

"Nineteen, my lady. I come, as you know, from the English Borders."

"Then," said Cyra, "many's the time you've played host to the Scots."

"Aye, my lady, many's the time, and most recently, before we left, we played host to King Jamie's rogue Lord Bothwell."

"Indeed," laughed Cyra. "I remember him well."

Marian continued, "I am the daughter of a well-to-do farmer. A year ago I was married to Alan Browne, my cousin. Alan is the younger son of a London merchant and was in great favor with the Countess of Whitley. Several months ago the countess decided Alan would benefit by working for her trading interests in the Levant."

"A countess in trade?"

"She was not born a countess, my lady. She was the only daughter of a wealthy goldsmith. The earl, her late husband, needed money, and the countess's father wanted a title for his daughter. She is very beautiful."

Cyra nodded. "Go on."

"We left England on one of the countess's ships. Our voyage was smooth and pleasant once we left the Channel and moved south. We were only two days into the Mediterranean when our vessel was attacked by pirates."

"Did they harm you, Marian?"

"Oh, no! I told them I was with child, and they said a slave who was a proved breeder was worth more, so I was left in peace."

"Are you with child?"

"I lost the babe before we reached Constantinople, my lady."

There were murmurs of sympathy all around for the English girl.

"Well, you are safe now," said Cyra. "Both you and your Alan."

A slave entered bringing a light supper for the ladies, who, after their afternoon of excitement, fell to it eagerly. Even Firousi, her nervousness gone, ate with gusto. As they finished, Sarina moved close to Cyra.

"Would you like to see my plans for the summer gardens tonight, Cyra?"

Cyra stared at her for a moment, then, realizing what the girl was trying to do, smiled and said, "Yes. Come to my quarters at nine. We'll make a party, just the two of us. I have some of those honey sesame cakes you love so."

Zuleika hissed in Sarina's ear, "If you cause her one instant's pain with your viper's tongue, I will personally slit your throat."

"What makes you think you and Firousi are her only friends?" whispered Sarina. "Do I not also have eyes to see her pain?"

At the ninth hour of the evening, a gilded litter waited outside the women's quarters. Lady Refet and Cyra conducted Firousi to it. Holding back her tears, Cyra kissed her friend and whispered, "Know only joy, dearest Firousi."

As the litter moved off down the hall, Sarina put an arm around her red-haired companion and said, "Where are those cakes you promised me? My mouth waters for them."

Cyra was touched by the thoughtfulness of the Spanish girl. There was no reason for the Sarina to be kind to her. Cyra was the favorite, the beloved of Prince Selim, the fortunate mother of his unborn child; and if Zuleika was correct, Cyra would have a son and would become Selim's bas-kadin. Cyra had everything and had been cosseted and petted since her capture. Sarina was merely one of Selim's gediklis, the girl who was clever at growing things and therefore of some use. And yet Sarina had somehow felt the favorite's anguish at seeing her best friend take her place in the prince's bed and had offered Cyra her garden plans as a diversion.

Sarina had been to the favorite's suite only once—on the morning following Cyra's first night with the prince. She had not stayed long, and now it gave Cyra pleasure to show the Spaniard about the lavishly furnished rooms, with their thick rugs, beautiful inlaid furniture, and rainbow of pillows.

Afterward, Sarina spread her carefully drawn plans on a low table and explained to Cyra exactly what would grow where.

"Of course," she said, "now that you have this suite, I shall change my plans for your garden to suit your tastes."

"What did you have planned?" asked Cyra.

"Roses. Gold of Ophir roses."

"Marvelous! They are my favorite. Against the green of the bushes and trees in my glen, the white marble of the balustrade, and the blue mosaic of the fountain, they will be perfect."

Sarina smiled. "Do you really like it, or are you just being the diplomat again?"

"No, I am not being a diplomat. I think the gold roses will be lovely. You are clever with gardens. I don't have the patience you do. You really love plants and flowers, don't you?"

"When I was a child I used to follow my father about the duke's gardens. I learned a great deal from him."

"Do you ever miss him?"

"He is dead," said Sarina. "He died the year before I came to Constantinople. My mother, brothers, sisters, and I returned to my mother's village. It is on the sea near the town of Málaga. Queen Isabella and King Ferdinand are freeing Spain from the Moors, but they often raid our coast, taking captives for sale as slaves. They lay waste to everything, and what livestock they can't carry off, they slaughter. The people of our village became tired of having their friends and relatives carried off, so we built a stone tower on a high hill overlooking the town. We kept a watch at all times, and if the Moorish ships were spotted approaching, the sentinel would ring the tower bell to warn the people. One day the bell rang, and, taking what we could, we fled into the hills. We were halfway to our hiding place when I realized my cat was missing. I thought I would have time enough to go back and get him. I reached my house safely, grabbed Pedro, and then was captured leaving. I was taken to Algiers, sold to a slave dealer from Constantinople, and then bought by a eunuch from the sultan's palace."

"They did not hurt you?"

Sarina tossed her chestnut curls. "Holy Mother! No! A beautiful girl is worth twice the price if she is a virgin."

Cyra decided to change the subject. As happy as she was, her own road to Turkey still pained her. "Do you really like cats?" she asked.

"Yes," replied Sarina. "Despite the fact a cat was responsible for my enslavement, I still love them."

Cyra called to Marian. "Fetch the basket by my bed, Marian."

The girl hastened to obey, and a moment later returned carrying a reed basket which she placed upon the table. Sarina cried out in delight and lifted from the basket a squirming, mewing kitten.

"Selim gave me a cat," said Cyra, "and several weeks ago the little vixen presented me with five kittens. Please take any two of them. The coal-black belongs to Zuleika. I was beginning to despair of finding them homes."

"Oh, thank you!" cried the Spaniard. She chose a tiger-striped kitten and a fluffy gray one and cuddled them, one against each cheek. "What darlings! Do you think Lady Refet will let me keep them in the harem?"

"Of course. Cats were the favorite animal of the Prophet. Are we friends now?"

"Yes," whispered the other girl. There were tears in her eyes. "I have been so lonely. You, Firousi, and Zuleika have been friends from the beginning, and Amara and Iris seemed to fall in so easily with one another. I know I have a sharp tongue, but I don't mean to be unkind. The words just pop out. Will you forgive me for being so mean?"

Cyra was taken aback by the girl's emotional outburst. "Of course we are friends. I know you don't mean what you say when you snap. Things will be better now."

Sarina rose, clutching her kittens. "It is late, and you must get your sleep, expecially now. May I come again?"

"You are welcome at any time, and *thank you*," said Cyra meaningfully.

Left to herself, the Scots girl called to Marian, who helped ready her for bed. Then, dismissing her slave, who she knew was eager to join her husband, Cyra lay alone in the vast bed, hot, silent tears sliding down her cheeks.

18

ALTHOUGH CYRA no longer shared Selim's bed, she still spent much time with him. The mornings were taken up by the prince's administrative duties. Once each week he held a court of judgment, allowing the people of his province to bring their grievances before him to be settled. Conscious of the fact that the child she carried was an imperial heir, and conscious also of the strong possibility that one day she might be the sultan valideh, Cyra frequently attended these courts in order to see Muslim law in action. Heavily dressed in her feridje and jasmak, she sat concealed by a carved screen behind Selim's throne, attended by Marian and the faithful Arslan.

All phases of the law interested her, but she found its treatment of women fascinating. Compared with Christian Europe, it was far more enlightened and fair.

One day there came before Selim a woman of about forty. Kneeling before the prince, she stated her case.

"I am called Cervi, my lord. At the age of fifteen I was married by my father to a young merchant, Razi Abu. I bore him two sons and a daughter. I have been a faithful and obedient wife these twenty-five years. Four months ago Razi Abu divorced me so he might marry a dancing girl he saw in a tavern. I bow to my husband's will, my lord, but he has cast me penniless into the streets. He will not return my bride price to me, and I must beg for my very bread. I plead for justice, my lord. The bride price is mine under the law."

"This is true," replied the prince, "but have you no one to whom you might turn? What of your sons and your daughter?"

"My daughter is married and lives in Constantinople, Prince Selim. As for my sons, they, too, are wed, and live with their wives and children within their father's house. He has forbidden them to aid me, though they would if they could."

The prince nodded. "Is the merchant Razi Abu in the court?"

"Razi Abu," called the court chamberlain, "come forward." The crowd stood silent.

Selim turned to his captain of the guard. "Go to the house of the merchant Razi Abu and fetch him, his wives, and all his children here. On your way, escort the lady Cervi to the small anteroom off the court, where she may wait in privacy."

While the court buzzed in anticipation, Selim turned slightly and spoke softly. "Cyra, see the woman is fed. She looks as if she has been starving."

"Yes, my lord. And perhaps I might give her some clothing. Her garments are in rags."

"Good girl," he answered.

Cyra left her hiding place and hurried to the harem. Arslan was dispatched to bring Cervi, who came trembling before the prince's wife.

"Do not be frightened," Cyra told the woman kindly.

Cervi had no time to be afraid, for she was whisked into the harem bath, scrubbed, and massaged by Cyra's own slaves. Then she was fed a delicious meal of hot rice pilaf, lamb kebabs, honey and almond cakes and, finally, dressed in clean, fresh clothes. Then, taking the woman's hand, Cyra hurried her out of the women's quarters and through the halls of the palace to the hidden chamber behind Selim's throne.

"You will not be called until your husband has stated his case, but here we may listen and observe."

The merchant had not yet arrived, and Selim was judging another case. It involved a jeweler who had several shops in Constantinople but lived on a large estate within Selim's province. The man was protesting his taxes.

"But, Highness, I am a citizen of Naples."

"Do you own land there?"

"No, my lord."

"Do you have any business there?"

"No, my lord."

"Do you pay taxes there?"

The jeweler hesitated, but Selim looked at him sternly.
"No, my lord."

"When were you last there?"

"I was born there, my lord. My parents brought me
to Constantinople when I was two."

"And when were you last there?"

"Not since I was two."

The crowded court rocked with laughter.

"So," said Selim, "you have not seen the place of your
birth since you were two. You neither own land, nor do
business, nor pay taxes there. Yet you claim to be a
citizen of Naples. Do you speak the tongue?"

"Badly, my lord," the jeweler said, shuffling his feet
nervously.

"By Allah!" roared Selim. "You are a fraud! Now
listen to me, Carlo Giovanni. The Koran states that those
who follow not the religion of truth must pay both a head
tax and a land tax. Until his death three years ago, your
father paid both these taxes for his family. You are a
non-Muslim living in a Muslim country. You are allowed
all the privileges of its citizens, including the right to
worship Allah freely in your own manner without harass-
ment. But as a non-Muslim, you *must* pay your taxes! I
could have you stripped of your shops and other proper-
ties, but I shall be merciful. You must pay your back
taxes in full, plus a fine of three thousand gold dinars,
which you will personally distribute, under my eye, to the
poor of this province. And do not whine that you cannot
afford it, for I know you can. If it comes to my ear
again, however, that you have tried to cheat the government, I shall regret my leniency and deal harshly not
only with you but with your entire family."

White-faced with relief, the jeweler kissed the hem of
the prince's robe and hurried from the court. He had
barely fled when the door opened to admit the captain of
the guard, who escorted Razi Abu and his household.

"The hussy!" hissed Cervi. "She wears my dowry
jewels."

Selim watched Razi Abu arrogantly approach his
throne. He was a small, portly man with eyes like black
currants. He was dressed in the finest brocade, and his
white silk turban held a sapphire the size of a peach pit.
His well-trimmed beard smelled heavily of scented oil,

and his pudgy fingers were heavy with rings. He was, to the casual observer, the picture of respectability; but Selim, looking more closely, saw the small, broken blue veins along his nose which indicated a secret drinker. The merchant's bow was inadequate.

"Do you know why you are called here?" questioned the prince.

"No, my lord."

"The lady Cervi, whom you divorced, claims you have refused to return her bride price and that you cast her out penniless, even forbidding her sons to aid her. All this is forbidden by the holy Koran."

"Highness, the old woman spent her bride price years ago. Age has addled her wits, and she remembers not."

Selim heard a snort from among the veiled women.

"But why," he continued, "did you forbid her sons the right to aid her?"

"They could aid her if they chose. A viper's bite is gentler than an ungrateful son," replied the merchant smoothly.

Another snort.

"Who makes that noise?" demanded the prince.

Silence.

"If you do not speak, how may I judge this case fairly? I will protect the teller of truth."

A heavily veiled woman stepped forward. "I am Dipti, the second wife of Razi Abu. He lies, my lord. Cervi's bride price was not spent by her. He gave it, along with my bride price and the bride price of his two other wives, Hatije and Medji, to *her* for her bride price." She pointed at a tall figure in an exquisite lavender silk feridje.

Selim noted that the other women wore the plain black alpaca feridje of the poor.

"Then," continued Dipti, "he threatened to disinherit Cervi's sons if they helped her. What could they do, my lord? They and their families live within our house. They work for their father and have nothing of their own."

The prince frowned. "These are grave charges, Razi Abu. What have you to say?"

"They are all jealous of my precious Bosfor, my lord prince. This flower of springtime has brought me happiness in my old age. She is naught but gentle and loving."

"Hah," snapped Dipti. "Listen to me, my lord. For his

gentle and loving Bosfor, he has robbed us all. Before she came into our house, each of us had, as the law allows, our own quarters, our own conveniences for cooking and sleeping, our own slaves. Now Hatije, Medji, and I are crammed into two small rooms because Cervi's quarters were not large enough for Bosfor, and Razi Abu must rebuild the harem to suit her. Our slaves were taken from us so she might have more and now just one old crone waits upon us. Any jewelry of value that we had has disappeared, to reappear on her person. We have not dared to complain for fear of being cast out like poor Cervi."

"Will any of the others substantiate your charges, Lady Dipti?"

Hatije and Medji stepped forward. "We do, my lord."

A young man moved before the prince. "I am Jafar, my lord, the son of Cervi and eldest of all Razi Abu's sons. The women speak the truth. They have been treated most shamefully—my mother worst of all. Our father has never been an easy man, but until he met this Bosfor he at least treated his family with respect. Had he taken the woman as a concubine, we would not have minded. Since she has come, we are all mistreated. Any imagined offense to her is reported to our father, and the offender is severely punished. We are in fear of our lives." He stepped back among his brothers.

The prince's eyes found Bosfor. He motioned to her to step forward. "I would hear what you have to say."

The lavender figure glided to the foot of his dais and sank into a graceful bow. Slowly she raised her liquid brown eyes to him.

"Why, the bitch," said Cyra softly. "She dares to flirt with him."

The woman's features were vague behind her sheer veil. Selim reached down and flicked it away. The face smiling up at him was the artfully decorated one of a whore. She was about seventeen. Selim was repelled, for he detested brazen women, but he did not show his feelings.

"Gracious prince." The voice was husky and low. "These charges are but the ravings of jealous old women and greedy sons overeager for their inheritance."

"Could you not have been content to be a pampered concubine? Surely you are not so ignorant that you did not know that in order for you to be married to Razi Abu, he must divorce one of his faithful wives. This would seem to me a hardhearted thing to do."

"I am a respectable woman, my lord."

"Hah," snorted Dipti.

Bosfor turned on her. "Old hag! You'll regret your meddling. I am to bear my lord a son."

"Aiyee! You add adultery to your other crimes!"

"*Hold!*" shouted the prince over the uproar. The room quieted. "Lady Dipti, these are serious charges you make. The law states that there must be four witnesses to such a charge. If you cannot provide proof, I must sentence you to eighty lashes. Do you wish to withdraw your charge?"

Bosfor smirked smugly at the older woman. "She has no proof, and she has besmirched my good name. She must be punished, the gossiping old crone."

"There is proof."

"No!"

"Yes! Bosfor moved into our house four months ago when Razi Abu divorced Cervi, though he could not marry her until a month ago. In all that time she has had no show of blood."

The prince smiled gently. "Sometimes, Lady Dipti, eager lovers consummate a marriage before the formalities. Could this not be the case with Bosfor and Razi Abu?"

Behind the dais Cervi squeezed Cyra's hand. "Oh, Allah! Poor Razi Abu. When Dipti is angry, nothing can stop her tongue. She will tell all."

Cyra glanced at the merchant, whose complexion had turned a sickly shade of green. Feeling a stab of pity, she whispered to Selim, "Clear the court, my lord, else the merchant will be shamed publicly. His crime is not that great."

Selim nodded and gave the order. Only Razi Abu and his family remained. Lady Cervi was brought back to the court.

Dipti drew a deep breath. "Razi Abu can no longer wield his weapon, my lord prince, and has not been able to these past five years. A severe fever killed his potency. He is as useless as a eunuch. But that is not all. When Bosfor had been in our house but a few weeks, five of the women sought her out to reason with her. As we reached her chamber door, we heard a man's voice and, peeking in, saw this shameless creature lying naked upon her couch with a man. We have watched her closely ever since, and twice more the same man has visited her in secret."

Selim turned to Razi Abu. "Is what she says true?"

Sadly the merchant nodded.

"You cast out a faithful wife to marry with this woman who cuckolds you beneath your own roof and is to bear another man's child? Why?"

The merchant was close to tears. "I did not know it until after I had made her my wife. When I learned of her condition and said I would cast her out, she threatened to make public my infirmity."

"This does not excuse your cruelty to the lady Cervi, so I sentence you thusly. First, you will return to her her bride price. Secondly, you will pay her ten times that amount in damages, and she will be allowed to return to your house to collect all her personal possessions and jewelry. Thirdly, you will sign over two-thirds of your business to your sons. And, lastly, I sentence you to one year in prison for so flagrantly breaking the law of the Koran. Had you been younger, I should have sent you to the galleys. You are a selfish and thoughtless man, Razi Abu. Perhaps a year in prison will give you the time you need to meditate on these sins, and you will return home in a year's time a kinder and more compassionate man."

Razi Abu turned angrily to Bosfor.

"No!" she screamed. "You cannot! My child will be born a bastard."

Slowly the merchant intoned, "I dismiss thee. I dismiss thee. I dismiss thee."

"You are legally divorced, Bosfor," said Selim. "Now hear your punishment according to the Koran. You have been proved an adulteress. You will be taken from this place to the public square in the village. There, stripped naked, you will be given one hundred lashes. However, I am a merciful man, and the fruit of your sin is innocent of any wrongdoing, so I will delay your sentence until the child is born. Until then you will be lodged in the village prison."

"My lord, have pity! Such a beating will kill me! What will become of my child?"

"It will be placed with a childless couple." He signaled the guards. "Take them away. The court is over for this week."

Rising from the dais, Selim graciously acknowledged the thanks of Cervi and her family and then disappeared behind the carved screen. Giving Cyra a quick kiss, he took her by the hand and hurried her off to his quarters.

She stretched herself out upon a divan while a servant removed Selim's heavy ceremonial robes and turban. Comfortably dressed in wide pantaloons banded at the ankles and a wide-sleeved silk shirt open at the neck, he sat down beside her. Silent slaves brought a bowl of fruit and thick, sweet, steaming coffee in tiny porcelain cups. Cyra made a face and pushed the coffee away.

"Cool water," she said, "flavored with tangerine."

It was placed before her, and Selim waved the slaves away. Cyra looked at him adoringly.

"Thank you, my dear lord, for your mercy to the woman Bosfor."

"I heard you gasp when I pronounced sentence."

"Poor little baby. His mother will die."

"The beating may not kill her."

"If she is whipped with a feather. Is that not the usual weapon?"

"The sentence is a just one, Cyra. The Koran is very clear on the matter of adultery. Had she named the man, he would have suffered an identical fate. That she did not, led me to believe there is some good in her and moved me to mercy."

"When you pronounced sentence, our son quickened within me, and I felt him move for the first time."

Selim grinned happily. "He approved my judgments." He pulled her up. "If I can influence him in the law, then perhaps I may turn him to the expansion of the empire, also." Leading her over to a large, square table, he pointed to the map upon it.

"Europe," he said, slamming his hand down on the table. "Someday I shall expand the empire to cover all of it, perhaps even the island your Scotland shares with England. I shall convert many to the true faith!"

"Show me where Scotland is," she asked.

He pointed to a small red patch in the blue sea.

"It's so tiny!" she exclaimed. "Where is San Lorenzo?"

His finger moved to a yellow section.

"It's even smaller than my homeland." She sighed. "I wonder how my father does. And Adam and my grandmother Mary."

He debated telling her, but then decided she should know. "Your father and his family have returned home. He was much distressed at your loss."

He saw the tears she would not allow to fall well up in her eyes.

"It is better, Selim. Father did not really like San Lorenzo. He missed his estates."

Noting the unspoken question in her eyes, he smiled to himself. Sure of her love and loyalty, he knew she would not distress him by asking, but he also knew her curiosity pricked her sorely, so he spoke.

"Rudolfo di San Lorenzo has married Princess Marie-Hélène of Toulouse."

Her outburst of giggles startled him.

"Oh, no!" she gasped. "Poor Rudi!" Her laughter lit up the chamber. Then, seeing his bewilderment, she gained control of herself. "One summer the heat was so unbearable that we went to the mountains to a village noted for its waters. Princess Marie-Hélène was there also. She was several years older than both myself and Rudi. She is fat and dark and given to numerous moles on her face. She spent most of her time eating and complaining about the lack of suitable companions."

"Poor Rudi, indeed," chuckled Selim. "Almost to have had you, and to end up with a fat princess."

Cyra peered again at the map. "How do you read a map?"

"The different countries are set in different colors, each marked with its name. The capital cities are also indicated."

"Here is Turkey!" she exclaimed gleefully. "And Constantinople! But where are we?"

His finger moved to a spot slightly northeast of the city.

"This whole green part is the empire?"

He nodded.

"By Allah! It is huge!"

"No," he replied. "Since my grandfather took Constan-

tinople, no new territory has been added. In fact, we have
lost territory since my father became sultan. The Egyptian
Mamelukes now control Cilicia, and Venice has
seized Cyprus. But someday I shall regain these lost lands
of ours—and take others."

"Will your father let you go to war, my lord?"

"My father is more interested in beauty than power. If
he wished, he could be a great warrior, but he prefers to
remain in Constantinople, adding to the palace and gardens of the Yeni Serai. Allah help us if the Christians
decide to start one of their dreary Crusades."

Cyra laughed. "Patience, my lord Selim. Your fears are
foolish. The French king, Charles the Eighth, is very busy
invading Italy. Henry the Seventh of England is attempting to subdue the Irish again. In Spain, Isabella and
Ferdinand divide their energies among the Inquisition, the
navigator Columbus, and the persecution of the Moors.
As for His Holiness, Pope Alexander the Sixth, it is rumored he secured his high office by bribery and is far
more concerned with amassing wealth for himself and his
numerous bastard offspring than with defending the
faith."

Selim was astounded by her speech. "You are remarkably well informed for the cloistered wife of an Eastern prince, my love. I doubt that the biggest gossip in
Western Europe has as much information as you do. What
is your secret?"

"No secret, my lord. Politics interests me. Knowing this,
Hadji Bey keeps me well supplied with information. How
else may I help you if I cannot be your ears? You have so
much to do."

He put an affectionate arm around her while his other
hand gently swept across the map of Europe. "If I allowed
it, you would don armor and ride into battle at my side,
wouldn't you? What lucky chance brought me such an intelligent and brave woman?"

"It was ordained long before our time, my Selim."

"By Allah, how I love you! There is not another woman
anywhere to compare with you!"

Sweeping her into his arms, he kissed her passionately.

"This son of ours already interferes with me," he murmured against her scented hair.

"My lord," she chided him, "does not Firousi satisfy you? She loves you deeply."

"Firousi is a charming confection and very dear to me, but it is a meal I crave, not sweets. Besides, the little turquoise may not be sharing my bed much longer. It is likely that she is with child."

Mischievously, Cyra looked up at him. "Who next, my lord?"

"You are impudent." He scowled at her.

"I am realistic," she countered. Then, suddenly jumping back, she cried out, "Your son has kicked me most rudely!"

"Ho," he laughed. "He warns you to keep your place, woman."

She folded her hands over her rounded belly. "Hear me, my son. Whatever may come to pass, I am always your mother, and you are merely my son."

Selim looked at her with admiring eyes. "What a sultan you would be, my love."

"What a sultan you will be, my Selim!"

19

Spring had come to Turkey with a kiss that year. Never had the rains been so gentle, nor the countryside so lush and green. The faithful in their mosques thanked Allah for his bounty and for their noble sultan. Peace and business prospered, and Ottoman culture, under the benevolent guiding hand of Sultan Bajazet, flourished.

By mid-June, to Firousi's delight, Selim's amusement, and Lady Refet's concern, the silvery-blond Caucasian girl was sure she was with child. Hadji Bey was hurriedly and secretly sent for. He arrived one glorious moonlit night, and was immediately taken to Cyra's private garden, where Selim, his aunt, and the Scots girl were sitting about the blue mosaic fountain enjoying the first fullness of the Gold of Ophir roses.

"Greetings, my daughter," said the agha, eyeing Cyra, who was now obviously heavy with child. "I see it goes well with you."

"I think I can take this small barbarian's insults a bit longer," replied the girl, patting her swollen belly.

"Insults?"

"He kicks, Hadji Bey. Not just gentle taps, but great and mighty kicks. I can assure you I am quite bruised from him."

"You are sure, then, it is a son?"

"Oh, yes! No Turkish female of gentle breeding would behave in such a manner. Only a big boob of a boy would dare," she said, smiling.

"She blooms like the roses, does she not, Hadji Bey?" asked Selim. "How is it possible for one already incomparable to become more so each day?"

The agha smiled. "Your joy brings me joy, my dear

Selim, but surely you did not bring me here merely to share it."

"It was I who sent for you," said Lady Refet. "You must help me before this vainglorious young cock is the death of us all. Cyra will give birth in less than two months, and not four months later the ikbal Firousi will also give birth. When word of this reaches Besma, she will be like a madwoman."

"It has already reached her," replied Hadji Bey, "and she has already tried again to gain the sultan's ear. Fortunately, the death of Selim's mother is still fresh in his mind and heart, and I intend to keep it so. In three nights the sultan gives a reception. He will be presented to an exquisite girl, a Circassian like yourself and your sister. I call her Kiusem, as your sister was called. She even bears a striking resemblance to the first Kiusem. I have been keeping her hidden for just such a moment, but I guarantee that the sultan will be enamored of her and will have no time for the lady Besma's complaints and ravings."

"Bless you for your foresight," sighed Lady Refet.

"However," continued the agha kislar, "I would advise you, Selim, to take a hunting trip for a few weeks, and *not* to take a new ikbal until Cyra's child is born."

"You would do well to heed Hadji Bey's advice, my dear nephew, before Besma convinces Bajazet that you and your burgeoning family are a threat to him."

"I do not feel like hunting."

"Nevertheless," thundered the agha, "you *will* hunt! We have not schemed and planned all these years for Turkey's future to have your whims destroy those plans. For myself I care not, but what future has your aunt, or Cyra, or Firousi, or your unborn children, should the sultan become suspicious? You will hunt, my son. Go toward the mountains. Take a few of your Tartars with you, but leave the main force to guard this palace. In two or three days' time, you will meet, 'by chance,' with Bali Agha and his troop of Janissaries. He is a young man about your age and holds the highest position in the corps. I can keep Besma from the sultan, but he who controls the Janissaries' loyalty controls the empire. The Janissaries know little of your good work in Magnesia. They remember only the dull boy of early days, and Besma has worked very hard to keep that image alive. Your half-brother grows more degenerate every day. Though he has been forced by his mother to consort with women, he still prefers boys, and he has no sons. Besma is becoming desperate, and she schemes for the sultan's overthrow so she may place her son upon the throne."

"I must be back in time for the birth of my son."

"I will personally guarantee it," replied the agha. "But remember, Selim—the birth of your child is a certainty; that you rule after your father is not."

The prince grimaced at the agha's words, but he was no fool, and Hadji Bey had made his point. So comfortable had he been these last few months with his life and Cyra that he had almost forgotten his goals.

The next morning Selim, with half a dozen of his Tartars for companions, left the Moonlight Serai and galloped into the hills to hunt—and for a "chance encounter" with the young chief of the Janissaries.

Bali Agha was thirty years old, of great height and commanding presence. Unlike many Janissaries, who, being of European origin, dyed their light hair black, Bali wore his shaggy dark-gold hair proudly. He had discovered early that his lighter locks won him considerable favor with the ladies. His face was square, with a strong jaw fringed with a yellow beard, a high forehead, a short nose, and snapping black eyes that peered from beneath bushy eyebrows, giving him the appearance of a stern lion.

Bali Agha was a disciplinarian, and under his command the Janissaries flourished, grew stronger, and were feared. He and his men were loyal to Bajazet but looked to the future. The future offered them three choices—the heir, Prince Ahmed, Prince Korkut, and Prince Selim—the last a devout Muslim, intelligent, and a good soldier.

Turkey had had two good sultans under the Ottoman dynasty—Mohammed II, conqueror of Constantinople, and his son, Bajazet II. The empire had grown powerful, and if it was to remain that way, it needed a strong sultan to succeed Bajazet. Bali Agha knew that neither Ahmed nor Korkut was that man, and from his powerful position he secretly began to sound out his captains and the more promising of their men on their choice.

The verdict was overwhelmingly in favor of Selim, and Bali Agha dutifully reported all of this to Hadji Bey. The stage was set, but as long as Bajazet lived and was capable of ruling, Bali Agha and his Janissaries would take no action. However, when the time came for a new sultan to put on the sword of Ayub, Bali Agha and his men would stand behind Prince Selim.

20

THE SUMMER brought with it searing heat. With the prince away, his little household settled into a quiet and uneventful daily routine. They might have been any well-to-do family on their country estate had the danger of their existence not been brought home to them by the ever-present sight of Selim's Tartars.

These loyal soldiers guarded their lord's home and family with a vigilance that was almost frightening. They had no love for the kadin Besma or her son, and though nothing had ever been said openly, it was their dearest wish that their prince and his heirs succeed Bajazet.

One day in mid-August the sun rose like a fiery ball over the Black Sea. By ten in the morning the roses, which had been briefly refreshed by the night dew, hung drooping.

Cyra sat on the edge of the mosaic fountain in her garden, dabbling her swollen feet in the water. Under normal circumstances the heat would have been unbearable, but puffed and bloated as she now was at the end of her pregnancy, it was devastating.

Entering the garden, Marian ran to her mistress. "Are you mad, my lady Cyra? Putting your feet in that cold water? You'll catch a chill."

"Not in this heat. Besides, perhaps a chill will wake that son of mine. He is slothful."

"What do you mean, slothful? All summer long you have done naught but complain of his kicking."

"I know," she sighed, "but for two days now I have felt no movement. Marian—you don't think he's dead? I could not bear it!"

"No, no, my lady! Do not fret. I once heard my old

159

grandmother say that when the child quiets, the time is near. Have you had any pain?"

"None. I feel strangely serene, and yet I wish to be active. I will check all the arrangements for my lying-in this morning. Please get me a cloth to dry my feet. The water has made me quite comfortable again."

"A cloth for my lady's feet," Marian called to the attending slave. The slave quickly obeyed, and, kneeling, Marian dried Cyra's feet and slipped a pair of green leather slippers onto them.

Entering her salon, Cyra called for the little cedar chest, and once again, as she had each day for the last two months, she opened the chest and lifted out the tiny embroidered shirts, diapers, and robes. Carefully she inspected each item and then tenderly laid it back. Their size amazed and frightened her. Could a human being really be that small?

At noon she ate lightly of fruit and soft white bread spread with thin slivers of cheese. She had scarcely finished when a messenger arrived with the news that Prince Selim would be arriving by nightfall. She sent the slaves scurrying to prepare for their master's arrival.

As the afternoon progressed, the sky began to darken with an impending storm. Lady Refet could see that Cyra's feverish activity was beginning to tire the girl, and she ordered her to her couch to rest.

In the stillness of her apartment, Cyra slept briefly. Awakened by a clap of thunder, she rose and slowly walked to the windows, opening them to allow the stormy breeze to freshen the stale air of the chamber. A sudden rush of warm water down her legs startled her, and, gasping, she cried out to Marian.

Quick to grasp the situation, Marian led Cyra back to her divan, where she propped up her lower limbs with pillows.

" 'Tis the babe," she said. "I thought your restlessness of the past few days boded his birth. Now, lie still while I fetch my lady Refet. I'll send Fekriye and Zala to keep you company."

"But there is no pain," Cyra protested.

"Time enough for that, my lady. Some begin their entry into this world with pain, others with water. I saw my mother give birth successfully both ways."

"Marian, have Yussef find Prince Selim's messenger and send him to hurry the prince. He'll know the road my lord takes. He is to tell Selim that his son is ready and eager to enter this world."

"At once, my lady, and I'll wager my lord outrides the storm," she chuckled.

Alone for a few moments, Cyra lay, scarcely breathing. Tomorrow, she thought, this time tomorrow, my son will be born, and I'll hold him in my arms. Then she remembered her mother. Meg had died in childbirth, and Adam's mother, too. Fear took hold, and she began to tremble.

"Allah—God—" she whispered, "let me live! I don't want to die. Let me survive to lie once again in my Selim's arms." She stopped. What kind of a thing was that to say to *Him?* "Oh, please understand," she began again.

At that point Lady Refet hurried into the room with Zala and Fekriye.

"I've sent for the midwife. Have you any pain?"

Cyra shook her head.

Issuing quick orders, Selim's aunt helped Cyra to rise, and, working quickly, the three women stripped the girl of her trousers and blouse, sponged her with herbed water, and wrapped her in a light robe. Assisting Cyra to her large bed, which Zala and Fekriye had freshly prepared, Lady Refet tucked her in.

Fatima, the midwife, arrived. Examining Cyra, she remarked, "It will be several hours yet, but not bad for a first child. This one is built for breeding."

Smiling wryly, Cyra remembered her innocent remark to her father: "But, father, Grandmother Mary says I'm meant to bear children."

Marian returned. "The messenger has left, my lady. He has promised to ride as though the seven jinns were chasing him."

Sighing with relief, Cyra felt a slight cramp in her back. "I think I had a pain," she exclaimed excitedly.

"Let us wait a few minutes to see if another one comes, my lady. Then we shall know for certain if your labor has begun," said Fatima.

The pains began coming with steady regularity but for a few hours seemed no more than the brief cramps that accompanied her monthly show of blood. Then they began to mount in intensity and duration.

The hours inched by, and the prince did not arrive. The wind was high, and the thunder rolled, peal after peal, but the rain did not come. Jagged lightning ripped at the fabric of the sky, giving it a weird illumination.

"I am going to die," Cyra said to Lady Refet. "Just as my mother before me did, I am going to die. I shall never see Selim again." She began to cry.

The older woman cradled the girl in her arms. "You are most certainly not going to die. Everything is proceeding normally."

"The pain is terrible, aunt. I do not think I can stand much more. I am so frightened."

"Pah," snapped the midwife. "Your pain is slight, my little bird. I have seen girls scream and shriek with real pain. All is well with you. This is an easy birth. You are frightened because it is something new to you."

The words were small comfort. Night fell, and suddenly they heard the clatter of hooves. Minutes later, Selim burst into the room.

"Beloved." He held her close.

"Selim," she sobbed, and then, smiling through her tears, said, "I can go on now that I have seen you for one last time."

Startled, the prince turned to his aunt for an explanation.

"It is all right, nephew," she soothed him. "Cyra is just a bit frightened. Everything proceeds normally."

"I should have brought a doctor from Constantinople," raged Selim.

Fatima sniffed audibly. "And what could a doctor do that I cannot? I am, Your Highness, the most famous midwife in the whole region. A doctor would drug the lady with opiates, and the baby would enter the world drowsy and weakened."

Selim glowered at her and turned back to Cyra. "Take my hands," he said. "When the pains come, squeeze hard. I will share your agony. I would see my first son born."

He stayed beside her until the end, refusing all food or drink. As the hour approached midnight, Cyra shrieked, and the midwife cried out. "The baby's head! I can see the baby's head!"

Lady Refet whispered to Selim, "I must go for the witnesses."

Hurrying out, she returned moments later with Zuleika, Sarina, Cyra's bodyguard, Arslan, her eunuch, Anber, and a harem slave she knew to be in Besma's pay.

Cyra shrieked again and doubled over. Leading the girl to the birthing stool, Fatima went swiftly to work, the witnesses surrounding them. It was midnight. Suddenly the skies opened, and the rain came in torrents. A huge clap of thunder shook the palace, and in the strange ensuing silence the cry of a child rent the air.

"Praise be to Allah and to Mohammed, His Prophet! It is a boy!" Fatima announced, passing the howling infant to Marian. She turned back to attend Cyra.

Quickly Marian cleansed the baby with olive oil, wrapped him in a warm blanket, and handed him to Selim. The prince stared down in awe at the small bundle in his arms. His deep-blue eyes were very solemn and seemed to say to Selim, "It is ridiculous that I should be so small and helpless when I have so much to do."

Cyra had now been helped back to her bed. "Give me my son," she whispered.

Fatima, finished with her duties, nodded to the prince. He laid the baby in Cyra's arms.

"Marian, help me to sit up." The girl gently raised her mistress. Unwrapping the infant, Cyra inspected him carefully.

"Everything is there, my lady. I counted," said Marian.

Cyra giggled weakly. "He has his grandfather's nose," she said. Then, "Look! Look at his palms. In the left is a bolt of lightning. In the right a tiny scale!"

Selim and Lady Refet peered down. "She is right, nephew. It is a sign. Zuleika said he would be a great warrior and have great wisdom. What will you name him?"

"A warrior with great wisdom," mused Selim.

"He shall be called Suleiman," said Cyra firmly.

The prince stared at her a moment, and then a smile lit his face. "Yes," he said. "He shall be called Suleiman."

21

AWAKENING the following afternoon, Cyra forgot for a brief moment all of the previous day. The sun made dappled shadows of the leaves in her garden, the fountain tinkled cheerfully, and the air was mountain-cool and fresh.

Gazing down at her newly slim figure, she remembered, and, turning on her side to call Marian, she saw the cradle beside her bed. "Praise be to Allah and to Mohammed, His Prophet," she exulted. "It is a boy! *My* son! My son, Suleiman!" She looked at the baby. He slept, his tiny hands curled into fists resting on either side of his head. His hair was black and wavy. Lifting the blanket that covered his little body, she noted that his limbs were rosy and sturdy, yet small-boned.

"You are awake." The voice startled her.

"Selim! What do you think of Suleiman? Is he not beautiful? Is he not the most perfect child you've ever seen?"

The prince smiled tenderly. "Yes, my dove. He is beautiful, but that is because he takes after his mother."

Her laughter was happy. "You great fool! He looks like an Ottoman, and bless Allah for it! He is you all over again."

"I love you, Cyra! Not simply because you've given me a son, but because you are the bravest, most adorable of women."

"I was not so brave yesterday. I was frightened, my lord, and yet today the sun shines, and all is well. I know now that my fear stemmed from the unknown. I shall never again allow myself to fear it!"

"I have brought you some gifts, my love." He proffered a flat leather box.

Taking it, she raised the lid and gasped. Nestled in the velvet was the most perfect emerald necklace and earrings she had ever seen. Each stone in the necklace was perfectly matched, and the earrings, oblongs of gold filigree, were scattered with smaller emeralds. "They are beautiful," she murmured.

"They match your eyes. Bajazet gave them to my mother when I was born. I wanted you to have them. I brought you something else." He handed her a thin gold chain, to which was attached a round medallion.

The medallion was half worked in a filigree of open, crisscross gold. The other half was intricately carved gold in the shape of a quarter moon. She fingered it gently, and the tiny bells attached to the openwork tinkled.

"I made it for you, Cyra."

"You honor me, my lord. The medallion will be all the more precious to me because it was your hand that created it."

"You are my bas-kadin. It is proper that I do you honor, but I must speak to you about my aunt. Since you are now officially head of my women, you may want her to return to Constantinople."

"Oh, no, Selim! Please let everything remain as it is. I love Lady Refet, and I could not get on without her. Besides, if we sent her back, Besma would make her life miserable."

"You have made me very happy, my beloved. It shall be as you wish."

Suddenly the baby wailed. The young parents looked startled.

"What is the matter with him?" cried Cyra.

"I think," said Selim, laughing, "that Prince Suleiman is hungry." Picking up the infant, he handed him to Cyra, who placed the child at her breast. And, smiling contentedly at each other, the young couple listened happily to the suckling of their son.

PART III

The Kadin
1501*1520

22

It was autumn. Snow had already appeared on the distant mountain peaks, yet by the sea the air was still warm. The vineyards and the orchards, bursting with ripe fruit, mingled their scents in a sweet potpourri of apples and grapes.

Lazy bees droned among the late flowers, and from the gardens of the Moonlight Serai came the sounds of children's voices. There were six little boys, ranging in age from seven to two, who played a rough-and-tumble game across the grass.

"Suleiman," called the beautiful red-haired young woman, "be careful of your little brothers! Remember, my lion, they are still very young."

"Yes, mother," the tall, slender, dark-haired boy called back.

Cyra turned to her companions. "He sometimes forgets that Abdullah and Murad are only two and three," she said.

Zuleika laughed. "Abdullah can take care of himself," she said. "He's so fat I'm surprised they don't use him for the ball."

"Murad is fatter," replied Cyra. "He can't even see his legs, he's so pudgy. We've never had that problem with the girls, have we, Firousi?"

"No. My girls are just perfect." She glanced lovingly at her two-year-old daughters, little silver-blond miniatures of herself. They sat playing in the grass at her feet. "I'm glad they are twins," she said. "If I'd had only one girl, she might have been lonely, and I actually think Selim was pleased with them after six boys."

"Of course he was pleased," said Cyra, "and he delights in spoiling them."

The three young women looked at each other and
smiled. Eight years in captivity had changed them little.
It was true their figures had matured with childbearing,
but their own self-discipline had prevented the usual
harem fat from setting in, and they were still slender. Their
faces, if it was possible, were more beautiful, but happiness accounted for that. They were truly happy.

Zuleika had been taught from childhood that she would
share her man, and Firousi and Cyra had been snatched
from their cultures early enough to change and accept the
Turkish way of life. Seated in the gardens of their home,
sewing and chatting, their children playing around them,
they presented a charming picture of domesticity.

Few changes had come about in the years since they
had first come to the Moonlight Serai. Two of their number had departed on the black camel of death—Iris in giving birth to a stillborn son, and Amara from a fever that
struck her down during their second winter there. The little maiden from the warm Indian plains had never ad-
justed to the Turkish climate.

Perhaps the only flaw in their contentment was the fact
that the terrible-tongued, softhearted Sarina had failed to
join them in motherhood. Selim had taken her often
enough to his couch, but she could not conceive. The children all adored her, and she loved and spoiled them in
return. Still, she was only twenty-four, so perhaps there
was some hope.

"Father! Father!" The shouts of the children rang on
the cool air. Selim was coming across the lawn. The boys
crowded about him, and he spoke to them each, giving a
pat on the head to the younger ones, an affectionate whack
to the older boys. Little Guzel and Hale hovered behind
their brothers, and, seeing them, Selim scooped them up,
one in each arm.

"And how are my littlest houris today?" he asked.

The twins giggled and, hiding their flowerlike faces be-
hind their hands, peeked at him through their tiny fingers.
Reaching his three kadins, he put the little girls down.
"They grow more like their seductive mother every day."
Firousi blushed prettily.

The prince turned to his oldest son. "Suleiman, find
your aunt Sarina and tell her I desire her presence. Then
return to your studies." The boy bowed to his father and

hurried off, feeling self-important. "Marian!" Cyra's slave appeared magically. "Take the children inside and tell their tutors they are to stay there."

The woman quickly complied. Selim was a good master, but he had been known to react harshly when not obeyed promptly.

Sarina joined the women, and, turning to them, Selim spoke.

"Word has just reached me that Besma has finally attained her first goal. My half-brother Ahmed has been returned to Constantinople, and the sultan has promised not to send him away again. He has been given a portion of the palace for his own court, and twelve of father's loveliest gediklis."

"Twelve!" exclaimed Cyra.

"A small slap at me, my dove. As a younger son, I was honored by receiving six maidens, but as heir, Ahmed has received twice the number."

"Allah help them," murmured Zuleika.

"Yes, my flower of the Orient. They will need Allah's help, but we have a more serious problem. Prince Ahmed will be arriving tomorrow night for a short visit while the workmen finish the renovation of his part of the Eski Serai."

"What mischief is this?" demanded Cyra.

"Besma's, I'll wager. I believe she hopes to arouse my brother's jealousy against me by showing him our way of life and my six fine sons—all of whom by law will supersede any sons Ahmed may sire."

"What shall we do, my lord?"

"We shall do nothing, Cyra. We shall behave as we always do. Ahmed has been envious of me since I was a child. Once he took from me a toy my father had given me, even though he was well past the age for such things. He will be jealous of my women and my sons without their doing or saying a thing. Simply stay as much out of his way as possible. When you must be in his company, be cordial, no more."

They nodded in agreement with him.

"Will he be given the freedom of the palace, my lord?"

"Except the harem, Cyra."

"Suleiman and Mohammed have their own quarters

now, my lord. Might he not seek to harm them? His ways with small boys are well known."

"It will be all right, my love. I have already instructed Arslan to guard your son and Firousi's. The household guard will be extra vigilant during my brother's stay."

"Thank you, my lord."

"You will have a great deal to do between now and tomorrow, my ladies. See that the household is prepared, and wear your loveliest costumes."

Bowing, they left him musing in the late-afternoon sun.

"The pot begins to boil," Selim muttered to himself. "With Allah's help I'll prove the better cook. Enjoy my hospitality while you can, my brother. We shall meet on the battlefield yet."

The following day the heir-apparent arrived at Selim's palace. Outwardly the relationship between the two princes was cordial. Though Besma had poured a constant stream of poison about Selim into her son's ear, Ahmed was not stupid. Selim had never exhibited any ambition or open hostility toward his older brother, and when Ahmed was away from his mother, he found he liked his younger brother. Selim, for his part, went out of his way to make Ahmed comfortable and secure.

On Ahmed's first evening, the domed and colonnaded dining hall of the Moonlight Serai was brightly lit. Brass braziers, their charcoal heat glowing bright red, took the chill off the late September night. In a corner a group of musicians accompanied a lithe dancing girl who weaved and undulated across the marble floor. Seated on soft cushions at a low table, Prince Selim entertained his older half-brother. With them was Lady Refet, for her years and her position afforded her this honor and respect.

The dancing girl finished her efforts, bowed, and ran from the room. Well-trained slaves removed the last dishes from the table and brought water pipes to the two men.

"Your hospitality is excellent, my dear Selim, but then so, I understand, is the beauty of your harem. Why is it I have not yet seen your women?"

"The sweets, my brother, should always be served at the end of the meal."

Prince Ahmed laughed. "Well said, Selim! I am prettily reproved. My mother has always said my manners were gross."

Selim nodded to a eunuch and then turned to his brother. "Join me on the dais, Ahmed, and I shall present my women to you."

They moved from the table to a raised, pillow-strewn marble dais. Lady Refet sat on a leather stool nearby. Two slaves swung wide the large doors to the reception hall, and a veiled figure in a gold-bordered, light-green wool caftan glided into the hall. She moved to the foot of the dais, where a slave removed her robe. Her trousers were striped in wide bands of gold and green, a bodice made from cloth of gold covered her sheer white blouse, and her feet were encased in green silk slippers. Red-gold hair flowed over her shoulders and down her back. It had been brushed to a sheen that caught the light and glowed. Around her throat glittered an emerald necklace, and emerald earrings bobbed from her ears. Falling to her knees before Selim, she pressed the hem of his robe to her forehead first, then to her lips.

"Rise," he said. "Ahmed, my bas-kadin, the lady Cyra. You may remove your veil before my dear brother, love."

Her slim ringed hand gently pulled the sheer green cloth from her face. "Welcome to the Moonlight Serai, Prince Ahmed. May your stay with us be a happy one."

Ahmed stared for a long moment into the cool, unwavering green eyes, then his glance took in the rest of her face and her slender body. "Brother Selim, I would give my inheritance for one night at her couch."

Selim laughed pleasantly. "My thanks, dear brother," he said, "but I prefer the life of a country gentleman. Your empire is safe. Come, sit next to me, Cyra."

A second figure appeared in the main doorway. She, too, wore a gold-bordered wool caftan, but in Persian blue. When the slave removed the caftan, Selim saw that her costume was identical to Cyra's except for the colors —blue and gold. Her silvery-blond hair had been dressed high on her head to give her the illusion of height. Around her throat she wore a necklace of sapphires. Kneeling in front of the dais, she made her obeisance, removed her veil, and flashed a dazzling smile at Prince Ahmed.

"My second kadin, the lady Firousi."

"Magnificent," murmured the visiting prince.

Firousi moved to the dais and settled herself by Cyra as Zuleika arrived. Standing in front of her lord, Zuleika allowed the slave to remove her gold-bordered, scarlet wool caftan, revealing gold-and-scarlet trousers, a cloth-of-gold bodice over a sheer white blouse, and scarlet silk slippers. A magnificent necklace of blazing rubies flashed fire from her throat. Her shining, blue-black hair was drawn back high on her head, to fall in one long, thick braid down her back.

Selim glanced at Cyra's costume, Firousi's, and Zuleika's. A little smile played at the corners of his mouth. "My third kadin, the lady Zuleika." Zuleika removed her veil, nodded coolly at Ahmed, and took her place next to Firousi.

"The first three are exquisite, my brother. If your other three kadins are as lovely, I shall be quite jealous."

"I have only three kadins, and one ikbal, Ahmed. My other two maidens are dead."

A fourth figure in a gold-bordered white wool caftan walked into the hall and to the dais.

"Ah, Sarina, come forward, my prickly rose."

Selim was not surprised to find that beneath her robe Sarina's costume matched those of her companions, her colors being white and gold. She wore only plain gold jewelry, for the lovely necklaces worn by her three companions had been gifts from Selim in token of the births of his first three sons. Sarina fell to her knees, her chestnut curls tumbling in delightful confusion about her face and shoulders. She then rose and removed her veil.

"My ikbal, the lady Sarina."

"Is it not unusual to address an ikbal by the title *lady*, my brother?" asked Ahmed.

"In this house it is not," returned Selim, a bit sharply. "Though Allah has not *yet* blessed Sarina with children, she is indispensible to my well-being and happiness." Sarina shot her lord a loving and grateful look, and then took her place on the dais. "When you visit my gardens tomorrow, think of Sarina," continued Selim. "She has been responsible for them since we came here, and my gardens are famous throughout the province."

"I don't suppose your hospitality extends to the point of sending one of these jewels to warm my couch during my visit, brother?"

Lady Refet looked shocked. Selim's women were startled, and Cyra saw the almost imperceptible but angry tightening of her lord's face that hid behind the pleasant, amused expression he turned to Ahmed. "You joke, of course, Ahmed," he said. "Our future sultan, above all people, knows that under our religious laws what he play-fully suggests is impossible. However, I have not been unmindful of your every comfort. Hadji Bey has sent to us three of your maidens. You will find them waiting when you return to your suite."

"Your thoughtfulness leaves me speechless, Selim."

Selim grinned wickedly. "Before we retire for the night, I would have you meet your nephews and nieces." He nodded to his head eunuch, who, disappearing out a side door, returned a minute later with the eight children.

Walking to the foot of the dais, they bowed low to their father and their mothers. The boys were dressed in long yellow royal robes, and the girls in tiny green caftans. They stood in a line, according to age, in front of Selim.

"My bas-kadin's oldest son, Suleiman. He is seven."

"Ah, yes," said Ahmed, "my heir. Did you know you will be sultan one day, nephew?"

"If Allah wills it, my lord uncle. May you live a thou-sand years!"

Ahmed stared curiously at the boy. Suleiman stared back, his gaze unwavering.

"My second son, Firousi's Mohammed. He is six and a half." The boy bowed. "Zuleika's son, Omar. He is five. And this little monkey is Cyra's Kasim. He is four. Here is Zuleika's second son, Abdullah, who is three. Finally, my youngest son, Cyra's Murad, age two."

"Most impressive, my brother. They are fine-looking boys, and it is comforting to me to know that the line of Osman will not die." Ahmed turned to the twins. "And who are these beauties?"

"Firousi's daughters, Hale and Guzel."

"Hale, 'light around the moon,' and Guzel, 'the beauti-ful one.' Charming," murmured Ahmed. "Come, little ones. Sit on your uncle's lap."

Hale stamped her small foot and shouted, "No!"

Fortunately, Ahmed was amused. He had been well-fed and was feeling expansive. "I retire defeated, brother Selim. Your small daughter has grievously wounded my heart." He rose slowly, bowed to Lady Refet and his brother's harem, and, followed by his personal slaves, left the hall.

Hale climbed into her father's lap and settled herself. "I don't like Uncle Ahmed," she announced. "He's a nasty man!"

23

To THE RELIEF OF Selim and his family, Prince Ahmed's visit to the Moonlight Serai was short. When word came that his apartments in the Eski Serai were ready, he departed, and for the next year or so the inhabitants of the Moonlight Serai lived in relative peace, their lives free from intrigue. Unfortunately, this state of affairs could not last.

The portion of the Eski Serai turned over to Prince Ahmed was not a pleasant place. He was not yet the father of a living son—stillbirths, miscarriages, and puny females had been the fate of his ikbals—and without a kadin, no one particular woman in his harem was dominant. His favorites changed hourly, with his moods, and this led to confusion. The ikbals of Ahmed were far too busy plotting against one another to oversee the household slaves, and the prince, in his eagerness to be free of his mother, would not permit Besma to do so. Consequently, the apartments of Ahmed and his women were filthy and disorderly.

Hadji Bey knew all of this but said nothing to the sultan. Instead, he allowed tales of the heir's slovenliness and decadence to filter across the empire. Biding his time, the agha felt that with luck, Selim, an obviously devout Muslim and the father of six healthy young sons, would inherit Bajazet's throne with no war and little bloodshed.

Aware of the enormous disparity between her own odious offspring and the handsome son of her dead rival, Besma decided to pay her son and his household a visit.

Entering the apartments, she noticed with distaste the dust balls beneath the furniture, the clothing carelessly strewn about, rotting fruit in a bowl, and the distinct smell of urine. A slave asleep on the floor received a sharp kick from her foot. He leaped up.

"Where is your master?"

The slave pointed to the gardens. Besma, her step extremely firm now, followed his trembling finger into the warm sunshine. She stood for a moment in the shadow of a column, viewing the scene before her.

Her son lounged bare-chested on a divan by a pool in which several young girls and boys were swimming naked. The years had changed Ahmed greatly. Short of stature, he had always been heavier than one might desire, but the excesses in which he had indulged had turned his neat pudginess to sloppy fat. He had developed breasts that flowed into great rolls of blubber that fell over his trouser top. Though liquor was forbidden by Muslim law, he secretly drank, and the secret was all too obvious in his beady, bloodshot eyes and the blue-veined, bulbous nose that had once been as straight and hawklike as Selim's. His graying hair and beard were untidy and badly needed barbering.

Besma's eyes now moved with sharp distaste to several others of Ahmed's suite. They were posturing in a most disgusting and all too obvious tableau. One called to him to look, and when he did, he laughed in delighted fashion.

Besma stepped into her son's view. She nodded curtly at him and turned to the group tableau. "Get out!" she commanded. "I wish to speak with my son!" They stared in astonishment at her. *"Get out!"* The prince's retainers fled.

"You forget yourself, mother. *I* am master here."

"You forget *yourself*, my son. Bajazet is the master here and everywhere else in the empire. You would do well never to forget it."

"What do you want?" he asked rudely.

"To speak with you about your conduct, and from what I have just seen, I come not a moment too soon. Your apartment is filthy! I find your slaves asleep on the floor and your women and boys disporting themselves in a vulgar fashion. Word of this incident will be all over Constantinople by nightfall. While your reputation grows worse, Selim's grows better. You openly break our laws, wallow in dirt, consort with boys, and mistreat your women. He is seen in the mosque regularly, his home is a place of joy, and his sons are legion. You would think he was the heir!"

"*I* am the heir, mother. *I* will rule after my father. Selim is merely a younger son."

"Selim is the darling of the people, you *fool!* Each time he rides into the city, they cheer. Lately he has taken to coming with his three older sons—the heir, Suleiman, and the princes Mohammed and Omar. The people cheer louder. If you took the time to come out of your pigsty, you would see for yourself."

"*I* am the heir," repeated Ahmed.

"Bah!" snapped his mother. "You will never live to rule unless you change your ways, and should you chance to outlive Bajazet, will your brothers let you rule?"

Ahmed's face crumbled. "What shall I do, mother?" he whined. "*I am the heir.*"

"Will you do exactly as I say?" she demanded of him. He nodded.

"I will install a woman here from the Pavilion of Older Damsels to oversee your slaves. At least you will give the impression of cleanliness. Your drinking must stop! As for your depravities, try to keep them to a minimum. The agha has spies everywhere, and he is no friend of ours. When you are sultan, the first thing I shall do is have his head lopped off."

"Is that *all*?"

"No! I am going to persuade Bajazet to bring Selim's four oldest sons to the Eski Serai. Suleiman is nine now, and the youngest of the four, Prince Kasim, is six. As your heirs they must be placed in protective custody and not be allowed to run wild in the countryside like peasants. Next year we shall get Abdullah. The year after, Murad, and as each of Selim's sons reaches the age of six, we shall obtain them. Here, under our watchful eye, who knows how they might develop?"

"Will Selim let them come?"

Besma smiled nastily. "He will have no choice," she said. "If he does not accede to his father's wishes, he goes against him; and if he does that, it is treason. We have him in a box!"

But Hadji Bey knew of Besma's plot within minutes of her decision. It had been ridiculously simple to plant several spies among Ahmed's maltreated slaves. The agha quickly dictated a message to his secretary, which was then enclosed within a small capsule, fastened to a pigeon's leg, and the bird was immediately dispatched to the Moonlight Serai. His next move was to see that the sultan was made unavailable to Besma for the time being.

Several days later, Selim arrived in Constantinople, with Suleiman riding at his side. They presented themselves at the palace, and the agha quickly arranged for an audience with Sultan Bajazet, who had not seen his oldest grandson since the boy's circumcision rites. He was delighted by the fresh-faced youngster who stood before him.

Suleiman was tall for his age, and very slender, with the young, hard muscles of a well-trained body. His eyes were gray-green, his skin tanned from the outdoors, and his short black hair curly. There was no doubt that Suleiman was an Ottoman, and the sultan was pleased with him.

The boy wore yellow trousers, bright red leather boots, a white shirt embroidered by his mother in green silk, and a green wool cloak. Stuck in the green silk sash that girdled his waist was a small, ornate gold dagger set with semiprecious stones. Bowing, he greeted his grandfather, "May you live ten thousand years, great sultan of the world."

Bajazet was delighted with his grandson, and Selim, noting this, quickly spoke up. "I have come with an invitation, my lord father. Never since the day I left your palace have you come to visit my home. I have six fine sons, and only one knows you. My wives complain that my hospitality is that of a beggar, not a prince, that my father is not invited to eat salt with me under my own roof. Surely the empire can spare you for a few days so you may honor my home with your presence."

"Oh, yes, grandfather," piped Suleiman. "Do come! I will take you hunting with me!"

"So you hunt, lad? What have you caught?"

"These, sire." He laid before the sultan six flawless white ermine skins. "Father took me hunting in the mountains last winter. I trapped them. They are a gift for you, grandfather."

The sultan carefully fingered the furs, but no trap

marks could be seen. He smiled down from his throne at his grandson. "Would you like me to come to visit, Suleiman?"

"Yes! Yes!" nodded the youngster vigorously.

"Then so be it," said Bajazet. "I shall ride out with you this very day." And he descended from the dais, took his grandson by the hand, and walked from the throne room.

The sultan was expected to remain at the Moonlight Serai for a week, but at the end of that time, Sarina, who had at long last to everyone's delight conceived a child, gave birth to a lusty boy. With the proud grandfather's permission, the infant was called Bajazet, and the sultan tarried in his son's household.

One afternoon as the sultan left the apartments of the new kadin and her son, Selim came to him. "Walk with me in the gardens, my father. I would speak to you, and there is less chance of our being overheard there."

"What troubles you, my son?"

"It is Suleiman and his brothers. They are past six, and as heirs to your throne they should go to your protective custody. I felt that before you returned to Constantinople we should discuss this matter."

Bajazet gazed across the gardens. Beneath a group of trees sat three of Selim's kadins. About them his six grandsons and his twin granddaughters, Hale and Guzel, played. The bas-kadin, Cyra, rocked a cradle containing her nine-month-old daughter, Nilufer. Though the sultan would have loved to have his grandchildren about him, he knew the risks involved. "No," he said. "They shall not go to Constantinople. I acknowledge the wisdom of protective custody, but your sons are far too happy and healthy here. It is like the old days before our time, when our people roamed the steppes of Asia. They will grow into better men outside our city. Besides, it will be many years, may it please Allah, before I turn my throne over to my successor. Let us wait until your sons are older, and then we shall discuss their coming to the capital again."

"Forgive my spurning your generous offer, my lord, but custom demands that Suleiman, Mohammed, Omar, and Kasim go. What will the people say if they do not? I would not bring criticism upon you, who have been so kind to me."

Bajazet gazed at his son. This was a game they were playing. Selim no more wanted his sons in Constantinople than he did, and the sultan knew it; but Selim had ever been loyal to him, so he let it pass and cleared his throat.

"The people will say I am an old fool, sentimental, and in my dotage, but never will they say I am not sultan. Because of our laws of succession, your sons will supersede Ahmed's should the idiot ever have any. In any case, his degenerate habits are ruining his health, and I doubt he will reign long, if at all.

"Between you and the throne stands your brother Prince Korkut. It is not known, but he will never reign. He does not want the responsibility. So you, my son, will one day be sultan, as your brother Mustafa should have been. You will be a strong sultan. I can see this. And after you, Suleiman, who must be stronger yet. The restraint of my court at so young an age would sap his strength. I will not allow it! This is my final word."

Selim fell to his knees before his father. Bending his body until his head touched the sultan's boot, he said, "I am your loyal and devoted servant, my lord. With my whole heart, I thank you."

Tears welled up in Bajazet's eyes, and, quickly wiping them away with his sleeve, he raised his son to his feet. For a long moment they looked at each other in silence. Then the sultan spoke. "It is *you* who should be my heir," he said, and, turning abruptly, he strode back into the palace, leaving Selim astounded.

Several days later, Sultan Bajazet reluctantly tore himself away from Selim and his family and rode back to his capital. He had scarcely returned when Besma Kadin swept into his suite.

"And how," she asked, settling herself comfortably on a low divan, "was your stay at the Moonlight Serai, my dear lord? You remained longer than we expected, and we missed you."

"It was delightful."

"And Prince Selim and his family are well?"

"Yes. He has a new son, born while I was there, and named Bajazet after me."

Besma gritted her teeth. "The oldest boy is nine, isn't he?"

The sultan nodded.

"It is past time for him and his next three brothers to be placed in our protective custody. When may we expect them?"

"You may not. I have forbidden their removal from Selim's custody. They will remain where they are. It is far healthier."

"What?" Besma leaped to her feet and paced the room. "Are you mad? They are the heirs! They must be placed where they can be watched. Ahmed must be protected!"

"From four little boys? Better the children be protected!"

"What do you mean, my lord? Protected from whom?"

"I do not think we need go into that," replied the sultan.

"What are you saying?" shrieked Besma.

"That accidents happen. Lower your voice, madam. I am still sultan here, and you are my slave. You forget yourself! Perhaps several good lashes will remind you."

She persisted, "Do you think that I would harm those children? What kind of a woman do you think I am—I, who have given you your heir?"

"I know what kind of a woman you are," he said coldly. "Kiusem gave me my heir. His name was Mustafa. He died, you will remember, at the age of two and a half, and some say you poisoned him."

"The ravings of a madwoman! Kiusem was driven insane by her son's unfortunate death."

"The accusation of a grieving mother. An accusation I knew to be true. Kiusem was *never* mad, nor her sons fools."

Besma's mouth fell open but, recovering, she asked, "If you think I poisoned Mustafa, why did you not kill me?"

Bajazet sighed. "I have asked myself that question every day for thirty-two years. Perhaps because Ahmed was a baby and needed his mother, or perhaps because your death would not have restored my dear son to me. But take care, woman. You could still end your days in a weighted sack at the bottom of the sea. Ahmed no longer needs his mother, and neither do *I*!"

A wiser woman would have departed at this point, but Besma's anger overruled her good sense. "You dare to call me a murderess?"

"I do, and I have heard men in the streets call you

worse. Beware, my kadin! Selim and his family are under my personal protection. If any harm should come to them, I would strangle you myself and leave your worthless corpse for the dogs."

The woman whitened, and discretion finally overtook her. Throwing the sultan a venomous look, she fled his presence.

24

THE SPRING OF 1509, which had begun so promisingly, gave way to strange May weather. On the morning of the ninth, the yellow sky reflected its image into a dun-colored sea. The wind was quiet, and for several hours there had been no bird song to break the monotony of the stillness. It was several minutes before noon.

The slaves in the Moonlight Serai scuttled fearfully back and forth, to and from their tasks. It had been thus for several days, and the nights had been no better. No breeze sprang up at sunset to cool the rooms after the heat of the day, and a fiery moon glared down, turning the shining white marble of the jewellike palace to a blood red.

Suddenly, a low rumble came across the hills from Constantinople. It increased in volume and intensity until it exploded in a roaring wind that bent the trees to the ground and tore across the water. The earth heaved and moaned like a tortured animal. The palace and its outbuildings shook to their foundations.

The slaves flung themselves to the ground, wailing in terror. Small fissures opened in the ground. They widened, inhaling whatever stood in their path, and abruptly closed again, crushing their prey.

Cyra was sitting in her salon playing chess with Suleiman when the first shock hit. Leaping to her feet, she cried out, "Suleiman! Quickly! The children! Bring them here!"

The boy ran from the room, only to run into Marian, who was entering her mistress's apartments carrying Sarina's wailing fourteen-month-old daughter, Mihri-Chan, and trailed by seven older children, two of whom held the littlest by the hand.

"Marian! Bless your common sense!"

"And where else would I bring them, madam? We cannot count on those worthless slaves. They are too busy hiding themselves."

The palace rocked again, and the littlest children began to cry. As the shock subsided, Lady Refet, Sarina, Zuleika, and Firousi rushed into the room, and the children, who had been huddling together, scattered to their mothers.

Nilufer, Cyra's six-year-old daughter, wandered out into her mother's gardens. "Mama," she called, "why is the sea running away?"

Hurrying to the child's side, Cyra gazed past her dainty pointing finger and saw the waters slowly receding into the bay. She was staring in amazement when Zuleika's voice broke in. "I saw the same phenomenon once in China. The waters will return shortly in one large wave."

"Will it come as high as the palace?"

"I think so. Hurry! We must get to Selim's tower observatory!" Each grasping Nulifer by a hand, Zuleika and Cyra ran with her back to the salon, and, quickly gathering their families and what slaves they could find, they fled, half running, half falling in their fear, across the palace lawns to the prince's tower. Gasping for breath, they stumbled up the stairs to the safety of the top. Once there, the slaves and some of the children collapsed in relief, but the kadins and the older princes gazed from the parapet at the scene below them.

The sea had stopped receding and, gathering into an enormous mass, now flung itself toward the shore, easily clearing the clifftop on which the palace stood, and swirled through the vast estate.

"My gardens," moaned Sarina. "The salt will destroy everything, and the roses just coming into bloom!"

Cyra suppressed a giggle. They had survived an earthquake and barely escaped from a tidal wave, and Sarina thought only of her gardens.

"The waters will quickly recede, and we can flush the gardens and fields with fresh water," said Zuleika soothingly.

And the waters did recede, cascading over the cliff like a giant waterfall, leaving in their wake struggling fish and small crustaceans that scuttled across the gardens. The earth rocked again, a clap of thunder rent the air as the sky turned black as night, and the rain gushed down in torrents.

"Zala," said Lady Refet, "light some lamps so we may at least see."

The trembling girl obeyed, but even the flickering lights could not dispel the air of disaster that hung over them. The tremors continued, softer now, but threatening still. Suddenly a slave began to scream hysterically.

The young princes looked at her in disgust. The younger children were simply wide-eyed. Cyra quickly stepped up to the girl and slapped her sharply. "Stop it this instant, Ferilze. It is a bad earthquake, and that is all!" The bas-kadin's voice was firm and assured, but her heart trembled and her mind repeated the same things over and over.

Where was Selim? He had been in Constantinople for a week. Was he still there? Was he safe? How had the quake been in the capital? She knew she must quiet these questions in her mind and tend to the business of keeping their lord's household calm and operational.

The sky began to lighten, and the rain stopped. Suddenly it was a perfect May afternoon. A fresh breeze blew down from the mountains, and the sun shone cheerily from the clear blue sky.

Cyra fell to her knees, and the others followed suit. "There is no god but Allah, and Mohammed is His Prophet. Praise to thee, o Allah, who has safely brought us through this danger," she said, then rose to her feet. "I think we can safely say the worst is over. Let us return to the palace."

On trembling legs Prince Selim's household descended the twisting stairs of the tower and slowly walked across the sodden lawns to the Moonlight Serai.

The main porch of the palace showed a large crack. Cyra bent to inspect it. "It isn't deep," she noted. "It can be repaired."

In the main court Cyra took a lambskin-covered gold stick and hit the large gong several times. The earth trembled slightly as if in reply. Silently they waited, and then slowly the slaves began to creep out of their hiding places.

The bas-kadin made mental notes. Only two were

missing. "Is anyone hurt?" she asked. "Where are Shem and Latife?"

The chief eunuch bustled forward with his usual annoying self-importance. Cyra deflated it quickly, her voice cutting.

"Where were you during the danger? We women had to see to the household while you hid your overstuffed carcass, Allah knows where—probably in the storage cellars. Two slaves are missing. What do you know of this?"

The chief eunuch began to bluster, "As head of my lord Selim's household—"

"As head of my lord Selim's household, it was your duty to see first to our safety," snapped Cyra. "You did not. Go to your quarters."

The eunuch drew his short frame to its full height. "Miserable woman," he squeaked, "who are you to speak to me thus?"

The other slaves gasped. Cyra answered slowly, deliberately, "I am our lord's bas-kadin and the mother of an imperial heir. Now go to your quarters, Ali. You are tired and obviously in shock."

Mortified, the small, fat man brushed past the other slaves. When he was gone, a farm slave came hesitantly forward. "Madam, when the quake struck, I saw Shem run to the pastures to free the master's horses. I do not know what happened to him after that."

"I do," said another slave. "He reached the pastures and freed the horses, but a large crack opened in the earth. He fell in, and it closed again before I could help him."

Another slave spoke up. "Latife is dead, I think, my lady. A hanging lamp came loose and fell on her head. She lies in the hallway between the harem and the prince's quarters."

Cyra quietly directed slaves to put the shaken household back in order. She sent other slaves to see whether the unfortunate Latife had indeed been killed. She had not. Sarina gathered up her gardeners and rushed off to inspect her precious gardens.

The high walls surrounding the prince's estate had been completely destroyed; there were several large fissures that had not closed on the grounds, and the fields were completely torn up. However, all the buildings had re-

mained standing, except two sheds. There were some
large cracks, but no serious damage. The slaves, save
Shem, were all alive, as well as the farm animals and
the prince's horses. This happy news was delivered to
Cyra and Lady Refet by the eunuch Anber. Cyra looked
at this dark man, who reminded her so much of Hadji
Bey and who was Hadji Bey's protégé.

"Where were you during the quake, Anber?"

"I gathered as many of the household slaves as I could
and led them to safety, my lady kadin."

"Are you loyal to our master, Anber?"

"I would do all within my power to protect him,
madam."

"I think we shall soon have a need of a new chief
eunuch."

A smile split the ebony face.

"How sad it will be to lose our good Ali."

"I hear and obey, my lady."

"It must be a completely natural death, Anber."

"Perhaps a bit of poppy," suggested Lady Refet
quietly. "Sometimes the hand is apt to slip."

They smiled at one another in complete understanding,
and Anber backed slowly from the room.

"Ali will be no loss," observed Cyra.

"He is Besma's best spy," replied Lady Refet. "I would
give my ermine-lined pelisse to see the look on her face
when she learns of his sad demise."

"I have a feeling," whispered Cyra, "that the time of
my dear lord's triumph draws near. We must surround
ourselves only with those who are loyal. We have allowed
Besma's spies their freedom for too many years."

Lady Refet reached out and took Cyra's hand in hers.
"How I bless that day seventeen years ago when you
came to us. You are more Turkish than I am, and so
good for Selim."

"Loyalty and ambition are not just Turkish traits, sweet
madam. They are Scots as well, and as to my being very
Turkish, why should I not be? I have lived more than half
my life here."

"We have spoken only once, dear child, of the time
you came to us, and it was so long ago. If it no longer
pains you, will you answer a question?"

"If I can," said Cyra.

"Were you never afraid? You, Firousi, and Zuleika were the calmest girls I ever saw enter the sultan's seraglio. I would have expected it from Zuleika, since she is an Easterner by birth, but you and Firousi were Christian maidens."

"The events in my life had moved so quickly that I was in shock," replied Cyra. "The night I was auctioned on the block in Candia, I did feel fear. It was warm, and yet, stripped naked on that platform, I felt frozen. My shame lasted but a short while, though it seemed forever. Hadji Bey bought me, wrapped me in his cloak, and whisked me off to his house, where I was given clothing and the immediate company of my two friends. We vowed that night that we should be true to one another no matter what our fate brought. If we were to be slaves, we would be powerful ones. After that, there was no time for fear. A whole new world opened for us. A stupid woman would have wept and begged for death at her supposed shame. We chose life, and all it could bring us. Too soon do we meet with death."

The older woman stared at the younger. "Through the ages there have been only a few women such as you, my child. How fortunate my nephew is to have you."

As darkness fell, the slaves lit the lamps and brought the evening meal. Tremors still shook the earth gently at intervals. The two women ate silently, each content in the knowledge that the danger was past, and each lost in her own thoughts.

The moon rose pure and white in a dark velvet sky, preening itself in the now quiet sea. Night sounds—the cry of the hunting owl, a soft, sighing breeze, the chirrup of young frogs in a nearby marsh—filled the air reassuringly. Nature was regaining her composure.

The following morning, young Suleiman visited his mother's quarters as she breakfasted. Sitting across from her and helping himself to some fruit, he announced, "Mohammed and I are going to ride into Constantinople to look for father."

"You are not," answered his mother calmly.

"But we must," cried the boy. "Father could be dead or injured! Who would care for him? Do you think that she-camel Besma would not use the earthquake as an excuse to murder my father?"

"Suleiman!" Cyra's voice snapped a warning. "I trust
your grandfather to see to your father's safety. Besides,
the sultan is at the Yeni Serai, and you know that the
harem lives at the Eski Serai." She spoke in English as
she always did when she did not want the slaves to understand her. "Besides, my son, your father is probably on
his way back to us by now."

Proudly drawing himself up, the boy said, "I am almost
fifteen, madam, and a man. In my father's absence I am
head of this household. Has he not always said so? It is
my decision to take Mohammed, my brother, and ride to
Constantinople to look for our father."

Two pairs of eyes, one green, the other gray-green,
blazed across the table at one another.

"Do not play the Grand Turk with me, my lad," said
Cyra. "You are now, and will always be, my son. Do you
think your father or grandfather would forgive me if
I allowed you this folly and you came to harm? You are
an heir! Where is your wisdom? Would you leave this
house of women and children unprotected?"

"The soldiers would protect you," the boy replied sul-
lenly.

"And who is to lead them should it be necessary? Am I
to put on armor and ride into battle while you wander
about the capital?"

The boy looked at his intensely feminine young
mother, with her undressed red-gold hair loose about her
shoulders, and burst out laughing.

"I fail to see what is so funny," she said.

He choked back his mirth. "Dearest bulbul, you are
so pretty, yet in your anger I see in your eyes the ghost
of your Scots ancestors. I can well imagine you ar-
mored and riding into battle."

Reaching across the table, she grabbed a handful of his
dark hair and yanked hard.

"Ouch!" he protested, struggling to escape her.

"Have you no respect for your mother?" she laughed.

"I humbly beg your pardon, bulbul."

She relinquished her hold and became serious again.
"Perhaps it is time you were kept more fully informed,
Suleiman. You are near to a man, though it amazes me
to see you so. After the quake yesterday, I sent a message
to Constantinople. Hadji Bey's pigeons are reliable under

any circumstances. We should have an answer soon. Let
us wait until then."

He gave in gracefully, knowing in his heart that she was
right and feeling a trifle foolish that he should have allowed his emotions to overcome his own common sense.

Toward late afternoon a weary bird fluttered through
the open portico into Cyra's salon. Picking the exhausted
creature up, she felt its heartbeat beneath her hand. Brave
soldier, she thought, removing the capsuled message from
its leg. Giving the bird to a slave, she instructed that it be
fed and watered before being returned to the cote.

She sat down and, opening the container, withdrew a
slip of paper. The message in Hadji Bey's familiar hand
was written in the dialect of the agha's native land. He
had taught Selim's kadins this ancient tongue when they
had first come to Turkey. It was used in all their personal
correspondence, thus confounding would-be spies.

The message was brief. Selim and the rest of the imperial family was safe. The palaces, public and government buildings were damaged, but not badly. The capital,
however, was in ruins. Huge waves had poured over the
city walls. Scores of people were dead or injured. The sultan and the court were moving to Adrianople. Selim would
accompany them before returning home. Under no circumstances were they to leave the palace.

Reading the message through twice, she placed it in a
small brazier and watched until the coals completely consumed it. She called to a slave and instructed him to as-
semble the family at once.

They came quickly, the adult women and the three
oldest boys. She told them Hadji Bey's message, and they
shared her relief regarding Selim. Cyra then sent for the
chief eunuch, Ali. Anber brought her word that the chief
eunuch was ill and could not leave his bed. Concern in
her voice, she instructed that Ali be looked after with the
utmost care. The listening slaves marveled that the bas-
kadin could be so kind to one who had spoken so rudely
to her.

Ali died peacefully the next day, and Cyra, with the
approval of Lady Refet and the other kadins, appointed
the eunuch Anber to his place.

Aftershocks continued for the next month and a half,
but they were mild and none so severe as the first quake.

There was a great deal to do regarding the repair of the estate. Selim sent word that he would remain with his father until things were more settled.

To assuage their loneliness, the prince's kadins threw themselves into an orgy of work. With the slaves and workmen from nearby villages already busy with the Moonlight Serai and its grounds, Cyra sent small troups of Tartars throughout the province to assess the extent of the damage.

Reports came in daily, and after the four kadins had carefully read them all, the soldiers were sent out again with gifts of dinars and food from Selim's own storehouses. Slowly the area returned to normal. Homes were repaired, farm animals rounded up or replaced, fields replanted, wounds healed—and, most important of all, bellies were filled. The name of Prince Selim, on the tongue of every man, woman, and child in the region, was blessed six times daily.

In mid-July the four wives of Sultan Bajazet's younger son could sit back and smile with satisfaction at a job well done. The aftershocks had stopped entirely. Everything was back to normal in their small world, and already the hot summer sun was encouraging the wheat to great height. It seemed that after the terrible devastation of early May, nature was on her best behavior.

One afternoon as Cyra sat quietly sewing, the chief eunuch admitted a dust-stained messenger to her presence. Selim was coming home! "He cannot be far behind me, my lady, though the people in the village will scarce let him by with the singing of his praises. I rode as fast as I could."

"You have done well," she replied through her veil. "Anber, see that the prince's messenger is offered refreshment before he goes to his quarters, and inform my aunt and sisters of his message."

Thus dismissing them, she called to her own slaves to prepare her bath and fresh garments.

Prince Selim, his troup of Tartar cavalry riding smartly behind him, arrived home to be greeted by his four lovely wives, who, forgetting protocol and decorum, ran from the main portico to meet him. Leaping from his horse, he

flung open his arms and managed, by a miracle known to
Allah alone, to enfold them all.

The soldiers nudged each other and grinned down from
their horses in delight. Here was a man—a prince to be
sultan someday! Four beautiful and devoted wives, for
though their faces were veiled to all men save their lord,
the slave girls spoke often of the kadins' beauty.

Selim stood there, travel-stained and weary, his four
women laughing and crying their joy at his return. Then
his sons, following their mothers' example and leaving
restraint behind, dashed from the palace to meet him.
Suleiman, fifteen next month, led the pack. Four-year-old
Prince Nureddin, the youngest, brought up the rear on
chubby, dimpled legs. Nine fine boys. The ten-year-old
princesses, Hale and Guzel, six-year-old Nilufer, and even
the littlest princess, Mihri-Chan, waited decorously beneath the main portico. As Selim and his party reached
them, Nilufer, who had inherited her mother's delicate
features and her incredible green eyes, flung herself on
him, smothering him with kisses, and then promptly
begged to be put upon her father's horse.

"She is learning your ways, my love," laughed the
prince. "First a compliment, then the request. She is not
so subtle as you, but then she is still young." He bent
down and lifted the child up into the saddle. "You may
take him to the stables, Nilufer. Can you do it?"

Her eyes shining, the child gathered up the reins. "Yes,
father."

"Selim," protested Cyra, "she is too little for such a big
horse."

"She is an Ottoman princess, and all Ottomans ride well
naturally." He tapped the horse lightly on the rump, and it
trotted off to the stable with Nilufer proudly on its back.
The prince turned to his men. "You have done well, my
Tartars. Go now and enjoy the pleasures of the bath. This
evening there will be feasting and entertainment for you
all." Turning back to his family, he escorted them into
the palace. "Tonight I shall dine with my oldest sons and
their mothers." A slave took his dusty cape while another
removed his dirty boots.

"Cyra, come with me, I want to speak with you." He
strode off to his quarters. "How is my aunt? Why did she
not greet me?"

"She is very well, my lord, but exhausted from her labors these past weeks. She bade me ask you to visit her when you have bathed and changed."

He nodded, then queried, "What in Allah's name did you do to the people of this province? There wasn't a village where I wasn't stopped and offered a selection of refreshments and nubile virgins."

They entered his apartments.

She laughed. "I simply distributed food and gold in your name following the earthquake. Did you not notice that the homes are all repaired and the fields filled with growing grain?"

"I did. Except for a few scars on the land itself, you would not know the quake had touched this region."

"But it did, dearest. The waters from the sea swept all through our estate. Had it not been for the storm that followed, we would have been a salt desert now."

"I thank Allah you were not in the city, my dove. The waters poured over the city walls. Hundreds were drowned. What wasn't ruined by the waters burned in the fires that followed. The sultan himself narrowly escaped death. The sea inundated his private apartments at the Yeni Serai. He had left them but an hour before. Three slaves who were cleaning the rooms were drowned."

"How horrible! We were lucky in losing only one slave."

The prince continued his story. "We set up tents in the gardens of the Eski Serai, but when it became apparent that the aftershocks would continue, the sultan moved the court and government to Adrianople. Before we left, he opened the granaries to the people of the city, and for the time I was with him in Adrianople, he did nothing but plan the rebuilding and repair of Constantinople. It has started already. Poor father was so worried about my family. However, Hadji Bey assured him you were all safe. Besma was naturally quite disappointed to hear you were all out of danger."

"That woman!" hissed Cyra, her eyes narrowing. Then, remembering, she spoke again. "My lord, you must forgive me for acting without your authority, but it became necessary to dispose of the chief eunuch, Ali. He was Besma's spy."

"Ali?"

"Yes, my lord. Once I told you I did not know who Besma's spies were. I spoke the truth. However, several years ago Hadji Bey felt it best that I know. The others were a white eunuch in your aunt's quarters, a bath attendant, and one of the slave girls attached to my suite. Ali died an apparently natural death." Selim raised an eyebrow, but Cyra continued. "I have appointed Hadji Bey's protégé Anber to the position of chief eunuch."

The prince nodded his approval. "And the others, my love?"

"The slave girl I rewarded for her service to me by marrying her to a prosperous farmer in the region who has always been of service to us. The bath attendant slipped while alone in the baths, hit her head, and drowned. The white eunuch was caught trying to run away with half of Lady Refet's jewels in his pockets. It was necessary to execute him as an example to the other slaves that we will not tolerate that sort of thing."

Selim whistled softly. "I shall be glad when I succeed to the sultanate, my dear wife, to have you on *my* side, and not against me."

"I regret having to take these actions, but I feel that the time is approaching when you will assume your fated duties. If we are not safe from Besma in our own household, we are safe nowhere. Bajazet will not live forever, and when he goes to Paradise, our battle begins. You cannot be held back through worrying about us. We are a household of women and children, but with this province loyal, and surrounded by faithful slaves, we can withstand anything."

Tenderly he drew her to him. He smelled of sweat and horses. "How I pity Rudolfo di San Lorenzo. With you at his side, he might have ruled all Europe."

"No, my Selim. I should have been merely his duchess. He has neither your vision nor your intelligence, and he would have treated me as a brood mare and chattel. Legally I am your slave, but never have you treated me thus. You have loved me as a woman, and yet respected me for myself. And despite the fact that you are Turkish to the soles of your feet, you have always acknowledged the fact that I have a mind." This last was said with a twinkle, for though Selim was a strong man and not one to be swayed, he often sought Cyra's advice.

"Impudent slave," he chuckled, "it is not your clever mind I admire, but your ripe, round body." His hand slid beneath her pelisse.

Squirming away in mock dismay, she exclaimed, "My lord! No Turkish gentleman would accost a lady with the filth of the road still on his person. What will the slaves say?"

"Damn the slaves," he muttered, tumbling her among the cushions. As if on cue, a slave entered, announcing, "Your bath is ready, my lord."

"*Damn* the bath!" roared Selim, glowering down at his favorite, who was biting her lip to hold back her laughter. "If you laugh, I'll strangle you."

"Yes, my lord," she gasped, choking back her giggles.

His own laugh then rumbled across the room, and her silvery one joined it. The slave stood open-mouthed, afraid to move.

Selim wiped the tears from his eyes. "Tonight?"

She smiled and, rising from the pillows, walked from the room.

25

THEY DID NOT KNOW IT THEN, but the next year was to be the last one they would spend together in peace and contentment. It was a happy year, for Selim was home more than he had been since those early days.

Occasionally he would ride into Constantinople, taking the three oldest boys with him. They came back full of tales of how the city was being rebuilt and how the people had cheered them and their father.

More often the prince would take his sons hunting. Even the youngest, Nureddin, was included, riding his shaggy pony, his fat little legs hugging the animal's equally fat sides.

Selim spent long, lazy afternoons sailing on the bay with his daughters. He came to know them as he never had. Hale, for instance, was like her mother not only in appearance but in temperament as well. Guzel, the other twin, was thoughtful and more sensitive. His youngest daughter he found mischievous and stubborn but completely winning when she chose to be. Mihri-Chan was spoiled, he knew, but then Sarina had only two children.

It was Nilufer, however, who was his favorite. She did not look like him, and though she had Cyra's delicate features, she was not merely her mother's replica. Nilufer was decidedly herself. She was bright, charming, and independent, yet extremely feminine. She was a natural leader, and even her older sisters deferred to her.

Selim spent the evenings in the company of his aunt and his kadins, enjoying quiet entertainments and talks. Sometimes there would be visitors from the capital or from outlying provinces. Then Selim would closet himself with them, sometimes for several days.

If there was anything to mar the perfection of their

lives, it was the fact that Selim, who had always been healthy and strong, began to suffer from a stomach disorder. In the beginning it appeared to be no more than indigestion. Cyra ordered a bland diet for the prince, and his symptoms disappeared, only to return a few weeks later. Worried, the bas-kadin sent a message to Hadji Bey.

Several days later, Alaeddin Cerdet, the sultan's personal physician, arrived. Selim protested but was firmly and completely examined by the doctor.

"Ulcers," Alaeddin said without any preamble.

"Nonsense," snapped Selim. "That's a disease of weak men. I've never been sick a day in my life."

"Nevertheless, Highness, you have ulcers, and as I have known you since birth, I am not surprised. Ulcers are not a disease of weak men but are caused by tension. Look at the atmosphere in which you were brought up. A weak man would have begun these attacks fifteen years earlier. Now we must keep them under control. I shall prescribe a liquid diet and bed rest."

"Liquid diet? Bed rest?" roared Selim. "Am I an old man to be tucked into my bed with warm bricks at my feet and a shawl about my shoulders, and fed broth? I am *the Ottoman.*"

Alaeddin Cerdet put his face close to the prince's and spoke softly. "You are *the son of the Ottoman,* Highness, but unless you do as I say, you will never live to reign."

Selim looked startled.

"Come, my lord," continued the doctor, "do you think Hadji Bey would send you any ordinary doctor? Trust me —and follow my advice. The liquid diet and bed rest are just temporary measures to get your ulcers under control. It will not be for long."

So Selim rested and, grudgingly, drank his broth. The pain subsided. Eventually his diet was expanded but kept simple, and as long as he followed Alaeddin Cerdet's advice, he was free from pain. Unfortunately he could not always do so because of the frequent visitors to the Moonlight Serai. Hospitality demanded spicy pilafs, lamb kebabs, honey-nut cakes, and hot, sweet Turkish coffee. Selim could hardly eat a separate diet in front of guests. If it were known he was ill, confidence in him might dwindle. So he ate the rich diet he served his guests, and suffered terrible attacks of pain afterward. Only the opium pills prescribed by Alaeddin Cerdet for these occasions helped. Unfortunately, as more visitors came to the Moonlight Serai, Selim suffered more attacks, and a change began to come about in the prince's personality. He began to be more stern and less patient.

Summer ran into autumn, and despite the earthquake of May, the harvest was good and the storehouses were filled to overflowing. The rains came, continued for a few weeks, then stopped. The days that followed were gloriously sunny and warm. Then, suddenly, winter was upon them.

It swept down from the mountains in a vicious temper of snow, wind, and bitter cold. It was the worst winter the peasants could remember. The cattle had to be brought in from the fields lest they freeze, and both day and night the peasants huddled in their homes feeding their ravenous hearths from a fast-dwindling supply of wood.

Then, just when it seemed it would be winter forever, spring arrived. Overnight the tulips, hyacinths, and jonquils were in bloom, and the almond blossoms, like pale pink clouds, perfumed the air.

Selim's family had been penned in the palace for many months and welcomed the opportunity to get outdoors. The women sat in the gardens enjoying the beautiful flowers, while the boys took to their horses, and the girls to games upon the fresh spring grass.

Selim decided to take the opportunity of riding into Constantinople before the spring rains set in, and one bright morning he left with his Tartars. The young princes stood disappointedly watching their father depart. They had wanted to accompany him and felt insulted at being left behind.

Evading their tutors, two of Cyra's sons, thirteen-year-old Kasim and eleven-year-old Murad, along with Zuleika's twelve-year-old, Abdullah, rode off into the hills to hunt. The day was balmy, and a salt-scented breeze blew in from the sea. They saw much game but contented themselves with the taking of a few rabbits. They rode, swam in a small, icy mountain pond, and lay back in the new grass, describing the shapes of the clouds to one another.

When they finally noticed the sun beginning to sink lower and a chill entering the air, they mounted their horses and turned toward home, racing each other across

the mountain meadows. Suddenly Abdullah pulled his
mount up short. Below, they could see their home set
above the edge of the sea, and the lonely road that led to
it. Abdullah had spotted a large group of horsemen attempting to hide themselves among the trees beside the
road. Kasim signaled silently that they would move closer
in an attempt to identify the intruders.

Tying their horses, they slipped stealthily through the
woods to within a few feet of the soldiers. There were at
least a hundred of them mingling in a small clearing. They
were garbed in black, with no identifying badges of
service.

"How much longer must we wait here, captain?" asked
one of the men impatiently.

"Until two hours after sunset," replied a large, evil-
looking brute. "The moon won't rise until after midnight,
and by then the Moonlight Serai will be a smoldering
ruin."

"And its inhabitants?" asked the first man.

"The men can have the women, but kill them when
they're through. As for Prince Selim's children and the
slaves, kill them at once. Those are Besma Kadin's orders.
It must appear that Tartars have done this deed."

The three young princes stared at one another in horror,
then, regaining their senses, slipped back through the
woods and quickly clambered up the hill to their horses.

"Abdullah, take Murad and warn the family. Go by
way of the beach and, in Allah's name, *hurry!* The sun is
near to setting." He mounted his own horse.

"But, Kasim," quavered Abdullah, "where are you going?"

"To Constantinople. To tell father. If I ride all night,
I can reach him by tomorrow morning. Go now!" Wheeling
his horse, he galloped off.

Abdullah and Murad quickly scrambled onto their
mounts and forcing them down a narrow cliffside path,
gained the beach. The dying sun glowed red across the waters as the two boys pushed their animals to the limits of
their endurance. They soon reached the Moonlight Serai.
The horses stumbled up the path and raced across the
gardens.

Cyra had been sitting in the dawn kiosk, enjoying the
beautiful peace of early evening. Seeing the horses racing

up the cliff path, she ran through her miniature glen to
the palace, reaching it just as the boys did. "What on earth
has possessed you two!" she shouted at the culprits. "First
you run off from your tutors, and then you tear up the
gardens with your horses. Allah help you both when your
Aunt Sarina sees her tulip beds."

"Captain Riza," gasped Abdullah, sliding off his horse.
"Get Captain Riza, Aunt Cyra! Hurry!"

Cyra saw the urgency and fear in the youngster's face
and immediately dispatched a slave. Within minutes, the
captain of Selim's palace guard appeared. Abdullah
quickly told him what they had seen and heard. Cyra
blanched, but the captain's face darkened with rage and
he exploded in a rash of oaths. "That mangy bitch," he
roared. "She's waited years to attempt this piece of treachery!"

"Can we hold them off?" asked Cyra.

"Not a chance, my lady kadin. I have only twenty-five
men here. I allowed twenty-five to go home for the spring
planting, and the prince took the other hundred with him
to the capital. You'll have to flee, and Allah protect the
slaves!"

"No! I will not leave those who have been loyal to us
to suffer certain death. They must be protected."

"Madam," replied Captain Riza, shrugging helplessly,
"the situation is hopeless. You must think of the children."

"Mother," piped little Murad, "why can't we all hide in
the Jinn's Cave. Father fitted it for an emergency."

"Of course!" cried Cyra. "It is the perfect answer! I
have allowed fear to paralyze my wits. Besma's assassins
will never find us there!"

Captain Riza looked puzzled. "The Jinn's Cave?"

"Yes, good captain. A large group of caves beneath the
cliffs on the beach. Selim thinks it was used by pirates
many years ago. It is hidden by brush, and its entrance is
blocked by a hidden door. Once inside, that door can be set
so that even if an intruder unknowingly touches the control, it cannot be opened from the outside. There is a fresh-
water spring within, and a high place that can be used as
a lookout which commands a view of both land and sea.
We will be safe there until our lord returns."

"By the Prophet's horse, this is a piece of luck." Captain
Riza turned to a slave. "Get the chief eunuch!" Then,

to Cyra, "We will wait until dark. Then the entire household will go under cover of darkness into the caves. I will send two observers out to warn us when Besma's murderers begin their move. With luck we can be hidden away long before they come."

The sun hovered for a last moment above the sea, then plummeted over the horizon.

"Go, my lady kadin," said Captain Riza. "Our time is short."

The darkness came quickly, and in the Moonlight Serai the slaves moved swiftly and calmly. Anber had explained the gravity of their situation, and although they were frightened, they knew the family of Selim Khan—their family—would protect them.

In the kitchens the assigned slaves gathered all the food and supplies they would need. Meanwhile, the house slaves hid what valuables they could, and in the children's quarters, the nurses packed clothing for their young charges.

Finally, an hour after sunset, a silent exodus began from the Moonlight Serai. Everyone carried a change of clothes, for Cyra feared that the assassins, finding their prey gone, would loot everything in sight. The young princes and princesses carried or led their household pets. Cyra thought this responsibility would lessen their fears. The kadins and Lady Refet carried their jewels.

The Jinn's Cave was actually several caves—a large main room, with two smaller rooms, one directly behind the other, opposite the entrance. A third, smaller cave stood to the left of the entrance.

The stone door was a miracle of balance. When shut, it fit so closely in its opening that no one could find it. Pressure in one corner would open the great door unless a large iron bar were jammed into a sunken stone cylinder inside the entrance.

Aside from its size, the cave had two other advantages. It had a source of fresh spring water which sprang from a rock and dripped into a time-smoothed basin. Its second advantage was a flight of natural stone steps that rose to an observation post where one could view both the sea and the surrounding countryside without being observed.

All this was as the young princes had found it. Selim

had oiled the mechanism that controlled the door, and installed metal torch holders in all the rooms. The boys had often heard their father say the cave would be an excellent hiding place, as no one could possibly find it. Selim had also added that the cave's original owners were most likely pirates of an earlier time who had used it to hide themselves and their booty from the authorities.

The princes had discovered it when Suleiman had thrown Omar's ball too hard, and it had rolled through the bushes and bounced into the entrance of the cave. They had, to their disappointment, found no treasure, but the cave had given them many golden hours, and tonight it would give them the greatest treasure of all—their lives.

Reaching it, they discovered that the farm slaves had transported the half dozen milk cows and all the goats and poultry from the farmyards into the farthest cave. Captain Riza's men had brought the few remaining horses and hunting dogs. Fortunately, Prince Selim's herds of cattle and sheep had already been taken to their mountain pastures for the summer.

The smaller side cave was assigned to the family and their attendants. Quilted cotton pallets were unrolled and the younger children put to bed, to be watched over faithfully by their nurses. The remainder of the women slaves were placed in the nearest of the back rooms, and, rank forgotten, they huddled together for comfort, while the male slaves and the eunuchs occupied the main cave.

The two soldiers assigned by Captain Riza to watch the intruders returned, followed by a third man who, using a wide rush broom, swept away all signs of foot and animal tracks. A final head count was taken, and then the great stone door was sealed shut from the inside. From the lookout post, three pairs of eyes scanned the blackness.

"Now, listen to me, all of you," spoke Captain Riza from the center of the main cave. "We are in mortal danger and will be safe only if you remain silent. You may speak softly now, but when I give the signal, there is to be complete silence. Only those in charge may speak then, and if I hear one voice I should not, I will rip the tongue from the offending one's head. Do you understand me?" His moustache bristled, and heads nodded.

The torches cast a rosy glow on the sand-colored walls of the cave. The frightened group spoke in hushed whispers as the excitement of their escape and the horrible reality of their situation had its full impact on them. Each had the same thought—somewhere out in the night was a band of violent men intent on murder. They did not want to die—at least not now. And certainly not in this manner.

Prince Suleiman stood in a corner digging a spear into the ground. His young face was strained and angry. He didn't want to be penned in this rock fortress. He wanted to be outside avenging himself on those who wanted to attack him and his family. It had taken several sharp words from his mother to get him to enter the shelter; and despite the fact that Captain Riza had taken the time to explain the logic of the situation to him, his young heart seethed with anger. Suleiman took his position as Prince Selim's eldest son and heir very seriously.

A hand fell on his shoulder. "I know, Suleiman, I want to be out there, too." It was Mohammed, his favorite brother. The closeness of these two was amazing. Only four months separated them in age, and only four months distinguished between the heir and the second son. Yet never had the younger resented the older. "Hammed the Happy" was what the slaves called him, and he truly was. Where Suleiman was dark-haired, Mohammed was tawny. Suleiman's gray-green eyes crackled with authority, but he was a somewhat shy young man. Mohammed's dark-blue eyes sparkled with laughter, and all would have admitted that he was the extrovert of the family. An imperial Ottoman prince by birth, but somehow more touchable and nearer to the common man than the rest of his kin.

Selim's children had grown up as no children of the Ottoman family ever had or ever would again. So strong was the bond of friendship among the prince's four kadins, and so well had the first three kept the vow made that night in Candia eighteen years before, that nothing would ever separate them.

Suleiman was the heir. Never had anyone questioned it. The nine boys and four girls had grown from babyhood

genuinely loving one another. They protected, fought,
and teased each other as average children in any large
family. They understood that they were princes and
princesses of a great line, but they always acknowledged
that Suleiman was the heir. In fact, they were proud of
it. One day their oldest brother would be sultan, and
when he was, he would do away with the barbaric custom of killing off all other potential heirs. It simply never
occurred to any of the brothers that they might do away
with Suleiman and steal the throne for themselves.

Their insularity from Constantinople and their grandfather's court had protected them, and they would retain
this attitude as long as they lived.

"Captain"—the voice of the tower observer cut through
the cave—"they're coming!"

"Silence, all of you," roared Captain Riza as he ran up
the steps. Peering into the darkness, the captain saw the
lighted palace and was then able to pick out the shadowy
figures of men and horses about it. Selim's four kadins
joined him. They could hear the savage shouts of the
men, their words carrying through the clear night air.

"There's no one here! The palace is empty!"

"It can't be! They must be hiding!"

"Look for a cellar beneath the palace. Search the
grounds!"

"Captain, the farm animals are all gone!"

"Then burn the barns! Burn everything! We must find
them. They cannot have gone far."

"Maybe they were warned and fled by boat!"

"No, captain, the boats are here."

"You, there! Take ten men and go back and search
that village we passed. These people love Selim. They'd
hide his family. Find them!"

Dark shapes raced across the estate. They poked and
pried into every nook and cranny, trampling the gardens,
smashing the statuary—and then a light appeared on the
horizon.

"Allah! They're burning the village," whispered Cyra.

"Don't worry, my lady kadin. We can rebuild, and the
people have an instinct for survival. They have long
since fled."

"Cyra," sobbed Firousi, "they are burning our palace!"

Through the night they watched in silence as the lovely white palace burned. The outer marble walls were not destoyed, but the interior, they knew, would be gutted.

The gray dawn heralded the arrival of the spring rains. The day was as dark as their mood. Captain Riza sent two of his men, garbed like the intruders, out to spy. Returning several hours later, they informed Captain Riza that the hostile captain had determined that Prince Selim's family had to be somewhere in the area, and had decided to camp on the palace grounds one more night to search further. His own spies had ascertained that the imperial wives and children had not fled to Constantinople, nor, for that matter, in any other direction. Several people caught in the village had been tortured but had revealed nothing.

The Jinn's Cave was naturally cool, and after a severe winter, coupled with the chill rains, it had not warmed up, but they could light no fires lest the escaping smoke betray them. As a result, they were cold and miserable. Most of the morning they huddled together in their quilts, torn between despair and the hope that young Prince Kasim had reached the capital and was now bringing help.

In Constantinople it was midmorning when a weary young horseman arrived before the great gates of the Eski Serai. He dismounted and pounded on the large doors. The grizzled head of an old soldier popped from the guardhouse above.

"Open the gates," called the boy. "I have an urgent dispatch for Prince Selim."

The gateman looked down at the dirty boy and asked, "Who demands entrance to the palace? Go away, boy! We have no time for games!" He moved to close the shutter.

"I am Prince Kasim, son of Selim Khan and fourth grandson to the sultan. Open the gates, or, by the Prophet's horse, when I get my hands on you I'll flay you alive!"

"Open the gates," said the old soldier to his younger companion.

"But how do you know the boy speaks the truth?" asked the other soldier.

"Listen, my lad. I've served the sultan's family these

thirty years, and only an Ottoman would dare to speak to a Turkish soldier in that manner. Open the gates!"

The young soldier signaled down to the guards, who swung the great doors open. Prince Kasim headed for his father's quarters.

"Get my father at once," he ordered the slave who ran to meet him.

"My lord Selim gave orders not to be disturbed until half an hour before midday prayers. I dare not disobey, young sir."

"Where is he?"

"His chambers, prince, but he is not—ah—he is not alone."

Young Kasim raised an eyebrow, brushed past the slave, and, running down the hall, entered his father's suite. The slaves guarding his father's bedchamber leaped up, but it was too late, Kasim was through the door.

Selim lay asleep upon his bed. Curled next to him was a young girl who awoke and gazed at the young prince with large, startled eyes. Kasim gazed back, his dark eyes expressionless. "Leave us," he commanded softly, and bent to waken his father. The girl opened her mouth to protest, but Kasim grasped her plump arm in an iron grip and pulled her from the divan.

"Who are you to send me away thus?" she whispered.

"Kasim, second son of Selim Khan's bas-kadin. Now go, or I shall have you whipped."

Gathering her clothes up, the girl fled. Kasim bent again and shook his father. Selim awoke instantly.

"Kasim!" His eyes darted across the bed.

"I sent her away. Father, I have urgent news and have been riding since sunset yesterday to bring it to you."

Selim listened, then sprang from the bed, swearing, "That daughter of the Devil! That spawn of pig's offal! She has gone too far this time." He roared for a slave. "Go to the sultan. Tell him I must see him at once, and don't let his servants bully you! Deliver my message personally. Then fetch the agha kislar. *Run!*" He sank down on the bed again, his head in his hands. "Cyra! Cyra! If a hair on your head has been harmed, I shall kill that bitch and her misfit offspring myself."

Young Kasim patted his father's shoulder. "Don't

worry, father. I sent my brothers by way of the beach, and it was not yet sunset when I left."

"How many soldiers were at the palace?"

"About twenty-five. Captain Riza let some go home for the spring planting."

"Damn!" shouted Selim. "Where could they all hide?"

"They probably sought refuge in the Jinn's Cave," said Kasim calmly. "It would be the best place, and no one knew about it except us."

The agha kislar arrived. "My son, what has happened? Your slave practically dragged me here." His eyes fell on the boy. "Kasim! Where did you come from?"

Selim quickly told Hadji Bey the boy's news. The agha's face became grave. "When my lord Bajazet hears of this, heads will roll. I had no warning of Besma's plans. She must have contracted directly with someone outside the palace. The sultan has often allowed her to go into the city, but usually she confides her plans to someone. Besma Kadin has overplayed her hand this time. Do not worry, my sons. I feel that your family is safe. I shall send word to my servant Talat to watch for one of our winged messengers. If they are safe, they will send word. Come! We must go at once to the sultan and tell him of this treachery. I shall have guards placed outside both Prince Ahmed's and Besma's quarters so they may not escape their punishment."

The two princes followed the ageless agha kislar through the corridors of the palace to the sultan.

Sultan Bajazet, having been awakened by Selim's messenger, was awaiting them. The sultan was sixty-three now. His hair and full beard had turned white, and his dark-brown eyes were kindly. He had always been a peace-loving monarch, his interests being more artistic than warlike, and he had done much to further Ottoman culture but little to advance Ottoman power. Nevertheless, he was a strong man. And despite the fact he had lost Cilicia to the Egyptian Mamelukes, and Cyprus to Venice, he was greatly beloved by his people. His reign was one of peace and prosperity. Recently having lost a minor war to Venice, he had rebuilt both his army and his navy, though his people, knowing his aversion to war, wondered why he bothered.

His visitors found him in a loose yellow silk sleeping robe, a small enameled cup of hot, sweet coffee in his hand. "Kasim," he smiled happily at his grandson.

"Tell him," Selim said coldly to his son. "Tell him how that she-devil who dares to call herself his kadin, not being satisfied at murdering my brother, has contrived to murder my wives and all his other grandchildren."

The sultan paled as he looked from the stricken face of his grandson to the angry face of his son.

"It may not be that tragic, my dear lord," said the agha, trying to soothe the sultan.

"No!" snapped Selim. "Perhaps some escaped like Kasim!"

The sultan recovered himself. "You make serious charges, my son, but you tell me nothing. What has happened?"

Young Kasim repeated his story.

Selim cut in. "Most of my own personal soldiers are here with me, my father. Of those left at my serai, Captain Riza allowed half to go home for the spring planting. My family and slaves were virtually undefended. The bitch planned this well!"

"They may have hidden in the Jinn's Cave," said Kasim, who understood the shock his grandfather was experiencing, and wished to ease it. "No one could find them there."

"But we do not know!" added Selim impatiently.

The sultan, who had listened to all of this with mounting anger in his heart, turned to the agha. "Have guards posted at the suites of Besma Kadin and Prince Ahmed. They are not to leave their quarters. They are to be told nothing!"

"I have anticipated your wish, my lord," replied Hadji Bey. "I have also taken the liberty of alerting five troops of Janissaries, and Prince Selim's Tartars. They, along with your horses, await you."

The sultan smiled grimly. "You are more valuable to me than all those who serve me put together. How I wish now I had taken your advice regarding Besma, but I will remedy that on my return. Stay here and see that my orders are carried out. I can trust no one but you. Now, leave me to dress. We go within the hour."

They bowed and left him. The agha took Kasim to see that he was fed before he began his long journey back home. Selim returned to his quarters and called his men to him.

26

TOWARD DAWN of the second day, the black-garbed soldiers rode off, tired of seeking their elusive prey, and now afraid of possible retribution. The villagers who had fled them were loyal to Prince Selim. Someone was sure to have reached the capital by now, and the sultan's Janissaries would be on their way. The black-garbed mercenaries had been paid to kill, not be killed, and so they departed.

From his hiding place, a young boy watched them go. When he was sure he could not be seen, the boy walked across the ravaged estate of Prince Selim. He was tall and lanky, with a thin, handsome face, and dark, haunting eyes. His dress was that of a peasant, and he meandered along as any young boy would who was out wandering on a fine spring morning. Occasionally he spun about as if in pure joy, but the more careful observer would have seen that he was really trying to see if he was being followed. Coming upon the serai, he gazed a moment at the devastation, then whistled softly.

The fire had completely gutted the interior, which had fallen within the now-blackened white walls in a charred pile. Although the main fire was out, the rubble still glowed despite the gentle rain. Content that he was indeed alone, the boy headed for the beach and went directly to the entrance of the Jinn's Cave. When the door refused to open at his touch, he bent down, picked up a rock, and tapped out a code against the stone door.

The noise reverberated through the cave, and for a split second the hearts of all within swelled in terror. The sound came again, and this time Suleiman ran to the door, pulled the iron bar from its cylinder, and swung wide the great stone. The tall boy entered quickly and without a word helped Suleiman shut and bar the door again. Then with a whoop they fell into each other's arms.

"Ibrahim!"

"Suleiman! I knew you would be here," said Ibrahim. "Kasim rode through the village on his way to the capital and warned us."

"Are the villagers all right? We saw the flames and knew they had been burned out."

"Yes, they're safe. There was plenty of time to hide anything of value. The herds are already in the high pastures for summer, so all that remained was for the people to disappear—which most of them did. A few stubborn ones remained and were tortured by the soldiers for their pains. The village was burned out of spite. But tell me, Suleiman, why? What was it all about? Those were not the sultan's men."

The young prince's face hardened. "Besma!" He spat out the name. "May she die a thousand times, and each death be more horrible than the last."

"By Allah!" exclaimed Ibrahim. "She grows bold! When the sultan hears, she is one already dead."

"I pray it with all my heart," murmured Suleiman devoutly. "But you, my friend. Is your mother safe?"

"Yes," grinned Ibrahim, "and absolutely delighted with the destruction of our house. Now my father has no excuse to keep her in the country while he dallies with those plump wenches he keeps in our house in Constantinople."

Ibrahim's mother was a constant source of gossip and amusement to the local village. Ibrahim's father was a wealthy merchant from the Greek portion of the empire who had settled his family in Constantinople. He had married early—a girl from his native village—and she had dutifully produced three sons and two daughters for him. However, as his wealth grew, his ideas changed, and after their move to the capital, he had taken first one, then another nubile concubine. When the usually meek mother of his children had raised her voice in violent protest, she had found herself shipped, complete with her three younger children, to a comfortable but distant country house. After all, she was now forty. Her dark hair was streaked with gray, and her figure was matronly from childbearing. She had grown older, and there was no help for it; but though her husband suffered the years, too, he was constantly buy-

ing and discarding maidens. She could hardly compete
with the plump, blond sixteen-year-old from Crete or the
dusky-skinned nineteen-year-old from Egypt who cur-
rently shared her husband's bed. So, having no means
other than what her husband gave her, she was forced to
remain in lonely exile with her youngest son and her two
daughters.

Cyra had met young Ibrahim on the beach several years
before. She liked this bright, amusing, and clever boy, and
after discreet inquiries into his family, character, and habits, had asked him to study with the young princes. As
Cyra had foreseen, Suleiman and Ibrahim had become
good friends, and because they were, Ibrahim knew the
secret of the Jinn's Cave.

Although the Greek boy had seen no one about as he
walked through the prince's estate, Captain Riza refused
to allow them outside the cave. Too much of an exodus
was likely to attract attention, and the secret of their hiding
place could be lost. Hopefully, Prince Kasim had reached
Constantinople safely, and even now would be on his way
back with a rescue party. In the meantime, the captain decided to send one mounted soldier out on the Constantinople road to meet their lord and tell him his family was safe.

The sun was now up, and in the confinement of the cave
the prince's household and family found it hard to keep
their dispositions even. The smell of the penned-up animals was overpowering. Everyone was getting restless.
Then, about noon, the tower sentry shouted down to Captain Riza that the prince was coming.

The five women dashed to the observation post, Cyra
and Zuleika helping Lady Refet. They could see Selim
mounted on his magnificent black stallion, Devil Wind.
Next to him rode the sultan, and beside the sultan, Kasim.

"Praise Allah," sighed Cyra.

Behind the royal horsemen rode several troops of
Janissaries and Selim's Tartars. They reached the palace,
and Cyra ordered Captain Riza to open the stone door.
"We are all safe now." Grinning, the soldier complied.

Selim and Kasim were the first to dismount, and they
ran across the gardens to the beach stairs. Cyra reached
the top of the stairs as they did. For a moment the prince
and his bas-kadin devoured each other with their eyes.
Then they flung themselves into an embrace.

"When I thought I should never see you again, my heart died within me," whispered Selim. He bent and kissed her hungrily. Cyra returned the kiss with equal passion, then raised a relieved, tearstained face to her lord. "I knew we would be safe, my love, but what frightened me was what Besma might do to you after she had moved against us"

"Do not fear, my jewel, her hours are numbered. The black camel of death will soon have a passenger."

The sultan bustled up. "My dearest daughter, praises to Allah that you are safe. Are the children all right?"

Cyra knelt and kissed the hem of the sultan's robe. "Yes, my gracious lord, and not only the children but all the slaves and the farm animals as well. We are most fortunate, but had we not had such a wonderful hiding place, we should all be dead. The assassins even burned a nearby village in an effort to find us."

He raised her up and wiped her tears away with his own handkerchief. "You will never know such terror again, my daughter. I, Bajazet Sultan, promise you this." The sultan moved on to his former ikbal, Lady Refet, and Selim tenderly embraced his other kadins.

The chief eunuch, Anber, began to organize the slaves into work parties. The ashes of the palace were cool now, and he hoped to salvage something from its ruins. The Janissaries began to set up tents on the trampled lawns to shelter the prince's family.

Selim stood to one side comforting the weeping Sarina, who after one look at her gardens had burst into tears. "There, my Sarina, do not spoil your beautiful topaz eyes with tears." He bent and brushed some earth aside with his hand. "See? Green shoots. Your gardens will grow again."

She sobbed harder. "Those are weeds! Will you never learn to tell the difference?"

Selim kissed the tip of her nose. "Good," he chuckled. "Your tongue is still sharp! You will recover."

"Oh, forgive me, my lord! Two days ago the blue hyacinths perfumed the air with their fragrance. The paperwhite narcissus and the yellow daffodils danced in the breeze. In the greenhouse I had several pots of your favorite tulips that I was forcing to adorn your quarters when you returned. For seventeen years I have worked to make our gardens places of perfect beauty and tranquillity, and in one night it has all been destroyed—destroyed by that bitch, whose only accomplishments have been to produce an idiot son and create chaos and death in her wake!"

"Hush, love, you will distress the sultan. He is already much vexed by Besma's evil."

But Bajazet had heard the impetuous Sarina's words, and the resolution to deal harshly with his kadin, weakened by his relief at finding Selim's family safe, renewed itself. The Spanish woman was right—Besma created chaos in her never-ending lust for power.

He stayed the night with his son and his family, but at the first hint of dawn he was up and on his way to Constantinople. He left with the promise to send workmen and materials to rebuild the Moonlight Serai. His mind was clear, thanks to a pleasant night spent in the company of Lady Refet, and his heart was hardened with the resolve of what he must do.

When the sultan reentered his capital, he went directly to his palace. The agha kislar came at once to his quarters.

"Is all well?"

"I have failed you, my lord," said the agha sadly. "Prince Ahmed fled the palace last night."

"How?"

"He had had an escape tunnel secretly constructed from his quarters to the outer wall. We did not know about it, as his pretty boys did it, and they are unbribable. My spy could not reach me until it was too late."

"And Besma Kadin?"

"She awaits your pleasure, my lord."

"Have her brought to me, and I wish you to remain also. I do not blame you for the prince's escape. I shall hunt him down myself. He cannot have been ignorant of his mother's treachery."

"My lord, the family of Prince Selim?"

"All safe. I shall tell you afterward."

A lesser eunuch advised Besma Kadin of the sultan's wish to see her. She made him wait while she put the finishing touches on her toilette, then followed him through the palace to the sultan's quarters.

At fifty-seven she was still a handsome woman. A Syrian by birth, Besma had rich blue-black hair that was now silver, and her smooth olive skin was just beginning to wrinkle, but her black eyes were still sharp and lively. She had dressed carefully in bright cerise trousers and a

long-sleeved, slash-skirted dress of dark-blue silk. A large
gold belt covered with sapphires and pearls girdled her
hips. Over this she wore a heavy cerise satin sleeveless
robe trimmed with ermine and embroidered with diamonds. Her hair was wound in a coronet of braids about
her head and covered with a small pink gauze veil.

As she walked down the tiled corridors, she was calmly
ready to accept her fate. By now, Bajazet would have
learned of the demise of Selim's family. He would be very
angry and suspicious, but she had been very careful. There
was nothing to connect her with the deed, since she had
used hired mercenaries, who by now would be well on their
way to Persia. No, there was no way—or no one who could
accuse her of the deed. Even if the sultan did suspect her,
he could prove nothing, but he would be greatly enraged
and would probably punish her by exiling her from court.

She laughed softly to herself. For years she had wanted
to get away from him, and now she would. She would, of
course, have her own palace, her own slaves, her own eunuchs who would all be entirely loyal to her—not spies for
that wretched agha kislar, Hadji Bey. She had won, as she
had known she would from the day the midwife had placed
her son in her arms for the first time. Ahmed would be
sultan now, and there would be no danger from Selim. He
would, she imagined, be quite a broken man. Bajazet
could not live much longer, and the first act Ahmed would
perform as sultan would be to sign Selim's death warrant.

The doors to the sultan's quarters opened before her,
and she entered.

"My dear lord," she began smoothly, "why have you
treated me in such a fashion? I have not been permitted to
leave my suite for almost three days now. Even my garden
was forbidden me, and my slaves were also held prisoner.
What have I done that you should treat me so harshly?"

Slowly Bajazet turned to face her. "You have failed,"
he said quietly. "Selim's entire family and household are
safe."

She paled, but, recovering quickly, asked, "Why should
they not be, my lord?"

"Do not pretend, you she-devil," he thundered at her. "I
know you are responsible! Your assassins were loose-
lipped!"

"Who dares accuse me?"

"Murderess!" he hissed, ignoring her question. "For too many years I have ignored your treachery and evil because you were the mother of the heir, but he is heir no longer. Last night your precious son fled the palace in secret. He is as one dead. I shall declare Selim my heir by the time of the evening prayers."

"You can't do that!" she shrieked at him. "My son is the heir! *My son!*"

"I cannot do *what?* I am sultan here, madam, a fact you have conveniently forgotten over the years."

"Even if you pass over my son, Safiye Kadin's son, Korkut, is legally next in line. What of him?"

Bajazet advanced toward her, his face dark with rage. "Do you dare to preach the law to me, you foul creature? Do you not remember that Korkut publicly renounced his claim to my throne two years ago? He never wanted the sultanate, and besides, he knew it was the only way he could live in peace from your schemes. He is happy as governor of the Macedonian provinces, and completely loyal to my wishes."

"You cannot disinherit my son!" she screamed again. "I have worked too long for him!"

He towered over her. "You poisoned my true heir, Mustafa, and I closed my eyes to it, breaking the heart of the sweetest woman who ever lived. Now you have attempted a worse deed—the slaughter of thirteen innocent children, four lovely women, and over two hundred slaves. All this in the name of putting *your* son on *my* throne? Is there no end to your evil? I should have had you killed years ago!" The veins at the sultan's temples stood out, visibly throbbing.

"But you did not kill me," she retorted, "thus condoning my actions. You are as guilty as I am!"

"I shall not go to my grave before I right that wrong," he shouted, springing at her. His powerful hands closed about her throat, and he squeezed with all his strength. Besma uttered a strangled cry and clawed at his fingers with her crimson nails. It was too late. By the element of surprise, the sultan had gained the advantage. Slowly he pressed harder, and she began to crumple to the floor. Her face, purple with trapped blood, began to turn blue. Her black eyes bulged from their sockets and then suddenly she went limp.

Hadji Bey moved quietly from the secluded corner of
the room where he had been standing, and gently pried the
sultan's fingers loose. Besma fell to the floor, and a strange
rattle came from her open mouth. The eunuch bent and
felt for a pulse. There was none. "She is dead, my lord," he
said.

The sultan stared down at the bejeweled heap of rich
clothing at his feet, then clutched at his chest, uttering a
cry of pain. Hadji Bey called to the guards. "Quickly, fetch
the sultan's physician!"

"Wait!" gasped Bajazet. "Selim—to be my heir—
Selim!"

"Did you hear him?" asked the agha. The guards nodded. "Then you"—he pointed to one guard—"fetch the
doctor. And you! Get my servant Talat. Tell no one of this,
or your lives are forfeit! Hurry!"

The guards raced from the room as the sultan, uttering
another cry, clutched at his head. Hadji Bey helped the ill
monarch to his couch and then casually covered the body
of the dead kadin with a rug.

Talat arrived. "Let no one but the doctor enter this
room," said Hadji Bey to the returning guard.

"Master," whispered Talat, "what has happened here?"

"The sultan has killed Besma and now suffers a seizure.
Send a message to Prince Selim that he is to come with all
possible speed. His family, too. We must secure the palace
before word of this reaches Prince Ahmed. The sultan has
declared in the presence of witnesses that Selim is to be his
heir."

"We have won, master! After all these years Kiusem
Kadin is avenged. If only she had lived to see her son sultan."

"Silence, you fool! Bajazet is still our lord, and only Allah has the right to call him to Paradise. As long as Prince
Ahmed lives, we are all in danger. Now go, and send our
fastest messenger. Swiftly! But arouse no suspicion by your
actions."

Talat left the sultan's suite as the doctor entered. Going
immediately to his royal patient, he made a swift but thorough examination.

"Will he live?" asked Hadji Bey.

"I cannot be sure," replied the doctor. "He has suffered
seizures of both the heart and the brain. He is now para-

lyzed from the waist down. I do not know yet whether the seizures have affected his speech, as he is in shock. I will give him an opium pill to help him sleep." He pushed a gilded ball between the sultan's teeth and, holding an amber goblet to his patient's lips, forced water down his throat. Turning to the agha, he asked, "How did this happen?"

Hadji Bey lifted the rug. The doctor's eyes widened at the sight of the woman's body. "Besma?"

"She defied him once too often," replied the eunuch.

"It is as Allah wills it," said the doctor. "Does anyone else know of this?"

"The two guards and my servant Talat, who at this moment sends a message to Prince Selim." He watched for the doctor's reaction.

The doctor smiled slowly. "How convenient that Prince Ahmed has fled the palace," he observed. "His fate is surely cursed. Do you know where he is?"

"On the Adrianople road, according to our latest reports," said the agha, "but he will be brought back."

"To what, my friend?"

Hadji Bey studied the doctor. He knew this man had always been loyal to Bajazet, but with the sultan's demise, where would his loyalties lie?

As if reading his thoughts, the doctor spoke. "I could never support Prince Ahmed, my friend. You of all people should know that. Do you not remember it was I, a young man then, who fought so hard to save Prince Mustafa? I sat by his bedside through the night while the child writhed in an unspeakable agony that I could neither cure nor ease. When he finally succumbed, I wept with joy that Allah had given him the release I could not. The sultan rewarded me by making me court physician. I know them all. Prince Ahmed has been weak, spoiled, and depraved from the beginning. He is as rotten as an overripe peach. Prince Korkut is a good man, but happy governing Macedonia and indulging his love of ancient artifacts. Prince Selim is the only logical choice, and, more important, he is the sultan's choice. I bow with a happy heart to my lord Bajazet's wisdom."

"Save the sultan if you can," replied Hadji Bey. "He must repudiate Prince Ahmed publicly, or there will be civil war. We must avoid that at all costs, and there are those who will support Ahmed in hopes of ruling through him."

"Not the Janissaries?"

"No, no," replied the agha. "Bali Agha is loyal first to the sultan, and then to Selim. The Janissaries will follow his lead."

"Then half the battle is won, and the people adore Prince Selim and his family."

"The people? Bah! The people will follow whom they are told to follow. It is certain jackals in this palace whom I fear, but I will root them out."

The doctor nodded his agreement. "I must get back to my patient."

"Good. I will make arrangements for the sultan's convalescence," said Hadji Bey, "and see to the posting of special guards. Word of how serious his illness is must not reach the wrong ears." The agha walked over to Bajazet's couch and stood staring down at his lord. The sultan slept the sleep of the drugged, but he looked more peaceful. Hadji Bey sighed softly. He, too, was getting old, and he was tired. He wished his master no ill, for the Ottoman ruler had been good to him; but he longed for the day when Selim, stronger and younger, could take up his father's burden, and he, Hadji Bey, could put down his own. Sighing again, he left the sultan's quarters.

27

THE GRAND VIZIER might be the man who helped the sultan dictate domestic and foreign policy, but Hadji Bey, agha kislar of the sultan's household, had a stronger hand in Ottoman family business. He acted in the sultan's name, and his word was law. He was greatly beloved for his kindness and patience, but equally feared for his swift and final judgments. Hadji Bey was one of the most powerful men in Bajazet's empire.

Under his guidance the word was spread that the sultan had suffered an attack of exhaustion and was upset following the exposure of his kadin's treachery. Besma, according to official court records had been strangled by an executioner, and her body sewn into a weighted sack and dumped into the sea.

There were some who were shocked, not by the alleged means of her death, for that was common, nor by the unceremonious disposal of her body, for that, too, was the usual practice, but by the fact that the woman who had tried for so long to rule had finally been caught, and justice had been administered at last. The few who had known in advance the kadin's wicked plans now trembled lest they be discovered and punished for not exposing her. Most, however, had underestimated neither the sultan's intelligence nor the agha's power, and they had merely waited for Besma to make that final, unpardonable mistake.

In another matter, however, the gossip ran rampant. Prince Ahmed had fled Constantinople, and Prince Selim was rumored to be entering the capital with great ceremony. Why had the heir fled? Was he part of his mother's plot? Was the sultan really suffering exhaustion, or had the heir attempted an unsuccessful or possibly successful as-

assination? Was Ahmed still the heir? All Constantinople waited eagerly for the answers.

The morning was clear and warm. Hardly anyone had slept, and the streets were crowded. There was nothing the people loved better than a spectacle, and the agha kislar had arranged to give them one. The populace would long remember Prince Selim's entry into the capital, and their sympathies would be carefully manipulated to be with him now and always. Should Prince Ahmed later try to take the city by any means, Constantinople would fight to the death for the sultan's younger son, Selim.

There were many who remembered the time years before when Prince Selim had left Constantinople to govern the Crimean province for his father. Now he was returning, and there was a great deal of speculation among the common folk as to why, but in the meantime it was a festival day, and the crowds were happy.

Suddenly an urchin high in a tree outside the main city gates cried out, "They come!"

Those nearest the gates strained their eyes and saw a cloud of dust in the distance. With agonizing slowness the dust cloud began to take shape as it came nearer. It was the Tartars, Selim's wild and fierce soldiers. Suddenly a troop of Janissaries, dressed in red and green and mounted on shining dark-brown horses, galloped from the city toward the incoming horsemen.

For a moment the crowds were startled. What was happening? Was Prince Selim being forbidden entrance to the city at this last moment? The Janissaries drew their scimitars. The Tartars madly brandished their spears as they galloped straight toward the Janissaries. Were they going to fight? The people stirred uneasily and pondered the wisdom of flight. Suddenly a collective shout rose from the throats of the Janissaries. "Selim! Selim! Selim!" The two groups of horsemen merged into one. "Selim! Selim! Selim!" The happy roar of voices filled the plain before the city.

The Janissaries and the Tartars were as one when they entered the city. They passed through the gates, those hard, disciplined young men, and for one of the few times in Turkish history, the Janissaries were cheered.

Behind them danced a group of gaily appareled children, their skin hues as varied as the colors of their costumes. Some carried baskets of flower petals, which they scattered on the ground about them. Others had baskets of gold dinars, which they flung to the crowds. The people went wild.

Following the children was Prince Selim, mounted on Devil Wind. The prince was dressed all in white. He wore tight-fitting silk breeches, a white silk shirt embroidered with gold thread, and a magnificent white silk coat styled in the Persian manner, which was embroidered with gold thread and dotted with small diamonds. His high boots were a soft, gold-colored suede. On his short-cropped dark head he wore a small white turban, the most predominant feature of which was a hen's-egg-sized yellow diamond from which sprang an egret's feather. A white wool cloak with a hammered gold clasp flowed down his shoulders and over the horse's dark flanks.

The crowds screamed themselves hoarse at the sight of their handsome, smiling prince. He rode with ease, holding himself straight and occasionally raising a gloved hand to wave at the sea of people. They cheered.

Behind him rode his personal guard, and following them were Selim's kadins and their children. The men in the crowd were merely curious about the unattainable, but the women of Constantinople were beside themselves with excitement at seeing these fabled creatures, their clothing, and their jewels.

Their anticipation was well rewarded. The prince's wives rode in gilded howdahs hung with pale-green draperies, each mounted upon the back of a dainty white camel wearing a red harness hung with gold bells. The kadins were ranked according to their standing in Selim's household, Cyra coming first. Each was followed by her sons mounted upon white horses; and following each prince came his sister or sisters in rose-garlanded, gilded willow carts drawn by little gray mules and led by small black boys.

The young princes were full of pride at their part in the procession and sat straight in their saddles, but of the four daughters of Prince Selim, not one acted the same. Nilufer, Cyra's daughter, sat alert and wide-eyed at her first visit to the city. Hale, one of Firousi's twins, laughingly threw sweetmeats to the urchins who scrambled amid the procession, while her sister, Guzel, sat shyly beside her, wishing they were in a litter and feeling no protection in her veil. Mihri-Chan, Sarina's baby daughter, cuddled in her nurse's arms, alternately throwing kisses to the noisy crowds and playing peek-a-boo with her chubby fingers.

The procession wended its way through the city toward the palace on the hill. The sun was high and hot, but the crowds lining the route stood their ground, and the water vendors did a brisk business.

Selim thought his face would crack with the strain of smiling. He did not feel like smiling, but the people demanded a happy prince, and at least this day they would have one. The painful events of the past week were etched sharply in his mind, and he pondered them carefully. His father lay near death, or so he thought. His brother had fled, and now he, Selim, was entering the capital in triumph. If Ahmed attempted to return to the city, he would kill him. He would probably kill him anyway. There was no doubt in his mind now that he would be sultan.

He chided himself for growing soft these past years. The softness was neither of mind nor body, but of attitude. For too long he had been separated from Constantinople. Thanks to Hadji Bey, he had always been informed on all state business, but it wasn't like being in the midst of it. Safe in the country at his Moonlight Serai, surrounded by the love and the warmth of his family, he had almost forgotten that his mother had borne him to replace his brother. Well, there was no longer a Moonlight Serai. It lay behind them in ruins, and the Eski Serai would now be their home.

The great gates of the palace loomed before him. He reined Devil Wind to a halt, and for a moment gazed up at the stone battlements that surrounded this city within a city. Then, putting spurs to his horse, Selim Khan entered through those gates, closing the door on his past and facing his destiny grimly.

He was greeted by Hadji Bey alone, for Selim had insisted that until the sultan made public the change in the succession, there should be no official reception. At that moment the only thing he wanted was to see his father, for during the years Selim had lived at the Moonlight Serai and had had easier access to him, Bajazet had become most dear to his younger son. Understanding this, the agha personally escorted the prince to the sultan's apartments.

Bajazet's speech had not been affected by his stroke, but he remained paralyzed from the waist down, and his mind alternated between clarity and forgetfulness. He had aged by twenty years, and it was with shock that Selim beheld him.

"My beloved son," whispered the old man from his couch.

Selim flung himself before his father in a gesture that was part respect, part grief. The sultan looked down on him for a moment, then said, "Get up, my son. I am an old man and have no regrets, except that I did not kill Besma sooner. Sit here next to me. My mind is not always clear now, and I must speak with you before it begins to wander again."

The prince rose from his knees and lowered himself to the cushions. "What would you have me do, my father?"

"Are your kadins and children safe? Ahmed is like his mother and will not hesitate to get at you through them."

"They are now within the palace, my father."

"My palace, I have discovered, is not necessarily a place of safety, but hopefully Hadji Bey will see that they are well protected. Hear me, Selim. I cannot rule any longer. My doctors either cannot or will not say whether I shall recover completely. I do not think I shall. When I am well enough to speak before the people, I shall publicly declare you my heir. If I tried to do so now, there are those who would say I had been forced or coerced in my illness, and we must avoid war at all costs. However, until I can speak out, you are my regent. I ask only one favor of you. I have, as you know, three kadins—Safiye, who is old now; the second Kiusem, whose son Prince Orhan is just ten; and Turhan, who has borne me the child of my old age, Prince Bahiteddin, who is five. Protect them all for my sake. Let no harm come to them. Remember your own mother and your frightened childhood."

Selim bowed his head and then looked up into his father's eyes. "I shall guard them as my own family. This I swear to you. No harm shall come to them by my hand. But what of Ahmed's children and women?"

"You will know what to do, my son."

So, Prince Ahmed's women and his three daughters were strangled by the court executioners and stuffed into weighted sacks to join Besma at the bottom of the Bosporus. No one mourned their loss.

And while Selim went about the business of running his father's empire, his wives began the business of settling themselves. The harem of the Eski Serai was far too small to accommodate all of Bajazet's women and their attendants, let alone the new arrivals. Lady Refet, although not officially named, was looked upon as the sultan valideh, and she set about straightening out the overcrowded situation.

Not counting the ikbals and the kadins, there were some two hundred women in Bajazet's harem at this time. Lady Refet ordered a large, comfortable house built at the edge of a forest on the palace grounds. In it she retired most of the older women. Here they would live out their lives in peace, comfort, and security. It was with little reluctance that these older ladies of Bajazet's harem retired.

New odas consisting of ten girls apiece were set up in the freshly refurbished harem. Each had its own oda mistress, an older woman on whom the younger girls could look as a mother figure, and the older ones as an experienced friend.

The keeper of records went over his entries, and all maidens who had been in the harem three or more years and had not yet caught the eye of their lord were honorably married to palace and government officials whom Selim thought it wise to honor.

This act created much support for Selim, as the serai girls were beautiful, well-educated, and highly accomplished. They would grace any man's home and, most important, give that man a link with the sultanate.

There were about fifty gediklis remaining. These girls were considered promising enough to remain to serve Bajazet and perhaps attract the next sultan. Divided into five groups and assigned to an oda, the young ladies continued their serai education. Each of the three kadins and two ikbals of Sultan Bajazet was each given a new apartment in the now spacious harem. Well-trained, courteous attendants and slaves were assigned to serve them. Though at first frightened by the sudden turn of events, having spent many years under the threat of Besma, they slowly realized that the new regime of Lady Refet was for everyone's good, and no harm was meant to them.

Selim's kadins were kept busy decorating and furnishing

their own new apartments. They had chosen for themselves a two-story building in the harem which was built around a quadrangle. It was called the Forest Court. At either end of the quadrangle were entry arches, the north ones leading to the main grounds of the palace, and the south opening onto a large private park. The park had been designed to resemble a partly formal, partly wooded garden. It rolled gently in some places and had a medium-sized lake which served as a refuge for waterfowl and as a place to boat. All this was surrounded by a high wall.

The quadrangle was planted. In its center was a rectangular pool with a fountain. Graveled walks with cream-colored marble benches were placed at strategic locations, and small fruit trees, flowering shrubs, and plants completed the charming retreat.

Each of Selim's kadins had chosen for herself a wing on the second floor of the building. The main floor housed the slaves, the eunuchs, the communal kitchens, and the baths. The building wings opened into one another, so Cyra, Firousi, Zuleika, and Sarina were not separated.

Selim had decided to remove his older sons from their mothers' care, and each was set up in his own quarters, but Cyra, speaking for herself and the other kadins, begged that the younger princes remain with them for the present. She pleaded the well-known lechery of some of the pages that could, and had, ruined many a child. It was agreed that only the boys who had reached their biological manhood would go to their own establishments within the palace walls. They would be given sterile harem damsels to sate their natural appetites.

Suleiman, who would be sixteen in two months, Mohammed, who was now fifteen, Omar, who was fourteen, and Kasim, now thirteen, left with no regrets, much to the annoyance of their mothers. Cyra had to admit to herself that her firstborn son was nearly a man. Twice recently she had caught him fondling her slave girls, and when she had chided him, he had merely grinned and asked her for what other purpose had Allah created pretty girls?

Of the remaining princes, only twelve-year-old Abdullah and eleven-year-old Murad objected to being left with the women. A few well-administered slaps from their annoyed mothers ended the rebellion. Bajazet, Hassan, and Nureddin, ages eight, six, and five, were too young to care.

Selim's sons were not, however, entirely separated from one another. They attended the newly formed Princes' School, along with their young uncle, Prince Orhan.

Selim's daughters were to remain with their mothers. Hale and Guzel, who had just celebrated their eleventh birthday, were assigned several learned older women who would broaden their educations. The princesses could speak, read, and write Turkish, English, French, Chinese, and Persian, and had been taught mathematics, history, and geography as well as both Eastern and Western literature. Their sewing and embroidery improved daily, and they played several instruments, sang, and danced, but they were painfully ignorant in the matter of their function as females, as well as court etiquette. Their first lessons in such manners left them weak with laughter. The only men they had ever known intimately in their short lives were their father and brothers, who had cosseted and spoiled them constantly.

Firousi was distressed to learn that there had already been several offers of marriage for the twins. Selim's second kadin vehemently protested that her daughters were far too young and, besides, were not yet capable of bearing children. The twins themselves were not overjoyed at the news of their possible marriages. Tears in their eyes, they begged their father not to separate them. When the time came, they would accept marriage, but only, they swore, to the same man.

Selim was not insensitive, and when he thought about it, the possible advantages of bestowing these exquisite girls upon one useful man far outweighed the disadvantages. He gracefully acquiesced, and the matter was dropped for the present.

Meanwhile, Cyra was formulating her own small plot. Suleiman's friend Ibrahim had returned to Constantinople, and she knew her son missed his friend. One evening as Selim relaxed with his water pipe in her quarters, she tackled the situation.

"Do you remember Ibrahim—Suleiman's young friend from the country?" Selim nodded. "He has returned to his father's house. The old fool is trying to make a merchant out of him, and he is very unhappy."

"It is a son's duty to obey his father in all matters," replied the prince.

"The boy is no more meant to be a bazaar vendor than Suleiman," she said in an exasperated tone. "He is bright and clever. If I might venture an opinion—"

"Do continue, my dear," said Selim dryly.

"Ibrahim should be trained for government service. He could be a valuable asset to us one day," she finished triumphantly.

"You are suggesting that Ibrahim continue his education in the Princes' School?"

"Why not? He had all his lessons with Suleiman when we lived in the country. The tutors report he is highly intelligent, and Suleiman would be very happy to have his friend with him again."

"It is not the custom for an outsider to study with the imperial princes. We are no longer at the Moonlight Serai. But," continued Selim, "there is no reason that Ibrahim and Suleiman cannot continue their military training together. We might also arrange for Ibrahim to have *some* lessons at the palace school."

She protested.

"No, his father has made a decision concerning Ibrahim's future. I will not interfere in those plans."

Cyra pouted, "But his family would be honored if we took an interest in him."

"Come now," teased the prince. "You are the most ravishing creature in the world. You have been taught to give pleasure, and here you sit like an adorable spider in the middle of your luxurious web, weaving schemes. Weave a spell upon me instead, my beloved. My mouth is parched for the cool sweetness of your lips."

Her eyes caught his as he plucked the jeweled pins that held her hair. It fell like a shining curtain around them.

"I never grow tired of you," he murmured, brushing her lips with his. "You have never become dull or boring like so many others. You are full of life and constantly changing. I have always wondered what kind of country your Scotland must be to breed women like you. You are my slave, and yet you are the freest woman I know. No man could ever own you."

Laughing softly, she nestled against him. "Perhaps it is our climate that makes Scots women as we are, or perhaps I am like my cats in having the ability to adapt to my situation, or"—and this more thoughtfully—"perhaps I re-

member that one day I shall be the sultan valideh. If I
stopped learning now, I should make a poor one."

"Do you look for that day?"

"I dread it," she replied, looking him straight in the face.
"For me to be sultan valideh, my son must be sultan, and
when he is—" She stopped, stricken. "Oh, my Selim! I
love you so! Never leave me! Rule a thousand years! I am
bas-kadin to the greatest prince who ever lived, but so
many times in my heart I have wished you were a simple
farmer or merchant so we might live our lives in peace and
grow old together as normal people do!" She burst into a
frenzy of uncontrollable sobs so great her body shook
harshly with them.

He gathered her into his arms and held her tightly, murmuring endearments. "There, my dove. Hush, sweet moon
of my delight. Don't weep, my love, my incomparable
love."

She always amazed him. That she loved him and their
children, he knew. That she put him and his interests first,
he did not doubt; but that she was capable of such deep
emotion with regard to him, he had not realized. His cool,
beautiful, competent kadin wept like a girl in the first flush
of love; he had not expected it, and it frightened him. Such
loyalty made him weak, and he needed time to think, so he
tried to cajole her out of this mood. He slid his hands beneath her thin night garments and caressed her smooth
body. She sighed contentedly, but then stiffened.

"Selim!" Her voice sounded exasperated.

"Heart of my heart"—his voice was sheepish—"you
frightened me. I have never seen you like this."

The storm was past, and her laughter rang clear in the
dim, scented chamber. Relieved, he grinned, and his own
laughter joined with hers. "Your proper kadin has returned
to you, my lord. Don't stop. Your hands are a healing
balm."

"Ill-mannered slave!" he replied in mock rage. "It is you
who should strive to please me!"

She applied a skillful caress. "Like this, my lord? Or
perhaps this, my lord?"

He looked at her through fierce, half-closed eyes. She
returned the look and, bending, placed a burning kiss on
his waiting mouth.

28

WHEN PRINCE AHMED fled Constantinople, he went to the palace at Adrianople and declared himself sultan. Civil war broke out. Most of the provinces, neither understanding the situation nor realizing how unfit Ahmed was to rule, supported him. The battle lines were drawn—Selim, the Tartars, and the Janissaries on one side, and Ahmed and the provinces on the other.

Now, two years later, the battle was over, and Hadji Bay, eager to give the news to the kadins, hurried down the corridor leading to the apartment of Prince Selim's baskadin. Brushing past the slaves guarding the door, he entered the salon.

They were all there, seated about the fire, embroidery in hand. He wondered silently why women were considered the weaker sex. In his fifty-seven years on this earth he had observed their strength over men many times. Not necessarily physical strength (although after watching the act of birth he wondered if men could be that strong), but their great strength of will.

It pleased Hadji Bey's vanity these twenty years later that his choice of women to help his prince become sultan had been correct. Not only had they produced among them nine fine sons, but they had accomplished a greater miracle in their unity and solidarity. Never in all the ages had four women shared one man without backbiting and betrayal. He wondered whether they could now maintain this serenity. He coughed softly. "Good day, my daughters."

Cyra rose and came toward him, hands outstretched. "Dear Hadji Bey. What news?"

"It is over," replied the agha. "Prince Ahmed is dead, and our Prince Selim is victorious!"

"Praise Allah!"

232

"Does the sultan know?" asked Zuleika.

"Not yet, my lady. He is having one of his bad days and would not comprehend. When his mind clears, I shall tell him."

"How did Prince Ahmed die?"

"Badly, my lady Cyra."

"This is no time for levity," she said sharply. "You know precisely what I mean."

"Yes, madam, but even in the sweetest victory it is wise to keep a sense of humor lest we become pompous and overimpressed with our own good fortune."

Cyra blushed. "I stand corrected."

The agha patted her gently and marveled silently at the blush. The woman before him was thirty-three years old, and the mother of four. She was sophisticated in the ways of the world, and yet she still had the good grace to admit a fault. He had waited many years to see Selim become sultan. Now he prayed Allah he could see Suleiman attain the same goal. This fantastic woman's son would indeed be great.

"Come, my lord agha. Sit by the fire and tell us of Ahmed's end," she said, leading him to a comfortable spot and helping to settle him. "Some peach sherbet?"

A slave girl placed a crystal goblet held in a filigreed gold holder in the eunuch's hand.

"Wherever Ahmed went, he lost his followers as quickly as he gained them. Realizing the battle was lost, he deserted his last few followers and fled to the nearest village, hoping to find refuge in anonymity. Poor prince! As usual, he made an unfortunate choice. The village he chose had been pillaged and ravaged by his own men but two nights before. He was recognized. The villagers held him until Prince Selim arrived."

Zuleika's eyes were shining with expectation. She reached for an apricot and bit into it so fiercely that the juice ran down her chin. "How did he die, Hadji Bey? How did the pig die?"

The eunuch smiled at her. Age had not softened this proud woman of Cathay. Once she had decided that Ahmed was her enemy, she had been relentless. "Patience, my dear, I am coming to that." He raised the goblet to his lips and sipped his sherbet. Refreshed, he continued, "Ahmed was brought before his brother. They say he blubbered and soiled himself like a child. Prince Selim spoke sternly to him, exhorting him to accept his defeat as the will of Allah and die like a true Ottoman. He assigned a black mute to hold his brother's sword, and ordered Ahmed to fall upon it. The unfortunate prince cried out in terror that he could not, and begged Selim to kill him himself. Our prince reminded his brother that the Prophet forbids brother killing brother. A storm was blowing up, and he was becoming impatient.

"The thunder came closer, and it began to rain. Still, Prince Ahmed could not bring himself to end his worthless life with honor. Then a streak of lightning struck a nearby building, shearing off its side. The assembled company turned to stare in amazement, and when they turned back, Ahmed was skewered as neatly as a chicken on a spit."

"Good," snapped Zuleika. "So should all traitors end!"

"There is more," said Hadji Bey. "The mute who held the sword may not be able to speak, but I myself taught him to write. He sent me a message saying that in the moment that all turned to gaze at the lightning, a hand shoved Prince Ahmed onto his sword. No one else saw it. The hand belonged to Ibrahim."

"How horrible," whispered Firousi in a frightened voice.

"Why should it be horrible that our enemy is dead?"

"Zuleika, you misunderstand me. It is good that Ahmed is dead, but why did our lord Selim have to be his executioner? Why could he not have left that task to the judges? Now the people will say he killed his brother to gain the throne."

Zuleika cast her eyes upward in exasperation, but Cyra put an arm about her friend. "No, dearest. No one will call our Selim murderer. Nor will they call him hypocrite. Had he not delivered the judgment against his brother himself, he *would* have been criticized. Technically, Ahmed was still the heir, since the sultan's illness has prevented him from publicly renouncing Ahmed and naming Selim. The thousands who fight, follow, and believe in Selim would have expected him to dispose of his rival. There was no other way. Selim might have tortured and dishonored Ahmed, but he did none of these things. He permitted his brother to die honorably and quickly. When our lord returns to us, we shall never mention this incident. Though

Ahmed was his enemy, he was also his brother. Selim cannot help but feel some anguish."

"Cyra, Cyra," said Hadji Bey. "You have lived a thousand years to have gained such wisdom! Perhaps when I named you I should have called you Hafise instead of Cyra."

"I think I prefer being called Cyra to being known as the 'Wise One,'" laughed the bas-kadin. "If you are called wise, then everyone expects you to be so. It would be too great a strain. I could never satisfy everyone."

"Aiiee!" cried the grand eunuch, rolling his eyes. "Every word a pearl!"

The other kadins giggled behind their hands.

"Hadji Bey! Really!"

The agha chuckled from deep within his throat. "Remember, my lady, levity."

"Out of my sight, you old schemer," laughed Cyra.

Hadji Bey rose to his feet and, smiling fondly at the ladies of the future sultan, bowed himself out of the room.

Several weeks later, Prince Selim returned home, to be happily greeted by his entire family; but the homecoming was marred by two tragedies. The first was brought by the prince himself, who, after affectionately greeting each of his women in turn, took his third kadin aside and spoke privately with her. A sharp cry from Zuleika caused the others to turn toward them.

For one brief moment the smooth, calm face of the Oriental woman contorted in agony, and Selim, his own face sad, put his arms about her and muffled the hard, dry sobs. It lasted but a minute, and then Zuleika drew away from the prince. She stood with her head bowed for a moment, and then, looking up into his face, brushed the tears from his cheek. Calling to her sons Abdullah and Nureddin, she asked permission to return to her quarters, and left the salon.

Selim returned to the little family group. "Prince Omar is dead," he said. "He was killed in that last foolish battle between my brother and myself. He died bravely. Suleiman and Mohammed tried to aid him, but my third son was mortally wounded by the time they reached him. There was naught they could do but slay the murderers."

There was nothing the kadins could say, but words were

unnecessary. They had been so fortunate these many years. They had lived as a normal family, and they had known happiness, warmth, unity, and love. Unlike most women of their time, none had lost a child before this.

The second sadness to mar their day was the messenger who brought word of Prince Korkut's death. This second older half-brother of Selim had, upon receiving word of the younger man's victory over Ahmed, taken poison. In a scroll delivered to Selim, Korkut reiterated once again that he had no wish to be sultan, but he knew that if he remained living, dissident groups would form to press a cause he could not espouse, bringing further civil war to the empire. Death, concluded Korkut, was the only answer. He closed by bestowing his blessing on his younger brother.

That night in Cyra's bedchamber, Selim wept. He had loved and admired the scholarly Korkut, who had administered the Macedonian province so well for their father. Of all the sultan's sons, Korkut had been the most like him, lacking only Bajazet's desire to rule; but, more important to Selim, Korkut had been his childhood friend.

"They will blame me for his death," said Selim. "No matter how it is announced, they will say I murdered him, too."

"Too?"

"Ah, yes. Already the gossips in the streets whisper that I murdered Ahmed. In two short years they have forgotten the depraved monster he was."

She shook her head vehemently.

"Yes, my flower, and there is more. They say I hold the sultan under guard. That my father really sent his Janissaries to make me a prisoner as I rode on Constantinople with my Tartars; but that, instead, the Janissaries welcomed me and betrayed the sultan." He sighed. "Ah, well. Soon they will call me a usurper. The doctors have told me that my father will never regain his health, and the council would declare me sultan. I put on the sword of Ayub in a few days."

"And about time!"

He looked surprised.

"My dear lord, Turkey needs a strong ruler. Without one, she will flounder and break apart. It is only providence that the kingdoms of Western Europe are too busy with their own internal troubles. Were this not so, they would descend on us like a pack of wolves. They think we are barbarians. Christian princes who for one political reason or another wish to add to their own prestige and treasuries undertake Crusades against the infidel. Look to Spain. Ferdinand and his late queen, Isabella, drove the Moors out with a vengeance. The Moors are a highly civilized people, but they are not Christians. How many of them died under that fanatical instrument of Christianity known as the Inquisition? Oh, no, my lord! That must not happen to Turkey! Our sultan must be strong. We need you!"

"You speak as if you were born a Turk."

"My lord, I lived only thirteen of my years in Western Europe. The greater part of my life—and all of my happiness—has been here with you."

He sighed. "If any other woman spoke to me thus, I should call it flattery or guile, but not when you do, my incomparable one. Your truth has been both my joy and my sorrow. Come, kiss me, beloved."

Her lips met his, and, as always, he felt the storm of desire sweep over him. He marveled silently at his need for her. Never did he grow bored or disillusioned with her, and never could he get enough of her perfumed body.

With Zuleika his lovemaking was always savage. Never could he forget that he was to be sultan, and never could she forget she had been a princess of Cathay. Their love was a battle of wills, and never had she shown herself vulnerable until today, when he had told her of their son's death.

With Firousi he could laugh, for although the Caucasian girl obviously adored him, she found the rather awkward positions of lovemaking amusing, and rarely could she control her mirth. He had on several occasions threatened to beat her, but instead of fearing him, his beautiful kadin had turned her gorgeous turquoise eyes up to him, lips twitching, and promised solemnly to behave. Then it would be he who would end up laughing.

Sarina, strangely enough, was the shyest of his wives. Afraid of displeasing him, she had always done exactly as she was taught. When it finally occurred to Selim that she was a bit frightened in their physical relationship, he, the sternest of warriors, had become the gentlest of lovers, and had won Sarina's undying adoration. He secretly wondered if this fear of Sarina's had prevented her from conceiving a child for so long.

With Cyra it was none of these things. She was, he had known from the beginning, his only true soulmate. It was to her he came to talk over his ideas and hopes, and although he would never have admitted it—and she would never have suggested it—Cyra often advised and guided him with great wisdom.

The night had grown cool, and she slept now, instinctively aware that for the moment he no longer needed her. Selim gently drew a cover over her and rose from their bed. The pain that had gnawed at his stomach these past two years seemed to be worse tonight. Walking onto the terrace, he thought of the task ahead of him, and his mouth composed itself into a grim line.

His father had rebuilt Constantinople after the earthquake, and it was much for the better; but the sultan had done litle to expand and strengthen the empire. Bajazet encouraged literature and the arts, but his provinces were near rebellion and unprotected from the nomadic tribes that of late had grown bolder. There could only be one sultan in Turkey, and, as Cyra said, he must be strong—not a sick old man of sixty-five. So Selim would ride in a few days' time to the tomb of the soldier-saint, Ayub, and put on the sword which symbolized the leadership of the house of Osman. Bajazet would retire with his three kadins to a quiet serai on the sea where the old man would receive the best of care.

His younger brothers had conveniently died natural deaths while he had battled Ahmed. There were no loose ends now. He would be sultan, and after him his son Suleiman would take up the reins of a stronger and more secure Turkey. As he stood watching the muted colors of the early dawn unroll across the sky, he heard Cyra stir behind him.

"Is it the pain again, my lord?"

He nodded.

"Have you taken the medicine the doctor prescribed?"

"It only makes me feel worse, my love. It eases the pain but addles my brain and makes me sleepy. If I must choose between pain and witlessness, then I choose pain. Should I show the least sign of weakness, there are those who lurk in the shadows only too ready to pounce upon me and bring the House of Osman tumbling down."

Cyra sighed but said no more. Selim's pain was obviously worsening, and of late he had become more irritable when suffering the attacks. The sun was now coloring the city below the palace, and the prince departed her chambers to make his preparations for the coronation.

Selim Khan put on the sword of Ayub on a windy spring morning. It was done hurriedly and with little pomp. He rode from the palace, his black garments of mourning for his brothers relieved only by the white egret feather in his turban. At the tomb of Ayub, the Mevlevi dervishes, a religious order who had been allied with the House of Osman from earliest times, awaited him.

The Mevlevi had always been the ones to declare a sultan to the people, and now, hastily gathered, they were reluctant to name Selim sultan over the still-living Bajazet. Selim grew impatient with their chatterings, and, unconciously paraphrasing his bas-kadin's words, he snapped at the head dervish, "While you fuss like an old woman, the northern tribes gnaw at our borders. Turkey needs a strong sultan. You yourself have seen my father's condition. Must I kill him to satisfy your conscience? If the price of saving Turkey is the death of Bajazet, then, by Allah, kill him yourself! I will not harm one hair of his beard, but I *will be sultan!*"

The head of the Mevlevi stared at Selim for a moment, then, grasping the prince's hand, led him to a raised platform and proclaimed to the assembled crowds that Allah had willed Selim Khan to be their sultan. He fastened the bejeweled silver-sheathed sword onto Selim and stood back to allow the people a good look at their new lord.

The crowds stared in silence at the tall, grim-faced man. Then a small cheer began toward the rear of the assembled crush and rippled forward like a wave until it reached a roar. Sultan Selim Khan flashed a brief smile at his people, then, leaving the dais, leaped on his horse and, surrounded by his personal guard, returned to his capital.

At the palace gates the Janissaries swarmed forward crying, "The gift! Make the gift!"

And the pages who rode with the sultan reached into their pouches and flung handfuls of precious jewels to the eager soldiers. It was a bold and generous gesture. The head of the Janissaries, Bali Agha, struck Selim on the shoulder—the traditional greeting to a new sultan—and demanded, "Can you lead us, son of Bajazet?"

The meaning was clear. The fierce Janissaries had been idle for several years now and were eager for battle.

"I can lead you," replied Selim, "and I will soon fill those noisy kettles of yours with enough gold to give them a more pleasant sound!"

Those within the sound of his voice began to chuckle, while others quickly repeated the sultan's words to the men in the rear. The courtyard erupted with laughter.

"Long life to our sultan, Selim Khan," came the cry as the new monarch, pushing his horse forward, rode through the mass of men.

Selim did not go to war for over a year. His first task was to straighten out the administrative workings of his government, which had grown lax during Bajazet's illness while Selim had been away, chasing his brother throughout the empire. Then, too, time was needed to greet the delegations that came to bring tribute and pay homage to the new sultan.

One of these delegations came from the city of Baghdad. It presented to Selim one hundred rolls of brocaded fabric, one hundred gilded baskets of tulip bulbs, one hundred perfectly matched pale-pink pearls—and the caliph's fourteen-year-old sister.

Knowing in advance the gifts of the Baghdad delegation, Cyra had suggested to the sultan that he give the girl to their eldest son, Suleiman. "She can be nothing more to you than a concubine, my lord, but if you give her to Suleiman, she may possibly become the mother of a future sultan, and you will do great honor to Baghdad. We shall need their friendship when we march on the shah of Persia."

So Selim watched with interest—and possibly a small feeling of regret—as the ambassador from Baghdad handed out of the bejeweled litter a slender girl of medium height. Her hair was the color of dark honey, her eyes velvety brown, her skin a rich, golden cream. She was dressed in all shades of pink, from the deep rose of her trousers to the pale mauve of the diaphanous veil that barely masked her features.

"The youngest and most beloved of my master's sisters, o sultan of the world. Gulbehar, the 'Rose of Spring.'"

"We are grateful for this touching demonstration of the caliph's loyalty," replied Selim, "but a man of my many winters could easily frost so fair and tender a bud. Therefore I shall present her to my eldest son and heir, Prince Suleiman. Like Gulbehar, he, too, is in the spring of his life. May she please him well."

From the latticed screen behind the sultan's throne, Cyra laughed softly at the incredulous look on Suleiman's face, and the expressions of delight on the faces of the Baghdad delegation.

"Well," said her slave and confidante, Marian, "are you satisfied with your meddling?"

"Very," replied Cyra. "I spoke with Gulbehar yesterday. She is a good and gentle girl, and will make my son a charming kadin."

"Suleiman is shy and easily led, my lady. He needs a strong wife, though not, perhaps, while he has a strong mother."

"You forget yourself," said Cyra coldly.

"No, dear madam. I forget nothing. Sultan Selim—may Allah bless him—will not live forever. One day you will be sultan valideh. I think you look to that day."

"Beware, Marian. You could lose your tongue."

"My lady, I mean only to warn you to take care. Your position as bas-kadin is an important one and therefore makes you a target. There will be those within the harem who will seek to discredit you."

Turning from the spectacle below her, Cyra asked, "What have you heard?"

"Nothing grave, madam. Bath chatter. There are those young gediklis in the harem who have been heard to say they will make Sultan Selim notice them. Beware, my lady. He is no longer cocooned in the Moonlight Serai with just four women, and he is, in all things, a Turk."

"I think it would be wise to distribute some bribes," said Cyra thoughtfully. "And Marian, keep your eyes and ears open when you visit the baths, but do not worry about the gediklis. Selim may take a hundred to his couch, but none will ever bear him a child except his chosen kadins."

Cyra was correct. Selim did take other girls to his bed, but none conceived—the kadins saw to that. When the first occasion arose, and a maiden named Feride became a guzdeh, the sultan's four kadins acted with the utmost decorum. They welcomed her graciously to the small apartment that was given her. When the time was chosen by the court astrologer for Feride to go to her lord's bed, the kadins themselves led her to the bridal bath, helped to dress her in the traditional blue-and-silver night garments, and sent her off to the sultan in a golden litter with their good wishes. They had even given the over-stimulated and nervous girl a soothing draft of cherry sherbet to calm her nerves.

Everyone agreed that the kadins were perfect models of Turkish female propriety, and they continued to be so. Feride became an ikbal, and they sent her small congratulatory gifts of jewelry and perfume. When other girls followed Feride to the sultan's couch, the kadins behaved in the same generous manner. Only a few trusted slaves knew that after each maiden went her way to the sultan, the four kadins gathered in Cyra's salon to laugh and make merry—and only Marian knew the reason for their mirth.

Of the female bazaar vendors who came to the harem there was one Esther Kira, a Jewess, who had become a favorite of Cyra. Usually the vendors left their wares with black eunuchs, who would show them to the ladies of the harem, but the tradeswomen came directly to the kadins.

Esther Kira and the bas-kadin had met soon after Selim's family came to Constantinople. Esther was seventeen, black-haired, black-eyed, olive-skinned, plump, and merry. She was scrupulously honest and carried only the finest merchandise. Moreover, on several occasions she had obtained special items for Cyra.

One of these items, purchased in utmost secrecy, was a special herb that Esther swore would prevent conception. So far, Esther's herb had worked, and her quilted coat jingled with the gold paid her by the kadins.

No one thought much of the new ikbals' barrenness, for in September of 1513 Firousi Kadin presented Sultan Selim with his fourteenth child, a daughter, Nakcidil, the "Print of Beauty." In October Zuleika followed with the birth of her daughter Mahpeyker, the "Moon-Faced One," and finally, in late November, a son, Karim, was born to Cyra.

Of all the bas-kadin's children the baby, Karim, was the most like her, and perhaps for that reason the dearest to her heart. Little Karim was, from birth, his mother's image. His skin was a pure Celtic bone-white, and within a few months' time his eyes had turned to the green-gold color of his mother's. His hair was red, but not Cyra's red-gold; it was, rather, a bright carrot color. His features were Cyra's in miniature.

"He reminds me of my brother, Adam," laughed the bas-kadin happily. "He is pure Leslie."

"An unfortunate thing for an Ottoman prince," remarked the sultan teasingly.

Karim's birth came at a time when the sultan badly needed diversion. Sultan Bajazet had died quietly at his isolated serai on the Bosporus, and once more the rumors of murder sprang up to haunt Selim. Then, Lady Refet, who had been ailing, died suddenly in her sleep.

Bajazet was mourned officially and noisily, but Lady Refet was mourned quietly and in the hearts of all those who had known her. The kadins were especially stricken by the death of Selim's aunt. She was, aside from Hadji Bey, their last link with a happy past. She had been their mother, their confidante, their friend. The thought of spending their future without her was devastating. If they had anything to be thankful for, thought Cyra, it was that Lady Refet had not had a long, drawn-out illness. In their last ten years at the Moonlight Serai, she had suffered several severe attacks of breathlessness, and had become weaker with each attack. The reorganization of Bajazet's harem, though largely administrative, took her remaining strength. In the last few months before her death, she had rarely left her suite, and when she did, she was always carried in a litter.

Cyra felt Lady Refet's death deeply, for she had loved and admired the woman greatly. Refet had been the most selfless woman she had ever known, seeing to her own daughters' happiness first, and then devoting the rest of her life to her nephew Selim and his family. Their happiness had been her happiness; their sorrow, her sorrow. She had asked nothing for herself, but instead had given generously of her love, her time, and her understanding to those around her. It was so typical of her to die quietly in her sleep.

The harem wore black for several months, and the kadins sent word to their lord that so red were their eyes from weeping that they could not possibly appear before him. Others were not so discreet, thinking this an opportunity to curry favor with Selim.

Unfortunately, the sultan was beginning to suffer almost constant pain from the stomach ulcers that afflicted him. He had never been the most patient of men, and the agony brought on by his illness caused his temperament to undergo a drastic change. Selim was becoming cruel.

One poor new ikbal, a Provençal called Pakize, expired from a beating administered by the sultan himself when she dared to appear before him dressed in reds and blues. Another unfortunate had two fingers of her right hand cut off when she was heard playing too gay a tune on her lute. The birth of Karim brought an end to the official mourning, but the sultan was not long diverted from his bad mood. The pains in his belly grew worse with each passing day. The physicians could do nothing short of administering drugs for his pain. Selim would not permit this.

He had changed. The sultanate weighed heavily on him. His temper grew short, and the slightest infraction of rules was punished quickly, though fairly. He still sharply resented the fact that the old shah of Persia had secretly encouraged his brother Ahmed by supplying him with weapons and food, thus prolonging the civil war.

Then one day the Janissaries overturned their kettles and began to beat upon them. Striding into their midst, the sultan demanded to know their complaint.

"Where is the gold you promised to fill our kettles with?" demanded a young soldier.

Selim glowered at the boy and toyed with the idea of lopping his head off, but, fortunately for all, his sense of justice remained intact. "Prepare yourselves," he shouted at them. "We march within a month!"

The Janissaries roared their approval. War! Glorious war had come to the Ottoman Empire.

29

THE OTTOMANS had consistently faced west in their conquests, yet Selim Khan chose Persia for his first war. There was a good deal of speculation regarding this move. Some said he marched east because Shah Ismail had supported his brother Ahmed. Others, because his son, Prince Omar, had been killed by the Persians, who had aided Ahmed. The latter appeared to be true, since his third wife, Zuleika Kadin, went with him.

In part they were all correct, but a greater motive lay behind the sultan's decision to war on Persia. Selim's spies had found a descendant of Baghdad's last Abbasid caliph, the man who was spiritual ruler of Islam. Selim believed that all the Muslim world should be united under one leader, both spiritual and temporal, and he intended that he and each Ottoman sultan who followed him would be that leader.

Technically he had no claim, and, more important, he did not have the murdered caliph's heir, who now lived in Egypt. There were others who also sought to become the spiritual head of Islam. Selim knew he must work quickly.

Selim, with a wisdom that had helped him to survive these forty-seven years, turned to Persia, where Shah Ismail, a convert to the Islamic schism of Shiism, now ruled. The sultan, like his Catholic counterparts in Europe now facing a similar problem in the form of Martin Luther, intended to stamp out this heresy, rescue the caliph's heir, and, based on his devotion to the pure and true form of Islam, have himself named hereditary Defender of the Faith.

In the month that followed Selim's decision to go to war, the great army was fully provisioned and the government set up to run smoothly in the sultan's absence.

Firousi and Sarina were to remain in Constantinople,
where in Selim's absence they were to take charge of the
children and the harem, while the sultan's new vizier
would see to the everyday affairs of the government.

Suleiman, Mohammed, Kasim, Abdullah, and Murad
were to accompany their father, as was Cyra. Zuleika,
reminding the sultan of her own secret quarrel with Persia,
also went with her lord.

They left Constantinople on a bright morning in late
winter. The air was crisp despite the sun, and snow still
clung to the distant mountains. Riding out from the Eski
Serai, Sultan Selim was a magnificent sight on his black
stallion, Devil Wind. The horse sported a beautiful gold-
embroidered and fringed-green silk throw, made by the
ladies of the harem, over his shining back and flanks. Selim
was particularly pleased with his dark leather saddle,
bridle, and heavy gold stirrups. Like all Ottoman princes,
Suleiman and Mohammed had learned a trade. The heir
was an extremely competent goldsmith. His brother was a
fine leatherworker. Despite their heavy schedule of studies, the two princes had found the time to make their
father this gift.

Selim was dressed in dove-gray silk embroidered with
silver thread and small emeralds. He was accompanied by
his Tartars and a troop of Janissaries. They would be
ferried across the Bosporus, which separated the European
side of the city from the Asian side where the army
awaited them. The crowds lining the streets cheered wildly
as their lord rode off to war with the Persians.

After two years as sultan, Selim still retained his popu-
larity. It was true he rarely smiled now, was becoming
more short-tempered, and had already disposed of three
grand viziers. But these failings were easily overlooked because of his one great virtue—he insisted on honest and
scrupulously fair judgments in his law courts. The Turks,
who already encompassed several races and nationalities
as well as many religions, knew they could trust him. He
was being called Selim the Just.

At that moment, the people loved their stern sultan, and
he could do no wrong. They cheered him as he rode off to
war and the beginnings of Turkey's greatest conquests.
How could they realize that, eaten with cancer, his person-

ality would change for the worse, and he would be re-
named Selim the Grim—the title that fickle history would
perpetuate?

In her heavily curtained litter, the noise of the crowd
adding to the pain in her already throbbing temples,
reclined the bas-kadin. Cyra did not want to make this
trip, and despite the fact that past Ottoman women had
accompanied their lords into battle, she was of the firm
opinion that women did not belong on the battlefield.

Zuleika had insisted upon going to personally claim her
vengeance, and so Cyra must go, too, lest the people misunderstand the sultan's taking Zuleika, and her own future
position be jeopardized and weakened.

It was not that she didn't wish to be with Selim—she did
—but at this moment she was annoyed with him. Of late
he had ignored his kadins in favor of an overblown
French ikbal who pandered to his dark moods. When they
returned to Constantinople, the girl would be dead. Cyra
had personally seen to that.

She had not done it out of jealousy or with malice,
but because the girl had flaunted her small yet favored
position to all in the harem, with particular emphasis in
the direction of the kadins. Selim would have grown tired
of her soon enough, but in the meantime the girl's rude-
ness might be emulated by others.

She was not a bright creature, or she would have
known better, and Cyra fully expected her to give Firousi
and Sarina trouble, but it would not be for long. She would
one day soon be given small doses of poison in her food,
sicken slowly, and it would appear that she had died a
natural death.

In all her years in Turkey, Cyra had arranged a death
only once before—long ago in those early days at the
Moonlight Serai. She had always tried to win her point
with reason, and it distressed her to have ordered a death.
However, she reasoned, the Frenchwoman was a trouble-
maker and must be disposed of lest she influence the
other girls in the harem to similar acts of disobedience.

The baby, Karim, stirred in the crook of her arm and
whimpered. Unbuttoning her blouse, she put him to her
breast. It annoyed her to take her five-month-old son on
this long trip, but when Selim had suggested she leave him
with a wet nurse, she had turned on him like a tigress.

It was no secret to those in the imperial household that the bas-kadin's youngest child was her favorite.

Six-month-old Mahpeyker also accompanied her mother, because Cyra had insisted Karim have a playmate of his own age. Zuleika, though amused at the idea of the two infants playing, had not dared to laugh, for she knew that without Cyra's presence she herself would not have been allowed to go. With unusual good nature, for she cheerfully would have left her daughter with a nurse, she, too, traveled with her child.

As the army made its progress through Asia, Cyra noted a change taking place in Zuleika. In the twenty-two years they had been together, the beautiful Chinese had rarely permitted her emotions to show. The bas-kadin liked and admired her friend, but she had always suspected that as happy as Zuleika was as Selim's third kadin, she had never been able to forgive fate for the insult it had dealt to her pride, even though it had gained her that happiness.

Now, as they drew close to Persia, Zuleika allowed her thoughts to drift backward in time, and spoke for the first time in many years of the events which had made her a sultan's third wife, rather than a shah's first. For the slave who was now queen mother of Persia, she had nothing but contempt. For the old shah's concubine, Shannez, her hatred burned hot. The sultan had promised Zuleika that she might name their punishment. Cyra knew she was putting a great deal of thought into it. The bas-kadin shuddered and thanked Allah that she was not Zuleika's enemy. If the Chinese's hatred could burn so steadily for so long, her punishment would be terrible.

Word came that Shah Ismail had left the city of Ispahan, and with his army was coming out to meet the Turks. Selim was delighted, as it gave him the opportunity to choose the battleground. The decisive battle was set in the valley of Chaldiran, high in the mountains of eastern Anatolia.

At the western end of the valley, the Turks set up camp—row upon orderly row of little yellow tents for the soldiers, several large cook tents and hospital tents, and, at the camp's center, the green-and-gold-striped pavilion of the sultan. Selim's quarters actually comprised several tents set upon a carefully constructed, tiered

platform. There was a small command tent where the
sultan met and conferred with his captains. Another tent
was used for cooking meals. A third housed the royal
infants and their nurses, and a fourth, the sultan and his
wives. This last was quite large and was divided into
several rooms—a public reception salon, a private salon,
and sleeping quarters for the sultan and his family. The
furnishings were quite elegant and rich. Thick carpets
covered the wood flooring. There were low, round
tables of ebony banded with mother-of-pearl, and tables
of highly polished copper inlaid with blue mosaic. Fine
brass lamps burned softly over the pure jeweled colors
of the plump silk cushions. The sultan's sleeping quarters
were the most Spartan in the pavilion. His bedchamber
contained a couch, a gilded leather trunk, a small writing desk, and a chair.

Cyra and Zuleika had each furnished her separate
quarters luxuriously with sheer hangings, rich velvets,
multicolored silks, and thick furs. Their sleeping couches
were gilded wood, their lamps, which burned fragrant
oils, were made of pure silver encrusted with precious
gems. Opening off their rooms was an entrance leading
outdoors and down a curtained way to a natural rock
pool where they might bathe in privacy.

The pavilion was quite comfortable, considering the
situation and the lack of slaves. Each night after he had
dined with his sons and officers, the sultan would retire
to the private salon and the comfort of his kadins. Sometimes the young princes would join them, and it would
become a warm and familiar family evening.

On nights when the encampment lay quietly in sleep,
Selim would come to Cyra's room and slip beneath the
soft white fur coverlet into the warmth of her arms.
Zuleika, with her fierce desire for vengeance, was not a
fit companion for her lord now. As always in times of
crisis, the sultan turned to his bas-kadin. Her slim body
comforted him, and he was able to forget for a time the
empire, the coming battle, and the fierce pain in his
belly. Often, after the delicious physical contact that so
delighted them both, they would lie facing each other
and talk.

How the Ottoman officials would have gaped in amazement if they could have seen and heard their great lord

speak to this mere woman of such varied matters as his
future plans for conquest, a new variety of peach tree he
had heard of that he must have for the orchards of the
Eski Serai, the building he was planning to erect in the
gardens of the Yeni Serai to house the treasures he was
collecting, and the fate of his children.

Selim knew that whatever he said to Cyra remained
with her and her alone. She was one of the few people
he trusted completely. He knew that his interests were
hers, and even after their many years together, her tact,
wisdom, loyalty, and sense of justice—which he found
equal to his—still pleased him.

The pain in his belly had eased to a dull steadiness
that he was able to bear. Morning would come soon,
and with it the battle that would be fought between
him and the Shiite upstart, Shah Ismail. At sunset the
previous evening he had seen a fiery sword in the sky
pointing east. His soldiers had become very excited, and
the mullahs had cried that it meant Allah was sending
His blessing upon Selim the Just, the true believer, Defender of the Faith. They would defeat the Persians.
Selim, though a devout Muslim, was not a believer in
signs. They would win tomorrow, but they would win
because for the first time in history the Ottoman army
would be using artillery. With this satisfying thought,
he fell asleep in the warm curve of Cyra's soft body.

The following morning, dressed in quilted, hooded
silk cloaks and heavily veiled, the kadins watched the
panorama from a specially constructed platform. At the
far eastern end of the valley, they could see the camp
of the shah of Persia. Between the two encampments
the battle raged.

The Persians fought valiantly, but from the start they
were badly outclassed by the Turks' new artillery. Over
and over again, groups of the sultan's swift horsemen
would dart in among them, draw them within range of
the Ottoman guns, and then dash off, leaving the shah's
soldiers to be shot to pieces.

Ismail's troops had neither seen nor faced artillery
before. They fought the Turks as they always fought
an enemy, and the results were disastrous for Persia.

The smells of blood, gunpowder, horses, and sweat
mingled in the wind to create a nauseating odor, and the

kadins held clove-studded oranges to their noses to block
the stench.

Watching as Suleiman's and Mohammed's soldiers
cut to ribbons a troop of Persian horsemen misled into
thinking that Prince Suleiman was separated from his
cavalry, Zuleika observed. "They are still small boys
who play at war."

Cyra nodded in grim agreement. She was angered
at her eldest son for taking what she considered foolish
chances, and a little frightened of the battle. The noise
of the guns deafened her, and seeing men fall dead
about her seemed unreal. The bearers ran back and
forth carrying the wounded from the battleground to
the medical tents. Some of the fallen were horribly maimed
and torn, for the simple Turkish soldier, as unused to the
guns as his Persian counterpart, was suffering also.

Cyra put her hands to her ears for a brief moment to
still the terrible din, and saw Selim on Devil Wind—in
the midst of the fray—his scimitar flashing like a bright
and terrible butterfly. His lips moved constantly, and she
instinctively knew he was shouting encouragement to his
men over the cacophony of the battle.

A messenger rode up to Cyra. "Madam, I regret to
inform you that Prince Kasim has been killed. His body
is being brought to the sultan's pavilion." The messenger
wheeled his horse about and galloped off.

As she swayed and the scene before her eyes swam,
she felt Zuleika's arm tighten about her. "It is the will
of Allah," she heard her own voice say. "Praises on
Allah and Mohammed, His Prophet." Zuleika led her
back to their tent.

The Battle of Chaldiran was a great victory for Sultan
Selim. Shah Ismail himself, along with his personal possessions and his favorite wife, Tacli Hanim, had been
captured. The victory fires burned high and hot throughout the night. The sounds of the drum and flute echoed
over the valley, and the laughter of women could be
heard among the tents. The shah had traveled neither
lightly nor without amenities, and Selim's soldiers had
found, much to their delight, a number of attractive female slaves and dancing girls in the Persian camp. Though

the officers had been allowed first choice, there were enough women left to satisfy the men's needs.

Selim, supping with his captains, drank from a goblet of black amber circled with gold flowers. To his amusement, the golden inscription identified it as the property of Shah Ismail. Selim had also appropriated the Persian ruler's belt and armlet—plates of gold set on iron and held together with a woven red-and-blue fabric.

The night was not so merry for Ismail. Quartered under heavy guard in a small tent, he wept bitterly, not for the battle lost but for Tacli Hanim. His beautiful young wife, along with her fortune in jewels, had been given as a slave to the sultan's handsome second son, Prince Mohammed.

In the sultan's private quarters, however, the scene was even sadder. Two biers stood upon the thick carpets of the private salon. Upon one rested the body of Cyra's seventeen-year-old son, Kasim. She had washed and dressed his body herself, allowing no one else to touch him. Gently she had brushed his dark-brown hair for the last time, and had wept, remembering the child he had been, the man he would never be.

She had gazed deeply into his vacant, dark-blue eyes, but he was gone. The eyes had stared back at her, seeing nothing. The spark that had given Kasim life had flown. Sadly she had drawn the heavily lashed lids closed, and, ripping her garments, had slipped to the floor, weeping bitterly.

It was here Suleiman had found her. Lifting her up, he had brushed the tangled hair from her face, kissed the tears on her cheeks, and led her to her room.

Crouched by the second bier in stony-faced silence, Zuleika mourned. Her second son, Abdullah, had perished this day at the age of sixteen. Zuleika's thoughts were not, however, of her son. They were of revenge, and she now knew what form that vengeance would take. Persia had humiliated her, and she would humiliate Persia in a way it would not forget.

She rose and gazed down at the still, ivory features. He had died honorably, and perhaps it was better this way. The kadins had always hoped to end the cruel slaughter of the reigning sultan's brothers, but who really knew what would happen when Suleiman became sultan? Power changes people, as Zuleika well knew.

Cyra, Firousi, and Sarina still clung to some of their Western ethics, but she, born in the East, knew the dangers of too many heirs, and the wisdom of their speedy demise. There would always be discontent between ruler and ruled, but the fewer roads to rebellion, the less chance of it.

"He was brave, my brother, Abdullah."

She turned to face Suleiman. "Cyra?"

"My mother sleeps, thanks to the juice of the poppy, and so should you, dear aunt. Tomorrow we leave for Tabriz. You would not wish to be weary when my father passes judgment on the Persian heretics." Their eyes locked for a moment.

"We understand each other, o son of Selim. Praise Allah, you are more a Turk than a Westerner."

"The Scots have never been noted for their mercy in blood feuds, Zuleika Kadin."

"You are a Turk," she replied firmly and, kissing him on the cheek, left him.

He stood, puzzled, for a minute and then, shrugging, walked out of the pavilion into the moonless night.

30

THE SHAH'S PALACE at Tabriz was brightly lit, and its throne room was filled to capacity with the entire Persian court. The Persians were frightened, and the sultan knew it. He also knew the first thing he would do after allowing Zuleika her revenge would be to ruthlessly stamp out the heretical Shiite sect adhered to by Ismail and his followers.

The Turkish soldiers had found hiding in the town a French Jesuit priest who claimed to be the representative of the French king, Louis XII. Selim let him go unharmed, but wondered if perhaps the European Christians were not secretly encouraging the split between the Muslims.

Seated on the Peacock Throne, the sultan was a resplendent and frightening figure. His black silk robe was embroidered with gold tulips, and he wore a cloth-of-gold turban set with a pigeon's-blood ruby. At his feet reclined his kadins; Cyra in peach-and-gold silks and gauze, Zuleika in amethyst and silver. Nearby stood Suleiman, Mohammed, and Murad.

Before the sultan stood the young shah. "I do not ask mercy for myself, my lord, but for my mother and the other ladies of my court."

"I do not war with women, boy," said Selim.

The shah flushed. "Then you agree to grant them safe conduct?"

"Nor do I make treaties with boys. Especially those whose foolish fathers could not even distinguish between slave girl and princess."

"You speak in riddles, Sultan Selim."

The sultan smiled. "Perhaps I do, but you will help me solve this riddle, boy." He clapped his hands, and the guards escorted a small, richly dressed woman into the room. The Persian court bowed as she passed through them to the foot of the throne.

"Mother!" cried the shah. The soldiers restrained him.

"Zuleika." The sultan nodded to his kadin, who rose languidly from her place and, moving gracefully, stood beside the Persian queen. "Now, my boy," said Selim, "before you stand two women. One was born a princess, the other a slave. Can you tell me which is which?"

"Is this a joke, my lord?"

"No, Shah Ismail. It is a riddle."

"There is no riddle! My mother was born Princess Plum Jade of Cathay."

"Like your father, Shah Ismail, you accept the obvious too quickly. Zuleika!"

"My lord Selim?"

"Face this women and unveil yourself."

Zuleika raised a slim hand to her veil. It fell from her proud face and slipped silently to the floor. The eyes of the Persian queen widened in horror, and with a terrified shriek she fell to the floor crying, "Mercy, mistress! Mercy, I beg of you!"

Brushing aside the sultan's guards, the shah rushed to his mother's side and frantically tried to raise her. "It is your victory," he said to Selim. "She is frightened. She has always been a nervous woman."

"Well she might be," replied the sultan. "Hark to me, Shah Ismail! I am going to tell you a true story."

The boy ruler managed to get his mother settled among some cushions, where she continued to tremble and sob softly.

Selim began, his rich voice holding all the hall. "Twenty-two years ago, a young princess left Cathay with a large caravan guarded by the emperor's soldiers. She was to be married to the king of a neighboring country. At the border between the two countries, her intended husband's soldiers replaced her brother's, and all the servants, with the exception of one slave girl, returned to Cathay.

"Unfortunately for the princess, her royal husband-to-be had a beautiful but evil concubine who had secretly left her harem and ridden out with the soldiers to get a look at the royal bride. This woman wielded great influence over the king. She feared that a younger, more

beautiful and intelligent girl—especially a queen—could
destroy her power. She decided to see the bride before
her lord did, and, if necessary, dispose of her.

"Greeting the princess warmly and with honeyed words,
she found her worst fears confirmed. Not only was the
maiden young and exquisitely fair, but she was highly
intelligent. Acting swiftly, that evening the concubine
slipped a powerful sleeping draft into the princess's cup,
and in the night two soldiers, bribed by this wicked
woman, took the princess, whom they believed to be a
slave, overland to Baghdad, where she was sold in the
poorest slave market.

"Fortunately, the princess was purchased by the agha
kislar of my father's household. He was passing by on
his way out of the city, and immediately recognized a
priceless pearl among the common stones. Meanwhile,
the concubine substituted the bride's slave girl as her
lord's bride."

At this point the Persian queen began to wail and rip
her garments.

"Miserable pawn of dog offal," hissed Zuleika in
their Chinese dialect, "control yourself! You would be a
queen, now act like one—if not for your son's sake, then
for my family's name, which you have usurped!"

"Oh, mistress," wept the woman in the same dialect,
"*she* made me do it! She said I would die a horrible
death if I didn't. I was alone in a strange land, and
frightened. I did not want to die."

"And you thought we should never meet again, eh,
Mai Tze?"

"I have suffered for my evil. The old shah hated me
and my plainness. Our marriage was not consummated
for almost five years. Only when he became convinced
by his advisers that his people would accept only a
legitimate heir did he come to me. Then he returned
to *her* bed! She even wields more influence over Ismail
than I do. Do not, I beg of you, kill me!"

"Do you think I would avenge myself on so insig-
nificant a creature as you?" snapped Zuleika. "It is
Shannez I have come for. And, in Allah's name, get
off your knees and stand up!"

The queen struggled to her feet and stood cowering

before the sultan, who now took up the thread of his story.

"When I was twenty-five, my father honored me by allowing me to choose six virgins from his own harem so that I might set up my own household. One of the maidens I picked was Princess Plum Jade—called Zuleika by our people—the very Zuleika who stands before you now, the mother of three of my sons. This woman you call 'queen'—the wife of your late king and the mother of Shah Ismail—is nothing more than a baseborn slave named Mai Tze!"

The throne room exploded into an uproar, and the queen fell into a faint as the Persian courtiers moved angrily toward her. Selim's soldiers forcibly restrained the threatening crowd as two slaves rushed to revive the fallen woman with rosewater.

"*Silence!*" thundered the sultan. The room quieted. "You owe this poor creature a great debt. She is not the villain here. Slave or no, she was your king's legal wife and is the mother of Shah Ismail. Had she not gone along with the deception, Cathay would have destroyed you, and the old shah would have died childless.

"She will retain her place in this court with all its honors. I, Selim Khan, command it." He glared down from his throne at the roomful of muttering Persians. "Now I shall deal with the one truly responsible. Bring the lady Shannez to me."

Proudly she entered the silent room, walked to the foot of the throne, prostrated herself, and then rose to face Selim boldly. She was tall for a woman, slender, and although well into her forties, looked like a girl in her mid-twenties. Her skin was a clear, light olive. Her hair, which was dressed high on her head, giving her a queenly look, was blue-black and showed no gray. Her eyes were glowing jets. She wore a simple plum-colored silk robe, no jewelry except heavy gold earrings, and was unveiled.

Selim gazed at the cold, sensuous face. His eyes moved slowly to the faintly visible pulse in her throat, to the high, cone-shaped breasts, the glimpse of a slim leg.

Zuleika, noting her lord's interested gaze, leaned forward and whispered, "Do not deny me vengeance, my lord. Remember our two sons dead by Persia's hand."

"It shall be as you wish, my tigress." He smiled grimly. "Lady Shannez, I present to you my bas-kadin, the lady Cyra. You have, of course, met my third wife, the lady Zuleika."

"The sultan is mistaken," came the smooth, cool voice. "I have never met either of his wives."

"It is you who are mistaken, Lady Shannez. I imagine it gave you great pleasure to dispose of Princess Plum Jade. No doubt you thought her dead these many years, or perhaps some desert savage's slave. Zuleika, my love, raise your face to the lady Shannez so she may better look upon you."

The kadin obeyed her lord's command. Shannez blanched deathly white but, recovering quickly, looked Zuleika straight in the eye, laughed softly, and said, "So, you're not dead. Your kismet must be very strong, and here you are to take your vengeance. Very well. I have lived a good life."

"I shall not kill you. Oh, no, Shannez! I shall show you the same mercy you showed me! However, I shall leave nothing to chance, as you so foolishly did." Zuleika gazed at the woman coldly, then turned to a guard. "Bring the man!"

Every eye in the room turned toward the door through which the guard had exited. He returned quickly, bringing with him an incredibly ugly, powerfully built little man, deformed by a hump on his left shoulder. The creature wore nothing but a loincloth and a small, dirty turban which perched on his head like a fallen cake. He was missing one eye, and the other eye moved swiftly to and fro in his head, taking in everything around him.

The heat of the crowded room had already brought forth the stench of nervous bodies, but the misshapen man brought a far stronger odor with him. Flinging himself on his face at the foot of the throne, he cried in a harsh voice, "Oh, lord, may you reign over us forever!"

"Rise," commanded the sultan.

The man scrambled to his feet.

"Your name?"

"Abu, my sultan."

"You are my slave?"

"Yes, most gracious lord."

"What is your work, Abu?"

"I sweep and shovel dung in my lord's stables."

Selim glanced quickly at Zuleika, an expression of gleeful admiration in his eyes. "You have done your work well, Abu. Your diligence has not gone unnoticed. The head groom tells me my stables are a place of beauty." Here Selim stopped and muffled a laugh. "Such devotion shall not go unrewarded. This day I grant you your freedom on the condition you remain in my service for one year. At the end of that year, you will be paid twelve gold pieces and may go where you please or continue to remain with my household."

Abu fell to his knees and, clutching the hem of the sultan's robe, kissed it.

"Wait, Abu. There is more. A free man needs a woman to look after his needs. This woman was the favorite of the old shah. Many years ago, she caused great harm to the lady Zuleika."

"The mother of little Prince Nureddin?"

"You know my son?"

"Yes, great lord. He comes to the stables to ride his pony. He gives me sweetmeats and figs. He is my friend. Shall I kill this woman for you, lord?"

"No, Abu. I have graciously granted her her life, but because you have been loyal to me, I give her to you as a slave. She is yours forever. Teach her your loyalty, and use her as you will."

In his whole lifetime Abu had possessed a woman only on a few occasions. His lowly rank, his occupation, and his own personal appearance left precious few who were willing to associate with the sweeper of dung. His good eye took in the beautiful woman who his lord had said was his. Selim was not known for practical jokes, so it must be true. "Oh, great sultan! The ages will speak of your generosity toward your humble servant Abu."

He turned to Shannez. "Come, slave!"

"Approach me, vile animal, and I will kill you," she hissed.

The humpback raised an arm and smashed her to the floor. Grasping her limp arm with his talonlike fingers, he half dragged the woman from the room.

For a moment the hall quivered in stunned silence, then Selim spoke. "You have seen my mercy toward one who would betray an emperor's true daughter. I granted her life. My vengeance is far more terrible to behold.

"There is but one true God, Allah. And Mohammed, may his name be blessed, is His true Prophet. Is there any of you who would deny this? Who among you mourns Husayn and follows the teachings of the Shia?" No one spoke. "I will strike down without mercy those who mock the one God and His Prophet, be it man, or woman, or child!

"I will spare you, Shah Ismail, because, having led your people from the true path of Allah, it is up to you to lead them back. Those who will not publicly recant this heresy shall die. I, Selim Khan, have spoken!"

The sultan then rose from the throne and walked from the room, followed by his two wives. Out of hearing of the others, he turned to Zuleika. "Are you satisfied, my blossom? Your vengeance was quite diabolical. I never knew you to be quite so ferocious. Have you been so unhappy with me?"

The Chinese woman caught the sultan's hand and brought it to her forehead, her lips, and finally to her heart. "For twenty-two years I have lived for you, and then for our children. Never have I known an unhappy moment with you, never have I had an unkind word from you—but never have I forgotten what that woman did to me. That her treachery brought me unspeakable happiness mattered not—only that she dared to lay hands upon a daughter of the emperor of China. My family is as great in their land as yours in ours. Would you not have done the same thing had you been in my place, my dearest lord?"

Selim put his arm about Zuleika, drew her close, and kissed her gently. "Yes, my tigress, I would have done the same. And now is your soul purged of its bile?"

"Not quite, my lord, but that small bit that remains I can exorcise quickly."

"I will leave you to do so." He turned and strode off down the tiled corridor.

Cyra had been standing quietly in the shadows. Zuleika moved to her side and asked, "Will you come with me? What I must see may be horrible, but I must know that Shannez is completely humbled before I can be satisfied."

Cyra nodded. They moved through several corridors, down a flight of stairs, finally reaching a small door that opened into the stableyards of the shah's palace. Here, Abu, the sweeper of dung, had been quartered. Immediately on entering the open court, they heard screams of outrage. Zuleika smiled.

"This way," she said, and Cyra followed her across the open yard to an almost-hidden staircase cut into the side of a wall. "Up here," said Zuleika, moving up the stairs and across the flat roof of the building. They came to a small opening in the roof. Here Zuleika stopped and motioned to Cyra. They lay down and peered into the stable below them.

Cyra's eyes widened, and she trembled at the sight. A naked Shannez lay spread-eagled upon a filthy blanket. Her arms and legs were held by means of leather thongs to four small pegs which had been driven into the dirt floor. Abu stood nearby, shaking his loincloth preparatory to rewrapping it about his hairy body. "A mighty weapon for so small a man," mused Zuleika.

Bending, Abu loosed the thongs about the woman's ankles and wrists and tossed her the now-soiled silk robe. "I'm hungry. Forage for food." He punctuated his words with a well-placed kick.

Shannez scrambled to her feet clutching the robe about her and, hurling invectives at her tormentor, ran out of the stable. Cyra and Zuleika rose and moved to the edge of the roof. Below them the woman stood hesitantly for a moment, then, spotting an open cistern, made for it. From the shadows a soldier loomed.

"Halt, woman! Where do you go?"

She paused. "To seek food."

"In a cistern? Come! I will show you."

"I will find my way."

"I *will* show you. Orders of Zuleika Kadin. I am to guard you at all times." Shannez stared at the man. "You're not a bad-looking wench," he said. "Perhaps we should go the long way." Leering, he moved toward her.

"Get away from me!" she shrieked, flailing out at him.

Abu appeared in the stable door. "What's all this noise? Where's my supper, you lazy slut?"

"Hello, Abu," said the soldier. "Who's the woman,

and how did you get so lucky, you ugly son of a she-camel?"

"She was the old shah's favorite," said the sweeper of dung proudly. "The sultan gave me my freedom, and the woman as a slave to care for my needs."

"By the beard of the Prophet," replied the soldier, "old Selim gets generous with the pretty goods." He thought for a moment. "Say, Abu. How would you like to make some money? Now you're a free man, you've got to think of the future."

"What do I have to do?"

The soldier drew the little man aside, then whispered to him.

"Well, it's fine with me, but I warn you, all she does is kick and scream. I had to tie her down."

"A fighter, eh? It adds more spice. Wait here while I get my comrades."

He returned in a twinkling with five other soldiers. Each placed a small purse in the dung sweeper's hand. Abu turned to Shannez. "Get back inside."

"But your food——" She stopped and looked wildly about for a means of escape. There was none.

"I'll fetch my own food. Get inside!"

Shannez tried to run, but the soldiers laughingly caught her and dragged her into the stables as Abu walked away.

The two women stood on the roof for a moment; then Zuleika spoke over the screams coming from below them. "Let us go. I am satisfied."

Silently the kadins moved down the stairs and across the stableyard. The little door closed with a quiet click on Shannez's shame and anguish. Zuleika Kadin never again spoke of her past.

31

THE SULTAN RETURNED to Constantinople with eight hundred and fifty camels and five hundred donkeys laden with gold, silver, precious jewels, and other booty. The slaves numbered over ten thousand. The boundaries of the Ottoman Empire had been widened by the annexation of Diyarbekir and Kurdistan. The Persian campaign had been very successful.

In his wake, Selim left the bodies of forty thousand Shiites who had been massacred because they refused to return to the pure form of Mohammedanism. The young shah was so horrified by this act that he was never known to smile again.

The Turks had wintered in the shah's capital of Tabriz. The annexation of Persian territory had occurred in the spring of the year 1515, with the return to Constantinople coming in early autumn of the same year.

The kadins had agreed on one thing—never again would they accompany their lord on campaign. They had missed Constantinople, they had missed Firousi and Sarina, but most of all, they had missed the children. With the death of three of Selim's sons, the family became more important to them than ever before.

For a time, the sultan's mood was as of old. The treasury building, begun in the time of Selim's grandfather, Mohammed the Conqueror, had been completed to the sultan's satisfaction. It was ready to receive the vast treasure he had brought with him from Persia. The gold was put in huge iron coffers, which were then placed in a vault beneath the treasury. The jewels and other booty were placed in the main rooms. The silver was dispersed among the various palace treasuries for the payment of accounts. A register was made, listing everything brought back, and finally the door of the treasury was sealed with the imperial seal of Selim I.

Selim said on that day, "I have filled the treasury with gold. If any of my successors fills it with copper, let the treasury be sealed with his seal. If not, let them continue to seal it with my seal."

The sultan now turned his mind to other matters, the first of which was his eldest son. Suleiman, Gulbehar, and their court were being sent to Magnesia, where the prince would govern the province for his father. It was to be a test of the heir and his abilities.

Prince Mohammed would go to Erzurum in the same capacity. Prince Murad, Cyra's third son, who was now sixteen, and Sarina's thirteen-year-old son, Bajazet, were sent to a distant army barracks for further training.

Of the sultan's living sons, there were but three left in Constantinople. Prince Karim, the baby, would remain with his mother; but Firousi's Hassan and Zuleika's Nureddin, aged eleven and ten, were removed from the harem and given their own households.

The kadins were not happy at this last of the sultan's orders. They did not trust the morals of the younger eunuchs, and both princes were fresh-faced children. Spies from the harem were quickly introduced into the boys' quarters so their mothers might be kept fully informed and be able to protect their sons should the need arise.

The sultan's next move was in the direction of his daughters. Hale and Guzel were now sixteen and practically past marriageable age. However, in this area Selim was pliable. The girls would marry, but not a foreigner, and the choice would be theirs.

Selim, ever indulgent toward his twin daughters, allowed them, heavily veiled and concealed behind a viewing screen, to see the selection of prospective husbands. Half a dozen were picked from the chosen list, and the others dismissed. The twins were then informed in detail of each man's qualifications. Finally the sultan announced that his daughters would marry the eighteen-and nineteen-year-old sons of Pasha Ismet ben Orman, a valued servant and soldier of the Ottoman Empire. The marriages were celebrated almost immediately.

Pasha Ismet had grown rich in the service of the Ottoman government, and in his delight at having as daughters-in-law not just one princess but two, he provided his sons with adjoining white marble palaces overlooking the Bosporus.

Each palace—of one hundred rooms—was set in a garden filled to overflowing with flowering shrubs and trees of every known kind. There were simulated streams, ponds, and tiled pools. The mother of the bridegrooms obtained an audience with Firousi Kadin so she might learn the decorative preferences of the princesses. They must be happy.

At the marriage ceremony, Hale and Guzel were represented by the aging agha kislar, who took their vows for them. The wedding feast, which was held in a hall of the Yeni Serai, lasted three days. It was here that the sons of Pasha Ismet first met their brides.

After the feasting ended the first night, the two girls quietly left the hall with the other women of the harem. Only the kadins and the brides' personal slaves were permitted in the adjoining nuptial chambers, where the two maidens were bathed and carefully examined to be sure they were completely free of all body hair. Sheer night garments were placed upon them, and their hair was brushed and perfumed with musk.

The ladies then withdrew, each wishing Hale and Guzel the traditional blessing, "May you know only joy." In the anteroom outside, the bridegrooms waited, for they could not enter the wedding chamber of their royal brides until called. An imperial son-in-law had few privileges, and his position was firmly established on the wedding night. Hale and Guzel had agreed that in defense of maidenly modesty they would keep their new husbands waiting two hours. So Hussein and Riza waited nervously for a summons from their new wives.

In Cyra's salon, Firousi wept. The other kadins tried to comfort her. "They're so young," she sobbed.

"Nonsense," said Cyra briskly. "You were two years younger on your nuptial night. Guzel and Hale have had the good fortune to choose their own husbands, and the young men are already enchanted and enamored of their young brides. They will all be very happy."

Firousi sniffed. "Do you really think so?"

"Yes! And I think you had also better stop weeping. What scandal there will be at tomorrow's feast if you appear with red and swollen eyes."

Later that night, Selim came to Cyra's apartment. He was happier than he had been in a long time and was feeling expansive and talkative. He was pleased with the wedding, pleased with his daughters, pleased with his sons-in-law, and considering marrying Nilufer off next.

Cyra protested, "My dearest lord, she is but twelve and has not even reached sexual maturity. Surely you will not marry her off for a few more years."

"She could be married now, but not given to her husband until she matures. There are several men who would be suitable and whom I would like to bind closer to the empire."

"Never will I allow you to use my daughter as a political pawn! Would you deny her the freedom of choice that you allowed Firousi's daughters?"

"It was different for the twins. They have been close all their lives and would have suffered terribly if they had been separated. It is for this reason alone that I allowed them to choose whom they would wed."

"You cannot wed Nilufer to a stranger. She already loves a certain young man, and has since she was a child."

"How can that be? Whom have you allowed to break the sanctity of my harem to meet secretly with my daughter?"

"No one. They first met when we lived at the Moonlight Serai."

"But she was just a child then, and aside from her brothers, there were no men allowed in the harem at the Moonlight Serai."

"You are forgetting young Ibrahim."

"Nilufer loves Ibrahim? Impossible! She has not seen him since she was seven."

"I beg to correct you, my love, but she has. You permitted our daughter the freedom of Suleiman's court, and Ibrahim was a frequent visitor. When you sent our son to govern Magnesia, Ibrahim went with him. Nilufer has been heartbroken and sullen ever since. She loves Ibrahim!"

"It is but a childish fancy. She will get over it."

"If she is childish, then you will agree that she is too

young to be wed," said Cyra quietly.

Selim threw up his hands. "You have trapped me as neatly as the hunter the hare, beloved. I bow to your wisdom and cleverness."

She leaned over and kissed him. "And you will consider Ibrahim as a suitor in a few years' time?"

"Perhaps."

"You have named Suleiman your heir. Ibrahim is his best friend, and someday—may Allah grant it be many years hence—our son will be sultan. I am sure that he will name Ibrahim his grand vizier. If Suleiman's sister—his *full* sister—is wed to his grand vizier, our son's interests will be well served."

Selim smiled slowly. "Were you a man, my beloved, I might make *you* my grand vizier."

"I am far happier being a woman, your bas-kadin, and the mother of your children."

He softly stroked her long hair. "Ah, my beloved! If only I had a friend like Ibrahim to serve *me*. Perhaps I was hasty in dismissing my vizier, Cem Pasha."

"Dismissing him? You had his head lopped off—which was just a bit ungrateful, considering how well he ran the government while you were in Persia."

"Perhaps, my sweet, but when I returned, the late vizier was loath to relinquish his power. I forgave him, but he continued to try to usurp my power. He had to be punished. Beheading him seemed the quickest solution. Now I discover this old man that I replaced him with is a doddering fool!"

"Ali Akbar has served the government well over the years. Retire him honorably, my lord. You have had five grand viziers since you took up the sword of Ayub. Four have been beheaded. This old man's only fault is his many years. Do not overlook the many good services he has performed. Already the people speak openly in the streets of your harshness."

"What do they say?"

"I will tell you only if you will grant me forgiveness beforehand."

"It is granted."

"A most popular curse these days among our people is 'May you be vizier to Sultan Selim!' "

He grimaced. "I will retire Ali Akbar with honors, but whom shall I choose to replace him?"

"Piri Pasha," she answered.

"Not another old man! Never! Piri Pasha was in Constantinople when my grandfather, the conqueror, captured it. He has seen more than sixty winters."

"Piri Pasha is no Ali Akbar. He is an administrative genius. He is a man without vices, has no delusions of power, and has always put his duty to the government above everything—even his personal life. You need him, especially since you plan to go to Egypt."

"Will you come with me?"

"No, my love. Not unless you command it. On campaign you are a different person, not the Selim I know and love. My lord is the poet, the father, the gentleman—not the stern sultan and fierce soldier. The soldier has little need of my softness. I can be of no use to you if I go with you to Egypt, but here in Constantinople I am your eyes and ears. Who can tell you the truth as I do?"

He kissed her lightly. "And what will you do besides be my eyes and ears?"

"Why, see to the harem and the children. Nilufer will be thirteen come spring, and there are things I would teach her that her tutors cannot. My little Karim has not yet reached the age where he can do without his mother, though he grows more each day."

"He is so like you, beloved. Of all my sons he is the least like a Turk, but we shall change that as he grows older. Has he not already accompanied his father on one campaign?"

"If he grows older," she said softly.

Selim, however, did not hear her, for his mind had turned from Cyra to the second step in his plan to become the head of all Islam. He would shortly take his army out again, and this time his objectives would be the holy cities of Mecca and Medina; then on to Egypt, and his "rescue" of the caliph. He would take Cyra's advice and appoint Piri Pasha as grand vizier. Her instinct about people was always good. Free from worry on the home front, he could concentrate on the campaign.

Knowing how secure he felt, Cyra let him go without telling him about Hadji Bey.

The agha kislar was dying, and all the residents of the Eski Serai knew it, and wept. There was no one in the harem from the humblest slave girl to the baskadin who did not love and honor this wise old man. Hadji Bey had served the House of Osman since the age of nine. He was now seventy-one years of age. He had lived through the reigns of Mohammed the Conqueror, Bajazet, and Selim I, and had hoped to see Suleiman rule. Now he knew that Allah had not wished it so, and he sent for Cyra.

For the first time in all her years in Turkey, she entered the apartments of the grand eunuch. She was surprised to find them so simply furnished, for the agha's taste in clothing had always been elegant, if a trifle flamboyant.

The bedchamber was dimly lit, and the curtains drawn. Hadji Bey lay on his couch. Unlike the average eunuch, he had never become fat, and now his lean body seemed to have shrunk beneath the coverlets. An attendant set a stool by the agha.

Seating herself, Cyra told the slave, "Disturb us only in case of emergency." The man nodded and left them.

"Well, my daughter," said the agha, his voice weakened, "it is almost time for the thread of my life to be cut. . . ." She made a small gesture of protest, but he took her hand in his and patted it. Cyra noted the once-slim fingers had become like a bird's talons. "No, my daughter, do not grieve. My only regret is that I shall not live to see Suleiman sultan. This is what I must speak to you of now. There is danger ahead for him. He has too many brothers."

"How can you say this, old friend? My beloved lord Selim once had ten sons, but Omar is dead, Kasim and Abdullah killed at Chaldiran, and now my son Murad fallen in Syria. Only six remain. Selim needs his sons."

"But Suleiman does not," replied Hadji Bey. "My child, you, the brightest of my pupils, cannot see the truth for the secure and rosy mist before your eyes. Selim will live only a few more years. Yes! It is true, Cyra! The thing that eats at his guts will soon have gorged itself, and the sultan's life will be snuffed out. Suleiman is heir, but once Selim is dead, this bond that has kept the kadins united all these years will dissolve. Mohammed is but four months younger than Suleiman. He is charming, gay, and popular. Do you think little Firousi would not advance her son's cause? And the fierce Zuleika? You think her incapable of the same thing? Sarina with her one son is as capable as the other two. When Selim joins his ancestors in Paradise, all his sons but Suleiman must be there to greet him."

"No!"

"It must be done, my daughter! This advice is my only legacy to you."

"Have you forgotten my little Karim, Hadji Bey? Do you think I could destroy him? Do you think I would permit either Selim or Suleiman to destroy him? *Never!* We did not bear our children to have them murdered to insure the succession. The slaughter of brothers must be stopped!"

"You will destroy Suleiman, Cyra. As bas-kadin, you have power. As sultan valideh, you will have more power, but even that power has its limits. You will not be able to prevent malcontents from using Karim and his brothers against Suleiman—and they will! You must begin to act now!"

"I cannot, Hadji Bey! I cannot!" She began to cry softly.

The old man raised himself slowly and painfully. "I did not pick you off the auction block in Candia, protect you, train you, and raise you to such heights to have you fail me now. For all but nine years of my life the House of Osman has been my house! I saved it from Prince Ahmed and his mother. I will not let your sentimental weakness destroy it! I am not asking you to dispose of Selim's sons personally, but they must go! If they do not, Suleiman will be forced to destroy them himself. From his birth he has been told he will be sultan, and if I know Suleiman, he will be!" With this, the agha fell back among the pillows.

Cyra held a cup of cool water to his lips. "I will do everything to protect Suleiman, Hadji Bey, but there must be something else we can do besides kill them. Let me think on it before I make a final decision."

The old man nodded. "Now, my child, I ask two final favors of you. First, will you forgive me my harshness of today?"

"A thousand times over. In my heart I remember the man who sired me, but it is you who have been my father since my thirteenth year. How could I be angry at you for speaking the truth to me?"

Hadji Bey smiled up at her with a trace of his old self. "Daughter of my heart, you warm this old man's bones. The second favor I ask is that you sit by me until I sleep." She nodded. "Cyra, my daughter, be brave, be strong, and let nothing deter you from your goal. Suleiman will be a great sultan, but you will be a greater valideh!" Taking her hand, he closed his dark eyes, the sound of his strained breathing the only discordant note in the room.

She sat for several hours by his side; perhaps she dozed for a few minutes. Suddenly she became aware of the deep silence around her. Taking a small mirror on a chain from about her waist, she held it to his nostrils. The face of the glass remained clear.

It was then she allowed herself the luxury of weeping. Sobbing softly, she remembered the coffee-colored gallant in Candia who in one bid had paid a fortune in gold for her and then, covering her nakedness, led her away. He had saved her from God knows what fate, and had raised her to the pinnacle of power. In his wisdom he had charted her course with Selim's; and with Selim she knew more love and trust than any woman could possibly know. Hadji Bey was responsible for all her happiness.

Her sobs slowly abated, and, composing herself, she left the room, saying to the guard outside the door, "The agha kislar is dead. See to the preparations for his burial."

32

Early in the year 1517, Selim's army triumphed again. In Syria, near the town of Aleppo, the Turkish forces met and destroyed the army of the Mameluke ruler. The Ottoman artillery had improved, and the Egyptians, like the Persians before them, were taken by surprise.

Unopposed, the sultan's victorious armies swept across Syria, through Palestine, and into the Nile River Valley up to the gates of Cairo. Here, Selim arrogantly demanded that the Mameluke sultan relinquish his authority. He was refused as arrogantly. The Turks quickly battered their way into the city, where the Ottoman sultan promptly hanged the Egyptian ruler and his sons. Selim was at his fiercest, but his rage was not entirely due to his rival. The campaign had cost him three more sons. Murad had been killed in Syria. Sarina's only son, Bajazet, as well as his favorite second son, Mohammed, had fallen in the battle for Cairo. He had four living sons left. Selim was a born soldier, and his sons had followed him eagerly, yet he felt guilt at their loss. He had not raised them to fall in battle, yet it was an honorable death. Still, he was glad he did not have to face his wives with the news.

His grief was partially assuaged when his soldiers brought to him the last Abbasid caliph. The elderly man, found hiding in a cellar, was terrified of the Turkish ruler. Selim put his fears to rest by treating him kindly and with deference. Overwhelmed, the frail old man gratefully accepted the four plump, pretty Nubian ladies of middle years the sultan bestowed on him. A man of his many winters should be properly cared for, declared the sultan, and each of the caliph's new slaves had a special talent. One was a fine cook, another an excellent seamstress, the third skilled in simple medicine, and the last a good masseuse and teller of tales.

The old man was tenderly carried to the baths, where he was washed, barbered, perfumed, and presented with a new wardrobe. He was given choice living quarters and would, of course, return to Constantinople with the sultan, to live the remainder of his years in safety, luxury, and honor.

Six times daily, accompanied by Selim, whom he had taken to calling "my son," he led the prayers to Allah. One wit among the soldiers remarked that the old fellow must have thought he had died and gone to Paradise.

In gratitude the caliph named Selim and the Ottoman rulers to follow him as his successors, thus transferring the title Defender of the Faith to the House of Osman.

The sultan was jubilant. His territory now included Greece, the Balkans, a good part of Eastern Europe, all of Asia Minor down through Syria and Egypt, and with it a good part of North Africa, as well as all Arabia, with its sacred cities of Mecca and Medina. His power was the greatest of any monarch in the world.

While he was in Egypt, there came to Selim's attention the feats of the Khair ad-Din, also known as Barbarossa, a pirate who was greatly feared. Khair ad-Din hated Christians, especially Spaniards, with all the fervor of a fanatic. They were infidels, decadent, illiterate, weak— and worse, they had killed two of his brothers.

Taking command of his dead brothers' ships, he harried the Spanish from Tunis to the Balearic Islands. Caught ferrying Moors from Spain to safety in Africa, he captured the attacking galleys and added them to his own fleet, which also included several Papal ships, now rowed by their original crews.

At one point Khair ad-Din learned that a new purge of Moors was to begin in Spain. Guided by Spanish Muslims, he swept inland into the soft, fat underbelly of Spain, sacking monasteries, convents, churches, garrisons, and castles alike. Getting clear with as much booty as his men and their prisoners could carry, he capped his achievement by rescuing Spain's remaining seventy thousand Moors and getting them safely to North Africa. The grateful Moors joined his crews in droves.

After learning of Khair ad-Din's feats, the Ottoman

sultan sent for him. Khair ad-Din came, for he was no fool. He might be a pirate of great fame, but as famous as he was at sea, the Ottoman's feats as a soldier were greater. The pirate chief was a peasant, and he knew it. With a commission from the Grand Turk, he would be respectable and honored in the Muslim world. Khair ad-Din had one weakness. He desperately wanted respectability.

Selim, standing on the top step of the dais, fought back the urge to laugh as the pirate admiral approached. He was of medium height, well-muscled, and fat as a wrestler. His bright red hair and bushy beard were oiled and perfumed. The sultan, whose only acquaintance with redheads was with Cyra and their youngest son, thought Khair ad-Din the ugliest and most ludicrous figure he had ever seen; but he maintained his grim composure.

"May you live a thousand years, o my padishah," came a deep, cannonlike voice.

Selim graciously acknowledged the greeting and quickly got to the main business. Khair ad-Din was given the rank of beylerbey, with its horsetail standard, a sword, and a fine Arabian stallion. When the new beylerbey agreed to escort the twenty-five ships full of the sultan's booty back to Constantinople, Selim added a regiment of Janissaries and a battery of heavy cannon.

Khair ad-Din was ecstatic. From this day forward, he would fight for Ottoman Turkey, proudly flying its flag on his topmost mast. Forty-five percent of all he took would go to the sultan. The remainder would be divided among himself, his captains, and their men.

Satisfied, Selim left Egypt for the long trek home to Constantinople. With Khair ad-Din the scourge of the Mediterranean, the Christians would be kept very busy, and he would have the time to plan his Western invasions. The journey took longer than he would have wanted, for accompanying him and the army were an additional one thousand camels laden with treasure.

Selim returned to his capital in the early spring of 1518, to find that Cyra had temporarily appointed Anber, the chief eunuch of the Moonlight Serai, as agha kislar. He confirmed this appointment, first to her privately when

they visited the simple tomb of Hadji Bey, and then publicly through his grand vizier, Piri Pasha.

Piri Pasha was everything Cyra had promised he would
be. It amazed Selim that she knew so much about his officials, but he trusted her and had learned long ago not
to question his good fortune.

In his absence, his twin daughters had made him a
grandfather for the first time, with two fine boys. Nilufer
was fifteen and finally ready for marriage. With little
prodding, he chose Ibrahim to be her bridegroom.

A messenger was dispatched to Magnesia. Suleiman
and Ibrahim were to come to Constantinople within the
month. In the meantime, the palace would be made
ready for the approaching festivities.

Sarina, no less peppery at forty, bullied the new agha
to the point of tears with her demands to be allowed to
supervise the gardens for the wedding. Cyra smoothed
things over by sweetly asking Anber to grant her request.
"It will help ease her deep sorrow over Prince Bajazet's
death," the bas-kadin said. Anber, grateful for an excuse
to get the sultan's fourth kadin off his neck, agreed, and
Sarina triumphantly bustled to the royal greenhouse to
oversee the quickly cowed gardeners.

By coaxing and bullying, she achieved miracles. On
Nilufer's wedding day, the Yeni Serai gardens were filled
with Gold of Ophir rose trees in full bloom, each set in
a tall turquoise-enameled pot, and thousands of paperwhite narcissus and pale-yellow tulips filled the flower
beds. The peach, cherry, almond, and pear trees were in
full bloom, as they always were each spring.

During the days preceding the nuptials, a gentle pandemonium reigned within the harem walls. Nilufer was
to have an entirely new wardrobe. This meant three hundred pairs of harem trousers, three hundred long-sleeved,
slash-skirted dresses, three hundred fur- or satin-lined
robes, three hundred silk, gauze, or sheer woolen blouses,
three hundred night garments, three hundred sets of un-
derwear, and three hundred pairs of slippers. Her jewelry,
gifts from her family, filled three coffers.

Ibrahim sent word to his bankers, the House of Kira,
to purchase a palace worthy of his bride. Being able to
come and go freely within the harem walls and the out-

side world, Esther Kira cheerfully acted as go-between for the princess and her relations-to-be.

Nilufer had seen on a small point along the Bosporus a delicate, cream-colored-marble palace, and nothing would do but she must have it. The owner of the palace, guessing the purpose of the inquiry, demanded an outrageous price for his property. The Kiras, however, were not without resourcefulness. Secretly investigating the owner, they discovered he had sold supplies to the army at inflated prices—an offense punishable by death under Sultan Selim's strict laws.

Warned by a friend of his imminent exposure, the owner of the little palace fled. The property was confiscated by the government and given to the Kiras as a reward for their loyalty. They in turn sold it to Ibrahim at a fair price.

The twins' wedding festivities had lasted only three days, since the sultan had been eager to start for Syria. Nilufer was Selim's favorite daughter, and he was determined that she should be wed in a manner never to be forgotten by his subjects. It was his last generous act.

The wedding was to be held in the gardens of the Yeni Serai. The newlyweds would spend their first nights in the beautiful shore kiosk newly built by Selim for the occasion. The small, one-story building was decorated with marble pillars hung with red silk curtains. It had three rooms, each furnished luxuriously, and its roof was topped by a gilded, windowed dome resembling a tent. Set just outside the gates and overlooking the Golden Horn, it was a lovely and private place for the princess and her new husband.

Suleiman, Gulbehar, and Ibrahim arrived a week before the wedding. The prince was quite pleased that his best friend would soon be his brother-in-law, and took great delight in teasing him about his forthcoming marriage to a mere child. Ibrahim, two years older than Suleiman, was twenty-six.

The wedding day arrived—a perfect May morning. The cries of the muezzins echoed in the clear air all across the city. At noon, after midday prayers, Ibrahim was escorted by Prince Suleiman and his brothers-in-law, Hussein and Riza ben Ismet, to the Great Mosque (which had been the Byzantine church of Hagia Sophia) just out-

side the walls of the Yeni Serai. There he was officially
and legally married to Nilufer Sultan, represented by the
new agha kislar.

The men then returned to the palace for the festivities.
A pavilion painted with red, green, and blue designs had
been set up in the gardens. It was shaded by a cloth-of-
gold awning. Here the sultan, his sons, and his sons-in-
law seated themselves. Nearby was a smaller pavilion for
the women.

Nilufer wore pale-lavender trousers banded with diamonds at the ankles. Over them was a slash-skirted, long-
sleeved dress of the same color, covered with diamonds,
pearls, and amethysts, and topped with a deep-purple silk
cape embroidered in gold and silver thread and diamonds.
The cape was lined with alternate stripes of gold and
silver cloth. On the back of Nilufer's head she wore a
matching cap. Her long, dark hair was unbound except
for a single pearl-tassled braid. About her slim neck
sparkled a magnificent diamond necklace.

Leading Nilufer to be formally presented to her husband, the bas-kadin almost eclipsed her daughter.
Cyra was resplendent in beige and gold, her hair shining in the spring sunshine, her famous emeralds blazing.
Bowing to the sultan, she kissed her daughter and looked
for a moment into her eyes. Nilufer gently touched her
mother's cheek and brushed away the single bright tear.

"It is from happiness," murmured the bas-kadin.

"I know, my mother."

They turned to the agha who, taking the princess's right
hand, placed it in Ibrahim's right hand. Ibrahim then
removed his bride's veil and, giving her a kiss, whispered,
"You certainly took your time growing up."

"Isn't it worth it?"

"We shall see," said Ibrahim, leading her to their private dais.

"You are still a pig," she replied, smiling happily up at
him.

"And you still have a spoiled-brat temper."

"We shall be very happy," said Nilufer.

"I think so," grinned Ibrahim.

When the seven days of feasting and celebration were
over, Ibrahim escorted his bride home to their palace.

Selim's good mood had vanished. A week of indulgence had wreaked havoc with his insides, and the pains in his belly, which could have been held at bay with medicines and a simple diet, returned three fold. He sent for Suleiman.

The prince's mood was gay when he entered his father's apartments, and unfortunately this merely increased Selim's anger. Gesturing to his son to be seated, he got straight to business. "The reports I have received on you from Magnesia are bad."

"Nonsense," countered Suleiman. "Both the city and province are well run and prosperous."

"Administered by Ibrahim, not you," shot back the sultan. "You spend your time hunting and amusing yourself with Gulbehar. Considering the hours you spend with her, I should have at least one grandson by now. You have failed me."

"How have I failed you? My province is in good order. What if that is more Ibrahim's doing than mine? Have you not always told me to use to my best advantage the men around me? Ibrahim makes no decision that I have not personally passed on, and as for Gulbehar, it should please you to know she is with child."

Selim sniffed. "You refused to come with me into Syria and Egypt. If a Turk dismounts from a saddle to sit on a carpet, he becomes nothing! *Nothing!*"

"Aha! Now we come to the real thorn that nettles you, my father. You are still angry because I refused to accompany you on your last campaign. How could I govern Magnesia and follow you at the same time?" (Secretly, Suleiman was remembering a message from his mother: "Do not go with your father into Egypt. There is a plot to kill you and make Mohammed the heir." Of course it had been Hammed, his favorite brother, who had been killed; and he had often wondered if there had really been a plot, or if his wise mother was simply being clever again. He had never asked her.)

"Mohammed came with me, and yet he governed Erzurum," said Selim.

"Erzurum is the worst-run city in the empire, and do not speak to me of Hammed! If he had not followed you, he would be alive today, and I should not have lost my best friend!"

"Piri Pasha will inform you if you are to return to Magnesia," said Selim wearily.

"I await your orders, padishah." He rose to leave.

"Suleiman!" The voice was sharp. "I have not given you permission to go. I want your opinion on a plan I have in mind. I am thinking about invading Rhodes. The Christians hold the fortress there, and it is too close to our borders. What do you think?"

"You are correct as always, father. If you want me, I'll come with you."

"No. I have kept you safe thus far. You have always been my choice as heir, Suleiman. If I lost you now, I would have to go on until one of your brothers grew up. I cannot fight my fate. I grow old with this disease, and weaken. Go, my son. Go back to Gulbehar. Did you know it was your mother who talked me out of that tasty morsel? Have I missed a great deal, my son?"

Suleiman smiled. "For me, Gulbehar is perfection, but for you, father, only my mother could be perfection. You have lost nothing, but you will gain a grandson in a few months' time."

The sultan looked at his eldest son for a long moment, then said, "You are not a great soldier yet, nor are you a good ruler; but by Allah, my son, you are a great diplomat!"

"I have never really failed you, my lord. I will never."

They rose together, and Selim saw his son to the door, patting his shoulder as he left. Turning away from the departing figure, he sank down amid the cushions to think. He had always been a man to face facts, and the fact was that he was dying. And he knew it. How long he had left to live he didn't know, and his stupid doctors wouldn't even admit his approaching death. He did know it would not be too many more months before he joined his ancestors in Paradise. With Muslim logic he accepted it, yet he was angered. He was fifty-one years old and had been sultan such a short time. Turkey needed him! Already he had greatly widened its borders, and, once he took Rhodes, he would turn again into Western Europe. There was so much to do, and he was not entirely sure he could trust his oldest son to do it.

Suleiman, Suleiman, he sighed to himself. He was such a handsome boy, gentle and kind; but was he strong

enough to take up the reigns of the empire? What choice
did he have now? thought Selim. All his older sons were
dead; only Hassan, Nureddin, and Kasim remained. Hassan was far too much of a scholar, as his own father,
Bajazet, and his half-brother Korkut had been. No scholar
made a good sultan. Nureddin had inherited the cruel
streaks of both his Turkish and Chinese ancestors. He
would never do. At five, Karim was simply too young. His
choice must remain with Suleiman, he who since birth had
been fated to follow him.

Now his mind turned to the question of Rhodes. It was
absurd and intolerable that this little Christian stronghold
should exist tucked into its corner of the Mediterranean
off his very coast! The year was almost half over, so he
would not be able to mount a campaign now. Besides, it
would take a great deal of careful planning. Rhodes was
virtually impregnable, and the men who defended her
were very, very brave. Selim gave credit where credit was
due. There was no satisfaction in fighting a cowardly
enemy. The knights of Rhodes would give him a good
fight, and he looked forward to it.

He would stay in Constantinople for a while to put into
effect some of the reforms he had worked out long ago
but never acted on. Of the six years he had been sultan,
he had been away four. Perhaps Suleiman was right. How
could a man govern an empire and fight at the same time?

He wanted to be near his family for a while longer. He
had fathered sixteen children—ten boys and six girls.
Now just the four boys and his daughters remained.

Thinking back over his life, he chuckled to himself. It
had been good back in those days at the Moonlight Serai.
His aunt Refet running the household along with Cyra.
Sarina buzzing about the gardens like an angry wasp, and
forever berating him for not being able to tell the difference between her precious flowers and the weeds. His
grandfather would have liked Sarina. The conqueror was
a fine gardener himself.

His mind wandering, he saw the children tumbling like
puppies on the lawns. The kadins, their legs showing
through their sheer trousers, tossing a bright ball back
and forth. He could almost hear their silvery laughter and
taste the salt tang of the air from the sea.

How long had they been together? Almost twenty-six

years now. He almost wished he could put down the burden of the sultanate and return to those carefree days; but if he had tried to turn back, he would have discovered behind him a vast, bottomless void across which glistened only fragile memories, both bitter and sweet. There was no choice but to go forward.

33

Selim again left his capital to go on campaign. Aware that the capture of Rhodes would require special attention, he moved his army to a small peninsula facing the island. His purpose was twofold—to allow him to reconnoiter at his leisure, and hopefully to inflict a certain amount of psychological damage on the islanders, who, seeing the vast army, might not be overly eager to help the Christian defenders.

In Constantinople the kadins settled into a familiar routine. Hassan and Nureddin had been sent to the army barracks at Scutari with the promise from their father that if the reports on them were good, they might join him when the invasion began.

Only the three young princesses and little Prince Karim remained in the harem with their mothers. The sultan had suggested before leaving for Anatolia that Karim be given his own court, but Cyra had forestalled him, asking that Karim remain with her until the Rhodes campaign was over.

It was summer, and the bas-kadin was twice a grandmother. Before Selim had departed, word had come from Magnesia of Gulbehar's safe delivery of a son, and much to the sultan's pleasure he was to be called Mustafa. Nilufer, too, had, just a week past, become the mother of a son, to be named Mohammed.

The days passed quietly. When the first small hint of plague appeared in the city, those in the Eski Serai did not pay a great deal of attention. Plague was commonplace each summer when the weather got hot. A few cases were reported among the slaves who worked in the stables, but as these men were never in contact with the harem staff, there was no concern.

Then one day Anber brought word to the bas-kadin
that the young princes at Scutari were ill. Had Cyra not
lived so long with Firousi and Zuleika, she would, perhaps
have acted differently; but the bond between them was too
strong. Ordering the horrified Anber to have the princes
brought home, she then broke the news to their mothers.

The isolated, little-used Tile Court was prepared to receive the royal children, and both mothers would have
rushed to nurse their sons had not Cyra, for the first time
in their years together, wielded her authority. Only one
might go, and she must be chosen by lot. Zuleika won.

Hassan and Nureddin were horribly ill. No plague
boil had appeared yet, and their suffering was terrible.
Word was sent to the sultan that his sons were not expected to live.

Remembering Hadji Bey's dying words, Cyra realized
that, in a few days' time, Selim's ten sons would have
shrunk to two—her eldest and her youngest. A daring
plan began to form in her mind.

She could not allow Karim to become a political pawn
and a threat to Suleiman; yet she knew her gentle oldest
son would not be able to destroy his little brother, nor
would she let him. If Karim remained alive, he could become the means of destroying Suleiman and the empire
—or worse, become a puppet ruled by Western Europeans
whose greed and fear of Turkey far outweighed their common sense.

When Esther Kira came on her biweekly visit to the
harem that afternoon, Cyra invited her to walk in the
kadins' private park. It was not unusual to see them thus,
for the bas-kadin often walked and chatted with the little
Jewess in this manner. Cyra, with unusual frankness, came
right to the point.

"Esther, I have an enormous favor to ask of you."

"Dearest madam, I will do anything for you."

"Do not commit yourself so quickly, my friend. I am
asking you to save a life and, at the same time, perhaps
endanger your own and that of your whole family. No.
Keep walking, and do not appear surprised at anything I
may say. Even I am continually watched.

"Prince Hassan and Prince Nureddin are dying. This
leaves my lord only two surviving sons. With Suleiman
heir, my little Karim is in terrible danger. I cannot allow

him to be used against Suleiman, but I cannot see him
ruthlessly killed to protect Suleiman. With your help, I
plan to pretend he has died of the plague, and smuggle
him to my homeland."

Esther bent to sniff a full red rose. "Yes," she said, "it
could be done, and fate must be with you, my lady. At
this very minute there is a Scots ship out of Leeds in the
harbor. My brother Joseph will be sailing on it in five
days' time. He goes to the Edinburgh branch of the House
of Kira to bring them a reserve supply of gold and to learn
their particular method of business. Dealing with the Scots
is a very different thing from dealing with other Europeans."

Cyra laughed. "Remembering my early years, I would
certainly think so."

"How long will the two princes live, madam?"

"We have had no word since yesterday, but I would
imagine that by tonight or tomorrow they will have joined
their brothers in Paradise."

"Then Karim must become ill tonight." She dug into
her robe. "Take this," she said, slipping Cyra a small
package. "Put it in his food or water. It will not harm
him, only give him a fever for twelve hours. In the morning use your position as bas-kadin to have the two princes
removed from the Tile Court, and take your son there to
nurse him."

"Zuleika has been nursing the children."

"Say she is too weary to go on and must have rest. You
are the authority in the harem. She will obey. Remember
to have the Tile Court disinfected before you enter it. Do
not be afraid of the plague. They say Jews do not contract
it, and this is true. Isaac ben Judah, the old doctor in our
quarter, says it is because we follow the law and are
clean. He says plague comes from filth. The only cases
you have had here in the serai have been in the stables
—hardly a sanitary place. The two princes contracted it
at Scutari, and what soldier—be he Turk, Christian, or
Jew—stays clean? In three days' time you will call for a
coffin and announce Prince Karim's death. On the evening
of the second day I shall visit you to bring medicines. Instead, I shall smuggle the body of a child who has died
a natural death. I shall take Prince Karim out as I brought
the other child in—hidden in my basket."

"He must be disguised, Esther."

"Yes. That carrot top is the only one of its kind in Constantinople. His skin must be darkened, too." Again she dug into her robe and brought forth two packages. "The blue will turn his hair jet-black, the red will rid him of his fair skin. Put them in your other pocket so as not to confuse them with the fever medicine."

Cyra slid the colored packets out of sight as they turned back to the serai.

"You will need someone to help you, madam."

"Marian and her young daughter, Ruth, will help me. Esther, the House of Kira must set up an account for Karim in Edinburgh. I will finance it secretly from here. He is to be known as Charles Leslie, and is to be taken to the Abbey School at Glenkirk, to be raised by the monks. I will send a message with him to the abbot, who was once our family's confessor."

"I promised I would help you, dear lady."

"Ah, my friend! This is a very dangerous thing we do. If we are discovered, it will mean a terrible death for all of us. Are you sure you want to take this chance? Will your brother?"

"Yes, my lady," said Esther Kira firmly. "When Joseph and I were orphaned and brought to Constantinople by our Kira cousins, we were simply poor relations for whom a duty was being performed. Your kindness and patronage have given us stature and wealth in our family. Joseph has now been given this important assignment, and I have been betrothed to the second son of the house. We would do anything for you."

"God bless you for it, Esther. You will never lack as long as I live."

The Jewess raised an eyebrow. "God, madam?"

Cyra laughed softly. "When I was thirteen, Esther, and came to the harem, I decided that Allah was simply the Turkish name for God. It saved me a great deal of unnecessary trouble."

The little vendor chuckled. "Yes, my lady. I imagine it did."

When Esther had gone, Cyra dismissed her maidens and returned to the gardens with Marian and Ruth. They sat by the little lake, and the bas-kadin told them of her plans. Although Ruth was only nine, Cyra knew that she could trust her, and as the bas-kadin unfolded her plans, Ruth listened, solemnly and silently.

Marian's reaction was startling. "Thank God you've come to your senses and heeded the old agha's warning."

"Hadji Bey spoke with you?"

"A few days before he died, madam. I doubted he suspected you would solve the problem in this manner."

Cyra chuckled. "He would be most shocked, indeed. Were Karim not so Scots in appearance, I should not dare to do this."

"Have no fears, my lady. Ruth and I will help you and go with you into the Tile Court. Give me the fever medicine. I will see that the kitchens bring Karim strawberry sherbet with his dinner tonight. He loves it and will not refuse to eat it. The medicine will be in it. Will you tell him?"

"Not until we are safely in the Tile Court. He is a bright little boy and will understand." She dipped her hand into the cool water. "Has Zuleika sent word yet about the two princes?"

"There has been no word in over a day, my lady."

"Have the eunuchs not inquired at the gate?"

"They are afraid of the plague."

Cyra frowned. "We must inquire. It is not like Zuleika to worry us. The crisis must have come, and she could not send word."

Moving quickly to the Tile Court, Cyra called out, "Zuleika! It is Cyra. How are the princes?"

Silence greeted her inquiry. She called again. "Zuleika! Are you all right? Please answer me!" Silence. "Marian, go to the main gate and call the eunuchs to come in here. Tell them the bas-kadin commands it and will flay the skin off their backs if they do not obey!"

The eunuchs came fearfully but quickly.

"Break the door down," commanded Cyra.

"My lady bas-kadin, the plague germs will escape!"

Cyra's green eyes narrowed angrily. "Open that door or I shall personally slit your fat belly and burn your innards before your very eyes!"

It took but a minute to break the door down, and when it was opened, a sickingly sweet stench poured out. Placing a perfumed handkerchief to her nose, Cyra stepped across the threshold, flagging the others back with her free hand.

Within the chambers the lamps burned low, their oil almost gone. She moved from the small outer room into the main room behind it. As long as she lived, Cyra would never forget the sight that greeted her. Hassan and Nureddin lay dead on their couches. Zuleika was on the floor, her lovely body contorted cruelly, her face darkened with blood. One arm was flung back over her head, revealing a swollen, unbroken plague boil. Cyra knew that unless the boil broke or was lanced, the victim died. Bending down, she held her mirror to the woman's nostrils. Zuleika was dead.

The bas-kadin rose slowly. Suddenly she felt very old. I can't spend three days here with Karim, she thought. She moved to the outer court and heard her own voice saying, "The princes and Zuleika Kadin are dead. See that coffins are brought for their bodies. Burn everything within, and see that the entire Tile Court is scrubbed with disinfectant. I do not want the plague to spread any further."

"But who is to do it, my lady?" quavered the eunuch.

"Do we not have slaves?" she shouted at him. "Fetch them this instant! And you, you fat, cowardly son of a female pig, will personally oversee them! See that you do this job in a better fashion than you guarded Zuleika Kadin and the imperial princes. Do not tell me she did not call for help when she realized she was herself stricken. May Allah help you when the sultan learns of this!"

The eunuch gaped in amazement at her. Never had he seen or heard the sultan's bas-kadin lose her temper. Mercifully for them both, Marian led her mistress away.

The next thing Cyra remembered was Marian stripping off her clothes and saying to Ruth, "Burn them all." Then she was in her bath, and Marian, having shooed the bath attendants out, was scrubbing her with some evil-smelling stuff and boiling water. She protested weakly. "Good! You're still alive," said her slave tartly.

"I can't take Karim there," she whispered.

"You can, you will, and you must. Unless you wish to see him end on an executioner's bowstring," hissed Marian.

"It is his only chance. Now be silent, lest the walls hear our foolish chatter."

A final splash of hot water, and she meekly followed Marian into the cool room. Stretching out on a marble slab, she allowed the woman to massage her numb body with oil of wild flowers. Then she fell into the blessed relief of sleep. Marian tiptoed out, speaking to the waiting bath attendants. "The bas-kadin has had a terrible shock. Zuleika Kadin and the two princes are dead. It was she who found them. Wake her in two hours and see that she has her coffee."

The little woman pattered off down the hallway to Firousi's apartments. Sarina was there ahead of her.

"What has happened to Cyra?" asked the fourth kadin. "Gossip is racing through the harem like fire."

"My lady will be all right, Lady Sarina. She is resting now. I have taken it upon myself to bring you the tragic news before some gossiping slave does."

"The two princes are dead?"

Marian nodded. "Zuleika Kadin, also. My lady became worried when there was no word for over a day. She went to investigate, and it was she who found them."

Clinging to each other, Sarina and Firousi wept. Marian quietly left the room.

Next, the little Englishwoman headed for the kadins' kitchen, where she gave orders from Lady Cyra that Prince Karim was to have strawberry sherbet with his dinner this night. The cook, who had already heard about the deaths from the kitchen gardener—who had it from a passing guard—marveled silently at the fortitude of the bas-kadin to think of her little son's sweet tooth under such sad circumstances.

When evening came, Cyra had recovered from the initial shock of her discovery and invited Sarina, Firousi, and the children to dine with her. It was a somber meal. The children were aware that their two older brothers and Zuleika Kadin were dead.

The bas-kadin had made it very plain that she was taking Zuleika's little daughter, Mahpeyker, into her care. Curled up in Cyra's lap, the child fully understood that her mother was dead. Cyra, feeling the little one's warmth against her, thought that God was showing his approval of her plan to spirit Karim away by giving her another child to raise.

At meal's end, the youngsters brightened with the arrival of the sweet liquid sherbet and almond cakes. Cyra did not even dare to glance at Karim, knowing that somehow Marian had slipped Esther Kira's potion into his sherbet.

She could not sleep that night, worrying about her son. Finally, at dawn, she rose to the muezzin's call, said her prayers, and hurried to Karim's room.

His little body bathed in perspiration, the child tossed upon his couch. She glanced at the nurse sleeping on the floor by the boy. Angrily Cyra kicked her.

"Get up, you wretch! You have slept through morning prayers, and my son lies here ill!"

The girl scrambled to her feet. "Madam, I watched all the night and had just dozed off for a moment."

"Liar! Look at the prince! He is bathed in sweat! No fever could come so quickly. You have been sleeping for hours!"

The frightened nurse looked down at Karim, then drew back shaking. "Plague," she sobbed. "The prince has the plague!"

"Stop that wailing and fetch the doctor!"

The girl fled, to return a few minutes later with Alaeddin Cerdet. Quickly the physician examined the moaning, unconscious child, noting his rapid pulse, high fever, coated and slightly swollen tongue.

"Plague," he said. "The prince has all the signs of the plague. He must be removed at once to an area of isolation, lest he infect the whole palace. I will send a nurse."

"No," said Cyra. "I will nurse him myself."

"Madam, I cannot be responsible for your safety. The sultan would kill me if you should die as did the lady Zuleika."

"I shall be in no danger, Alaeddin Cerdet. I had plague as a child," she reassured him, lying smoothly. "I shall not go alone. My two slaves, Marian and Ruth, will accompany me."

"In that case, I cannot deny a mother the privilege of caring for her sick son. I shall inform the kitchens of the diet the prince must have. Try to get him to take some nourishment. If a plague boil rises, give it several hours to break. If it does not, lance it. Perhaps it will save him." He handed her a small, sharp instrument from his case. "If there is no boil, then Allah have mercy, for the child will surely die."

The newly scrubbed and furnished Tile Court was ready within the hour to receive them. A procession made up of Cyra, Marian, and Ruth, who carried the prince on a litter, entered the building. At the gate Cyra stopped to speak with the cowardly eunuch. She graciously apologized for her anger of the previous day and gave him a small purse of coins for his diligence in cleaning the court. Her eyes filled with tears when she said she had never expected to see it again, let alone under such circumstances. The eunuch was immediately sympathetic and swore to guard them with his life.

"Let no one enter," were her final instructions. "When our meals come, ring the bell by the gate and push them through the slot." Patting his arm and smiling a brave, sweet smile, she entered the Tile Court.

They were alone. Within a few hours, Karim's fever was gone, and he awoke as refreshed as from a good night's sleep. "Where are we, mother?" he asked.

"In the Tile Court, my son."

"Didn't Hassan and Nureddin die here?"

"Yes."

"Then why are we here?"

"Because everyone believes you have the plague."

"Do I?"

"No."

"Then let us go and tell them."

"Karim, I want you to listen very carefully to me. Do you know who will be sultan after your father?"

"My brother Suleiman."

"That is right. Do you know what will happen to you when Suleiman is sultan?" Karim shook his head. "He will kill you."

The little boy looked frightened. "Why, mother? I love my brother, and he loves me. He has told me so!"

"Yes, my darling, he does love you, but the law says he must destroy his rivals, and that there can be only one heir. If he does not kill you, there are evil men who would use you to threaten his power. In the end he would have to obey the law or he would not be a good sultan. You want Suleiman to be a good sultan, don't you?"

The child nodded vigorously. "I will go away, mother. Then Suleiman can be a good sultan."

"It would not be allowed, Karim. That is why we must pretend you are sick. Then we will pretend you have died —but you really won't," she quickly added. "Instead, you will be smuggled out of Turkey. You will be taken to my homeland, and you will pretend to be an ordinary little boy. You will go to a wonderful school with other boys your own age. You have often said you wanted to visit Scotland."

"Oh, yes, mother!"

"You must be very brave, Karim. You cannot tell anyone who you really are. There are wicked men in Scotland, too, who, if they knew your true identity, would use you to hurt your father and Suleiman. Do you understand me?"

"Yes, mother. But if I am not Prince Karim, who am I?"

Cyra smiled and thought to herself, Thank God he is bright. "You will be Charles Adam Leslie, my son. Charles, so you have a name of your own. Adam, after your uncle, my brother. And Leslie, which is my family name."

"Can I be a Christian, mother?"

"Do you want to be?"

"Oh, yes! Marian and Ruth have told me all about the dear Jesus and his mother Mary. I have often thought she must have been like you. Warm and soft and kind."

"Perhaps, my son." She glared at Marian. "You could have been killed for speaking to him of Christianity."

"Nonsense," returned Marian. "Sultan Selim has always approved of the princes' learning about other religions. I often spoke to him of the Jews, too."

"He does not evince any desire to be a Jew," said Cyra dryly.

Karim was growing impatient. "What will I tell people if I cannot tell them who I really am?"

"You will tell them you come from a land far to the east. On your journey to Constantinople, you fell from your pony, and now you can remember only your name.

Always tell those who ask this story. Never vary it. Say nothing more. Do you understand me?"

"Yes, but how will I get to Scotland?"

"Esther Kira's brother, Joseph ben Kira, leaves for Edinburgh in a few days' time and will accompany you. He will tell those who inquire that you were brought to his house in Constantinople with instructions to convey you to Scotland. I have set up an account for you with the Kiras in Edinburgh to cover your expenses. You will never lack for money."

"Will I ever see you again, mother?"

"I do not know, Karim. I realize I am asking a great deal of you. You are still just a small boy, but you are not an ordinary little boy. You are intelligent and wise beyond your years. Though you may never speak of it from the moment you leave the serai, remember that you are a prince of the House of Osman, that your great-grandfather was Mohammed the Conqueror, that your father is Selim the Just."

"I will not forget, mother." He threw his arms about her. "Even if some of the boys at school brag about their puny families, I shall remain silent."

"Good," smiled his mother, "but fear not, my son. You will not be entirely alone. Take this ring. My brother, Adam, gave it to me on my thirteenth birthday. See the inscription inside? You speak my native tongue, Karim. Read it to me."

Karim took the ring and read: "To my own dear sister, Janet, from her brother, Adam."

"Wear the ring always. *Never* part with it. Show it to the abbot at Glenkirk Abbey—though one look at you, and he cannot fail to know you are a Leslie. He will, when he deems it wise, introduce you to your uncle Adam, and to your grandfather, if he still lives."

Karim, his Ottoman and Highland blood now stirring with excitement at the thought of his dangerous impending adventure, announced, "I shall have to be disguised to leave the city, mother."

"So you will," she laughed, grabbing a handful of his hair and yanking. "This will be dyed black, and your skin will be darkened to a nut-brown."

"Will I look like a Moor?"

"I hope not, but probably you will. When you arrive in

Scotland, Joseph will see that your hair and skin are restored to their normal colors. Now"—she spoke in his own tongue—"what is your name, boy?"

"Charles Leslie," he answered in the same language.

"Where do you come from?"

"A land far to the east."

"What is its name?"

"I don't know."

"You don't know? You must be a very stupid boy not to know the name of your native land."

"I am not stupid. I fell from my horse on my way to Constantinople and injured my head. My memory is gone. I can remember only my name and that my country is in the East."

"Well done, my darling! Never, never change your story! Should your father and brother find out what I have done, I should be killed in a most terrible manner. My life is in your hands, Karim, as well as the lives of many others. It is a great responsibility to place on one so young, but then you are of the House of Osman and the House of Leslie. Both are breeders of brave men."

The little boy gazed up at his beautiful mother. "I will never betray you, mother. Never!"

She gathered him into her arms, holding him close, savoring the incredible sweetness of him and feeling her own heart break. My youngest and dearest child, she thought. I simply cannot let him go. I cannot! He is so little. What will become of him without his mother? There must be another way!

Then she saw Marian, her lips set sternly, her brown eyes speaking the terrible truth of the matter. Her own green eyes closed, and, burying her face in her son's soft neck, she saw the mute executioners, their black bodies oiled and glistening obscenely in the torchlight, the bow-strings swinging evilly in their strong hands.

Shuddering, she released Karim and, looking down at him, said, "You must not leave this room, my child, lest someone see you. Nor may you go near the windows. Ruth has brought some of your toys and will play with you."

A day and a night passed. Late in the afternoon of the second day, Cyra went to the gate of the Tile Court and

requested that Esther Kira and her famous herbs be sent
for at once.

"She may enter in safety. Jews are known not to catch
the plague. May Allah grant that her herbs work."

"My lady, may I ask how the little prince fares?"

"I am afraid, good eunuch," she replied softly.

By evening, when Esther Kira, with a wicker basket
some three and a half feet in length strapped to her back,
arrived at the Tile Court, the word was all over the serai
that Prince Karim was dying.

"I knew I could trust that fat slug to chatter," chuckled
Cyra.

The night deepened, and as the moon set, the final
touches were put on the little prince's disguise. Dressed
in simple but costly garments, he stood before his mother
for a final inspection. "He does not look like the same
boy," she approved.

The others nodded. Suddenly Karim flung himself into
his mother's arms. "I don't want to forget you," he sobbed.

Cyra gritted her teeth. "Do not cry, Karim," she said
sternly, "you will make the stain run." Then, more gently,
"I will not allow you to forget me, my son."

Drawing a thin gold chain from her pocket, she opened
the little locket on it to reveal an exquisite miniature of
herself. "Firousi painted it several years ago," she explained. (The second kadin had done the portrait in secret, as the portrayal of the human image was against
Muslim law.) "This locket will keep my face ever bright
in your memory, beloved."

She turned to the disapproving Marian. "Outside these
walls my face is unknown, and it will help to identify him
further to my family." She slipped the chain about his
slender neck. "There, my dearest son. When you are
lonely for me or are tempted to reveal your identity, gaze
upon my face and remember—my life is in your keeping."

Tenderly she kissed him a final time, and then, helping
him into Esther Kira's basket, spoke her final words to
him. "Remember, Charles Leslie. The motto of the clan
is 'Stand Fast.' Remember, and abide by it!"

A tray of herbs was placed over the crouching boy,
and the basket lid was closed. Cyra walked with Esther
to the gate.

"May Allah rain blessings on you, Esther Kira, for the help you have given me," she said loudly.

"I am desolate my remedies have failed, madam. If only you had called me sooner."

"At least his pain is eased, and he will slip quietly into Paradise," replied the grieving mother.

Walking through the gate, Esther shook her head sadly at the eavesdropping eunuch, who was so busy thinking how he would tell this new and deliciously tragic piece of information that he did not see the bas-kadin hidden in the shadows, the tears streaming down her lovely face.

34

THE HAREM was in deep mourning for the three imperial princes and Zuleika Kadin. Selim hurriedly returned from Anatolia to comfort his remaining wives and to privately mourn his great loss. He remained in his capital throughout the autumn.

During these months Cyra spent a great deal of time weeping. The residents of the serai attributed the baskadin's tears and loss of weight to the deaths, but Cyra was secretly fretting for word of Karim.

Finally it arrived, and on a sunny afternoon in late autumn, Cyra sat in her garden by the lake with Marian, Ruth, and Esther Kira. The pale, lemony sunlight dappled the dark waters, and a sharp breeze made the three of them pull their woolen cloaks tightly about their bodies.

"I have received a letter from Joseph," the little Jewess began, "but I dared not bring it. I have memorized its contents and burned it."

"Tell me!" begged Cyra eagerly.

"Their voyage was smooth and uneventful. At first the captain protested about the extra passenger, but Joseph said Charles might sleep on a pallet in his own little cabin, and that he had brought with him double the food ration required. The captain, after hearing these facts—and receiving a generous purse—relented.

"The first night, Joseph tried to give Charles his own bed, but the boy refused, saying, 'I am an ordinary boy now, Master ben Kira,' and nothing could dissuade him. They arrived at Leeds in early September, and went straight to Edinburgh. Two days later, Joseph obtained horses, and they rode north to Glenkirk, where Charles was safely installed at the Abbey School.

"My brother has been to see him once, and reports that

he is well and very happy. He has met his grandfather,
his uncle Adam, and two young cousins, one eight years
older than he, and the other three years older. He will
spend Christmas at the castle with your family.

"There! Is that not good news!"

"Dear Esther! It is the best possible news! How can I
ever thank you?"

Esther smiled and shook her head. "You are my true
friend, sweet lady. You have been more than generous to
the House of Kira over the years. I need no other reward. Now, I think it is best that I leave you to calm
yourself and meditate upon your happiness. Perhaps Marian and Ruth will walk with me?"

Cyra nodded absently, already lost in her imaginings
of Karim's trip and reception in Scotland. Her thoughts
were happily near the reality of what had actually occurred.

Joseph ben Kira and Karim were ushered into the
presence of the tall and austere abbot, James Dundas.
Joseph introduced himself and told his carefully rehearsed
story.

"My lord abbot, I am Joseph ben Kira of Constantinople. Before I departed from my home several months
ago, a child was brought to me by a black slave. He gave
me a letter, a chest of gold, and disappeared into the
night. The letter asked that I bring the child to his mother's homeland and take him to the Abbey School of Glenkirk to be educated and raised as a Christian. He wears
a ring and a locket about his neck to identify him to you.
I know nothing more of the matter."

"Come near, laddie, so I may get a better look at you,"
said the abbot. "I am an old man, and my sight is nae
what it used to be."

Karim stepped forward. The abbot visibly whitened.

"What is your name?"

"Charles Leslie, sir."

"Give me the letter you carry, my son."

Karim took the letter from his doublet and handed it
to the old man. With trembling fingers, the abbot opened
and read it.

"Now, child. Show me the locket."

Karim drew the gold chain from beneath his shirt and,

opening the locket, revealed the miniature to James Dundas. The abbot smiled.

"She is a beautiful woman. When she was a child, I could see she would be. Now, laddie, the ring." He took it, read the inscription, and returned it to Karim. "Well, my son, we shall do our best to make you happy in your mother's homeland."

Ringing a bell, he instructed the attending brother, "This is Charles Leslie, Brother Francis. He is to be our new pupil and is a cousin to Donald and Ian Leslie. He will share their room. See that he is settled. Then send a messenger to Glenkirk Castle. I must speak with the old earl at once!"

Joseph ben Kira rose. "If you no longer have need of my services, my lord, I will begin my return to Edinburgh. I can be reached at the House of Kira in Goldsmith's Lane."

"Thank you, Master ben Kira. You have done us a great service. I will commend your kindness to the earl."

Joseph bowed low, smiled, patted Karim on the head, and departed.

In her private garden by the lake, the bas-kadin rose from the marble bench. Yes, surely that was how it had gone. Now Karim was safe to grow to manhood, and her duty must return to her beloved lord Selim.

His ailment had grown worse, manifesting itself in a new and infuriating symptom—partial impotence. He never knew when it would strike. Many maidens were sent to his couch. Most returned weeping and in disgrace, for the sultan of sultans could not admit his disability.

Despite it, he continued to treat his three kadins with courtesy, affection, and favor. But having only one remaining son, he suddenly became desperate to father another; however, the kadins were more than ever united behind Suleiman, and no maiden went to the sultan without first sipping a soothing draft of their cherry sherbet. Though it was practically unnecessary these days, they took no chances.

In midwinter, Selim felt it his duty to return to Anatolia, as the invasion of Rhodes was planned for the spring. Before his departure, as was his custom, he would spend one night with each of his kadins.

Cyra was to be with him the night before he left, and from the stories brought to her by Firousi and Sarina, she was worried. Selim was totally impotent now, and he resented it deeply. Two nights before, he had taken leave of Sarina. Unable to perform as a man, he had grown furious, called his kadin an "old woman," and loudly demanded a young maiden be brought to him. Sarina, who loved Selim deeply, had gathered the shreds of her dignity about her and fled her suite for the gardens, where she wept bitterly.

Firousi's leavetaking of Selim had been equally disastrous. Again, the sultan could not function. Enraged, he had slapped the second kadin. Both were stunned by this action. Never in all their years together had Selim physically abused any of his wives. Without a word, he left her bedchamber.

The following morning, Selim made it a point to greet both Sarina and Firousi publicly, and with a great show of affection. Later in the day, slaves were seen entering the golden court laden with gifts. The sultan was wise enough not to go off on a military campaign leaving the status of his two lesser wives in doubt. He wanted no problems in his household.

Cyra spent a frantic day. Her apartment must be cleaner than clean. The gold, silver, copper, and brass accessories and ornaments must shine, the tile floors sparkle. Refreshments needed to be selected—small, hot pastries filled with lamb and kasha, glazed honey cakes, apricot sherbet, and sweet, hot coffee—all Selim's favorites.

Speaking to the various oda mistresses, Cyra selected four of the most beautiful and talented musicians the harem had to offer to soothe and entertain her lord with their melodies.

Then off to her bath to be scrubbed, plucked, massaged, and perfumed. An hour's nap to refresh her, and, having been dressed in the sultan's favorite peacock-blue, she was ready to greet Selim.

Their evening began pleasantly enough. The musicians played well and pleased the sultan. The light, late supper was enjoyable to him. Finally, the slaves dismissed, the lamps trimmed to burn low, Selim and Cyra retired to her bedchamber, where he attempted to claim his conjugal rights. He failed and promptly became angry.

Cyra, who had been expecting this problem, threw herself into his arms, sobbing piteously, "Alas! I have grown too old to please you, my dearest Selim. Would that Allah had struck me down before I lived to see this day. Forgive me, my lord! Forgive me for the sake of the five children I have borne you!"

Selim knew she lied. Her beauty and body, even at forty years of age, would have aroused a marble statue. But her performance and her attempt to save his ego and take the entire blame pleased him and helped to restore his sense of proportion.

"I forgive you, you exquisite liar," he growled.

She looked up at him, her green eyes clear and tearless.

"Don't you even have the decency to shed a real tear or two?" he grumbled.

She twinkled at him, "My love, I could not be so hypocritical." Then, sensing the worst was over, she spoke again. "If I may presume on our twenty-seven years together, my lord?" He nodded. "It is this illness that has rendered you feeble. When you are well again, there will will be no problem. How can I accuse you—or how can you accuse me—when we have spent so many nights together in an ecstasy of love, a love that has borne the precious fruit of five children? We are no longer youth and maiden, and though I look forward to the night that you return to me well and strong as of old, can we not this night—the night before you leave us again—simply enjoy the warmth of just being together?"

In reply, he held her hard against his chest. "Now I know why I chose you first those long years ago. You and only you have always had the talent to put me at my ease, and the wisdom to speak honestly to me. Praise Allah that He saw fit to present me with such a treasure as you, my beloved Cyra."

Raising her up, he gently kissed her sweet lips and settled into her arms. For some time, their voices whispered silkenly through the room as they talked together as had always been their habit. Then he fell asleep against her breasts.

In the darkness of the chamber, she heard his even breathing, and, knowing he finally slept, Cyra allowed herself the privilege of tears. Silently they ran down her cheeks. She wept neither for him nor for herself, but because she knew instinctively that this would be the last night they would ever spend together. Tomorrow he would leave for Rhodes, and she felt that he would not return. The Celt in her knew that he would soon die.

Where had all the years gone? Was it not only yesterday that she had come to him a cool but frightened virgin? She could see his even white teeth flashing against his sunbronzed skin as she first tasted the pleasures of womanhood, his relief and delight at the birth of Suleiman and all the other children who followed, his anger at his brother's treachery, and his deep belief that he alone could raise Turkey to the heights of power that had been foretold for it.

Of all those in the serai, she had seen the greatest changes in him. He had never been a heavy man, but lately she had noticed that his legs and face seemed thinner, although his belly, always flat, was now swollen. He had not been sleeping well, and this, coupled with the terrible pain he felt, had turned him into a raving despot when crossed or disobeyed.

Upon learning that Zuleika and his three younger sons had died in the Tile Court, he had had it destroyed. Discovering that the Persian captive Shannez, still among his slaves, had openly rejoiced at Zuleika's death, he had wreaked terrible vegeance. The woman had been publicly beaten, and salt had been rubbed into her open wounds. Then Selim had personally tied her limbs to four horses, which were then driven in four different directions, executing the unfortunate woman in a most horrible way.

His judgments, always fair in the past, became increasingly harsher. The slightest infractions of rules among the serai slaves were punished swiftly and often with brutality. Cyra's heart ached for the unhappiness he felt and the unhappiness he was causing.

The soft gray light of dawn began to filter into the chamber. Still he slept on, and she was grateful. He would awaken refreshed, and the day would go well for him. A slave entered to wake them. Catching the old woman's eye, Cyra nodded and waved her away.

"My lord." She gently shook him. "Dearest, it is time to wake."

Opening his eyes, he smiled at her and was instantly

awake. He rose. "Come to me after prayers, so we may say our good-byes privately."

She went to him at the appointed time, and he looked almost like the Selim of old—well rested, bathed, shaved, and ready to undertake the long journey back to Anatolia. For a moment they gazed at each other, then kissed fiercely and gazed again.

He knows, she thought wildly. He knows this is the last time we shall ever see each other in this life. She struggled for the right words, but he was too quick for her. "Guide Suleiman as only you can, my love." Then, turning on his heel, he left her.

She ran all the way to the secret balcony that overlooked the main gate. Firousi and Sarina were there ahead of her, but she was in time. Passing through the entrance, he turned, looked back, and raised his hand in a quick salute. The salute was for them all, but the look, Cyra knew, was for her alone.

Several weeks passed, and spring began to make itself felt along the shores of the Bosporus. A secret communiqué arrived from Piri Pasha, who had accompanied his sultan. Selim was very ill. The doctors did not believe he would live. No one was aware of this. She was forbidden to come to the sultan. She must remain in Constantinople to give the appearance of normalcy, and, more important, to hold the serai and the city for her son.

Cyra died a thousand little deaths. Her every instinct nagged her to go to Selim. What did anything else matter as long as she was with her beloved husband? If they punished her afterward, she cared not. Without Selim, she might as well be dead. But common sense triumphed. She could not help Selim, nor could she keep Azerael, the Black Angel of Death, from claiming his victim. It was Suleiman who counted now, the son she had borne to follow his father. If it were known that the bas-kadin had hurriedly left the city for the south, the secret would be out, and unthinkable troubles might erupt. The transition from Selim to Suleiman must be made swiftly and with a minimum of fuss. Only she could prevent a possible rebellion in the capital, and the capital was the key to the Ottoman Empire. The price of her son's success was almost more than she could bear.

Then, several weeks later, as she sat quietly embroidering with Sarina and Firousi, she felt the room go icy cold. Suddenly her face was wet with hot tears that coursed silently and uncontrollably down her cheeks. Guiltily she glanced up to see if the other kadins had noticed, and discovered to her surprise that they, too, were silently weeping.

No words were said—no words were needed. The sultan's stricken kadins knew in that one moment the sad and awful truth. Selim of Turkey was dead.

PART IV

Hafise

1520–1533

35

THE SULTAN WAS DEAD, and all of Western Europe, heaving a sigh of relief, waited to see what kind of a ruler his son would be. For now, however, there was time to breathe.

Thanks to the cleverness of Piri Pasha, the transition between sultans had been smooth. Selim's grand vizier had managed to keep the sultan's death a secret from his soldiers—and therefore from all of the empire—for almost six days. By that time, Suleiman, having been notified, and riding hard from Magnesia, had reached Constantinople and put on the sword of Ayub.

For three weeks Cyra lay on her couch, hardly moving. Marian and Ruth were desperate. Coaxing, they tried to feed her broth and soft white bread, but for every three meals they brought her, she picked at one. Desperate for a solution, Marian went to the agha.

"You must help us, my lord Anber. For three weeks she has lain prostrate with grief. We cannot rouse her."

"I will come and speak with her," replied the agha. "I think I have the key to unlock her self-pity."

Waddling into her bedchamber, he seated himself by her couch. "My lady, it distresses me to see you so. Especially when your help and wisdom are needed."

There was no response.

"I must know when you will be well enough to move to new quarters. The lady Gulbehar demands that you vacate these apartments now that she bears the title of bas-kadin."

A flicker.

He continued, "What a pity your son has not found the time to declare you the valideh. By right the title is

307

yours, but alas, since you do not hold it, Gulbehar rules supreme in the harem."

"What do you mean, Gulbehar rules the harem?"

"You know the etiquette, my lady Cyra. She is the sultan's bas-kadin. You are merely the former sultan's bas-kadin."

She sat up. "Leave me. I would dress and see my son, who seems to have forgotten who made him sultan."

"As you will, madam," replied the agha, smiling archly. Entering the salon, he said to Marian, "Attend your mistress. She wishes to dress and see her son. I think our young sultan is about to lose his first battle. May it not be a portent of things to come."

Cyra dressed carefully. She would never again wear the slash-skirted dress of a kadin. Instead, she put on the tunic dress of a valideh. Though she had lain for weeks in grief, her servants had not been idle. The tunic was of black brocade embroidered in gold thread and teardrop pearls. Her beautiful hair, still bright, was braided into a coronet and held with pearl pins. A sheer black silk veil edged in fine lace covered her head.

Carefully she outlined her eyes in kohl, lightly dusted her face with powder to accentuate her pallor, and then reddened her lips. The years have not changed me, she thought, carefully searching her mirror for signs of age. There were none. Though her first youth was long gone, she could pass for a young woman of twenty-five, and it pleased her vanity and gave her confidence.

She knew exactly where to find Suleiman. Sweeping into Gulbehar's chamber, she glanced scornfully at the girl and commanded, "Leave us. I wish to speak to my son in private."

Gulbehar, not quite sure how to react, and not wishing to face down her mother-in-law in Suleiman's presence, hastily scrambled to her feet and slipped out.

Cyra turned to Suleiman. "For three weeks I have lain ill with grief, and not once have you visited me!" Her voice was cold.

"There has been much to do, mother. I had no time."

"You have time for Gulbehar!"

"Gulbehar is my kadin, and she is feeling frightened by her new position."

"I am your mother! Without me you would not have

had life. Without me you would not have had Gulbehar! Do not forget that, my young lion—even in your high place. Now, why have you not declared me valideh? Is the harem to be ruled by a mere chit of twenty-two who wears garnet glass in her hair while I am shunted off to the Pavilion of Older Women? Already your kadin has had the bad manners to demand my apartments."

Suleiman flushed. "I am truly sorry, mother. Of course it is out of the question for Gulbehar to move into the Garden Court. It is the home of my mother and my aunts as long as they choose. I shall speak to my kadin."

Cyra, somewhat mollified, changed her tactics. "Do not be harsh, my son. Gulbehar is young. She has not had the guidance of an older woman these last few years. She is spoiled and has not had the chance to mature in the company of other women, since you have no others. She has given you your only son. Is it any wonder she is puffed up?"

"You are right, mother. Living away from court has not helped, either."

"Your father had four kadins, and the lady Refet was there to guide us. Gulbehar has had no one. You must declare me valideh. Only then will I have the right to school her—and in fairness, my son, it is my right."

"I shall do it, mother!"

"Today. Before the sun sets over the Golden Horn, Suleiman."

"Before the sun sets, mother, I shall declare you the sultan valideh Hafise."

"Hafise? I am called Cyra."

"No one outside the serai knows the names of its women. Hadji Bey named you Cyra, the 'Flame.' He saw in you things no proper son would see in his mother. On the few occasions you have traveled through the city, the people have given my father's kadins names of their own. They called you the 'Fiery One.' Firousi was the 'Fair One.' Zuleika was the 'Woman of Cathay,' and Sarina was known as the 'Dark-Haired One.'"

"I have always looked up to you, mother. You have been the source of my wisdom, and so I shall publicly call you Hafise, the 'Wise One.' If you would be valideh, you will bear this name and no other."

"Very well, my son. To please you, I shall be Hafise.

I only hope I will not disappoint those who take my new name seriously."

Suleiman smiled down on her. "You have never disappointed me, mother. I know you never disappointed my father, even at the end when he was so changed. If you can please two Ottoman sultans, how can the people be disappointed?"

"Selim was right. You are a diplomat. Now, if we can make of you as good a soldier and judge, perhaps history will be kind enough to remember you. Allah! I am ravenously hungry! I have hardly eaten these last few weeks." Kissing him lightly, she reminded him, "Remember—by sunset," and she left him.

No sooner had Cyra gone than Gulbehar crept back into the room. "What did she want?"

"Her rights, which I have too long overlooked," answered Suleiman. "She will be declared sultan valideh by day's end."

Gulbehar pouted. "Oh, my lord! That is so old-fashioned!"

Suleiman looked at his honey-haired kadin with her petulant little mouth. He could not help but notice the shimmering garnet glass that his mother had so acidly mentioned, nor the fact that Gulbehar had become undisciplined. Once again, his mother was right. *She* never failed him.

"You will obey her," he said, "and give her your respect. She is the 'Crown of the Veiled Heads' and will be treated as such. Go to her this afternoon, and take Mustafa with you. Give her your felicitations on her appointment. Perhaps she will teach you how to dress. You do not look like a sultan's kadin, but like a country wife!"

Gulbehar's mouth opened in surprise. Then she began to cry. "You are cruel to me! You have never before complained of the way I dress! It is your mother who has set you against me!"

The young sultan took Gulbehar in his arms. "Do not weep. My mother likes you. It was she who pointed out that I do not dress you as the bas-kadin of a sultan should be dressed. She feels your beauty is not sufficiently adorned," soothed the young diplomat.

Gulbehar, placated, sniffed softly. "Do not look at me," she said. "My eyes are all red and swollen."

"Your eyes are beautiful, my little flower. Now I must leave you. I have work to do."

He rose, kissed her, and strode from the room. Gulbehar watched him go, then picked up a mirror and began to contemplate her reflection.

By that evening, everyone in the serai and throughout the capital knew that Suleiman had publicly declared his mother the sultan valideh Hafise. The older women of the palace were relieved. In the few weeks that Cyra had lain ill and powerless with grief, Gulbehar's ignorance had slowly begun to erode the carefully set up system of harem government.

Without firm adult authority, the young girls had grown lax in their behavior, and petty quarrels had been the order of the day. Now uncertainty was the mood among these lovely creatures. They were well aware that Cyra Hafise had a sharp eye and brooked no nonsense.

The following morning, the valideh woke to eat an enormous breakfast. Her head was clear and her mind whirling with plans. She had carefully thought before sleeping the previous night of her position now. She was the first wife of a dead sultan and the mother of the current sultan. Never again would she live and love as a normal woman might. There was nothing left but power—but such power! She was inviolate. Not only throughout the harem, but throughout the empire, her word was law. There would be times when even her son would defer to her. In a woman of lesser character this might have given rise to fearful abuses, but Cyra Hafise had been well schooled by both Hadji Bey and Selim. Her common sense prevailed.

Conferring with the agha, she decided that all maidens over the age of twenty would be honorably dismissed from the harem. They would be given as wives to those Suleiman wished to honor or reward in commemoration of his accession as head of the House of Osman. Each girl would be given a good dowry, not only of clothes and jewels but also of money. Maidens raised and schooled in the harem were highly prized as wives, and the gesture was met with general approval.

Of the remaining women, many were past the age of childbearing and other usefulness. They were retired to the

Pavilion of Older Women, where they might live out their days gossiping happily in security and comfort.

Firousi and Sarina were delighted to see Cyra her old self again. The combination of Selim's death and their friend's prostrate condition had badly frightened them. They, too, had loved Selim, though never so deeply as Cyra.

For Firousi there had always been the memory of the childhood bridegroom from whom she had been snatched on her wedding day. Sarina, on the other hand, had realized that Cyra was Selim's great love. Afraid to love a man too deeply who loved another, her passion had been reserved for her children. Nevertheless, both women had wept genuine tears at Selim's death, and they missed him greatly, for he had been the pivotal force in their lives. No longer wives of a living sultan, they wondered what the future held for them. They dreaded the thought of inactivity, but here Cyra was ahead of them.

Of the women left after the valideh's housecleaning, the older ladies were given positions of varying importance within the harem administration that Cyra now set up. Two new and very important positions were created for Selim's second and fourth kadins. Firousi became the kahya kadin, or head stewardess. Next to the valideh, she was held most in respect, and carried an imperial seal, making her a powerful ally. Sarina was honored with the new post of haznedar usta, or mistress of the treasury. She would control all the expenditures and monies for the harem, making her another strong ally for Cyra.

Of the young girls, only the cream had been kept, and more female slaves arrived at the Eski Serai every day. The most promising of the new captives joined the other gediklis, and all the maidens were reassigned to new odas, each presided over by its competent and older oda mistress.

There was to be no more idleness. Each gediklis was assigned a household task which she was expected to perform daily. Personal interests and talents were sought out and encouraged. If a girl showed a talent for music, she studied music. If her aptitude was languages, she was taught as many as she could absorb. If her forte was embroidery, she was set to work making underclothes and other fine garments for the imperial family. Kept busy, these young, nubile creatures were less apt to involve themselves in troublemaking and intrigue. Cyra Hafise had seen enough of that in Bajazet's days.

The discipline was strong. Diligence and honest effort were always rewarded. Laziness and minor misdemeanors were chastised by the oda mistresses. Major faults were brought to the attention of the valideh. Those who had appeared before the formidable Cyra Hafise had to admit that, though severe, she was fair.

However, the greatest incentive for excellence was the fact that the sultan had only one favorite. To his mother's chagrin and the frustration of the entire harem, he seemed satisfied with the bland and spoiled Gulbehar. It was the one thorn in Cyra's side.

The favorite was twenty-two. She had changed in the eight years that she had been with him. Gone was the little girl who had meekly stood before Selim. The innocent sweetness that had so charmed Cyra had disappeared, and in its place was a cloying, clinging sweetness that—it seemed to the valideh—would suffocate her son. Gulbehar was spoiled and apt to be petulant when denied her own way. Worst of all was her stupidity and complacency. Having produced little Mustafa, she was satisfied that nothing else could possibly be required of her. She spent each day in complete idleness, playing with her son and winding garnet glass in her hair.

Cyra could not understand Suleiman's fascination with the girl, but she suspected that he saw in Gulbehar what he imagined was the perfect young mother. The valideh knew that her son treasured his own childhood memories of the warm and close family at the Moonlight Serai. He also adored his own mother and probably believed that with Gulbehar the happy pattern was repeating itself.

Soon enough he would learn how unimaginative the girl was, but in the meantime the valideh decided to get her son off to war. In an effort to keep him safe for the crown, they had insulated him. Selim had seen it too late, but she would correct it now.

Choosing her time carefully, she waited until Gulbehar was unavailable to her lord for several days. Then Suleiman was asked to the Garden Court to partake in a simple family evening with his mother, aunts, and three young sisters. It was an intimate party, as of old. The slaves had been dismissed, and only Marian and Ruth remained to serve them.

Suleiman's favorite sister was Mihri-Chan, the daughter of Sarina Kadin. She was twelve now and showed every sign of being a beauty—a petite, tawny creature like her mother, with tumbling dark, Gypsy curls and clear golden eyes. The sultan had not seen her in some time and was delighted with the change from little girl to half-grown woman. She danced for him with great grace, and sang like a nightingale while accompanying herself on a small lute.

"We shall have to find you a very special husband, but not quite yet. You have such charm, little sister, I am loath to let you go."

"I want to choose my own husband, as did my sisters," replied the princess, who, like her mother, was quite outspoken.

"Have you anyone in mind?" laughed Suleiman teasingly.

"Ferhad Pasha."

Suleiman raised an eyebrow but said nothing further. Instead, he turned to his two little sisters, Nakcidil and Mahpeyker, who were now six and a half. The youngest of Selim's children knew their older brother only slightly and were in great awe of him. The sultan, however, loved children and easily overcame their shyness. His pockets seemed filled with an endless variety of treats guaranteed to delight little girls. He was also extremely facile at making funny shadows on the wall with his fingers and telling stories to go with the amusing shapes. The two tiny princesses were soon dissolved in giggles of delight and protested mightily when the hour grew late and their nurses came to take them off to bed. Sarina, Mihri-Chan, and Firousi also begged the sultan's permission to retire. Cyra and her son were alone.

Suleiman smiled at her. "And now that we are alone, my mother, what is it you would speak to me about?"

She smiled back. "Turkey's future, my son. It is several months since you became sultan, and yet you make no move to strengthen and expand our borders to the west. Your father had great plans."

"I am not a soldier, as was my father."

"Selim Khan was many things. A soldier, yes. But also

a poet, a lover, a scholar, a father—but most of all, he was a great ruler! Are you so different? Western Europe is terrified of us. How long will they remain so if my young lion becomes a house cat? If you do not move to protect our borders, they will advance into our lands beneath the blood-soaked banners of their faith and bring death, famine, and destruction to all the House of Osman has built.

"Now is the time for you to strike. They are occupied with their own internal problems and are unsuspecting."

"As sultan I must lead the army with intelligence. How can I do so when the least among my soldiers has had more battle experience than I?"

"Your father's plans are carefully written down, and it is all mapped out for you. Piri Pasha has them. All you need do is follow them. The Janissaries were loyal to him. If you are clever, they will be loyal to you. They understand your lack of experience and will be patient if you will but lead them. Now they grow restless penned within the city."

Suleiman was thoughtful. "I should have to leave Gulbehar."

"My son, it is Gulbehar's duty to await her lord. You cannot live forever as we once did in the cocoon of the Moonlight Serai. You must enter the world and be a man! Listen to me, and I will tell you how to win the loyalty of the Janissaries.

"When the drum of war is sounded and the Janissaries go to draw their pay, go among them on foot and take a handful of silver aspers from the paymaster. I know this breaks with tradition, for the sultan always takes his pay from the cavalry. However, if you do as I say, you will win them over. You will not lose the cavalry's support, since you ride with them."

Suleiman marveled at the simplicity of his mother's words and, following her suggestion, discovered she was right. The Janissaries roared their approval of his small action and vowed to follow him forever.

Studying his father's plans, Suleiman found that he had intended to take Belgrade when Rhodes had fallen. The sultan reversed the plan. Rhodes could not help Belgrade, but the Western Europeans, using Belgrade as a jumping-off spot, could aid Rhodes by attacking his flank. With Belgrade safely in Ottoman hands and Barbarossa holding sway on the seas, Rhodes could expect no help at all.

In the spring of 1521, with the snow still melting on the distant mountains, a vast army marched westward from Constantinople for Belgrade. It was actually the grand vizier, Piri Pasha, who led the main attack force. Several days after the sultan's arrival outside the city gates, its defenders fired the town and retired into its citadel. Suleiman quickly countered by ordering mines placed under the towers of the fortress.

One week later, on August 17, 1521, Belgrade surrendered. It was the sultan's twenty-seventh birthday, and he was inclined to be merciful, allowing the Hungarian defenders to cross the Danube to freedom. Bali Agha, head of the Janissaries, was made the city's governor. With the coming of the first frost of September, the Ottoman army began its long return march south to Constantinople.

Western Europe was stunned but helpless. The Holy Roman Emperor, Charles V, was busily at war with France. Henry VIII of England, after making the expected statement of distress and sympathy, went hawking with his Spanish queen. Venice, more concerned with her lucrative trade with the Turks than the fate of Belgrade, turned a blind eye. The way to Rhodes was open.

It took almost a year to plan and provision the next campaign. Then in late summer of 1522, the last of Suleiman's army landed on Rhodes, and the Turkish batteries opened up. They were expecting another quick victory but were due to be sadly disappointed.

August passed and September. The Turkish casualties were higher than expected, not only among the common soldiers but among the officers as well. Suleiman grew impatient and angry with those around him, as well as with himself. Having taken full command from the beginning, he realized his errors. Belgrade had made him overconfident. His father would never have been caught in a situation like this. Selim would have marched quickly and struck swiftly. Suleiman had overprepared.

The autumn rains came, lashing the island with their razor winds, turning the trenches into slimy bogs. It was cold, and the water seeped into everything, rotting and molding clothes and rusting equipment.

For every man killed in battle, another died of fever in

the trenches. Suleiman, fully committed now, would not retreat. Shivering in his lean-to of tree boughs, he gave orders that the ancient ruins of Rhodes be restored to make decent winter quarters for the army. The siege would continue.

October. November. Then, in early December, the sultan, whose army had been slowly squeezing the Christian circle of defense smaller and smaller, sent word to the Knights of Hospitalers of Rhodes that his original terms of surrender still stood. If Philippe Villiers de l'Isle-Adam, grand master of the knights, would surrender the island to Suleiman, de l'Isle-Adam, his men, and the Christian inhabitants of Rhodes might remain in peace. They would be free to practice their religion, and the churches would not be turned into mosques. No slaves would be taken. Should they choose to leave, they and their possessions would be transported by the Turkish navy to safety in Crete.

De l'Isle-Adam had less than a twelve-hour supply of powder left. His force was cut down to one hundred and eighty knights. There was no other choice. He surrendered, and to his complete and unbelieving surprise, the Turkish sultan kept to the terms of the surrender. De l'Isle-Adam was grudging in his respect for Suleiman and secretly liked him. He knew that had the boot been on the other foot, he would have slaughtered the Turks, and it disturbed him to think that those who fought beneath the banner of the good Lord Jesus could be less worthy than those who fought in the name of the Prophet.

The Knights Hospitalers of Rhodes, their wounds tenderly and skillfully treated by Arab doctors, were safely carried to Crete by Suleiman's ships. The Christian inhabitants of Rhodes remained. With nothing to fear from Suleiman, they were loath to leave their homes and goods, and besides, they knew that life under the Ottoman government had more advantages than life under a variety of Christian kings.

With the surrender of Rhodes, the pretense of Christian unity passed, and the Ottoman Empire gained an important base upon the sea. In Western Europe, Charles V, Francis I, and Henry VIII cast a wary eye toward the East and wondered what was to come next.

36

WHILE SULEIMAN occupied himself with war, his mother occupied herself seeking clever and beautiful girls to attract him. Already she had several in mind that she hoped would appeal to her son, for she felt his having only one kadin was not a healthy situation. There were a lovely blond Venetian, a merry, petite Provençal, a lovely, voluptuous Syrian, and an exquisite Circassian. Surely one —or, hopefully, all—of these maidens would appeal to Suleiman when he returned.

At the same time, she offered her friendship to Gulbehar. She felt no malice toward the girl and, indeed, liked her. She simply knew her son and realized that eventually he would need more than a pleasing body to delight him. Then, too, there was the question of the succession. Little Mustafa was Suleiman's only child.   . .

When the pressure of running the vast harem weighed heavily on her, Cyra would call for her litter and go to visit Nilufer and her children. These now numbered three, all boys. On one such visit, she noticed a petite girl dressed in plain garments who sat quietly sewing amid a group of maidens. There was something about the girl that struck Cyra. Despite her obviously humble rank, she laughed easily and refused to be bested by the others. Finally the valideh's curiosity overcame her.

"Who is that girl?" she asked her daughter.

"Which one, mother?"

Cyra pointed impatiently. "That one!"

"Oh. Russalanie. She's one of the Tartar captives who came in as tribute last year. Suleiman always sends me a few to supplement my staff. I never seem to have enough slaves."

"I want that girl," said Cyra, drawing a ruby ring

318

from her finger and handing it to Nilufer. "She isn't worth the price yet, but one day—or I miss my guess—she'll be worth ten times more."

"What on earth do you want her for?" Nilufer's eyes widened at her mother's look. "Surely not to tempt Suleiman? His harem is overflowing with several hundred lovely girls, and there are a dozen maidens here in my own household with more beauty than Russalanie. She is a savage!"

"You are young, my daughter, and can see only the obvious. Besides, the girl can be trained. I'll take her with me."

"In your palanquin? Really, mother! I will send her to the serai tomorrow."

"And have everyone who watches wondering why I, who have more slaves than I need, have brought one from my daughter's house? Gulbehar would waste a month's slipper money trying to buy information. No! The girl comes with me today. Then I can control the situation."

Nilufer flung up her hands. "You are impossible!"

"I am your mother, and I will thank you to remember it. Now I see why your sons lack manners. You have obviously forgotten everything I ever taught you. See that the girl is told and is ready for my departure."

Shortly afterward, Nilufer stood on the portico of her palace and watched as her mother's palanquin disappeared from sight. The valideh's conveyance was a magnificent thing. Built of solid oak, it was covered with thin sheets of hammered gold encrusted with precious jewels in a floral design, and hung with midnight-blue curtains lined in pale-yellow silk. Eight perfectly matched coal-black slaves, wearing green satin pantaloons, leopard skins across their shoulders, and heavy gold collars, carried it.

As the bearers wended their way back to the palace, Cyra coolly observed the girl, who huddled in the corner farthest from her. Finally the valideh spoke.

"They tell me your name is Russalanie."

"The other women called me that because I come from the plains of Russia. My name is Roxelana."

"How did you become a captive?"

Roxelana smiled mischievously. "I did not run fast enough," she said.

"You wanted to be caught?"

"Yes."

"Why?"

"Each year the Tartars raid the villages in our region for virgins for their tribute to the Grand Turk. Look at me! I am tiny, yet what more was there for me in my village than for any other girl? Marriage. Babies. Hard work in the fields. I am too small to do my share, and besides, I hate farming.

"We had a priest in our village who could both read and write. He taught me. I read the few books he owned, and learned there was more in the world than my village could offer. Then one day a peddler came, and he had been in Constantinople. He told wonderful stories of how the girls in the sultan's harem lived lives of great luxury and ease. Of course the other girls thought it was a wicked, ungodly life, but I didn't.

"So, when the Tartars came last year and all the women ran to hide, I waited until the last moment to run. Naturally, I was caught." She shrugged and laughed. "And look at me now! Instead of being pampered in the sultan's harem, I am the humblest of slaves in his sister's house. I would have been better off in my own village!"

"You are an absolute barbarian and are not fit to enter my son's harem now, but perhaps someday you will be. You will not return to my daughter's home. You have a great deal to learn before I can even consider allowing my son to see you."

Roxelana's eyes flashed at the valideh's words, but she said nothing. Good, thought Cyra. They have not broken her spirit, but she is wise enough to hold her tongue. Aloud, Cyra said, "You read and write your own language. I see you have learned Turkish, too, though your accent is atrocious. This is a good start, my child. We will work on that first. What else can you do?"

"I am told I embroider well." She drew a small square of silk from her bodice and gave it to the valideh. The little cloth was covered with pretty fruits and flowers, cleverly done animals, and castles.

Cyra nodded. "I shall put you in the care of the keeper of the linen. You have much to learn, but if you trust me, you may well rise to a high position in your world.

You must be discreet and never draw attention to yourself. Obey the eunuchs and the women in charge. We shall find your talents and develop them until there is no girl in the harem who is as accomplished as you. Then possibly you may attract the sultan. Do you sing?"

"A bit."

"A bit, *my lady.* Your manners are bad! However, you are not, I can see, a stupid girl, Roxelana. You will learn quickly, I am sure."

"To gain all that you promise, my lady, I will study hard!"

"I promise you nothing, child. I have said only that with work it is within the realm of the possible. Obey me, and at the proper time you will be brought to my son's attention. If we move too soon and you displease him, there is no second chance. Do you understand me?"

The girl nodded.

"Good! Now, the first improvement we shall make is your name. Roxelana. Russalanie. It is not Turkish. From this moment on, you will answer to the name Khurrem. I have on several occasions watched you at my daughter's home. You laugh easily and are cheerful and merry. Khurrem means the 'Laughing One.'"

Khurrem smiled happily. "Thank you, my lady. I like it!"

Cyra leaned forward and peered through the curtains of the palanquin. They were approaching the palace. "One last thing," she said. "I will show you no obvious mark of favor in the serai, but that does not mean I am not watching and encouraging you. Now sit back and be silent. We are almost home."

The bearers trotted their burden through the gates of the Eski Serai and went directly to the Garden Court. Once inside her apartments, Cyra sent for the keeper of the linen, a motherly woman in her early fifties. Rising as the lady entered, she held out her hands in greeting. "Ah, Cervi! How good it is to see you. I wanted to tell you how exquisite the undergarments your girls did for me were, but alas, I am so busy!" Opening a casket by her side, she paused for a moment and then casually lifted out a rope of creamy pearls with the faintest hint of pink in them, and slipped them over the woman's neck. "A small token. Sit down, and Ruth will bring us some coffee."

The keeper of the linen, flustered and delighted at the same time, settled herself while happily fingering the pearls. Coffee was brought, and, pouring, the valideh handed her a tiny enameled cup. For a while they chatted idly, then Cyra asked, "How many girls are in your oda, Cervi?"

"Five, madam. Most of the maidens are not clever enough with a needle to suit me. Perhaps I am over-critical, though," she apologized.

Cyra handed her the silken square that Khurrem had embroidered. "What do you think of this work?"

Cervi took the cloth and examined it carefully. "It is very good, madam. Very good indeed."

Cyra called to Marian, "Send the slave Khurrem to me." She turned back to Cervi. "If you feel the work is truly good, you may have this girl in your oda. There could possibly be bigger things in store for her, and you would certainly profit by having an oda that produced a favorite."

Cervi nodded in agreement as the girl entered, bowed to her and the valideh, and stood quietly, her eyes lowered modestly, her hands folded.

"Ah," smiled Cyra. "This is Khurrem. She is one of the Tartar captives brought in as tribute last year. She has been doing simple sewing at my daughter's home, but when I saw how clever her embroidery was, I brought her back. Though she is clever with her needle, she is incredibly ignorant in all other ways. I think under your care she may become an accomplished maiden."

Cervi knew she had no real choice. At least the girl was clever with her needle, and, as the valideh had pointed out, there were distinct advantages in being in charge of a possible favorite. Cervi had no doubt that if Cyra Hafise wanted this girl to become the sultan's kadin, she would indeed become his kadin.

"I am pleased to cooperate with you, my lady," Cervi said.

"Khurrem is to be treated like any other maiden, Cervi. Show her no favor unless she merits it, and punish her when she deserves it. I will not have her spoiled."

"Of course, madam."

"And, Cervi, make no mention of this. Do you understand me? She is simply a clever seamstress."

Cervi smiled. "Yes, madam. I understand you perfectly."

Such was the entrance into the harem of the "Laughing One."

On the first day that Cervi's oda was scheduled for the baths, the valideh secreted herself in a hidden room overlooking the gediklis' bathing area in order to get a good look at her purchase. She was not disappointed.

Khurrem was a blond, and after her hair had been scrubbed and rinsed several times with lemon juice, it shone bright as a gold piece. It was a wonderful foil for her heart-shaped face with its little pointed chin and large, smoky-violet eyes.

Her figure was perfection. Standing barely an inch over five feet, she had firm, globe-shaped breasts, a tiny waist, and round, rosy buttocks. Her slender legs were well-shaped and surprisingly long for her stature. Complementing her lovely hair, eyes, and figure was her creamy skin color.

As the months slipped by, Khurrem improved in many ways. She learned to speak Turkish smoothly in her soft, rich voice. As clever as she was with a needle, she was more so with music. She learned to play both the lute and the guitar and had an amusing way of tapping her heels while singing to her own accompaniment. Her manners became flawless, and, taking the valideh's advice, she seemed never to appear twice in the same costume. Actually this was not true, for as a mere gediklis the Russian girl had a small wardrobe, but she did have a knack of adding small touches that distinguished and gave variety to her clothes.

If she had one fault, it was that she never forgot a slight. When whipped for a misdemeanor, she would not weep like the other girls; instead, she would rise and stare at her tormentor for a moment with a look that clearly said, "I will not forget." Still, Cyra Hafise was pleased with Khurrem's progress and sure she had found a girl to lure Suleiman from Gulbehar's constant attentions.

With Belgrade and Rhodes safely within the Ottoman fold, Suleiman returned to his capital. He had changed, and Cyra was delighted. Two years of campaigning had turned her polite, intellectual, and somewhat hesitant son into a man of strength. He now understood the need for conquest in order to protect his borders, and was certainly capable of ruling an empire.

His people welcomed him joyously, his family warmly. Being family-oriented, he spent his first evening at home within his mother's court. This seeming act of respect was highly approved by the Turks, but the truth was that Suleiman wished to speak of all he had done and was planning to do, and Gulbehar was simply not a good audience for such talk.

The valideh felt genuine sympathy for her son's kadin, who, having been educated only in the arts of physically pleasing a man, thought that this was enough. Cyra knew that the women most successful with their lords were the ones who appealed to them mentally as well as physically. She also knew that Gulbehar would never comprehend this.

As the evening drew to a close, Suleiman turned to Mihri-Chan and said, "You are to be married in the summer, my sister."

"Did I not tell you," snapped the little firebrand, "that I will choose my own husband as did my sisters?"

"Then you refuse your sultan's choice?"

"I do!"

"Ferhad Pasha will be most disappointed," murmured the sultan with mock sadness.

A look of joy lit Mihri-Chan's golden-brown eyes. "Ferhad Pasha! You have chosen Ferhad Pasha as my husband?"

Smiling, Suleiman nodded.

"Oh, my sultan! I hear and obey!" cried the happy princess. Then she launched herself at her brother, grabbed a handful of his dark hair, and pulled hard. "You beast! You frightened me to death! I thought you were foisting me off on some dusty old emir! How could you terrify me so? You don't love me at all!"

Laughing, the sultan loosened her grip on his hair and, slipping a sweetmeat into the offending hand, said to

Sarina. "Aunt, this maiden's manners are appalling. Perhaps she is not ready for marriage."

Sarina, joining in the game, replied, "I cannot say I disagree with you, Suleiman, but she is growing old—fifteen this March—and if we do not marry her off now, we shall have to retire her to the Pavilion of Older Women."

Mihri-Chan looked from her mother to her brother. Both wore grave faces, and suddenly she wondered if they could be serious. "Ohhh! I'll be good, I promise!" she wailed.

Suleiman hugged her warmly. "I know, little sister," he said reassuringly. "You will have your own way, but tell me, for I die of curiosity, why did you set your heart on Ferhad Pasha? You don't know him."

"I saw him once," answered the princess, "but," she quickly added, "he did not see me. He was walking in our father's garden. They stopped to talk, and I was hidden nearby in the rosebushes. He is very handsome—and brave, too. I thought it was wonderful how he sent you the rebel Ghazali's head from Syria when you first became sultan."

"Yes," said her brother dryly, "a most courteous gift."

So, the plans were set in motion for the wedding of the sultan's fourth sister.

This was the first chance Suleiman had had since becoming sultan to show his hospitality, and the wedding was magnificent. Throughout the entire empire, lawbreakers were pardoned. In all the major cities, government-sponsored feasts were held, and each girl of fifteen who chose to marry on the same day as Mihri-Chan was given a dowry of ten gold pieces, a bolt of fine cloth, and a small pearl necklace. To the wedding feast came officials, both high and low, of the Ottoman government—and, for the first time in Turkish history, distinguished Western European foreigners who resided in the city. Suleiman realized the advantages of having his wealth reported to Charles V, Francis I, and Henry VII by their nationals.

The wedding day was beautiful. The bride was radiant in her soft garments of willow-green silk, with a fortune in diamonds and pearls on her pelisse. The bridegroom, a tall, handsome man with an elegant clipped moustache, seemed happy and pleased—and well he might. Not only had he had the luck to marry his sultan's favorite sister, but Suleiman's gift to him had been the position of third vizier, and he had been assigned the pashalik of Syria. After the five-day celebration, the bridal couple would sail east under the protection of Khair ad-Din's fleet.

The ship that would carry them from Constantinople had been especially outfitted for the trip. Decorated with gold and silver leaf, its decks were enameled in bright colors. Great purple sails billowed from its silver masts, the tops of which flew green pennants. In the holds beneath the deck only a small area had been set aside for the hapless crew. The rest of the space bulged with wedding presents and Mihri-Chan's household goods. Only a minimum of slaves would travel with the third vizier and his bride. A separate ship would carry the bulk of their household servants.

Toward the stern of the ship, a spacious cabin had been constructed for the bridal pair. Of finest cedar, it was trimmed with gold and hung with silken curtains of crimson and sea-green. Jeweled lamps bobbed on solid silver chains hanging from the beams.

The sultan and the imperial family bade Mihri-Chan and Ferhad Pasha a private farewell in the Yeni Serai. The young princess was obviously blissfully happy, but Sarina Kadin was hard put to keep a cheerful face. Happy as she was for her daughter, she was saddened to have her only child going so far from Constantinople.

Then the yellow barge was ready, and, after a flurry of swift good-byes, they were gone—bobbing across the sparkling, deep-blue waters of the Bosporus to the waiting ship.

37

Now CAME A SHORT PERIOD of relative stability and peace for Turkey. The Janissaries, sated for the time being with Belgrade and Rhodes, were silent. Piri Pasha was honorably retired, and Ibrahim Pasha was named grand vizier, to the delight of both the valideh and her daughter, Nilufer. The graybeards, of course, grumbled at the sultan's choice, and thought the Greek too young—but, the sultan would be obeyed.

Suleiman now had time to spend with Gulbehar and their son. Of late, Cyra had noticed his eyes were more for little Mustafa than for his kadin. With delight she realized that the time had come when her son might be tempted by a female other than the soft and foolish Gulbehar. Khurrem began to be seen more in the valideh's company.

Then one day, while visiting his mother, Suleiman laughed so hard at an amusing song sung by the petite Russian that tears rolled down his cheeks. At a barely perceptible sign from the valideh, the girl handed her lord an embroidered silk handerchief so that he might wipe his eyes. Afterward, he noticed the lovely design on the cloth, and Cyra said, "Khurrem made it. She is wondrously clever with her needle."

"You will make all my handkerchiefs from now on, Khurrem," said Suleiman graciously.

Cyra was delighted. Her protégé had been noticed. A small compliment, true—but recognition, nevertheless. In the next few weeks Khurrem could be seen among the maidens who sometimes accompanied the sultan on his walks through the palace grounds. The valideh warned the girl, "Be modest at all times. Your beauty cannot fail to speak for you. I know my son. Already he is intrigued by you. If you are clever, he will want to know more."

Then came an evening when Suleiman, feeling moody, asked that Khurrem be sent to sing her merry songs to him. She remained in the sultan's quarters for almost three hours, and those who attended the sultan whispered it was more than the girl's singing that attracted him. There was now no doubt—Khurrem was "in the eye" of the sultan.

She was immediately elevated to the rank of guzdeh and given a small apartment of her own, consisting of a small anteroom and a bedchamber. A personal slave was assigned to care for her needs.

Cyra was jubilant, but Marian warned, "Beware, my dearest lady. That little cat has long, sharp claws."

Cyra paid little heed to her old slave's words, but instead began to plan for the night when Khurrem would be called to her lord's couch. It could not be for at least several weeks, she knew. It would be bad manners for the sultan to appear overeager, and then, too, the court astrologer had to be consulted.

Remembering her own happy bridal night, the valideh decided that Suleiman's and Khurrem's would be as happy as hers and Selim's had been. Determined that Khurrem should be the first to replace Gulbehar in her son's affections, she spared no effort.

Each day the Russian guzdeh was bathed in rosewater and massaged with precious oils distilled from wild flowers. Her hands and feet were creamed until they were soft and whiter than white. There was not a square centimeter of Khurrem's skin that did not make silk seem rough in comparison.

Her diet was carefully supervised by the valideh herself. The new guzdeh must walk in Cyra Hafise's private park two hours each day to keep her young muscles firm and supple.

The weeks went by, and then one afternoon Khurrem burst into the valideh's apartment waving a yellow silk handkerchief and crying, "It has come, madam! The summons has come! I am called to my lord's couch Friday—tomorrow night!"

It was a bad moment. Gulbehar had chosen that same

afternoon to visit with her mother-in-law. The young bas-
kadin was furious and hysterical by turns.

"I hate her! I hope she dies in childbirth!"

"But why? You do not even know her," replied the
valideh.

"I do not trust her."

"Nonsense!" snapped Cyra. "You are jealous. It is that
simple, and I will not stand for it! On Friday after
noonday prayers, you will, as your position demands, escort Khurrem to the bridal bath."

Gulbehar raised her tear-stained face to Cyra. "You
have been behind the Russian girl from the start. Do not
deny it, for I know it is true. There will come a time
when you will regret this intrigue. Khurrem is ambitious,
and one day her ambition will reach out to destroy even
you."

Cyra was distressed. Despite the fact she considered
Gulbehar a silly creature, she was fond of her and did not
wish to see her upset. The following day, however, Cyra's
sympathy turned to annoyance when Gulbehar refused to
leave her apartments, claiming illness.

Never had the valideh felt more angry. She had been
openly and publicly defied by her son's wife. As ruler of
the harem, she could not allow it. Her orders were swift.
Guards were posted about Gulbehar Kadin's apartments
until further notice. No one inside would be permitted to
come or go, and, harshest of all, Prince Mustafa was removed from his mother's care and placed in the custody
of his grandmother.

Noon prayers over, the valideh's servants hurried to
dress their mistress in her most elegant clothes.

Cyra had chosen a magnificent velvet tunic dress the
color of ripe apricots, its broad front panel embroidered
in gold thread and topazes. Over this she wore a cloth-of-
gold cloak fastened with an enormous emerald clasp. Her
hair, fashioned as a coronet, was topped by an ornate gold
crown studded with topazes, diamonds, and emeralds.
From it flowed a golden gauze veil. Since Gulbehar would
not escort Khurrem to the baths, Cyra would honor the
new guzdeh by doing so.

The ceremonial route would take them past the bas-
kadin's windows, and the valideh had given orders that
Gulbehar was to be made to stand and watch the festive

procession. Having developed the habit of seeing out of the
corners of her eyes while appearing to face straight ahead,
she briefly viewed with annoyance her daughter-in-law's
puffy, tear-swollen face as they glided by.

That evening, Cyra rehearsed Khurrem a final time in
the procedure for entering Suleiman's bed. Khurrem
laughed. "It's so silly," she said. "Are you going to tell me
you entered Sultan Selim's bed that way?"

The valideh secretly agreed with her pupil but replied
tartly, "It is custom and a mark of respect. If my son has
one weakness, it is his strict observance of tradition. When
you have entered the sultan's bedchamber, make your
obeisance. Show me."

Khurrem flung herself gracefully to the floor, her golden
head touching the rug.

"Excellent! Next, the eunuch who accompanies you will
remove your garments and depart. When this has been
done, go to the foot of the imperial couch. Take the coverlet in your hand—so—and place the corner of it first to
your forehead, secondly to your lips. Only then may you
enter the bed. Do so by crawling up from the foot until
you are level with the sultan."

"I shall do this only once," said Khurrem. "In the future
when I visit the sultan, I will not humble myself in such a
debasing way."

"*If* you go again, my dear. Unless you follow protocol
and your manners are flawless, you will repel my son. You
must fascinate him completely, or there will be no second
time. Remember that when you are tempted to let your
pride overrule your common sense. If you displease Suleiman, you will receive no help from me, and certainly
Gulbehar will enjoy adding to your humiliation. Is this not
the moment you dreamed of back in your barbarian village? Will you allow pride to destroy it? If you do, then I
have greatly misjudged you, my daughter."

Khurrem's smoky-violet eyes filled with tears of distress,
Cyra knew she had made her point. The valideh
cupped the girl's heart-shaped face in her hands. "Do not
weep, child. Conduct yourself as I have taught you, and
you cannot fail to win my son." She gently dabbed at the
girl's eyes with her own handkerchief. "Now return to your
chamber. In two hours I shall come to escort you to your
lord. I shall send Marian and Ruth to help you dress."

Khurrem fell on her knees and, catching the valideh's
hand, kissed it fervently. "Go," said Cyra, pulling her
hand away. Allah in His Paradise, the girl made her feel
old! Power was a marvelous toy, and she thoroughly enjoyed it, but at times like these a longing for the hills of
her native land reared its head in a way she had never felt
before.

At a few minutes to ten o'clock that evening, Cyra
Hafise was leaving her apartments when there came a terrible wailing sound. The startled valideh sent a eunuch to
discover the source of the appalling noise. He returned to
say that Gulbehar, garbed in black, had locked herself in
her bedchamber and was now weeping.

Cyra frowned angrily. "She should be beaten, but I suppose that would only worsen things." She turned to the
eunuch. "Break the door to Gulbehar's bedchamber open,
and bind and gag her."

The eunuch nodded and hurried to carry out the
valideh's orders. He had been in the harem a long time
and knew the customs surrounding the sultan's romantic
liaisons. Every door and window in the harem must be
shut. Only the way from the favorite lady's chamber to the
sultan's apartment was left open. Above all, there must be
silence. Nothing must distract Suleiman and his chosen
one from their pleasure.

Shortly afterward, Cyra entered Khurrem's chamber
and, drawing from her pocket a necklace of golden flowers
studded with tiny pink diamond chips, fastened it about
the surprised girl's neck.

"Madam," whispered Khurrem, "it is beautiful."

"Its owner far outshines it," replied the valideh.

She stood while her charge was placed in the golden litter, and, escorting it to the doors of her son's quarters,
said to the Russian, "May you know only joy, my daughter." The litter entered, and the doors to the sultan's suite
closed.

Returning to her own quarters, Cyra stopped at
Gulbehar's apartments. The kadin's attendants, huddled
around the tiled corner stove, turned frightened faces to
the sultan's mother. The valideh entered the bedroom and
stood for a minute, staring down at the younger woman.

"Cut her bonds," she commanded the kadin's eunuch,
"and remove the gag."

Gulbehar sat up and began to rub her wrists.

"Khurrem is now with her lord and master," began the valideh.

Gulbehar shrieked wildly.

Cyra raised her hand and slapped the girl. "Be silent!" She turned to the eunuch. "Leave us. I will speak with Gulbehar Kadin alone." She turned to the girl. "Control yourself! Khurrem is now a fact. Face it!"

Gulbehar's voice was low. "I am lost."

Cyra was becoming more annoyed as the minutes slipped by. "You are still the sultan's bas-kadin and mother of his heir," she snapped. "This day you have behaved disgracefully, and you have failed in your duties. Khurrem is but the first of my son's harem to grace his couch. There will be others, but no matter the number, it is your son who will follow my son—may Allah grant that be many years hence."

"Ah, my mother," replied Gulbehar sadly, "do you think I would have objected to my lord's taking another woman to his couch if he had made the choice himself?"

"But he did make the choice. From his entire harem he singled out Khurrem."

"No. You chose her. You placed her strategically, and trained her, and favored her. How little you know this man who is your son. For eleven years I have held him, and I knew he was bored with me, though his fondness for me would never diminish. Soon he would have chosen another maiden to share his bed, and I would have rejoiced that he found joy. But you have given him a viper. Khurrem is ambitious and cruel. She will never be satisfied with being merely the second kadin."

"How can you say that Khurrem is cruel? Ambitious, I know, but certainly not cruel."

"Your spies have obviously not told you of what your protégée did to the keeper of the linens. When Khurrem became a guzdeh, she had her eunuch force Cervi to kneel before her, and then she placed her foot upon the woman's neck. This was not cruel?"

Cyra had not known of this incident but pretended she did. "A childish prank," she said.

"Khurrem will try to destroy us all," repeated Gulbehar.

"Bah! I am mistress here, and I promise you that she will not harm you or your little Mustafa."

The morning following the Russian's first visit to her lord, Cyra joined her pupil for coffee, and was thus there when the sultan's gifts arrived. Wrapped in a handkerchief of gold-embroidered cloth with diamonds and rubies, they were outrageously extravagant. By tradition, Suleiman should have included among his gifts one bag of gold coins. He sent two. There was a sapphire the size of an apricot that hung from a thin gold chain, a necklace and earrings of deep-purple amethysts, a book of Persian love poems, a nightingale in a silver cage, and a small guitar covered in gold leaf and studded with pearls and turquoises.

Several weeks later, Khurrem announced to Cyra that she was with child. Remembering her conversation with Gulbehar, the sultan's mother quietly increased her grandson's bodyguards and added a food taster to his suite.

As for Suleiman, he was ecstatic over the prospect of becoming a father once again. Gulbehar's barrenness had given rise to doubts he dared not voice even to himself. He had quickly fallen under Khurrem's spell, and was so besotted with her that he forgot all else. During the months that followed, Suleiman would not take another maiden despite Khurrem's condition. Nor did he visit Gulbehar at night, though he often visited her suite during the day.

Cyra was furious. "By introducing Khurrem into Suleiman's bed, I was trying to keep him from being influenced by one woman, but he has only exchanged a soft, sweet fool for an ambitious beauty. Allah! what am I to do?"

"This is what comes of your meddling," scolded Marian, "but you need not fear. As long as you live, Suleiman will heed you above all others."

"That is small comfort, my friend. I would have him be a man as his father was. If he is influenced by his women, how long before he gives me only a mother's respect but heeds not my words? I cannot let that happen!"

As Khurrem became swollen with her pregnancy and less attractive to the fastidious eye of the sultan, she begged Suleiman's permission to withdraw to the lake kiosk. With Khurrem less available, the valideh firmly reasserted her influence with her son.

In the autumn of 1524, Khurrem presented Suleiman with their first child, a son named Selim. Eleven and a half months later, another son, Bajazet, was born to the

Russian. He was followed by his sister, Mihrmah, and a third brother, Jahangir.

With three healthy sons—young Mustafa and the little prince Selim and Bajazet—the line of Osman was assured. Little Jahangir, born sickly and a hunchback, could never become sultan, since the law forbade the anointing of a deformed man.

However, animosity grew daily between Gulbehar and Khurrem. And as if the trouble between Suleiman's two kadins were not enough, Cyra had another—and to her mind, more serious—worry. Firousi was not well. The court physician, Alaeddin Cerdet, diagnosed a heart difficulty, complicated by a retention of fluids. If she were not taken away from her duties as kahya kadin and the constant excitement of the court, she could easily die.

The solution was, of course, painfully simple. The valideh discussed it thoroughly with Hale and Guzel, and in the end it was decided that Firousi would leave the Eski Serai to live with Hale and her family. Riza ben Ismet, Hale's husband, warmed Cyra's heart with his enthusiasm. Now, he told the sultan valideh, he would have three beautiful blonds in his house—his wife, his daughter, and his mother-in-law—and he would, of course, be the most envied man in the empire. My lady Cyra was not to worry, either, he continued, for he would personally see that Firousi Kadin followed the diet prescribed by Alaeddin Cerdet and took plenty of exercise.

Unfortunately, Firousi was not inclined to be cooperative in this matter. "How," she asked Cyra, her turquoise eyes flashing, "how can you send me away?"

"How can I not? You have heard the doctor's diagnosis."

"We have been together since the very beginning. We have never been separated since that one time you and Zuleika went to Persia with our lord Selim. When you returned, we vowed never again would we be apart."

"Zuleika is dead. Dead, because I allowed her to go into a plague-infested court to nurse Hassan and Nureddin. I could have forbidden it and sent slaves, but I allowed my heart to overrule my head, and Zuleika died before her time because of my weakness. I will not allow you to die because within my heart I want you to stay. After Selim died and Suleiman made me sultan valideh, I dreamed of

you and Sarina and I growing old together in peace and
contentment, but how can I be content if I must worry
about your health? I will not let you die, Firousi! I ask
you, my dearest friend, to leave the Eski Serai and live
with Hale and her family. But if you will not go voluntar-
ily, I shall order it in my capacity as sultan valideh. I will
not let you die! I will not!"

Firousi stared in amazement at Cyra. She had rarely
seen her friend cry in all the years they had been together,
but now the tears were pouring down Cyra's cheeks.
Wordlessly, she clasped Cyra to her bosom and, sighing
deeply, said simply, "I shall go."

The sultan's troubles with the women in his family increased. His brother-in-law Ferhad Pasha was recalled
from Syria for misuse of his power. He had used his position to execute several personal enemies. Suleiman, like
Selim, scrupulously upheld the law, and so Ferhad was
dismissed and retired to his estates along the sea.

The valideh, ever watchful of her son's best interests,
knew that the dashing Ferhad Pasha would not stay quiet
long. She argued fiercely for the pasha's reinstatement.
"He has a well of energy. It is better that that energy work
for us, not against us. You cannot expect the wild horse to
pull the plow. It is better to turn him loose among our
enemies and cause confusion."

Suleiman was reluctant. "My instinct tells me that
Ferhad is hungry for, yet corrupted by, power. If I trust
him again, he will betray me again."

"As Allah wills it," replied Cyra. "But should this happen, you will execute him, and who will say you have
done wrong? In the meantime, you must think of your sister Mihri-Chan. Is this how you would treat her now that
she is finally with child?"

"I did not know. Very well, I will reassign Ferhad for
the sake of my sister and their unborn son, but only to a
small post somewhere in his homeland along the Danube.
If he does well and there is no repetition of his old tricks,
I shall restore him completely. However, Mihri-Chan may
not join him until after the birth of my nephew. She will
move back into the harem with her mother."

Mihri-Chan was not pleased to hear that she must
remain in Constantinople, but suffered it for her husband's

sake. At their parting, Ferhad said tenderly to her, "When I return, the first thing I would see as I enter the palace is you, my love, holding our son within your soft arms."

In seven months' time, Mihri-Chan was safely delivered of a healthy son, who was named Suleiman in honor of his uncle. Three months later, Ferhad Pasha rode through the gates of the palace, and the first thing that he did see was his wife, their son nestled in her soft arms. One hour later, Ferhad Pasha was dead—judged and bowstringed by order of the sultan, who had recalled him for the very abuse of power that had brought him back from Syria.

That night Suleiman entered his mother's court and was accosted by his sister, now garbed in black. For a long moment they stared at one another, and finally Mihri-Chan spoke. "I hope it will not be long before I wear mourning for you, my *beloved* brother." Then, turning, she melted into the night. In the morning they found her dead. Mihri-Chan had swallowed poison.

Desolate, Suleiman retired to his quarters and wept bitterly. His sadness was increased by the fact that Sarina, resigning her position as haznedar usta, had requested his permission to take her orphaned grandson and leave the serai. His sister Guzel had offered them a home. Sarina was eager to go, and Suleiman could not refuse her.

Taking her leave of him, she somewhat eased his guilt. "Do not grieve, my nephew. Mihri-Chan was grief-stricken. She would not have done it otherwise."

"She would be alive today, aunt, if I had forgiven Ferhad."

Sarina surprised him. "Ferhad was a mad dog, and mad dogs must be killed. Ah, do not stare so. It is true. My daughter told me many things. Her weakness was that she loved him consumingly. Better that Ferhad remained a soldier, for power corrupted him. He would not have stopped until all of Turkey was embroiled in civil war. I will always be near should you need the services of this old woman. Perhaps in a few years' time little Suleiman will enter the Princes' School. There he may be trained for service to his sultan and thus wipe away his father's shame."

They embraced, and he watched as she walked slowly from his sight. Like his mother, Suleiman questioned the quick passage of time. Only yesterday Sarina had been a slim maiden, her chestnut curls shaking, her golden eyes flashing as she scolded and chased him from her tulip beds. Now the chestnut hair was steel-gray and the lovely golden eyes faded and sad. Lines of grief and age marked the once-smooth face. She was growing old, and he had not noticed it until today.

Aside from his mother and Firousi, Sarina was his last link with the past. His father, his grandfather, Zuleika Kadin, the lady Refet, Hadji Bey, and his brothers were all dead. And the silvery-blond Firousi, like Sarina, had gone from the serai to live with her daughter Hale.

Sighing, he realized that he, too, was growing older— he would be thirty-two on his next birthday. It was early in the year 1526, and the battle for Hungary loomed ahead.

38

As USUAL, the princes of Western Europe were embroiled in their own petty quarrels. Charles V, the Holy Roman Emperor, had trouble on three fronts. In Spain, the Moors were regrouping and stubbornly resisting the church's efforts at conversion. In Germany, Martin Luther had not only the peasants but the landed aristocracy on his side, and all was in turmoil. To the south, France fought the emperor's troops for possession of northern Italy, and only the capture of the French king, Francis I, ended the conflict.

To the east, the Hungarians had held off the invading Turks for five years. Exhausted, they now appealed to Charles V, but despite the fact that Charles's sister Mary was married to the Hungarian king, Louis, the Holy Roman Emperor demurred and dragged his royal feet. He was far too occupied with his own troubles to be overly concerned with those of his brother-in-law.

In August 1526, Suleiman led his men against the Hungarians at the village of Mohács. He won a sweeping victory which he quickly followed by taking the Hungarian capital of Buda. The Ottoman Empire now reached to within one hundred and forty miles, as the crow flies, from Vienna. The pashas counseled pressing onward into the soft underbelly of Europe, but winter was coming, and Suleiman returned home to Constantinople instead.

Earlier in the year, the sultan had received a letter from the queen mother of France, who asked his help in gaining the release of her son. On learning of this, Charles V released Francis, but not without gaining heavy concessions, claiming he had been forced to sign them. He also

disavowed his friendship with Suleiman and declared he
would lead a Crusade against the infidel Turk.

Still, Suleiman demurred on pressing further into Europe. The young diplomat who had become such a great
soldier was again becoming a diplomat. Cyra disagreed.
Only if he took Vienna would the rulers of Western Europe view the Ottoman sultan seriously. But Suleiman was
adamant. He hoped to gain the friendship of the West by
remaining at peace.

Unfortunately, the less sophisticated rulers of Christian
Europe could not see the wisdom of an alliance with the
Ottoman Empire. In the name of their religion they insulted and harried the Turks until Suleiman was forced
to march on Vienna in order to protect his western boundaries.

For several weeks he had attempted to lay siege to the
city, but for the first time in his military career he was
faced with a well-trained Christian army. Fortifying
Vienna, its defenders retreated within and held the sultan
at bay for twelve days.

Arriving at the city in high spirits, Suleiman had sent
the following greeting to the Austrians: "On the third
day I shall eat breakfast within your walls." On the
afternoon of the third day, the Austrian commander,
Nicholas, count of Salm, sent a message back to the sultan.
It read: "Your breakfast is getting cold."

At any other time Suleiman would have laughed, but
winter was coming on. He remembered the terrible winter
siege of Rhodes. Fodder for the horses was getting scarce,
and within days the snows would begin blocking the
mountain passes back to Turkey. His lines of supply cut,
he would be forced to defend himself instead of attacking
the Austrians.

The sultan did not hesitate. Giving the order to pull out,
he marched his army home, where another defeat of
sorts awaited him. He could not keep peace even in his
own harem. His kadins had become openly hostile to
one another, and only the strength of the valideh prevented the serai from splitting into two camps.

For several years, Cyra had constantly changed attendants in the suites of her daughter-in-law's to prevent them
from forming friendships that might grow into partisan-
ship. Though this policy had helped to some extent, it

had not prevented Khurrem from attracting allies. Who could resist the beautiful blond Russian, compared to the sulky, embittered Gulbehar?

One morning the valideh and the two kadins were seated out-of-doors taking advantage of the late autumn sunshine when Prince Selim, a short, pudgy child of six, came howling to his mother.

"Mustafa pushed me down," he wailed, wiping his runny nose on his sleeve—a habit Cyra found disgusting and had tried without success to eradicate.

Five-year-old Bajazet trotted up. "No, he didn't. We were playing tag, and Selim fell over his own feet as Mustafa reached to tag him. He always ducks to avoid being 'it,' but this time he fell and skinned his knee on a stone."

Prince Selim grew red in the face. "Liar Liar!" he shrieked at his younger brother. "You always take his part! When I am sultan, the first thing I'll do is cut off your head!" He punctuated this last remark by a chopping motion of his hand, and then, giving Bajazet a shove that sent him sprawling on the lawn, ran off. The younger prince scrambled to his feet and gave chase.

Gulbehar turned slowly to face Khurrem. "So! You've been telling your fat little brat he is to be sultan. How dare you?! Mustafa is his father's heir! *Mustafa, not Selim!* It was settled years ago."

"Was it?" drawled Khurrem. "I do not recall Suleiman officially and openly declaring Mustafa his heir. Why should he? Simply because you had the good fortune to bear *my* dearest lord a child before I did is no reason for making your son heir rather than my Selim."

"*I* am the bas-kadin, and so acknowledged by our lord. Is your knowledge of Turkish still so poor, foreigner, that you do not know that bas-kadin means 'mother of the heir'?"

"I always thought it meant 'favorite,' though you are certainly not that. My many children are proof of my lord's love for me."

"Your children?" replied Gulbehar. "Three sons, and only one of them fit to bear the title of prince. As for the other two, one is an overfed, overindulged, overbearing little monster, and the other a cripple! Then we have your precious daughter, a wise child who screams at the very

sight of you. Bajazet is the only decent son you have
spawned. If our lord Suleiman had coupled with a dog,
the bitch would have produced a better litter than you!"

Cyra saw it coming but could not rise quickly enough to
prevent it. Like a springing tigress, Khurrem attacked
Gulbehar. Screaming threats, the bas-kadin fought back,
but, though smaller, Khurrem was the better fighter. She
kicked, gouged, pummeled, and used her nails to great
effect.

Frantically, over the screams of the two women, the
valideh called to the eunuchs, who came running to separate the sultan's wives. In that last moment, Gulbehar
struck her only real blow. As the eunuchs pinioning the
second kadin's arms pulled her up off the bas-kadin,
Gulbehar reached up and raked her long red nails down
the Russian girl's face. Khurrem screamed wildly in rage
as she was borne off, still struggling, to her own apartments. Gulbehar, brushing aside the eunuch's hand, rose
and walked silently away.

Cyra could not conceal the incident, for there had been
far too many witnesses, but she must try. Hurrying indoors, she sent for the agha kislar. He had already
heard.

"Bribe everyone you can," she told him. "Word of this
shameful incident must not go beyond the palace walls."

"Madam"—his brown face puckered like a baby's—
"madam, I do not know if I can. Already the tale runs
through the palace as a virgin runs from marauding soldiers."

"You must try, Anber Bey. If it is known that my son
cannot keep peace in his own household, he will lose
face. This must not happen!"

She had intended to keep this domestic crisis a secret
from Suleiman but was forced to speak to him that very
night. Taking coffee with his mother, as was his habit, the
sultan sent a message to Khurrem that he desired her presence later in the evening. Khurrem sent back the message
that she could not possibly appear before her lord when
she was so disfigured.

Cyra could not help but laugh at the cleverness of her
Russian daughter-in-law. The valideh had personally seen
to Khurrem's wounds. The scratches on her face were

not deep, would leave no trace, and would heal within a
week.

Gulbehar, hearing that Khurrem had been sent for and
had refused to come to her lord, swiftly appeared on the
scene and began to pour out a string of unintelligible complaints to the sultan. Cyra quickly sent her away. Confused, the sultan turned to his mother for an explanation.
Using the moment to her own advantage, Cyra placed the
blame squarely on Suleiman.

"This is your fault," she said. "For eleven years you
favored no one but Gulbehar. For the past seven years,
you have looked only at Khurrem. There has always been
animosity between them, and this afternoon it broke into
open physical combat. Had you taken other favorites, as
I often suggested, each would have been far too busy trying to lure you from the others, and Gulbehar and
Khurrem would not have had time to concentrate on their
hatred for one another."

"I must go to Khurrem. She must be badly hurt if she
will not present herself to me."

"You are a fool, my son! Khurrem has naught but a
few minor scratches. She is wise enough to gain your
sympathy by not complaining and by denying you her
company, while poor Gulbehar is a mass of bruises and
bites."

"In Allah's name, mother, what am I to do with them?"

"Is Mustafa your choice as heir?"

"Yes."

"Then officially declare him so at once. Do you still
care for Gulbehar?"

"I am fond of her, mother. She is a good woman. But
I shall not seek her bed again."

"Then, after declaring Mustafa your heir, send him
and his mother to Magnesia. It is time the boy began to learn how to govern. What more fitting place than
the province that was yours in your father's time?" He
nodded his agreement.

"As for Khurrem, no wonder she is overproud. You
have spoiled her outrageously. You *must* take more favorites. The harem is full of lovely and talented maidens. I
cannot believe there are not some who would please
you."

"I do not want more children, mother."

Cyra's eyes twinkled mischievously. "My son, I am going to tell you a secret. Do you think that it was by accident that, having sired ten sons and six daughters by his four kadins, your father had no other children by the ikbals he took when he became sultan? Only in the end was it impossible for him to have normal relations with his women. In the beginning of his reign he took many maidens to his bed, but we had decided that your status as heir had to be protected, and so we saw to it that Selim's ikbals remained barren. There are ways, my son. If you wish to maintain the status of your family, it can be arranged."

Suleiman's first reaction was amazement. Then he roared with laughter. "By Allah, my mother, you are a wicked and devious woman! But I love you. Very well, I shall do all you suggest, but you must keep your part of the bargain. See that my favorites do not prove fruitful."

So Prince Mustafa, accompanied by his sad mother, left Constantinople for Magnesia. Khurrem's first annoyance at having Gulbehar's son named heir turned to joy when her hated rival left the city. It quickly turned back to rage when Suleiman, ignoring her for the present, began taking other maidens to his bed. Four were swiftly elevated to the rank of ikbal.

Still, the Russian reasoned, except for the valideh, she was now first lady in the harem, and the valideh was in her fifties. How much longer could she live? Unfortunately, patience was not Khurrem Kadin's greatest virtue.

One warm afternoon when the air was heavy with the scent of roses, jasmine, and marigold, Cyra sent for a cooling fruit sherbet. When it came, the young white eunuch who carried the little tray attracted her immediate attention because his hands were shaking. It was not very noticeable, but she saw the faint quiver as, kneeling, he offered up the cup. It did not take a great deal of thought for her to decide the reason. The sherbet was poisoned.

She spoke one word. "Who?"

The eunuch began to tremble.

"You have a choice," said the valideh. "You may die swiftly, or you may die slowly and painfully."

"Khurrem Kadin," he cried, and, falling to his knees, begged for mercy.

"Drink it," she commanded. Her face brooked no refusal.

Mumbling a prayer to Allah, the eunuch drained the cup and minutes later fell dead at her feet.

"Where is Khurrem Kadin at this hour?" she asked a frightened attendant.

"At the baths, madam," she replied.

"Have this slave secretly carried to her chambers and left upon her bed," said Cyra. Slowly rising, she walked out into her gardens.

The valideh was annoyed with herself. She had underestimated her son's kadin. She had not believed that Khurrem would dare an attempt on her life, and had been lulled into a false sense of security.

Of all those connected with Suleiman's early life, only she remained near him. Gulbehar lived her lonely exile in the city of Magnesia. Firousi and Sarina had made new lives for themselves. Dearest Firousi! She hadn't wanted to leave Cyra, but it had been for the best. She was completely recovered now and would live to a ripe old age, the doctors assured the valideh.

They were all safe, and for that blessing she was grateful, but was there not a place of peace and safety for her? Suddenly she remembered Gulbehar's warning that one day Khurrem's ambition would reach out to destroy even the valideh. Disquieted, she was trying to organize her thoughts when the voice of Esther Kira cut through her consciousness. She turned to see the plump little Jewess bustling toward her.

"Ah, my dearest madam, Marian has told me everything! How could she do this to you, to whom she owes all? You must retaliate, of course. I have the most marvelous new poison from Italy. It leaves no trace."

Cyra laughed. "Marian was told to keep silent, along with my other servants. Oh, Esther! You do cheer me. But no, I shall not destroy Khurrem. She means far too much to Suleiman."

The gold bracelets on Esther Kira's plump arms jingled in annoyance. "I *thought* you would be merciful, and I disapprove," she said sternly. Then, reaching into the purse attached to her girdle, she drew out a little box, opened it, and removed a small gilded pill which she handed to Cyra. "Take one of these daily. They contain an infinitesimal dose of poison and will build your resistance to anything Khurrem can give you."

The valideh hugged her friend. "It will not be necessary. Many years ago Selim gave me as a gift an old Egyptian who was my food taster. He was a specialist in poisons and taught me this trick. I have been taking doses of poison ever since. Khurrem's sherbet could not have hurt me."

"Then why did you not drink it? What a fright it would have given her to learn you had drunk the sherbet and suffered not even a bellyache. I wager she administered the dose herself so there would be no chance of your escaping."

"I did not take it because I wanted her to know that I knew of her treachery. If I had accepted the cup and not died, she might have thought someone had changed the sherbet. This way, she knows I am aware of what she has done. Fear is a greater weapon than doubt. Poor Khurrem. She lacks subtlety. To properly administer poison, it must be done in small doses and over a period of time to avoid notice. There was enough death in my cup to kill an elephant."

"Ah, my lady, you are the wisest of women! A pure jewel among stones!"

Cyra laughed again. "Esther, Esther! What would I do without you?"

The Jewess sniffed, and without further ado, announced, "I bring news from Charles Leslie."

Cyra sat down and eagerly beckoned her friend to do so. "Tell me."

"He is well and has been knighted by his king. He is now Sir Charles Leslie. He also writes that he is betrothed to his cousin Fiona, your brother's daughter."

Cyra frowned. "I have never liked these marriages between first cousins."

"Rest easy, my lady. The girl Fiona is not your brother's blood child, but his adopted daughter. She was born to your distant cousins, the Abernethys. Charles writes all of this. When she was orphaned, your brother took her into his own house. He says her hair is red-gold like yours, but not so lovely.

"Ah, madam. For thirteen years he has been separated from you, and yet he remembers you with love. How fortunate you are to have such a son!"

The valideh's face became sad. "Yes," she whispered. "I am the most fortunate of women."

Esther Kira said nothing more.

The months passed, and Cyra began to notice a subtle change in Khurrem's attitude toward her. Nothing had been said by either woman regarding the incident of the poison, but invisible battle lines had been drawn. As Cyra had noticed years before, Khurrem never forgave those who punished her. The Russian felt that by inducing Suleiman to take other maidens to his bed, the valideh had chastised her unfairly. Khurrem had lived too long in her own world to become Turkish. Though she professed the faith of Mohammed, she was still an Orthodox Christian at heart, and she did not willingly share her man with others. She considered herself the sultan's legal wife, discounting Gulbehar with a logic that defied all reason. Though Suleiman had other favorites now, she still remained on top of the pack. He frequently visited her bed, but, nevertheless, the situation nettled Khurrem. This was Cyra's fault, and the Russian kadin would repay her in kind.

But Khurrem had not reckoned with the valideh's iron will. Cyra Hafise was made of far stronger stuff than Khurrem—or any other woman, for that matter. The Scotswoman had not survived thirty-nine years in the House of Osman on luck alone, but the years were going faster now, and Cyra wondered if she really wanted to continue the battle. She had known such happiness and love that for her it would last through eternity. She had known complete fulfillment and had wielded great power. Now all Cyra wanted was to live out her portion in peace.

Khurrem's very existence made this impossible, and the valideh was faced with a painful decision. To dispose of Khurrem or to expose her crimes to Suleiman would break her son's heart. Besides, Cyra Hafise had never liked being responsible for the taking of life. She could, of course, retire to her own serai away from Constantinople, but that would not really solve the problem. Suleiman, she realized, was still far too attached to her. Death, therefore, was the only answer—and as she was in good health, that seemed unlikely. Her will to live was far stronger than her will to die.

Then one day a greatly agitated Esther Kira came to the palace asking to see the valideh privately. Once again they walked in the gardens where they could not be overheard.

Esther began by asking a question. "Your brother is the earl of Glenkirk?"

Cyra nodded.

"A man perhaps four or five years younger than yourself?"

"Four years, Esther."

"Is he a great gawk of a man with reddish hair and a stubborn nature?"

"Esther, how would I know that? I have not seen Adam since he was nine years old."

"But, my lady—if you met a man today who claimed to be your brother, how would you know it was he?"

Cyra thought for a moment and then said, "He had a small black mole just at the end of his eyebrow, and as a child he looked like my father. I suppose if I met a man who said he was the earl of Glenkirk who looked like my father and had a mole at the end of his left eyebrow, I would strongly suspect he was my brother."

Esther clasped her hands together. "It must be he! It must!"

"Esther, what is this all about?"

"At this moment, my dear lady, the earl of Glenkirk is a guest in the House of Kira!"

The valideh blanched and gasped.

Esther rushed on. "You know the sultan has given trading concessions to France and that he is slowly opening the way to other countries in the West. Your brother is here representing the king of Scotland. He is our guest because of the House of Kira's involvement with Charles Leslie. He is asking questions, madam. It seems that your family knew from the beginning that you had been sold to the sultan of Turkey's household, but they were warned to do nothing as their cause was hopeless. When Charles arrived those many years ago, they knew you were still alive, but he would not tell them where. From the story he told, they deduced you had been given as a gift to another sultan. Your brother has taken it into his head that he can find you. It was all we could do to prevent him from marching up to the palace and demanding an interview with the queen mother, as he puts it."

Cyra giggled. "My brother was always one for going to the heart of the matter. But, Esther, why does he want to see the valideh?"

"He is a sharp one, madam. He learned that several months after you entered Sultan Bajazet's harem, Prince Selim was given six maidens and sent to govern a province in the Crimea. He feels that Sultan Selim's favorite wife might have known you, his sister, and can help him. Only the fact that I am considered an intimate of yours and could possibly arrange an interview for him prevented him from banging on the serai gates."

"So he wants an interview with the sultan valideh," mused Cyra. "You told him, of course, that it was impossible."

"I could not, madam. I did not have the heart. His hopes are so high. I thought when I returned to my home today I could tell him then, and perhaps you would send him some sort of verbal message."

"No," said Cyra. "Lord Leslie will have his interview with the sultan valideh."

"Madam! How can this be? No normal man other than the sultan may enter the harem or even speak with his ladies."

"Have we two not accomplished the impossible before, Esther? I am the sultan valideh, and my word is law. Even Suleiman defers to my personal wishes."

Esther Kira nodded. "But where?"

"The palace would be far too dangerous. Neither my son nor anyone else must know of Adam's existence until I have spoken to him—and determined my course of action. Perhaps it will never be necessary for Suleiman to know of the existence of the earl of Glenkirk. I have visited in the city at your house many times. We are known to be good friends. Who would think it odd if I chose to visit you again? I shall come in two days' time, but you must impress upon Lord Leslie the need for secrecy. Make him understand what an honor it is for the valideh to speak to him. Above all, do not tell him the truth. I shall decide whether or not that should be done."

On the following day, Cyra's youngest grandson, the hunchbacked Prince Jahangir, came to visit her. He arrived with his nurse, who apologized profusely to the valideh for their unannounced visit at the hour of her midday meal. Cyra brushed the words aside. "My grandchildren are always welcome, whatever the hour." She smiled down at the boy. "What brings you to visit this old woman, my child?"

"Mustafa sent me a gift!"

The little prince's hero was his older half-brother, and when Mustafa had been sent to Magnesia, Jahangir had been heartbroken. However, Mustafa had not forgotten the child.

"See, see what Mustafa has sent me!" Opening his shirt, he revealed a splotch of dark fur which, springing forth, became a monkey. Chattering madly, the little creature leaped upon the valideh's table, and, grabbing an apricot, shoved it whole into his mouth. Discovering the pit, the monkey spat it out. Laughter rippled across the room.

"Your pet is most charming," chuckled Cyra, "but alas, my grandson, his table manners are terrible. Please remove him from my dining table, and I shall see that he is fed."

Jahangir reached for his monkey, but the nimble little imp scrambled to the other side, where he stuffed a handful of pilaf into his mouth and promptly fell dead. The prince began to sob. "My monkey is dead! My monkey is dead!"

"No, he is not," replied the valideh firmly. "He is merely ill from overeating. Leave him with me, and I shall make him well again. Return with your nurse to your own quarters, and I shall bring you your monkey this afternoon."

Jahangir's dark eyes widened. "Truly, grandmother? You can really heal my monkey?"

"Yes, my child. Now go along like a good boy."

The little prince dutifully trotted out after his nurse. Cyra turned to her chief eunuch. "Dispose of the monkey as you did the white eunuch. Then go to the marketplace and find me an identical monkey. The rest of you will keep silent about this matter."

Fate had decided for her. She now knew what she must do, but first she would see her little brother. She laughed softly, remembering Adam as a child. But Allah! He would be forty-eight years of age now! What did he look like? she wondered. Why did he seek her after all these years? Tomorrow would answer all her questions.

39

UNLIKE THEIR COUNTERPARTS in Western Europe, the Jews of Constantinople were respected and equal members of the Ottoman community. The Kira family, though they could have afforded to live in a palace along the sea, preferred to remain in the old quarter where their ancestors had lived as far back as the Byzantine Empire.

When the sultan valideh Hafise arrived in her palanquin early in the afternoon, there was only a mild stirring among the neighbors. After all, was not Esther Kira a dear friend of the sultan's mother? And hadn't she visited the Kiras before? Cyra appreciated their sensible attitude. The one thing she had never really gotten used to in all her years in Turkey was the sumptuous pomp of this nation, and Suleiman was carrying the pomp to greater heights because of his love of a good show.

From the outside, the Kira house, though slightly larger, was like any other in the quarter. It was built of a light-colored brick, and the side facing the street was windowless, the only opening a large, brass-studded double door with a small iron grille on one side.

The closed palanquin was expected, and it was quickly waved through. The valideh stepped out and stood for a moment to accept the ceremonial greeting from the patriarch of the family. Then she was escorted into the women's quarters of the house. Esther had taken every precaution. The area was deserted, the rest of the women in the house having gone to the public baths for an afternoon of happy gossiping.

"Go into my private salon, dear madam. I shall bring Lord Leslie to you, and then stand guard outside the door while you talk."

Cyra thanked her and entered the room. Her heart

was beating wildly. What in Allah's name would she say to him? She had lain awake all last night planning the words, but suddenly they had all fled. She heard a step behind her. The door opened and closed. A deep, familiar voice spoke.

"Madam, I am Adam Leslie, earl of Glenkirk." The language he used was French. Esther's doing, she imagined.

Her back was to him, and she did not dare to turn and face him as yet. She replied in French, "I am well aware of your identity, Lord Leslie, and have been somewhat informed of your circumstances by my good friend Esther Kira. I do not understand why it is you should seek an audience with me. However, I am an old woman, and undue curiosity is a prerogative of old age."

"Thank you," said Lord Leslie. "I shall try not to take a great deal of your time, my lady. I have been given to understand that you were in the harem of Sultan Bajazet in the year fourteen ninety-three." She nodded. "Then perhaps you knew my sister and can tell me of her fate. She was just thirteen but very, very beautiful. Her hair was a red-gold, her eyes green. She was fair of skin. She had been kidnapped by slavers and was sold at a private auction where she was purchased by the grand eunuch of the sultan's household."

"How can you know all this?" interrupted Cyra.

"Because an envoy of the duchy of San Lorenzo attended the auction to try to ransom her back. She was betrothed to the heir of San Lorenzo. You must have been in the harem at the time she was brought in, and perhaps you can remember her."

The valideh said nothing for a moment. Instead, she removed the second piece of her yasmak and repinned it over the first, obscuring her features completely. Remaining in the shadows, she turned to face him.

"Describe her further to me, my lord." He began, but she did not listen. Instead, her eyes secretly devoured him. How he had changed! And why shouldn't he have changed? He had been nine the last time she had seen him. How long ago was it—thirty-nine years! How she had missed him!

He was a tall man, as their father had been. His hair, which had been russet when he was a child, had dark-

ened slightly, and was now liberally streaked with gray.
His features were like their father's, but his blue eyes
were a gift from their mother. She vaguely heard his last
words.

"Is it possible you knew her, madam?"

"Yes," she said. "I knew her."

"Then in the name of whatever God you worship, I
beg you to tell me where she is?"

"We worship the same God, Lord Leslie, though somewhat differently," said Cyra tartly. "Allah is simply our
name for him. But tell me—how can you be sure your
sister still lives?"

"I am privy to certain information that I cannot reveal
to you, but she lives. I would find her and, if she wishes,
take her home with me."

"Why do you want her back? Surely you are man of
the world enough to understand that the wife of an Eastern prince is his wife in every sense but the Christian—
and only because she has had the good fortune to bear
him a son. Is this not considered wicked and shameful
among your people? In your intolerant land, our customs
are thought of as immoral. Your sister would be called
a whore, a concubine, or worse. Would you subject your
sister to scorn and ridicule merely to satisfy a childhood
memory?" She was being harsh, and she knew it; but if
her plan was to work, he must have no regrets, nor must
she.

"Only four people knew her fate, and two of them are
now dead. We have told people that she was bought by
a good Christian merchant who took pity on her. We
have said they were married. There will be no shame for
her when she returns, and we shall say she has now returned because she is widowed."

"How can you be sure she will want to return?"

"Madam. My sister is a Scot. She would want to die in
her own land if it were possible."

Cyra resisted the urge to laugh at the coincidence in
their thoughts. "And you, Lord Leslie? How do you feel?
Do you consider your sister a whore? How would you
greet her return? As a Christian soul gone astray and now
reclaimed? A duty done? A burden?"

He said it simply. "I would greet her with love,
madam."

She felt tears welling up in her eyes, but, forcing them back, she persisted. "Are you sure? Once you have taken her home, there can be no going back for either of you."

"I am sure, madam. Just tell me where she is, and I shall prove it to you." Then his eyes widened in amazement as he heard the valideh's voice speaking his native Highland tongue.

"When we were children, Adam, you never could find me when we played hide-and-seek. It is comforting to know you have not changed." Stepping into the light, she removed the veils from her face.

For a moment she thought he would faint, so white had his face become. "Janet?" His voice was choked with emotion. "Oh, Janet! God be praised, I have found you!" Falling to his knees, he caught at the hem of her dress and wept like a baby.

She stooped down and hugged him. "You still weep easily, you great boob!" Pulling him up, she commanded, "Stop it, you clod. Are you so sad at finding me? What of all your fine talk? Bah! You do not really want me at all!"

The big earl wiped his eyes on his sleeve. "The lady Esther told me I was to speak with the sultan valideh Hafise. I am stunned to find you instead."

"Adam." Her voice had grown serious now. "I am the sultan valideh Hafise."

"You? You are Sultan Suleiman's mother?"

"I am."

"But then how can I take you home?"

"You can, and it will be arranged. I shall communicate with you through Esther. When do you leave?"

"In three weeks' time."

"Good. I shall have the time I need. Now listen to me, my brother. No one must know of our meeting or what has been said in this room. In this land the sultan is all-powerful. Only his mother may influence him. I am the most powerful person in the empire next to my son, but even that power could not save me or you or the Kira family should anyone find out our secret. What I am doing violates all our traditions." He gazed at her questioningly. "Yes, Adam. Our traditions. I have lived all but thirteen years of my life in Turkey, and though I am Scots-born, I am more Turkish than my own son. Speak

to no one of this. Go about your mission, and Esther will
advise you. Do you understand me?"

He nodded.

"Very well. Go now. When you leave Turkey, I shall
be with you. Trust me!" Kissing her cheek, Adam Leslie
left the salon.

One hour later, the valideh concluded her visit with
Esther Kira and returned to the Eski Serai. She had
spoken brave words to her brother, but for the first time
since she had come to Turkey, she had serious doubts.
She had not realized until recently how dependent
Suleiman was on her. In a sense she had failed him
with the very strength that had helped to put him on his
throne. Only if she left him could he become his own man
—and how convenient, she thought, that her reasoning
coincided with her plans.

For almost a week, Cyra thought about the meeting
with her brother. She pondered the correct way to approach the problem with her son. Yet it was Suleiman who
provided the opening she needed.

One evening while they sat sipping their sweet, burning
coffee, the sultan told his mother of the Scots lord to whom
he had that very day promised the concession of coming
twice yearly to Constantinople for trade.

"A large man, and quite open and friendly as Christians go, but I could not dismiss the feeling that we had
met somewhere before."

"I am not surprised you felt that way," said Cyra. "He
is your uncle."

"What!"

"The earl of Glenkirk is my younger brother. Suleiman,
he is your uncle," she repeated.

"Allah," he whispered, "if he but knew you were alive
—" He stopped, then turned wonderingly to her. "Is there
nothing that goes on in my empire that you do not know
about?"

She laughed happily at his chagrin. "No, my son. Very
little escapes me."

"If this large, bluff man is my uncle, then perhaps I
should double the concession," he answered her teasingly.

"You could scarcely acknowledge each other, my son.

Besides, Scotland is a small, poor country. Turkey already has the worst of the bargain."

"Always, you place the empire first," he said admiringly.

"Yes," she replied. "I do. That is what I must speak to you of tonight. Lord Leslie's visit presents me with an opportunity I cannot overlook. I am growing old, my son. I want to live the years left to me in peace, without responsibilities. I want to die in my own land."

"Mother—" Her hand stopped his mouth.

"Within the last year, two attempts have been made on my life, but in each case fate has intervened. Is this not proof that Allah would grant my desires? How much longer can I tempt fate? I would retire as Firousi and Sarina have."

He tore her hand away. "Who has done this, mother? Tell me, and I shall punish the offender. If you would retire, you may choose any palace I have and go in peace. Only stay near me!"

"Do you think if I wished punishment upon the offender, she would still live? Nay, my son."

"She?" And then he knew. "Khurrem? My kadin has done this?"

"Yes, Suleiman. Khurrem. Do not blame her. In her eyes I am a threat. She is as ambitious as I once was. She does it for you both. You are far too attached to me. You divide your love among your kadin, your ikbals, and your mother. I somehow think it is unhealthy for a man of your years."

"Paradise lies at a mother's feet," he quoted.

"Do not preach the holy Koran to me! It was I who taught it to you! If I retire to a nearby palace, I shall still be an influence in your life. There are those who will say that Khurrem has driven me from you as she did Gulbehar. Someday Khurrem might be valideh. She is not very popular now as it is, and an unpopular valideh may mean an unpopular sultan.

"If you are to be free without complications, I must appear to have died. Only then can I spend my old age in peace. I have already spoken to my brother, and he wants me to return to Scotland with him. Did you know that he came to Constantinople in hopes of tracing me?"

"You spoke with Lord Leslie? How?"

"Let the arrangements of our meeting remain a secret, my son."

"No wonder he looked at me so strangely today," mused Suleiman. "I thought it was simple curiosity at meeting the fabled Grand Turk. Allah! My own uncle!" He looked at his mother. "I cannot let you go. I cannot!"

"You would prefer that Khurrem murder me?"

"I shall punish her."

"She will, nevertheless, try again—and what is worse, Khurrem never forgives an insult. Your action will only make her redouble her efforts."

"Then I shall send her away."

"My son, my son! You have not understood a word I have said. It is either Khurrem's life or mine. You must make the choice, and you cannot. I have made it for you. Would you deny your four children their mother? Have you no feelings? Is this how I have raised you?"

"You plead for leniency for Khurrem, saying I must not separate my children from their mother; yet you, my own mother, would go from me."

"Suleiman!" Her voice had taken on an unaccustomed sharpness. "You are no longer a child. You are a man and sultan of the Ottoman Empire. Your eldest son is almost fifteen. He will soon take maidens of his own and make you a grandfather. Do you not think it is time you rid yourself of the influence of women? Mustafa is more independent than you. This should not be!"

"I am not influenced by women, mother!"

"My son, the fact that you can neither see nor feel the hands that have led you is proof enough of your need to be rid of me. From the moment you were born, I have guided your destiny. Others have helped me. Without Firousi, Zuleika, and Sarina, would your childhood have been safe? They, too, bore your father sons. Hammed was barely four months younger than you. Yet always our efforts were for you, and you alone. When our father officially became sultan, it was I who saw that Gulbehar became yours rather than his. When the Persian campaign was won, I was responsible for seeing that you were sent to Magnesia to learn how to govern. Who warned you not to follow your father into Syria and Egypt? I did! When my beloved Selim died, who held Constantinople in check until you had safely arrived? I did! Without my help you would have faltered a thousand times. Who brought you Khurrem? It was I who trained her to catch your eye. When the feud between Gulbehar and Khurrem reached epic proportions, to whom did you turn for help? To me! I solved your problem. Your father's last words to me were, 'Guide Suleiman as only you know how.' I have done it, but you are now a man and I am tired. I would like to live out my days in peace!"

For several minutes, neither of them spoke. Suleiman was wise enough to realize that his mother had worked herself into a frenzy. He had never seen her this way, and he was a little frightened. Her beautiful hair had become unbound as she spoke, loosened by her passion. It had never grayed, but rather had lightened with her advancing age until it was now a soft, pale-peach color. As she paced back and forth, it swung, catching the light.

Suddenly Cyra Hafise turned and faced her son. "I have given nearly forty years of my life to the Ottoman Empire!" she shouted. "I shall give no more! Will you, for whom I have done so much, deny me this? You are surely a most unnatural son!"

She could see that her words had stung him. Torn between his great pride at being the sultan and the pride of being her son, he pondered her words. She knew she would win. Like a flea, she had bitten at his most tender spot, his ego, and only her removal would now salve his wound.

He patted the cushions by his side, and she sat down. "How can this scheme of yours be arranged?" he asked.

"Thank you, my son." She caressed his cheek, but he turned away. Sighing, she spoke. "In a day or two, I shall become ill. I shall vomit my food and complain of pains. The doctor will come, and though he will find nothing wrong, my very position as valideh will force him to make a public diagnosis. I shall hover for several days between life and death. You, professing great concern, will visit me each evening.

"Finally I shall claim that the Angel of Death hovers near me and demand that my coffin be brought. By this time the doctor will be diagnosing my imminent demise.

"On the evening of the eleventh day, I shall call for my family to be brought to me for a final farewell." She stopped, then chuckled. "How I look forward to seeing

Khurrem's face! I shall be hard put not to laugh. That night I shall die. You must give orders beforehand for the coffin to be sealed. Only Marian and Ruth will attend me at the end. They will announce my death.

"Just before dawn, three old women in peasant black will depart the serai through a secret gate in my private park. No one will see them, but if anyone should, who would question their presence?"

"Three?" asked Suleiman.

"I am taking Marian and Ruth with me. Marian is English and has been with me since before you were born. Her husband was an Englishman and was secretary to your father for many years. You remember him. Their daughter, Ruth, has never seen her native land. I cannot leave them behind. To those who ask, merely say it was my dying wish that they be freed and returned to their own country."

"How will you live, my mother? I cannot have you dependent upon your brother's charity."

"Secretly deposit with the House of Kira the sum of twenty-five thousand gold dinars. Each year add an additional five hundred. The money will be credited to my account in Edinburgh and administered by the Kiras. As for my jewels, aside from a few parting gifts, I shall take them with me. To any who ask, say you buried them with the valideh."

He nodded. "You have thought this out carefully, my mother. You must really want to return to your native land."

"Suleiman, I was born a Scot, and I shall die one. But I have lived my life as a Turk, and I do not regret one moment of it. If Allah gave me the choice of reliving my time as I chose, I would choose the same path again."

He leaned across the table and took her hands in his. Gray-green eyes met green-gold ones, and he would have spoken had she not forestalled him. "No, my lion. My mind is made up. When you come to my apartments again, say nothing of this. Khurrem has placed two spies among my servants. This evening I had them removed, but I shall not be so fortunate again."

She rose and led him to the door. "Let this be our private farewell, my son. I have loved you from the moment you were conceived. All I have done has been for you.

May Allah guard and guide you in the days and years to
come. Always know my thoughts and prayers are with
you."

Her slender fingers reached up and touched his face.
They moved lightly from his forehead, across his eyes and
nose, and down his cheeks to his short, perfumed black
beard. Then, pulling his head down, she kissed him gently
on the forehead.

Two days later, the harem was mildly distressed to
learn that their healthy valideh had taken ill. The doctor's
diagnosis was "a mild digestive ailment." The valideh
would be well in a few days' time. But when several days
had passed and her condition had not improved, concern
began to spread among the inhabitants of the Eski Serai.

In her suite, Khurrem Kadin received regular reports.
The valideh was pale and wan. She vomited her food and
grew weak. She was now complaining of shooting pains in
her head and her chest.

Khurrem prayed for her antagonist's swift demise and
thought with chagrin of her two aborted murder attempts.
She was extremely hard pressed to conceal her joy when
word came that the Cyra Hafise, seeing the Angel of
Death near her bed, had called for her coffin.

On the evening of the eleventh day of the valideh's
illness, Khurrem and her children were sent for to bid
the mother of Suleiman a last farewell. Entering the bedchamber, Khurrem thought the older woman looked
strangely well, but then she was not the doctor. What did
it matter, so long as Cyra died? Khurrem knelt by the
bedside and felt a hand upon her head.

"My daughter," came the familiar voice—it was quite
weak, the Russian noted with satisfaction. "My daughter,"
the valideh repeated. "You have far exceeded my ambi-
tions for you." Was there a hint of mockery in the words?
"But whatever our differences during these last years, I
forgive you. You have been a good wife to my son and a
good mother to his children. I know you will continue to
be."

For a moment Khurrem felt a twinge of regret for this
woman who had lifted her from obscurity, but when her
eyes met the valideh's, she could not conceal her naked

triumph. "I shall not change my ways, my mother," she said solemnly.

Cyra almost laughed. She had been sure that Khurrem would not change her ways. Recovering herself, she turned her attention to her grandchildren. She blessed them all, beginning with her son's heir, Prince Mustafa, who had come from Magnesia. Pulling him close to her, she whispered, "Do not trust Khurrem Kadin under *any* circumstances. Remember my warning. It is the only legacy I can leave you." He nodded.

Next came Selim, still fat and nasty. He was his mother's son and would never change. Of all her grandchildren, he was the only one she had failed to get close to. Then came Bajazet, his eyes full of tears. A good boy. He was very much like her husband. He was followed by Princess Mihrmah, silent and overawed by her part in this drama. Last was little Jahangir, whose lower lip trembled as he said, "My monkey thanks you for healing him, grandmother."

Then they were gone, and she was left to say her final words to Suleiman in private. The sultan was visibly shaken. Grasping his sleeve, she drew him down to her, and the sound of her voice had its firm authoritarian ring.

"Listen well, my lion. These are the last words I shall say to you. Trust Mustafa and guard him well. Do not be misled by any accusation that Khurrem may make. The boy loves you and will always be loyal. If, Allah forbid, the heir should die, name Bajazet, not Selim. Selim is weak and warped. He is easily led by Khurrem. Bajazet is like his grandfather and Mustafa. He is wise enough to placate, but not to be influenced by Khurrem. Remember! Bajazet, not Selim. Watch over Jahangir. He is a good boy. When she is old enough, marry Mihrmah to someone who will be of use to you. A daughter is valuable in her own way. Allah's blessings on you, my Suleiman. Now go!"

"Mother—"

"*Go!*"

Tears pouring down his cheeks, he left her, giving orders to her staff that when the time came, the coffin should be sealed by her two faithful slaves, Marian and Ruth. He had, as his dying mother had requested, given them their freedom. They would leave the serai immedi-

ately following the valideh's death and return to their native land.

Cyra's servants were desolate. The valideh had been a
good mistress, and they loved her. Earlier in the evening,
she had called them to her one by one and had given
each a small purse. Everyone connected with the sultan's
mother, from the humblest kitchen slave to the agha
kislar himself, had been remembered. To each of her
maidens she had also given a small piece of her own jewelry.

Within the bedchamber of the valideh, the "dying"
woman arose from her couch and dressed herself in warm,
sturdy garments. Pulling on a black peasant feridje, she
said to her faithful Marian and Ruth, "It is time. Announce
my death."

The sobbing and tearing of garments that followed
touched her.

She could not have left her dearest friends, Firousi and
Sarina, without telling them the truth. Like her, they were
old now, and allowing them to mourn with breaking hearts
might have shortened their lives. She had told them the
truth about Prince Karim several years before, and on
the day of her "death" they received a message that read:
"Pay no heed to the gossips of the marketplace. For the
sake of peace, I have chosen to follow in Karim's footsteps." A secret visit from Ruth had confirmed the message. She brought with her a parting gift for them from
Cyra. Even now, as it had always been, they were united.

Gazing at the things that were hers, Cyra moved
through her apartment a final time. She had spent many
years collecting her furnishings and decorating her home.
Tenderly she ran her hand across a rosewood chest inlaid
in mother-of-pearl that Selim had brought her from Egypt.
The valideh wondered if Khurrem would attempt to claim
the Garden Court for her own. She would probably try, but
as besotted as Suleiman might be by his favorite, Cyra
knew he would never allow her to touch his mother's
things. The Garden Court would be closed and sealed.

In a way, it was a pity. Never again would a slipper
tred softly across the thick carpets, or a hand place a taper
to the lovely old lamps. No longer would the now-silent
rooms gather laughter and secrets to its walls.

For a moment, anger welled in Cyra Hafise. Why

should she be forced in her old age from the place and people she loved? This was *her* home. She had fought for it, and it was hers by right! Because her son was weak-willed in his personal relationships, she must leave him, her grandchildren, her country, and all else she held dear to return to Allah knew what in the dark land of her birth. If only she had believed Marian's warning about Khurrem those many years ago—but no, if it had not been Khurrem, it would have been someone else.

She must put her old life behind her and reach eagerly for the new one. She was leaving Suleiman and his family; but Charles Leslie and other grandchildren awaited her in Scotland. At this moment Khurrem believed she had won the battle. My only regret, thought Cyra wryly, is that she will never know that the victory was really mine!

Dawn was beginning to pull at the shade of night when a small, overgrown gate to the valideh's private park was opened. Three old women dressed in the black feridje and yasmak of the poor emerged and, clutching their bundles, walked out into the city. As light began to fill the eastern skies, they reached the docks and boarded a vessel flying the ensign of a foreign country. The gangplank was raised, the sails hoisted, and slowly the ship began to pull away from the shore.

In the Yeni Serai, Suleiman stood in the shore kiosk and watched as the ship sailed by him, its white sails catching the colors of the dawn. It carried his mother out of Constantinople and back to her cold, northern land.

From the minaret of the Great Mosque came the call of a muezzin. "Come to prayer. Come to prayer. The sultan valideh Hafise is dead. Come to prayer."

Falling to his knees, the sultan of the greatest empire of its time wept.

PART V

❦❅❆❄❧

Janet

1533∗1542

40

IT WAS STILL DARK when the ship entered the Firth of Forth, and Janet Leslie, standing on the deck, smelled for the first time in almost forty years the damp land smells of earth, sea and heather that to her meant Scotland. Shivering, she gathered her sable-lined cloak about her and peered intently into the darkness. The small lump to her right would be the Isle of May. Ahead was Leith and the end of her journey. No, not the end for there was still the long overland trip to Glenkirk.

What is the matter with me, she thought impatiently. I am frightened to death of this new life. Yet, when I was stolen from my family and sold into slavery I wasn't half so afraid. Of course I wasn't, she answered herself. Then I was too young and innocent to know better.

"Madame!"

She started.

"Madame, you will catch your death out in this damp air. Come inside at once!"

"Marian, you frightened me."

"I shouldn't wonder, madame, standing out here all alone in the cold and dark. Come inside now!"

Putting an arm around Janet, Marian drew her into the warm, lighted cabin.

"Shame on you," she scolded. That damp air could give you a chill. Do you want to be sick for your reunion with Prince Karim?"

"Charles," corrected Janet. "Prince Karim no longer exists."

"Yes, m'lady. Now give me that cloak and come lie down. We will not dock at Leith for several hours yet."

Taking the cape she folded it lovingly and laid it on the trunk by the floor. "That Esther Kira," she chuckled.

"Imagine her having two trunkfuls of lovely new clothes in the latest French fashions made up for you. And then secretly sending them aboard before we left Istanbul! She must have had a dozen seamstresses working round the clock. And clothing for Ruth and me, also! Now at least we'll not arrive at Glenkirk looking like beggars." She tucked a blanket about Janet's legs and propped pillows at her back. "There now, m'lady. Try to rest."

Janet nodded absently, then spoke. "Marian, are you sure you don't want to go back to England? You don't have to share my exile. You may still have family alive, and Ruth is entitled to know her people. You will never want for anything. I'll see you have a generous yearly pension."

Marian sniffed. "Now listen to me, madame. If I still have a family, they would not rejoice to see me. My parents would long be gone, and those of my brothers and sisters left alive have long thought of me as dead. I should have some explaining to do. You have been my family since I was seventeen. I will not leave you! My daughter," she glanced at the sleeping Ruth, "is more than old enough to marry, but what chance would she have in England? She could not keep her entire past life a secret, and people here have small minds. With you she retains her respectability and her virtue."

"I had not thought about it," said Janet.

"No, you did not," replied her tart-tongued servant. "Since we left the Eski Serai you have been sunk in self pity. The valideh Cyra Hafise is no more, but you are alive, madame, and you have not changed. Only our situation and circumstances have changed. In a few hours we will arrive in Leith; and after your brother has reported the success of his mission to the king of Edinburgh, we will be on our way to Glenkirk. In just a few days' time you will see your son again. Will you break his heart with the sight of a pitiful, broken woman, or will you greet him happily with the knowledge that you are here by your own choice?"

"I am afraid, Marian. More afraid than I have ever been in my whole life. I do not know this world to which I am returning. I have no place in it."

"What nonsense you speak, madame! You spent the first years of your life in this world; and as for a place in it, are you not the sister of the earl of Glenkirk, the mother of Sir Charles Leslie?"

"It is not enough, Marian! I must have more! I cannot spend the rest of my days being nothing more than a doting grandmother sewing tapestries!"

"Then you must make it more, my lady. Did you not make our lord Selim love you above all women? Did you not direct Sultan Suleiman's future? And save the life of Prince Karim so he might grow to manhood in this land? I have never known any such as you. You have the power to make things happen. My old granny came from Ireland, and she often spoke the Gaelic tongue. She had a word she used for a woman she admired. She would say that she was fit to be a 'ban-righ.' I never knew what it meant, but you, madame, are surely a ban-righ!"

For the first time since they had left Istanbul Janet Leslie laughed. "Ban-righ is the Gaelic for queen, dear Marian—and I thank you. You are right. No one placed me on the heights which I attained. I did it myself. I shall do it again here. I am a very rich woman now, and the first thing I will do is build myself a house. I do not intend to live with Adam and his family."

"A good beginning, my lady, for I do not like what I have heard about the earl's wife."

"Marian, you haven't even met the Lady Anne."

"I have listened, madame. The Lady Anne doesn't approve of this, or that, or the other. She feels that Christmas revels are wasteful. And Anne has converted the castle rose garden to a vegetable garden, and she sells them! Pah!"

Janet laughed again. "Perhaps you are right. What I fear most is the strain of living under someone else's rule. I am far too used to running my own home. I shall buy from my brother a piece of Glenkirk land, and I know just the place I want. I want Glen Rae where I played as a child, the hills about it, its loch, and the island in the loch. That island is just off the shore and would be ideal for a house. I shall begin as soon as we land. I can hire an architect in Edinburgh."

"You had best make the trade with the earl legal before you return to Glenkirk, my lady. From what I've heard of her, the countess is a grasping woman, and when she sees her husband's sister is no pauper, she is sure to try and get twice what you offer."

"You have been with me so long, Marian, that you begin to think as I do. Those were my own thoughts."

Marian smiled to herself. She knew that her mistress would be all right, for she had begun to make plans for the future. Now they could go about the business of getting settled and making a place for themselves in Scotland.

Janet had fallen asleep, her hair strewn about her face on the pillow. Lord, thought Marian, she is but three years younger than I, yet she still looks like a girl. Her skin is smooth and unmarked while mine is beginning to wrinkle. My poor brown eyes are fading in color, but her green ones are as bright as ever. My mouse brown hair is shot with gray, but her lovely red-gold tresses have just lightened at bit. I am plump with all the good food we ate in the Eski Serai, but my lady is still willow slender. If the men of Scotland are as I remember, she will be overwhelmed with marriage offers before the year is out—especially when word of her fortune is bruited about. Already Captain Kerr has made a fool of himself over her each time he's seen her.

With all these thoughts tumbling in her head, Marian fell asleep. She awoke to the sounds of men's feet tramping about the deck outside their cabin. Janet was gone from her bunk, but Ruth still slept. She went to her and shook her.

"Wake up, daughter! We are entering the harbor."

Ruth stretched and yawned sleepily. She was a pretty, sweet-faced girl of twenty-three with her mother's brown hair, and her late father's bright blue eyes. An only child, she had been born when Marian, in her early thirties, had long past given up hope of having children. She barely remembered her father, who had been Sultan Selim's private secretary and had died of a fever while on campaign with his master.

She had grown up with the sultan's three youngest children for playmates. She was barely nine when she had helped her mother and Lady Cyra smuggle the six-year-old Prince Karim out of Turkey to safety in Scotland. It was at that point she had become a woman, for had she once slipped and even hinted at this secret, many lives would have been lost—including her own.

On several occasions after she reached puberty, she had been offered the chance of marriage. She had refused. She hadn't wanted to leave her mother or her mistress. Ruth had inherited her father's intelligence and her mother's strong streak of common sense. She was virtually a free woman while a handmaiden to the sultan valideh Cyra Hafise. As the wife of a Turk, she would be cloistered from the world. Now, however, she was a free woman in actual fact and should the opportunity present itself, she would marry without hesitation.

As her mother bustled about the cabin making sure that everything was packed, Ruth quickly dressed. After a lifetime of underdrawers that reached to her knees, long Turkish pantaloons, sheer blouses, embroidered waistcoats, silk overgowns and waist shawls worn by Turkish gentlewomen, Ruth felt almost indecent in the simple drawers, stockings, petticoats and light wool dress she now put on. Picking up her cloak she called to Marian, "Let us go out on the deck and see this new land we have come to."

It was a fine, clear and crisp, late May morning that greeted them. Lady Janet called to them from the upper deck.

"Come and see Leith! The mists have just lifted."

Adam Leslie and Captain Kerr stood by her side. The two women joined them.

"Remember the day we left Scotland for San Lorenzo, Jan?" Adam asked.

"I do," she laughed. "It was raining so hard we couldn't see from one end of the ship to the other. Grandmother said it was an ill omen—that we should not be leaving our own land. As I remember, we thought it was high adventure."

"The fates wept to see you go, madame, knowing how long it would be before you would see your native land again. Today the sun shines with joy at your return," said Captain Kerr.

"God's nightgown," muttered the earl of Glenkirk.

A giggle escaped Ruth.

"Why thank you, captain," said Janet sweetly, as she stepped with force on her brother's foot. He grimaced.

"Come, Adam, we must not keep the captain while he goes about the docking." She stepped lightly down the stairs to the cabin deck.

"I think you've broken my toe," he grumbled at her.

"It serves you right!"

"You haven't changed, Jan! You are still a hoyden! A mother five times over, and a grandmother to ten, or eleven if Fiona's safely delivered and still a hoyden! God help me, Jan. How did you even keep your head on your shoulders all those years in Turkey? What will my wife, Anne, think of you? You must be more reserved. I want peace in my house."

"And so you shall have it while I am there, Adam."

"While you are there?"

"Yes. Now tell me, brother. How much money did father leave me?"

"A thousand pounds gold. What did you mean while you are there?"

"Two hundred fifty are yours if I can have Glen Rae, the hills about it, and its loch—including the island. I am going to build a house!"

"No!"

"Yes, I am! It is something to leave Charles and my grandchildren when I die. I have a right to Glenkirk land. Had I lived my life here, Charles would have inherited from his father, but my son was not born a Scot and has nothing. If you do not sell to me, I will buy land from one of your neighbors."

"They wouldn't sell!"

"Money, my dear brother, especially bright gold, has a habit of convincing people. Never forget that! Are you so wealthy you can afford to scorn my money? Perhaps I should discuss this with your wife."

Adam Leslie frowned, then said, "All right. The land is yours!"

"When we arrive in Edinburgh, we will see a lawyer immediately to make the transaction legal. When I arrive at Glenkirk, I would be my own mistress."

"Very well. I would recommend Fergus More. He's been handling Leslie family matters for many years."

She nodded her agreement. The ship was now firmly docked, and its sailors put the gangway down. Several porters hurried aboard to begin the unloading of the cargo. Adam Leslie offered his arm to his sister.

"Well, Janet, shall we go?"

She hesitated for a moment, and then moved forward to the gangway. At that moment a tall, elegantly dressed young man rushed aboard the ship, and brushing past her enveloped the earl in a bear hug.

"Uncle Adam! Welcome home!"

Janet Leslie felt her legs buckle beneath her. Staggering, she grasped at the ship's railing for support. The hood of her cape fell back revealing her face, drained of color. It had been fourteen years, but she knew him.

"Karim," she gasped softly.

The young man whirled, and whitening, he stared at her.

"Mother! God in heaven! Mother!" Enfolding her in his arms he wept.

"Hush, my little lion," she comforted him. "Hush now. I promised you we would be together again one day."

"Words spoken to a six-year-old child being sent far from home," he sobbed. "Oh, mother, I never thought to see you again! I have missed you so!"

Wordlessly they hugged each other until Janet pushed him away.

"Let me look at you, Sir Charles Leslie. You're a giant, and you *do* look like your grandfather!"

Holding her by the shoulders, Charles looked down into her face. "And you, mother, you are the same! But how do you come to be here?"

"I will tell you in private, my son. Like you, my true identity is secret from all but your uncle."

He nodded, and then his eyes strayed to the two cloaked figures emerging from the cabin. With a whoop he descended upon them and grabbing the smaller of the two he swung her up with a shout.

"Marian! You're here, too!"

She shrieked. "Put me down, you great oaf!"

He lowered her to the deck and with a loud smacking noise, kissed her on both cheeks.

"You haven't changed at all since you were six," she sniffed, reaching for her handkerchief.

"Neither have you, you exotic creature!"

Marian slapped at him playfully, "Greet your old play-mate, Ruth, you mannerless boob," she commanded.

He turned to the young woman who was standing next to Marian. "Why, Ruth," he gently pushed the hood from her face, "how pretty you've become." Kissing the blushing girl's cheek he smiled down at her. "Welcome to Scotland."

"Thank you, my lord."

"Enough," interrupted Adam Leslie. "Let us go. I must get to Edinburgh today and report to his majesty. You have arranged for transportation, Charles?"

"I was not expecting mother, uncle. Your horse is waiting, but I will have to arrange something for mother."

"No need, my lord," said Captain Kerr, who had been standing waiting to bid farewell to his passengers. "Madame," he bent over Janet's hand, "allow me to offer you my own horse for your trip into Edinburgh. If you'll tell me where you are staying, I will send a wagon along later with your baggage and your serving women."

Janet looked to her son.

"My mother will be staying at the Rose and Thistle, captain. I thank you for the loan of your mount. We shall see he is safely returned."

The distance between Leith and Edinburgh was a short one. It seemed to Janet that little had changed during her absence, but one thing she did note—the Scots capital was more bustling. When she had left Scotland, James IV had been king. Now his son, young James V, ruled.

Upon arriving in Edinburgh, Adam dispatched a messenger to his wife with the news that his search for his sister had been successful, and that Janet would be staying with them at Glenkirk. Then, he went to report to the king.

When Adam returned from court to the inn where Janet was staying, he brought an invitation for his sister to meet the young king. Janet could not refuse, but Adam was distressed. His sister laughed at him.

"It would seem strange if you tried to hide me, Adam. If you stick to our story, no one will know my 'shameful' past."

Charles laughingly agreed with his mother and personally escorted her to James' reception. She took the court by storm. She wore a low-cut black velvet gown, the floral design on the bodice embroidered in pearls and gold thread. Her gold tissue underskirt glittered with rubies and pearls, as did the white silk showing through the slashes in her gold embroidered sleeves, the wrists of which were edged in fine, wide, Venetian lace. Around the base of her neck was a flat necklace made of alternating gold squares each with a ruby center. From the center square hung a large gold and ruby square with a large teardrop pearl. A second necklace, similar to the first but without the pendant, hung below the other into her bodice.

Her hair, parted in the center, was hidden beneath a beautiful cap matching her gown. It was set half way back on her head and from it flowed a sheer black silk veil.

The king was enchanted. Lady Leslie might be old enough to be his mother, but by God she was a beauty! Half-Stewart, half-Tudor, James would not have been his lusty parents' son had he not made an overture.

Putting her slender hand on his, Janet smiled warmly up into his eyes. "My lord, were I ten years younger I should seriously consider your offer. As it is I am extremely honored by Your Majesty's kind favor."

"The rogue," she later laughed to her son and her brother.

Charles laughed with her, but Adam was shocked. "You could be his grandmother," he said.

"I most certainly could not!" she snapped back. "God's bones, Adam! What a prig you've become. Father would have laughed as does my son."

Several days later, they left for Glenkirk, but not before Fergus More had paid them a visit. As they rode from the city, the earl of Glenkirk was richer by two hundred and fifty pounds gold, and Lady Janet Leslie was the owner of Glen Rae, its surrounding hills, lake and island. Each was well satisfied.

Janet Leslie was returning, after more than forty years, to her ancestral home, and as the cavalcade wended its way down the hills that surrounded Glenkirk Castle, Anne MacDonald Leslie, countess of Glenkirk, sat in her bedchamber receiving reports of its progress. She was a handsome woman of forty-five with a clear peachy complexion, beautiful dark brown hair, and cold gray eyes.

"They are almost to the bridge, my lady," said her chief waiting woman. "We will just have time to reach the courtyard."

"No, Hannah. I am not going down. It is vital that my lord's sister learn immediately her place in my house as a poor pensioner is of no importance. If this lesson is not made clear in the beginning, I shall have a querulous old woman upsetting the routine of my household. I want you to secret yourself somewhere where you can see, but not be seen. Report back to me as soon as possible."

"Yes, my lady."

Moving swiftly through the stone corridors, Hannah slipped into a small enclosure that overlooked the entry court. She was just in time to see the lord of Glenkirk and his party enter the castle yard. She waited while the men-at-arms guarding the convoy dispersed. She could identify the earl and his nephew, Sir Charles. There were three women, but two were obviously servants. The third wore an elegant, dark hooded cloak. As Sir Charles helped her to dismount, the hood fell back, and Hannah gasped in amazement. I must get closer, she thought. That cannot be my lord's sister! Squeezing out of her cubbyhole, she scampered down to the courtyard.

"Welcome home, my lord. My lady is indisposed and begs to be excused."

"Thank you, Hannah. Nothing serious?"

"Nay, sir. She will be up by dinner."

The earl drew the beauty forward. "Janet, this is Anne's waiting woman, Hannah. Hannah, this is my sister, Lady Leslie. She will show you and your women to your apartments."

"Och, my lord, Lady Leslie will think us terribly ill-prepared, but we were not sure when to expect you, and several of the maids have been ill with the flu. If my lady and her companions will follow me, there is a good fire going in the Great Hall, and she may wait there while I finish the preparations."

"Thank you, Hannah," Lady Leslie said in her musical voice. "Adam, go see to Anne. You also, my son. Now, Hannah," she spoke as she walked, "since naught is prepared for me, I would reside in the apartments in the West Tower. They are available?"

"Yes, my lady, but—"

"Good! This is my Marian, and her daughter, Ruth. They will help you. I have brought draperies, rugs, featherbeds, linens, and all manner of things to make me comfortable. See that the trunks are carried up to my tower. Be sure there is plenty of wood for my fires. And you don't have to escort me to the Great Hall. I remember the way quite well. After all, I grew up here. Thank you, Hannah."

Stunned, Hannah watched the beauty leave her. Then turning to Marian she asked, "Is she always like that?"

"She ran a household a hundred times the size of this one," snapped Marian. "My, but you're a quick one, my dear. What shabby quarters did your mistress prepare for mine? My lady was not fooled, you know. However, she does admire your loyalty."

Janet walked into the main hall of the castle and up the stairs to the Great Hall which was on the second floor of the building. Four steps led up from the anteroom to a landing. Four steps led down from the landing into the hall. To the right and to the left were enormous fireplaces flanked on either side by tall, high glass windows. In front of her was the dining board in the shape of a T, on either side of which were also windows. It looked the same as it had when she had left it, except for two large, full-length portraits that hung over each fireplace. The painting on the right was of her father as she remembered him—a big, sensuous male animal. Tears clouded her vision for a moment, and she said a silent prayer for him.

Over the other fireplace hung her own portrait—the one her father had commissioned in San Lorenzo. It pictured her in her betrothal gown and had been finished just before she was kidnapped. She couldn't help smiling at the innocent, haughty little face that stared out of the picture.

"Except that your hair is lighter, you look just the same, madame. You must tell me your secret."

Janet descended the steps into the hall and saw on a long bench by the left fireplace a tiny blond woman with laughing gray-blue eyes.

"I am Jane Dundas Leslie, your nephew Ian's wife. Forgive me for nae rising, but," she patted her distended belly, "it would take too long."

Janet laughed. "I was in the same position five times, child. Soon?"

"Last week according to the midwife; however, my son refuses to obey the midwife! Fiona was due after me, but she may birth her second afore I hae my first."

"Patience," counseled Janet sitting down next to the girl. "How old are you, Jane?"

"Just seventeen. How old were you when you had yer first?"

"Almost fifteen."

"Oh, Jane!" cried a disappointed voice. "You hae met her first."

A slender girl flew down the steps and across the room to Janet. "Welcome home, madame belle mère. I am Fiona." She chuckled as Janet's startled eyes swept her figure. "I never show except the littlest bit." She pulled her gown tight across her middle revealing a gentle swell of belly. "Awful, isn't it? I am so proud of bearing Charles' children, and no one ever knows it till I appear wi' a bairn in my arms!"

"So, mother, ye've met my wench," said Charles entering the hall.

"Barely. And I've met Jane too. I have been so very sad about leaving your brother and sister, and all their children behind; but I can now see I have a lovely family right here. Sit down, Fiona, and let me look at you."

If she had picked the girl herself she could not have been more delighted. Masses of tumbling blue-black hair surrounded a rosy face. She had dark blue eyes, a straight little nose, and a rosebud mouth set with a sweet expression. It was an intelligent face, and a kind one.

Janet turned to look at her son. "You hae yer father's eye for beauty, my son."

"Aye," he said, "I do. I also look as he did for loyalty, intelligence and spirit. Like you, Fiona has all of these qualities."

For a moment her eyes filled with tears, but she held them back. "Where is my grandson?"

He laughed, "I thought you would be unable to contain yourself for very long, mother. Ah, here is his nurse now."

A pink-cheeked young woman descended the steps into the hall. She carried a plump, dark-haired baby boy with a serious expression in his bright eyes. Janet held out her arms, and without a murmur the child went to her. For a minute they looked at each other, then the child touched her cheek with his tiny hand, and said, "Mam!"

"Yes, Patrick. I am your grandmother. I am mam."

Sitting down on the settle, she placed the baby on the floor and handed him a gold bracelet from her arm, which he began to chew on vigorously.

"I do not believe it," said Fiona. "Patrick never goes to anyone but his father, nurse or me. Even Uncle Adam cannot thaw him, and the Lady Anne sets him to screaming."

"But I am his grandmother," replied Janet with aggravating logic.

And for the next hour the little group sat talking, reminding Janet very much of the evenings she, Selim, and the Lady Refet had made a family party. Then Ruth came to escort her to her apartments.

Marian, Ruth, Hannah, and several maids had worked quickly. They had swept the entire tower apartment which consisted of three floors. The first contained an anteroom and two small bedrooms; the second floor was a dining room and a little kitchen. The top floor of the tower held the master bedroom and garderobe. All of the rooms excepting the garderobe had fireplaces, and all of the fireplaces were blazing merrily, taking the chill off the long-unused tower.

The garderobe bulged with Lady Leslie's clothing, shoes, and jewels. On the sideboard a great silver charger gleamed, and crystal decanters sparkled with golden sherry and ruby wine. And everywhere pure, faintly scented bceswax candles twinkled.

"A miracle," said Janet upon finishing her tour of inspection. "Thank you for all your help. If I might ask one more favor, Hannah, would you have hot water brought for my bath? Marian, has the tub been put in the garderobe?"

"Yes, m'lady. Shall I have it set up by the fire?"

"Please." Turning to Hannah again she said, "Go to my sister the Lady Anne and tell her I am now comfortably

settled. I shall look forward to meeting her at the dinner
hour."

It was at least another half an hour before Hannah
was able to return to her mistress's apartments, and then
she had to wait as the earl was with his wife. When he
had finally left, she bustled in.

"Where have you been? It's been three hours! I understand my lord's sister brought wi' her two servants. She
will have to dismiss them. I will not feed idle mouths.
Such airs! She is little better than a servant herself. It is
bad enough I must feed and house her, her son, his wife
and children."

"M'lady. I think Lady Janet can more than well afford
servants, and these women—a mother and daughter—
hae been wi' her for many years."

"I shall speak wi' her myself, Hannah. Has she been
settled in her room in the North Wing?"

"Nay, m'lady. The Lady Janet wanted the apartment
in the West Tower."

"Did she? I see that we hae an autocratic old woman
who would try to run my house. Have her baggage put
into the room I had prepared, Hannah! I must be firmer
than I thought. Well, what is it?"

"Madame, I think I would suggest that you meet the
Lady Janet before making any decisions. I cannot force
the lady, my lord's sister, from her chosen place."

The countess looked outraged, then said, "Aye. It
would be better for me to make my position clear at
once with this old woman."

"She is nae old, m'lady."

"Not old? Of course she is old. She has passed the half
century mark."

"My lady Anne, the earl's sister may have lived fifty
years, but her face and form are those of a much younger
woman. She is the most beautiful woman I've ever seen!
And what's more, she is, I believe, extremely wealthy!"

"Hannah! You've been bewitched! Come along! I shall
go and meet this wonder."

Upon her arrival at the West Tower, the countess was
told by a firm Marian that she would have to wait until
the Lady Janet was finished bathing. Ten minutes later
she was ushered upstairs to Janet's bedchamber. The
woman who greeted her literally took her breath away.

She wore a loose pale green silk garment the top and
sleeves of which were embroidered delicately in gold
thread and tiny seed pearls. There were matching slippers
on her feet, and her hair flowed loosely, thick and pale
red, down to her knees.

"My dear Anne," said the beautiful woman, "how
kind of you to shelter me in your home." The countess
felt herself kissed on each cheek. "I do hope," the voice
went on, "you will forgive me for appropriating the West
Tower, but your good Hannah said it was not being used.
I am sure you worked hard to prepare charming quarters
for me, but I thought I should be less trouble to you here
out of the way. It will only be until my own house is
built."

"Yes, yes. Whatever pleases you," Anne heard herself
say. "You are building a house? Where?"

"Adam has sold me some land. Glen Rae, the loch and
its island for 250 pounds. I know I am wicked to spurn
your hospitality, but I shall not be happy until I am in
my own home again. Besides it will be a fine legacy for
Charles and his family, don't you agree?"

"Oh, yes! A fine legacy. I hope you will forgive me for
invading your privacy, but I did want to be sure that
everything had been done for your comfort."

"How kind you are," murmured Janet sweetly. "I see,
dear sister, that you admire my caftan."

"What?"

"My gown. It is called a caftan in the East. A loose
garment for relaxation. I have brought you one. Ruth,
the scarlet caftan, and matching slippers."

Before Anne could protest, Ruth was hurrying out of
the garderobe carrying a folded scarlet gown and slippers.
She held it up for her mistress's inspection, and Anne
gasped. The caftan's embroidery was of tiny diamonds,
turquoise and gold thread.

"When Adam told me of your wonderful dark brown
hair and fair complexion, I had this made for you." Instinctively Janet had played on her sister-in-law's vanity.
"Dinna refuse me, Anne."

For a moment the countess's features softened as she
fingered the lovely silk. "Thank you, Janet. It is the
loveliest thing I hae ever owned."

"I am so pleased I chose well," said Janet. "Now,

dear sister, you must excuse me. The day has been a long one, and I would rest before the dinner hour."

"Yes, yes, of course," replied the countess allowing herself to be led out.

A few minutes later Marian returned to her mistress. "Ah, madame, the Lady Anne came to cause trouble, but you have confused her completely."

"For the moment, my friend. I was expecting an attack and acted accordingly. However, dear Anne will recover quickly and try to attack again. It will be amusing to play with her. She is her own worst enemy."

"I am happy to see you have recovered from your melancholy," chuckled Marian. She drew the coverlet over her mistress. "I will call you in time for dinner madame."

Janet lay quietly, her green-gold eyes closed. I am home, she thought. I have fulfilled a childhood promise and come home. I wonder what will happen next?

41

By THE TIME ANNE LESLIE reached her apartments she was beginning to recover from the severe shock she had received upon discovering that her sister-in-law was not only beautiful, but obviously extremely wealthy. It would take a readjustment in her thinking to decide what to do and how to handle the situation. In the meantime she needed someone upon whom to vent her frustration. Unfortunately the earl chose that moment to appear in his wife's rooms.

"Ah, my dear, I was looking for you."

"I have been wi' your sister—if she is yer sister. For a woman over fifty, she is remarkably youthful."

"Isn't she?" smiled Adam. "But then father was eighty when he died last year, and yet no one would believe his age. Most took him for sixty-five or so."

"You look your age!"

"I also look like my mother's family. Jan is pure Leslie."

Anne took another tact. "I can believe she's pure Leslie. She has high-handedly appropriated the West Tower!"

"It wasn't being used," he replied. "I thank God my sister dinna see the room you *did* prepare for her! What were you thinking of, Anne? A tiny room no bigger than a nun's cell next to the servants' quarters in the oldest part of the castle—wi' no fireplace and only a pallet bed and one chest."

"I believed I was receiving an elderly woman who would need peace and quiet."

"But no heat," finished the earl wryly. "Anne, yer a bitch! Janet is my sister, and the odds that I would find her were incredible. My father grieved most of his

life for her. I only wished to heaven he'd lived another
year to see her safe home. She is to hae whatever she
wants in this house!"

"From what I gather she already had, m'lord. How
could you sell part of our son's inheritance? And for only
250 pounds?!"

"250 pounds *gold*, my dear avaricious wife."

"Gold?"

"Gold," smiled Adam Leslie. "And Janet is entitled
to Leslie land. Like our son, she, too, was born a Leslie."
So saying, he turned on his heel, and left his countess
openmouthed.

But Anne's ordeal for the day was not quite over.
She went down to dinner to find her beautiful sister-in-
law the center of a happy family gathering. Janet was
clad in a simple, high-necked, long-sleeved gown of midnight blue silk with creamy lace showing at the neck,
and cascading from the wrists. Her lovely hair, center
parted and braided in a three tier coronet added elegance. Around her neck was a simple gold chain. Seated
on a wooden settle by a fireplace she was surrounded
by Fiona, Jane, and—much to Anne's surprise—Agnes, her
daughter, home from the convent. The earl, Ian, and
Charles, dressed in their kilts, stood on the outside of the
group.

For a moment Anne was enchanted by the charming
picture, but then a stab of jealousy went through her.
Never since she had come into this house as a bride
had the hall rung with merriment like this. Never had
her own daughter, or daughter-in-law, or even Fiona,
laughed with her as they were doing now with Janet. The
woman was obviously a witch!

The countess walked to the dais. "If ye dinna come
to table, the dinner will be burned," she said sharply.
Angrily she watched as her own son seated Janet to his
father's right in his own place and then sat next to her.

During most of the dinner, Anne remained silent, listening as they all plied Janet with questions about the
East, its peoples, and their ways. Wretched godless infidels, thought Anne Leslie. They ought to be burned
to ashes. Lewd, lustful creatures openly debauching innocent Christian virgins, male and female. She had heard
stories! They should all be destroyed including her sister-

in-law who had lived among them. What kind of a woman lived for almost forty years in a non-Catholic land and came back unscathed?

Within a week, Janet was thoroughly at home again. To Anne's dismay, she even allowed a tribe of gypsies to camp for a few days on the estate, and when they left, Janet was the owner of a large, half-wild black stallion that she took to riding at breakneck speed all over the district. He was a magnificent beast, and she knew it was considered outrageous that she owned him. Women were supposed to ride dull, docile brown creatures named Lady, or Princess, not big, sweating black brutes called Devil Wind. Selim had owned such a horse with the same name, and when she had seen her own Devil Wind, she had known she must have him. She had bought him in late June—a skinny, half-broken two-year-old— from a tribe of passing tinkers. She had known at once that he was pure Arab, and consequently had barely haggled the price with their leader. And despite Anne's carping, Janet had offered the gypsies the hospitality of Leslie lands. The headman had thanked her.

"Majesty, we are grateful for ourselves, and for the horses." Falling to his knees he made her obeisance.

Startled, she told him to rise. "I am no queen, man!"

He looked at her, his eyes startlingly clear, and bottomless.

"Ye shouldna left him, my lady. He will be great, but had ye stayed, he would hae been greater."

For a moment she could neither speak, nor breathe. "I see things, my lady. I canna help myself."

She nodded and, feeling able now to reply, said, "Bring the horse to the castle tomorrow. I'll pay then— in gold—and dinna try to cheat me by switching horses."

He flashed her a smile. "And be hunted through half the world, madame?"

She laughed. "Ye see too much, tinker."

"I see the truth, madame."

She turned and walked away.

"Allah go we' ye," he called softly.

"And ye also," she replied as softly, never turning back.

When she went riding, Janet was invariably accom-

panied by Adam's bastard, Red Hugh More, who had
trained Devil Wind.

Anne, on the other hand, had spent a good part of
her married life avoiding Hugh More. Despite the fact
that he was Adam's only byblow and had been born
before she even came to Glenkirk as Adam's wife,
Anne hated Hugh, and his mother Jeannie.

Jeannie's family had lived and worked on Leslie lands
for as long as anyone could remember. Jeannie had been
a sixteen-year-old milkmaid when she had caught Adam's
eye. She hadn't been a virgin since she was twelve, but
she was no wanton. When she told Adam she was expecting his child, the fifteen-year-old boy knew she spoke
the truth. When the child was born at Michaelmas, it
was obvious that he was Adam's son; he had his father's
nose, mouth and birthmark on one buttock and his
paternal grandfather's red hair. The Leslies recognized
him, and Patrick Leslie held him at the christening while
Adam acted as godfather to his son. Jeannie was offered,
and accepted, a small cottage on the estate, and a yearly
annuity.

She lived quietly with her child, who saw his father
quite regularly. Occasionally Adam even sought solace
in her bed, for his bride was a cold, proud girl. Jeannie
was careful, however, that there were no more children.
Hugh was eight when the countess discovered his existence.

Heavy with her second child, mourning the death of
her first son, Donald, she had several times passed a boy
exiting the family vault in the chapel. Upon entering
she had found wildflowers on her baby son's tomb. She
was touched, and after this had happened several times
she stopped the boy.

"Do you put flowers on Lord Donald's tomb?"

"Aye, madame," came the reply.

"Why?"

Red Hugh More had never seen the countess in his
life, so it was in all innocence that he answered, "The
bairn were my half-brother."

Numbed, Anne asked, "Who is yer mother?"

"Jeannie More," said the boy. "We hae a wee cottage
in the glen."

"And yer father?" Her voice shook slightly.

"The lord Adam, ma'am."

"Do ye ken who I am?"

"Nay, madame."

"I am lord Adam's wife, and," her voice rose shrilly, "I forbid ye to ever come here again! My children are nae related to any peasant whore's bastard! Get out! I never want to see yer face again!"

The lad fled, and several days afterwards her father-in-law came and spoke to her.

"Leslies acknowledge their own," he said quietly. "Ye hae been wed wi' my son six years, and never has he shamed ye as other men do their wives wi' their amours. I dinna think he will unless ye try his patience greatly. Ye are his lady, yer children my heirs. Only ye can change that."

It was enough. She never spoke of it, and neither did Adam. However, once when visiting a sick woman in the glen she noticed a tall, big-boned woman with brown hair and straightforward blue eyes staring at her. "Who is that?" she asked her waiting woman, Hannah. Hannah hesitated, then replied, "Jeannie More." Strangely the countess was relieved. She had pictured her rival a lush peasant beauty, hardly this plain, big woman. The knowledge soothed her vanity.

Anne was sure that her sister-in-law had chosen Red Hugh More to captain the men-at-arms she was hiring simply to annoy her. Janet knew her bastard nephew annoyed Anne, but she had chosen him because she knew that the most trustworthy captain of one's own guards was likely to be a relative. Besides, Janet liked Red Hugh. The big, blue-eyed red-haired giant was loyal, charming, and was already paying court to Marian's daughter, Ruth.

For the next few months, Janet spent much of her time checking on the progress of Sithean, her new home. Sithean, pronounced "Shee-ann", meant Fairy Knoll in Gaelic, and Janet had given the estate that name because it was being built on a tiny island believed by the peasants to have been inhabited in ancient times by the fairies.

The island was located almost a quarter of a mile off the main shore of the loch, and an elaborate, heavily fortified bridge had been built linking the two. The castle, built at the narrow end of the island, was surrounded on three sides by water. The remaining land was carefully gardened and terraced with two small pastures set aside for the horses, sheep and cattle. Then as a final precaution, a stone wall, interspersed at even intervals with watch towers was set around the entire island.

"The expense," moaned Anne one day. "Ye've built it to withstand a siege."

Janet could feel her temper rising, but knowing that sweetness nettled her sister-in-law more than a sharp retort, she replied, "I am a woman alone. Easy prey for the lawless in these hard times. Would you prefer I stay wi' you and Adam?" She laughed at the look on Anne's face. "Come, Anne, be honest wi' me for once. Ye count the days till Sithean is habitable."

"Ye spend yer gold as though it were endless."

"It is."

"Think of yer son."

"My son?"

"If ye waste yer gold, what will be left for him to inherit?"

"Charles will inherit Sithean, *and* my gold."

"Ye speak as though ye were a queen!"

"I am," replied Janet, and for the barest moment a sad look touched her eyes. But Anne Leslie was neither quick nor intuitive enough to see it.

"Bah," she snapped at Janet. "Yer mad!"

"Then ye shouldna be troubled wi' my company any longer," said Janet as she turned and left the room.

I don't know what Adam sees in that woman, thought Janet. My God, if they don't finish Sithean soon I shall kill her! Snatching up her cloak she headed for the stables. "Ho, Gordy! Saddle Devil Wind!" The groom scrambled to obey her, and a moment later Janet, mounted on her big, black stallion and accompanied by Red Hugh, galloped away. The wind tore at her hood, but it was anchored firmly. The gray wildness of the day helped to restore her temper, and she turned the horse into the woods towards Sithean. The wet, matted leaves beneath his hooves muffled the sound as they raced through the forest. As they neared the hills above the loch, she slowed the horse.

"Easy, laddy," she crooned, patting his neck. They had reached the crest of the hills that bordered the loch. For a moment she stopped, and looked down on her domain. She was thankful that she would soon have her own home again. It would be ready before Christmas, and Charles, Fiona, and the children would be coming. She intended telling Charles that since Sithean would be his one day, he and his family were welcome to make their home there now.

Had it not been for the small house off High Street in Edinburgh that Fiona's parents left her, she and Charles would have been totally dependent on the hospitality of Glenkirk. Janet knew, however, that both Adam and Fiona hated living in Edinburgh. With this in mind she had had one large wing at Sithean constructed so that her son's family might have their privacy and she might have hers. If Charles accepted her offer, the house in town might be let for a fine price.

Devil Wind was straining at his bit now, so loosening her hold on the reins, she cantered down the hill to the loch and across the bridge. Red Hugh helped her dismount.

"Yer in a fine tearing temper. I dinna have to ask who ye've been talking to this day."

"My God!" she exploded. "That woman would try the patience of a saint! Nag, nag, nag! Now she claims I spend too much money building Sithean. Is it her money? No! 'Tis mine! Mine! The bitch!"

Red Hugh laughed. "Aye," he drawled, "I've oft felt that way myself. My father would come to the cottage to see me and mother, and there were times he'd look so angry I'd hide until mum had softened him up."

"And how did she do that, my lad?"

"The same way you undoubtedly softened your own lord out of a fit of the glooms," he grinned.

"Wretch!" She swatted at him. "Come along, nephew. If I am to move in by Christmas, I had best see how the work is coming along. Find the foreman for me."

While he went to do her bidding, she walked up to the second floor of the house which was built in the shape of an H. Walking into the gallery that made up the crosspiece of the H, she smiled in satisfaction. The sun had come out, and golden light was pouring in through the windows, which were staggered on both sides of the long room so that no two faced each other. They were tall, mullioned windows shaped like inverted U's and between them were expanses of wall that would soon be covered with paintings and tapestries. At each corner of the gallery she had had fireplaces built. Filled with lights, it would be a lovely place to sit.

It was here Hugh and the foreman found her, and after a few minutes of discussion, she was satisfied that the house would soon be ready. Riding back she turned to her nephew.

"I think I shall annoy Anne tonight and wear my new green velvet gown."

"I trust it is sufficiently low cut in the newest fashion."

"Very. Ye've been talking to my Ruth."

"I like talking to Ruth."

"Unless you decide to marry her, make sure talk is all you do, my fine buck. Marian is my friend, as well as my servant. I look on Ruth as I would my own daughter. She is not to be seduced."

"Yes, m'lady," he grinned at her.

"Arrogant ape," she chuckled at him. "I mean it. Now, let's race! My Devil Wind against your Thunderer!"

Both horses surged forward. Neither rider saw the lone horseman on the hill above them. He had been there several times in the last few weeks, but so secure were Janet and her nephew in the safety of their own land, they had not noticed.

"I think," said the master of Grayhaven to his horse, "that it is time I paid a visit to Glenkirk."

42

Had Anne Leslie not been so openly interfering of
Janet, and constantly annoyed that the sister-in-law she
had expected to be old, and poverty-stricken, was, instead,
a beautiful and wealthy woman, Janet might not have
taken such pains with her appearance that night. Her
late entrance into the Great Hall at the dinner hour
momentarily stopped all conversation.

She wore a velvet gown of forest green, its low-cut
bodice embroidered in gold thread, tiny topaz, and pearls.
On her head was a green velvet cap edged in gold
lace and pearls with a soft gold gauze veil that flowed
behind her, covering her pale red-gold hair. Around
her slender neck she wore a magnificent rope of creamy
pearls.

Adam rushed from the dais to lead his sister to the
main table where Anne barely nodded to her greeting
of "Good even, sister." But before she could be seated,
Adam was introducing her to his guest.

"Janet, this is Lord Hay, the master of Grayhaven."

Automatically she extended her hand and raised her
green-gold eyes to a pair of heavy-lidded leaf-green ones
that lingered a moment too long on her décolletage.

"Colin!"

"So you remember." He smiled. "You were but a
wee bit of a little girl when we last met."

"And you a great, gawky boy, my lord."

Seating her, he drew his chair next to hers and offered
Janet his goblet. She drank sparingly, grimacing as she
did.

"Aye," he chuckled. "The lady Anne knows naught
about wines."

"A kind way of saying my dear sister-in-law keeps a

391

poor table. In my father's day we bought the best, but Anne buys what is least costly."

"You havena changed, my dear. You are as open as ever. It seems I remember a wee maid at court who fought the beauteous Lady Gordon over that rogue, Lord Bothwell. What were you? Ten? Eleven?"

She laughed. "I dinna know ye were at court then. It was just before we sailed for San Lorenzo."

"I was a squire to my cousin, the earl of Erroll. I was in the Great Hall that night you fought wi' the Gordon woman. It was talked of for months after, and then when you were lost, it was talked of again."

"I wasna lost, my lord Hay. I was stolen from my family and sold into slavery. I was fortunate enough to be married to a great lord, and have lived a good life." She said it simply and with dignity. "Of course, you married too, did ye not?"

"Three times—once I got over the disappointment of losing you."

"What?"

"I admired ye greatly, and my father thought he might be able to talk to your father and arrange a match between us. But alas! Before he could, ye went away to San Lorenzo and never returned."

"So instead ye wed three wives and outlived them all. I consider myself lucky to hae escaped ye, my lord. What of yer children?"

"Only three living, though there were several started that died. I hae two sons and a daughter who is a nun. And you?"

"I bore my lord four sons, two of whom were killed in wars. Only the eldest, and the youngest live. I also hae a daughter. I left nine grandchildren behind. And then, of course, I have Charles's two here."

His eyes again caressed the soft swell of her breasts. "I find it hard to believe ye are a grandmother, let alone to eleven brats."

"Ye are overbold, my lord."

"As are you, madame. If ye dinna want yer breasts admired, ye shouldna display them so openly. I should, however, like to see more."

She flushed and to cover her embarrassment bit into

a chicken wing. "I wore this dress," she said quietly
between bites, "to annoy Anne."

"Ye've succeeded admirably, my dear. She's not
stopped looking daggers at you since you made your entrance. She has always fancied herself a beauty, and ye
hae stolen her show."

"From the moment I arrived she has been furious wi'
me. She had pictured some poor, beaten and elderly hag
who she would begrudgingly feed and house—and she
expected plaudits for her Christian generosity! She canna
forgive me for being reasonably attractive in my old age,
and a rich woman to boot!"

"Yer hardly old, madame. In fact I am seriously con-
templating the delights of bedding ye."

"Sir! I am widowed ten years, and a grandmother."

"Madame! I see the full breasts of a young woman, a
tiny waist that my hands could easily span; and I'll
wager beneath yer skirts are long legs, and soft, round
hips. I would explore it all, Janet." He leaned over
and kissed her neck. She trembled, for his lips burned
her skin, and turning quickly away she began to talk
to her brother. Beside her she heard Colin Hay laugh softly.

His admiration and obvious desire embarrassed her.
The Turks were a sensual people, but never showed
affection publicly. She wasn't used to the freedom enjoyed
here. She blushed to see the men around her openly admiring the women, and even caressing them.

Later an old minstrel sang songs that brought back to
her memories of a childhood spent in this very castle.
She stood, her back to the hall, gazing into the orange-
red flames of a roaring fire and thinking about her life.
Suddenly she jumped. Coming up behind her, Colin Hay
had clamped his arm tightly around her waist. He drew
her back against him.

"I want you!" he whispered.

"Let me go," she hissed at him, "or I shall shout
the hall down!"

"I shall come tonight," he said quietly, and loosed her.

Angrily she stomped away to find her brother and bid
him good night. Adam Leslie and his wife sat on the dais
listening to the songs.

"I bid ye good night, Adam, and ye also, Anne."

"So early, my dear," said Adam.

"Adam," said Lady Anne sweetly, "let yer sister go. At her age she needs her sleep."

"But I go not to sleep, Anne. I go to bathe. For the last half hour yer servants hae been lugging water up to my tower. Ye might try it sometime. Not only does it soften the skin and keep it young looking, but it also banishes bad odors." The lady Janet's honeyed voice fooled no one.

Ruth appeared from the shadows to escort her mistress to her apartment. "Ye look like a thundercloud, madame."

Janet whirled on her. "Of course I look like a thundercloud! I hae spent a lovely evening fending off my sister-in-law's shrewish tongue and Lord Hay's indecent proposals!"

Ruth began to giggle. "My lady is more than a match for Lady Anne. As to Lord Hay, all the men are lusty here. It is very different from our old home."

A little smile touched Janet's lips. "You like it, don't ye Ruth? Ye are happy?"

"Oh yes, madame. I do, and I am!"

By now they had arrived at Janet's tower apartment, and passing through the anteroom they climbed the last flight of stairs to the bedroom where Marian waited, dozing in a chair. The fire in the hearth burned high and hot, for Janet, with a complete disregard for her sister-in-law Anne's sparing ways, had insisted on plenty of wood. Before the hearth stood a large, steaming, round oak tub.

"Let yer mother sleep, Ruth. Help me to undress and then take her to her bed."

The younger woman helped Janet to disrobe and assisted her into the tub. Carefully Ruth brushed the green gown and placed it along with the rest of her mistress's clothing and jewels in the garderobe off the bedroom. Gently she laid a sheer, black silk nightgown and robe at the foot of the bed.

"Marian," called Janet quietly. The older woman woke. "Go to bed, my friend. Ruth, help yer mother to her bed and then come back to help me."

Alone, Janet luxuriated in the warmth of the bath, the creamy, sweet-scented soap, and the quiet of the night. She was having a proper Turkish bath put into her own house, but until then, this great, tall wooden tub

would do her. Suddenly she felt a draft as the door to
her bedroom opened. Lord Hay walked into the room.

"Good evening, my dear. Is yer tub big enough for
both of us? Aye. I see it is." He removed his doublet
and shirt and began to strip off his trunk hose.

"Get out!" she shouted. "I'll scream the castle down if
ye dinna get out!"

"Dinna be foolish, my dear. No one will hear ye high
up in yer tower." He was completely naked now.

"Ruth is coming back. She will go for help."

Mounting the two steps to the tub, Colin Hay stepped
into the hot water and faced her. "I have dismissed Ruth
for the night. She has gone to her virgin bed."

"You dared?!"

Reaching out he drew her resisting body towards him.
Bending he found her mouth, and gently, but pos-
sessively, kissed it. He released her. "Now, sweetheart,
scrub my back."

She screamed her rage at him in Turkish, but Colin
Hay just laughed.

"All right," he said. "I'll do yer back first."

Spinning her around he lathered her smooth, long back
with the soap, then washed and rinsed it. Finished, he
pulled her against him, and cupping her breasts in his
hands began to tease the nipples. She squirmed away
from him, and grabbing the bath brush brandished it at
him.

"You bastard!"

"My back, madame."

"Will ye get out of my tub, then?"

"Aye."

Angrily she attacked his back, scrubbing it so hard it
turned beet red. When she had finished, he calmly climbed
out of the tub and began to towel himself dry. She
could not help but look at him, for other than Selim, she
had never seen a naked man.

Colin Hay was big, standing at least six foot three
inches. She knew he was fifty-five, but his body was
lean and well-muscled, its smoothness marred only by
a few old sword scars. His wavy hair was still midnight
black with just a touch of silver at the temples. His
wind-tanned face was handsome and craggy, with a
high, wide forehead, long straight nose, a generous mouth,

and those strange, leaf-green eyes which looked out from beneath thick-lashed eyelids that were always half-closed.

He stood straight now and faced her, and of his masculinity there was no doubt. She flushed as under her fascinated gaze his manhood became large and swollen. She could not seem to draw her eyes away from it.

He laughed softly and holding out his hand commanded her, "Come."

"I have no intention of getting out of this tub, Lord Hay, until you dress yourself and leave my apartments," she returned coldly.

He reached the tub in two strides, and mounting the steps hauled her dripping from the water. Wrapping her struggling body in a towel he forcibly sat her in front of the fireplace. So black was his look that she dared not speak. Her heart was pounding violently with rage and fright.

"Madame, you try my patience! I told ye earlier I intended making love to ye tonight, and I do. God knows I've waited forty years to do so!"

"Do ye take me for a fool?" she exploded. "Do ye expect me to believe that because ye watched me at court when I was but a child, ye hae been pining for me all these years? Aside from your three marriages, I'll wager ye've been in every bed between here and the border, up to the isles and back! And now ye would add me to yer collection. I'll kill ye first!"

As she launched herself at him, the towel that was covering her fell to the ground. As she reached to pick it up, the master of Grayhaven had snatched it away, and before she could stop him, he tumbled her back onto her bed and flung himself on top of her. She fought him violently, clawing and scratching.

Cruelly he forced her legs apart and sliding between them, he drew them up and over his shoulders. Shrieking as she realized his intent, she tried to squirm out of his reach, but he held her buttocks in his big hands. Like silken fire his tongue touched her here and there —teasing, tantalizing, taunting. Sobbing, her control lost, she moaned her desire and shame as his tongue plunged repeatedly into her throbbing softness. Her body arched to meet his mouth, but he slipped up and over her, and kissing the tears on her cheeks, plunged into her. He moved smoothly and rhythmically until she cried out her relief. He quickly followed.

For a few minutes only their rapid breathing broke the stillness. Then Janet rose shakily from the bed and stood by the fireplace. Tears ran silently down her face. Finally she spoke.

"You Westerners call the peoples of the East uncivilized infidels, but never in all my years in Barbary was I treated by any man as you have treated me tonight. As a maiden my innocence was cherished and respected. As my lord's wife and later as his widow I was honored. You are the barbarian, Lord Hay! You have had you way wi' me, now get out!"

Instead he rose from the bed and moving quickly lifted her up and lay her back on the bed again. She tried to escape him, but he laughed at her futile attempts. Slowly his mouth traveled the length of her body burning deeply each spot it touched. Now his big body blotted out her slender one. She could feel her own desire mounting again, and head thrashing from side to side, she moaned and tried to fight it down. He would not let her, and with a skill that terrified her, the master of Grayhaven raped her once again.

Exhausted for the moment, they lay wordlessly upon the bed. Then mustering the little strength she had left, Janet crawled to the farthest corner of the bed, and pulling the coverlet over herself, fell asleep. He knew the battle was not yet over but left her alone for the moment, and wrapping the rest of the coverlet around his own body, he, too, slept.

When he awoke, the early dawn was just beginning to chase the night. Rolling over, he found her sprawled, still sleeping, on her back. Awake she did not look her age, but asleep she was a girl again. Her lovely hair billowed about her. He allowed his eyes the pleasure of traveling the length of the lovely body he had so cruelly loved but a few hours back.

"My god, Jan," he whispered softly. "You are extravagantly beautiful."

"My husband once said the same thing, Colly."

He started. "I dinna realize ye were awake."

"I was not until ye spoke. For many years I was wakened each day by a slave telling me it was time to

arise. The sound of a voice always wakens me." She
reached out to draw the coverlet over herself.

"Don't!"

"Please, my lord."

"What do ye hide I havena already seen?" Gently he
drew her close, and while one arm cradled her, his other
hand began to fondle her breasts.

"Colin, no! No more!" she pleaded. "Until last night
I knew only one man, my husband. Ye have twice
shamed me. I can bear no more."

"Ye hae been widowed ten years, sweetheart. Had
it been he who was left, would he have been so celibate?"

"Ye hae made me a whore."

"I would make ye my wife."

"Never!"

"By God, madame! Ye act as if I had insulted ye
by offering ye my name!"

She started to laugh. "Oh, Colly! Don't ye understand? My whole life has been controlled by men. This
is the first time I've ever been in control of my own
destiny. Neither Adam nor Charles would dare to interfere wi' me, and I am wealthy in my own right. I like
it! If I married ye, then ye would hae the right to control both me and my money. I should never be free
again."

"My God, Janet, I want ye for my own!"

As she cradled his head against her breasts she thought,
Why not? I shall be an old woman soon. Why should
I not take my pleasure while I may. He had no wife
to hurt, and I want him as much as he wants me. Perhaps even more!

She said quietly. "Ye shall have me for yer own, my
lord; and ye shall be the envy of every man in Scotland
—including the king himself—for the beautiful and
wealthy Lady Leslie will be yer mistress."

"Janet!"

"But betray me even once wi' another woman, my
lord, and ye'll nae enter my bed again."

Her hand wound into his dark hair, and she pulled his
head down to her. For the first time she kissed him
willingly, and her lips were softly fragrant beneath his.
He caught his breath in surprise as she scattered little
kisses over his body. Now she was beneath him, her

body moving more voluptuously as each minute went by.
"Not yet," she murmured in his ear, holding him back.

"My God, Jan," his voice was thick, "sweetheart,
please! Yer driving me mad!"

She laughed softly. "But a moment, my lord. Let me
find my own paradise."

Minutes later it was he who cried out his relief, and
again her laughter echoed in the chamber. He slept
deeply, never hearing her rise from the bed. The tub
still stood before the fire, and dipping water from it
into a large kettle, she swung it over the flames, and
when it was hot, poured it back into the tub. Climbing into the water she found the soap, a soft mass, in a
corner. She scrubbed herself swiftly for the lukewarm
tub cooled quickly, and the morning air was cold. Toweling herself dry she slipped into the nightgown and robe
that Ruth had laid out the night before, and turning back
to the rumpled bed lay down and drew the coverlet
over herself. A little smile played about her lips as she
fell asleep.

Ruth for all her innocence had recognized the look
in Lord Hay's eye the evening before. Awaking before
her mother, she dressed quickly, and silently she
slipped up the stairs to her mistress's bedchamber. Hearing nothing she gently opened the door and peeked inside. Janet lay curled on her side sleeping peacefully.
Lord Hay slept sprawled on his stomach. Softly closing
the door Ruth went downstairs to the kitchens. It was still
early, and few people were stirring.

Ruth helped herself to a large joint of cold meat,
freshly baked bread, a large honeycomb, and a pitcher
of ale. Placing it all on a tray, she hurried upstairs again.
She was extremely relieved to have passed no one, and
therefore not had to explain the large meal she carried.
Her relief turned to horror when she reached Janet's
bedroom and found Dumb Jock, the castle's slavey, lugging buckets of water into the room.

"Don't drop that tray, girl, or I'll slap ye!"

"Mother, I—"

"You thought I would be shocked so you meant
to keep it from me. Lord, child! I knew she would take
a lover sooner or later. We're no longer in the harem,
and she needs a man. She has been lonely without one.

Don't slop, Jock lad! Don't look so worried, daughter.
Jock will nae tell on her. She's the first that's been kind
to him. At the sound of her voice, his whole face lights
up. What a pity he canna speak. Take that tray into
them now and get the wine from my lady's cupboard."

The fresh tub steamed before the newly kindled
fire as Ruth set her tray down upon a table. She had
added the crystal wine decanter and two goblets from
Janet's own service.

"Come here, Ruth," said Lord Hay.

Shyly, eyes lowered, she approached the bed. The master of Grayhaven sat up, and reaching out dropped two
gold pieces down the girl's bodice. Hands to her chest,
Ruth blushed.

"Colin!" Janet's voice was amused, and mildly repri-
manding. "Please dinna tease my Ruth."

Colin's eyes twinkled, and he replied, "I thought she
might help scrub my back, hinny. Would ye, Ruth?"

Ruth looked terrified and gratefully fled at Janet's
dismissal.

"Colly! She's a virgin and gently raised."

"She'll nae be a virgin long the way Red Hugh looks
at her." He turned back to Janet and enfolded her in
an embrace. "You are warm, and soft, and," he sniffed
appreciatively, "you smell delicious."

"I bathed before I slept."

"Bathe wi' me now."

"I have no need to bathe again."

"Ye will, soon enough." Laughing he kissed her hungrily, his kisses becoming deeper and sweeter.

"Pig," she murmured weakly at him, her own body
beginning to move in rhythm with his.

Minutes later he grinned down at her, and said, "Ye'll
need a bath now, sweetheart."

She laughed in spite of herself, got up, and climbing
into the tub she asked him, "Don't ye ever take no for
an answer?"

"No," he replied, joining her.

Marian had thoughtfully provided a fresh, hard cake of
soap that smelled like wildflowers, and Janet lathered herself liberally. Handing the soap to Lord Hay, she rinsed
and climbed out of the tub. Drying off, she walked to the
garderobe and emerged a few minutes later wearing a pale

pink silk caftan and soft kid slippers. He had already toweled himself dry and was drawing on his trunk hose as she moved across the room and sat down at the table.

"Wine, or ale, m'lord?"

"Ale." He sat down across from her.

Filling a goblet with ale and a plate high with meat, some bread, and half of the honeycomb, she handed it to him. He ate with gusto, not speaking, quaffing the ale in three gulps. She refilled his goblet.

"Yer not eating?"

"I'm waiting for Marian to bring me my coffee maker. I think she may hesitate to invade our privacy."

"Nonsense," snapped the little woman bustling through the door. "I have simply been too busy fending off the lady Anne."

"Jesu! Is she here?"

"Was, madame. Was. I have sent her packing in a fine huff."

"What in God's name has possessed Anne? She has visited my tower only once since I arrived. Why now? Why this morning?"

"Because, m'lady, she knows ye bathed last night, and this morning she caught Dumb Jock hauling water up here again. Then, too, no one has seen my lord Hay since last night. She is suspicious of ye."

"She is envious of me! How did ye get rid of her?"

"I simply told her ye were bathing, and she could not go in. She was very angry." Marian chuckled.

Janet couldn't help but chuckle back. "Thank you, old friend."

Marian sniffed and placed the coffee making equipment on the table.

"I'll do it," said Janet. "Go back, and guard my door from that dragon."

"Is that Turkish coffee?" asked Colin when Marian had left them.

"Aye. My friend Esther Kira sent it to me."

"Can ye make two cups?"

She nodded. "Where did you learn about Turkish coffee?"

"I've done my share of traveling about the Mediterranean. Being born into the lesser branch of the family meant that I had to acquire money on my own. Each time I married I married richer, and wi' each dowry I mounted a trading expedition to the East. Like you, madame, I am very wealthy."

"Didn't ye love any of yer wives?"

"Moireach, my first wife was a colorless and dull little thing who died bearing me my equally dull and colorless daughter, Margaret. Margaret is a nun. She visits me regularly every two years, sighs over my way of life, my current mistress, and the state of my soul. She goes away promising to pray for me which I am quite sure she does.

"I killed my second wife, Euphemia, when I found her in bed wi' my head groom. Insatiable little bitch! Fortunately there were no brats.

"I came closest to loving my last wife, Ellen. She was a sweet, gentle, kind woman who kept my house, and my life, in perfect order. She gave me my two sons, James and Gilbert, and never complained about my mistresses providing I was discreet—which I was. She died five years ago in the winter." He turned to her. "And you, my dear. Did ye love yer lord?"

For a moment there was perfect silence in the room, and then Janet spoke one word. "Yes."

"Just yes?"

She struggled to gather her thoughts. "I loved my husband more each day he lived. When he died I would have died, also. Had my son not called me back from the brink of the grave, I should not be here now."

Reaching over he took her slim hand in his own great paw. Their eyes met. "If you could gie me but a hundredth part of that love, my dear, I should be well satisfied."

She smiled and handed him a tiny enameled cup of steaming coffee. "Ice, m'lord?"

He took a piece from the bowl she proffered, and dropping it into the coffee drank it down.

"Now, my lord, before Anne forces her way in and causes a painful scene—"

He grinned at her, and standing up walked over to Ruth who had come in and was busying herself by the sideboard. "Make sure the dragon isna lurking about, luv." He patted her backside. Giggling, she slipped from the room.

"Yer a most outrageous man," laughed Janet. "Ye hae

both Marian and Ruth eating out of yer hand. Especially my dearest Marian, who I thought would nae forgive me if she found I had taken a lover."

"Was she with you from the beginning?" he asked.

"Not the first year. My husband gave her to me as a gift when he learned I was to bear him a child. He bought both her and her husband."

"What was his name?"

"Marian's husband? Alan Browne."

"Yer husband," he said quietly. "You always refer to him as 'my husband', or 'my lord'. Ye never use his Christian name."

"No," she replied. "I don't."

Their eyes met, and then he said, "Yer Charles and my younger son, Gilbert, were close friends at the Abbey School. About a year after Charles came, some epidemic ran through the school. Every child there had it in some form, and the good brothers could nae keep up wi' the nursing. Parents were asked to come, but my Ellen had just lost another babe. There was nothing for me to do but pack up and go to nurse Gilly. Charles was also sick, and as Anne was busy at the castle nursing both Ian and Agnes, I cared for both my son and yers. In his delirium Charles spoke Turkish, and having traveled the Mediterranean I understand Turkish."

She sat very quietly, listening to his deep voice.

"There were," he continued, "several things he said that puzzled me. He spoke of 'my father, the sultan,' his Aunt Zuleika who died in the Tile Court, his brother, Suleiman, and his sister, Nilufer. He talked the most of his mother the bas-kadin. He wept because he must leave his mother and father and perhaps never see them again. He worried constantly that no one must know who he really was, or his mother would die. I have never spoken to anyone, even Charles, of these things."

"I thank ye for that, Colin. These things are in the past, and not important."

"I'm a curious man, Janet. I want answers to my questions."

"Ye hae not the right, my lord Hay."

"But I do," he replied quietly. Sitting down on the tumbled bed, he drew her down beside him, and turned her so she faced him.

"Last night I told you I had waited forty years to bed you, and ye accused me of a number of things, but the fact is, my dear, I spoke the truth. I watched you every moment I could the weeks ye and yer father were at court all those years ago. I was at the age where girls were beginning to interest me greatly, and you particularly interested me. I remembered playing wi' ye several times as a child; but now ye were neither a child, nor a woman; and I was on the brink of manhood. God's toenail! Ye were a pert minx the way ye stood up to the king's cousin! Leslie's fiery little wench they called you at court for weeks after you left for San Lorenzo. Then came the word that ye were betrothed to the heir of that damned duchy, followed a few months later by word of yer kidnapping. The king offered to make a match for me, but I would hae none of it. I dinna take my first wife until I was twenty-five, and only then to please my father, for he so desperately wanted grandchildren, heirs to Grayhaven.

"My second wife, Euphemia Keith, was a redhead. I think I married her because I imagined she looked like you would have when ye grew up."

"Did she?" Janet asked.

"Nay. Not at all. When Charles and I had become friends, he showed me that exquisite miniature you gave him to remember ye by. Who painted it?"

"Firousi."

"Who was she?"

"My sister-in-captivity."

"Was she beautiful, too?"

"She was exquisite! Far lovelier than I. A tiny silverblond with eyes the color of turquoise. Firousi was my best and dearest friend."

"And Zuleika?"

Janet laughed. "Yer as persistant as a terrier after a rat."

"Tell me!"

"Nay, Colly. There are others involved. Political implications that ye canna imagine."

"If what I believe to be true really is, then such information in the wrong hands could be very dangerous, my love. I dinna for one minute believe ye were married to a kindly Christian merchant. Ye were probably one of a number of wives of some potentate. I imagine Charles is a prince in his own land."

"Charles is a Scot. This is his land," she said sharply. "He has spent more of his life here than there. He would be dead now had I not smuggled him out. There are malcontents in every land, and if it were known that Charles were alive, his brother could be endangered. Enough of this, Colly! I will discuss it no more!"

Before he could pursue her further, Marian bustled into the room. "Madame, that woman is back. I canna budge her from the anteroom."

Janet rose and calmly walked across the room to a large hanging near the fireplace. Reaching up she touched a thistle carving on the mantle and pulled the hanging aside. A hidden door was revealed.

"Walk down two flights, my lord. Take the door to yer left on the second landing."

He raised her hand to his lips, and turning it quickly kissed the palm. Pushing him through the door, she closed it behind him. Turning to Marian she said, "You may tell the lady Anne that I will receive her now."

43

Autumn deepened, and the trees turned glorious shades of yellow, gold, scarlet, russet, and brown. The crisp, short days turned into long, chill nights. Janet had promised each workman a bushel of white flour and a fattened pig if her house was finished by Saint Margaret's Eve. It was, and after mass on Saint Margaret's Day she personally presented each workman with his bonus. To it she added a gold piece, and the foreman found himself richer by five gold pieces. The master builder was astounded and delighted to find that he, too, was included in the festivities.

His bill, presented with much ceremony, was paid on the spot, and in full. His delight was somewhat tempered when his satisfied client insisted on waiting while he paid off his men. The workmen chuckled with delight for had the Lady Janet not pressed the matter, they might not have been paid. Now their families would be safe over the long winter.

Sithean was to be dedicated on November thirtieth, Saint Andrew's Day. During the next two weeks the house would be furnished and the servants hired. Anne claimed that her sister would have great difficulty hiring servants as the Leslie peasants were lazy and did not want to work. However, this was not the case. The people flocked to Janet, and within a day her servants' hall was full. Lady Leslie was known to be a fair employer who paid the yearly wage on hiring and at Michaelmas thereafter. Her servants' quarters, according to the workmen's gossip, would be warm and dry for there were fireplaces everywhere.

A week before Janet was due to move into her house she asked her son to visit with her after the dinner hour. The fire burnt high in her bedchamber fireplace. She prepared coffee Turkish fashion for them both.

As they sat and sipped the sweet, thick coffee, Charles said, "You've never told me why you came home. You've been here six months, and you've never said a word to me."

"Thanks to my meddling, your brother took a second wife—Khurrem—'the Laughing One.' She was the one I had chosen to lure him from Gulbehar. Suleiman, however, seems to have an unfortunate tendency towards monogomy. He simply switched his allegiance from a passive kitten to an ambitious tiger cat. Khurrem presented your brother with three sons and a daughter. Gulbehar is now exiled to Magnesia where yer nephew, Prince Mustafa, governs for his father. When yer uncle Adam arrived in Istanbul seeking me I took it as a sign and staged my death so I might return home. It had reached the point where either I must go, or I must dispose of Khurrem. Twice in the last year she tried to poison me. Suleiman adores her, and I could not have hurt him. So I chose to come home to Scotland."

"I would have had the girl bowstringed," said Charles grimly.

"Ahhh," smiled Janet. "There speaks the Turk! You are yer father's son, Prince Karim."

"I was only six when ye sent me away, mother, but I forgot nothing. As a child I whispered my memories like a litany in the dark of night. Tell me. Are my aunts Firousi and Sarina still alive?"

"Yes. They live with the twins and their families. Sarina is raising her grandson, Suleiman."

"And my father? How did he die? We only heard that the Grand Turk Selim was dead. There was much rejoicing and masses of thanksgiving until Suleiman showed his teeth and attacked Belgrade."

"He died of the cancer that had been eating at his belly all those years. He was on campaign."

"I'll pray for him, mother."

"Then there will be two of us. I pray for him each day."

"And yet ye've taken a lover."

For an instant her eyes blazed green fire at him. Then she laughed softly. "Yer shocked, aren't ye, my son? How typically Turkish. Yer Aunt Anne is firmly convinced that the peoples of the East are evil, debauched creatures. How surprised she would be to find them highly moral, even more so than the Scots. Aye, Charles, Lord Hay is my lover, and more than that I willna say. It isna yer business. I do, however, expect ye to be courteous to Colly."

"I like Lord Hay, mother. I always have. I hope that perhaps ye'll wed wi' him if he asks ye."

"He has already asked."

"Mother!"

"But I refused. I dinna wish to marry anyone. Enough, Charles! I did not ask ye here to discuss me. I am moving into Sithean after it's dedicated on November thirtieth. I have furnished the entire East Wing for you, Fiona and the children. Since ye'll inherit it some day, ye might as well hae part of it now. I dinna want ye dependent upon Glenkirk's hospitality, and I know Fiona hates living in Edinburgh. Rent the house there. It should gie you a nice income."

"Mother! What can I say to you? I dinna even hae to ask Fiona. Thanks to ye, we'll hae a real home at last!" Then his face fell. "But we canna afford the upkeep."

"Ye shouldna have to, my son. Sithean is mine. Its upkeep and the servants are all my responsibility. Yer brother is having an extremely generous amount deposited yearly wi' the Kiras for my use, and I took all my jewelry wi' me."

He took both her hands in his and kissed them. "Thank you," he said simply.

"Go tell Fiona. And dinna worry for yer privacy. The entire East Wing is yers. The West Wing is mine. I shall speak to you further in the morning." She walked him to the door and kissed him. "Good night, my son. Send Marian to me on yer way down."

"You have done a good thing, madame," said Marian when she entered the room a few minutes later. "Sir Charles is floating, so happy he is."

"Come, Marian, ye surely never thought I was building that large stone barn for myself alone."

"It's a castle fit for nobility, madame."

"Yes, isn't it," purred Janet.

"And how will ye accomplish that? No! Don't tell me. You'll have an earldom for him before yer through. When you get that look in yer eye—"

Janet laughed. "I want the pale gold silk nightgown and robe. There's a border moon tonight, and I think Lord Hay will come."

After helping Janet remove her gown and petticoats, Marian placed a small tub from the garderobe in front of the fireplace, and filling it with warm water from a steaming kettle, added to it several drops of scented oil from a crystal flacon. Janet stood quietly in the tub as her waiting woman sponged her entire body with the fragrant water.

"It's outrageous that a woman yer age should look as ye do," muttered Marian wrapping her mistress in a warm towel, and thoroughly drying her. Next she poured a pale green cream from a gold bottle into her hand and massaged her lady's skin starting at the soles of her feet, and working upwards to her neck. She then sat Janet at her dressing table and brushed her beautiful hair till it crackled and glistened.

"Stand up, madame."

With a large lamb's wool puff, she dusted an extra fine scented powder over Janet and rubbed it into the skin with a silk cloth. Marian helped Janet into her nightgown, sheer pale gold silk held up by ribbons at the shoulders, the low bodice covered in a fine lace, and a ribbon at the waist. Janet then put on a matching cape edged from neck to hem in a thin band of dark sable. It tied at the throat with a single silk ribbon.

"I don't know why you bother," said Marian tartly. "He'll have it off you quick enough."

"Was not my lord Selim the same?"

"Aye. Men are alike that way."

She carried the little tub into the garderobe. Coming back into the bedchamber she said, "I had Ruth put wine, bread and a joint o' mutton in your cupboard. I fancy his lordship will be hungry after his cold ride."

"Where is Ruth?"

"In her bed. Alone. I saw to that! Earlier, however, I caught Red Hugh sniffing about her."

"I wouldna disapprove a match between them, Marian, but I've warned him not to seduce her."

"Thank ye, madame. He's a good lad, but—experienced, and my Ruth is so innocent."

"Dinna worry, my old friend. I love Ruth as my own Nilufer. I'll let no harm come to her."

"I know, m'lady. Good night now."

"Good night, Marian."

Janet walked to the fireplace, and reaching into a jar on the mantel, drew out a handful of aloes, which she threw on the fire. Standing by the window she gazed into the silver-lit black night. The moon rode high. He would come she knew. For over a month now he had been paying her secret visits, entering Glenkirk by a hidden door at the base of this tower. Besides herself and Colin, only Marian and Ruth knew of the door's existence. She had discovered it when she was a child.

Feeling a draft she turned. He stood, the tapestry to his back, stripping off his gloves. He tossed them along with his cloak on the wooden settle by the fireplace.

"Jesu, sweetheart, it's cold tonight!" He opened his arms. "Come warm me."

"And be frozen to death? No thank you, m'lord. When ye've thawed, I'll consider yer offer." Walking to the cupboard she took out a decanter and goblet, and pouring him some wine, handed it to him. "Are you hungry? Marion has left fresh bread and some mutton.'

"Later." He drained the goblet. "That gown screams rape. If ye dinna want it ruined, take it off."

Sprawled on the bed he watched her. Her slender fingers undid the ribbon on the cape, which slipped to the floor. She shrugged the ribbons off her shoulders and untied the one at her waist. He caught his breath as the gown slid slowly to the floor caressing her ripe breasts, hips and long legs as it sunk into a mass around her ankles. She stepped out of it, and joined him on the bed. Laying back she looked up at him. "Good evening, my lord Hay."

"Madame." He chuckled, and bending kissed the tip of each breast. Instantly they sprang erect. "So," he smiled lazily, "that's how it's going to be." Standing up he stripped off his clothes.

Hungrily she drew him down, and a few moments later they both lay spent and exhausted. For a while only their breathing broke the stillness. Then Janet said, "Are ye warm now, my lord?"

"Aye, and hungry too." Grinning he stood up and helped himself to the bread and meat in the cupboard.

"Gi' me some wine, Colly." He handed her a cup which she sipped slowly. "I told Charles he might have the East Wing of Sithean. He's delighted."

"He should be! Yer damned generous, but I'll feel better knowing that there's a man in the house."

"Red Hugh is a man. He'll be living there, too."

"Still after little Ruth, is he?"

"Aye, but he'll have to wed wi' her to get what he wants. Marian's daughter is no wanton ready for a quick tumble under a hedge."

"Will he?"

"I think so. What he wants of her no other woman, even a virgin, can gie him. My nephew hasna realized it yet, but he's in love!"

"And young Ruth," said Colin, "following yer instructions, no doubt, will first drive poor Hugh wild and then drive him to the altar. Yer a wicked lass, my Jan!"

She laughed. "Ye make it sound so odious! I simply want them both happy."

"If yer for them, they will be, my dear. Now if ye would agree to marry me I should be happy, also."

"Colin, my hinny, ye may have my love, my body, my undivided attention—and aye!—even my money! But I'll nae wed again! It's extremely pleasant being yer mistress, but 'tis even more pleasant being my own mistress."

"I'll keep asking." His eyes twinkled.

Putting her goblet on the table by the bed, she held out her arms to him. He accepted the invitation. They made love tenderly, slowly, each striving to prolong the other's pleasure, and as the moon began to set, they fell asleep.

44

SITHEAN WAS DEDICATED on Saint Andrew's Day in the year fifteen hundred and thirty-three. Janet had been home six months. Afterwards there was a feast. The Lady of Sithean had taken into her household a cook, a bailiff, a dozen housemaids and kitchenmaids, a laundress and two assistants, a spit-boy, three byremaids, a head groom, three undergrooms, a head gamekeeper, two assistant gamekeepers, twenty men-at-arms, their captain, her own personal body servants, two nursemaids for the nursery, and a priest. In all she was to be responsible for feeding, clothing, and housing fifty-three souls, not including her own family which now consisted of herself, Charles, Fiona, and their two babies, Patrick and baby Charles. It was not, however, considered a large household.

The celebration was for the family and a few friends. The earl of Glenkirk came with his countess. Ian, and his pretty Jane, who was again with child, came with their five-month-old son, Patrick. He was called "Wee Patrick" to distinguish him from his older cousin, Fiona and Charles' Patrick who would be two in January. Sister Mary Agnes, Janet's niece had come from her convent near Edinburgh in the company of her friend, Sister Margaret Mary, Colin's unfortunate daughter. The master of Grayhaven arrived with his two sons—his heir, James, who brought his bride, Jean Gordon, and his younger son, Gilbert, who was betrothed to Alice Gordon, Jean's younger sister.

Gilbert Hay was twenty, and though twelve-year-old Alice Gordon might some day be attractive, she was not of interest to him now. How he occupied his time became obvious several months later when two of Janet's house-

412

maids confessed to being pregnant, and each tearfully named young Master Gilbert as the culprit.

"Could he not have kept his cod in his breeches for one night?" she raged at Lord Hay. "Not one girl, but two! Do ye know how hard they are to train? For God's sake why did ye betroth a lusty cock of twenty to a child of twelve? It will be two years before they can marry. In that time he'll seduce every virgin for fifty miles around and start his own clan!"

That year, Twelfth Night revels at Sithean were particularly merry, for Janet's younger serving woman, Ruth Browne, was married to Adam's bastard son. As Lord Hay had predicted, Ruth first drove Red Hugh wild, and then she drove him to the altar. Actually it was Hugh's mother who had turned the trick. Out of the blue she had married a prosperous local farmer who had been recently widowed.

Speaking frankly to her son she told him, "Ye'll always be welcoome in our home, Hughie; but ye can see how busy I am wi' Geordie's puir motherless bairns. Cooking and putting up fur this great lot is more work than it was fur just the two of us. I dinna ken why ye dinna wed wi' Lady Janet's sweet Ruth. She's a guid girl, and will make ye a guid home. Perhaps my lady will even gie ye a small cottage."

"Och," he replied, "the one we've lived in will do for me."

"Nay, my son. Yer grandfather gie us that cottage, but we never owned it. When I wed wi' my Geordie, I returned it to yer father. Unless ye wed, yer only home is a barrack."

Red Hugh More thought about that on the long cold ride back to Sithean. All night long he tossed in his chilly, lumpy bed, listening to the snores and moans of his men who were off duty. All the next day he thought of the sweet-faced girl with her soft brown hair and the merry blue eyes that looked so regretful when refusing his bolder advances. By evening he had made up his mind and going to his aunt came bluntly to the point.

"I want to wed wi' Ruth Browne."

"Have ye spoken to her?" Janet inquired.

"Nay. First I wanted yer permission. If ye'll gie it me, I'll speak to Mistress Marian, and then wi' her permission, I'll ask Ruth."

"Very well, Hugh. Ye hae my blessing. Marian, come here." Marian came in from the garderobe where she had been brushing Janet's gowns. "Hugh seeks yer permission to wed wi' Ruth. I hae given him my blessing, but unless ye truly want him for a son, dinna be influenced by my decision."

Marian eyed the big man. "And what," she demanded acidly, "hae ye to offer my daughter except a dubious name and your fine self? Where will ye live? Ye hae no house. My Ruth is gently reared and wouldna take kindly to being a camp follower."

Tongue-tied, poor Hugh stood silently shuffling his feet. Janet, knowing the next move was up to her, spoke up.

"I will, for a wedding present to Hugh, build a small house in my new village of Crannog. They shall also have rooms here in my house for the times when they must remain here. As a wedding gift to Ruth, dear Marian, I will gie her her dowry." She turned to Hugh. "Your bride comes well dowered, nephew. Besides all her clothing, linens, pots, and kitchenware, she has eighty-five gold pieces; her jewelry which consists of a pearl necklace and one of blue Persian lapis; a pair each of pearl, garnet, Persian lapis, and plain gold earrings; and two gold bracelets. And, Hugh, my brother has promised me that ye'll be legally recognized—without the right of inheritance, of course—and from now on, ye'll be known as Hugh More-Leslie. Now, if ye are both satisfied and in agreement, I think we should see if Ruth will hae ye."

"If she won't, I will," chuckled Marian. "Ye hae my blessing too, my son; but treat my daughter well, or ye'll regret it."

Hugh was dismissed to find his prospective bride. With the privilege granted old retainers, Marian sat down on the settle opposite her mistress. The fire blazed merrily.

"Eighty-five gold pieces," she said. "It took me a moment, madame, but I think I've figured it out. Forty years I shared yer captivity. My husband, Alan, may God absolve him, spent twenty-two years before his death a slave to my lord Selim. Our only child was born into captivity, and is now twenty-three. Do not these figures add up to eighty-five?"

Janet smiled. "It was not for nothing that ye helped Alan wi' my lord's accounts. Yes. Yer deduction is quite

correct. I wanted Ruth to have money in her own right,
and so the marriage contract shall read. This way my
nephew must behave himself lest his wife cut him off!"

"Only you would think of that, madame."

At that moment Hugh More-Leslie was pouring out his
heart to Ruth. After hesitating just long enough to make
him believe that she might refuse him, Ruth accepted his
proposal. The wedding was set for Twelfth Night.

The wedding day dawned fair with a bright sun that
sparkled on the new snow. The religious ceremony was
held in Sithean's Chapel of Saint Anne, with the castle
chaplain, Father Paul, officiating. Sir Charles Leslie gave
the bride away. Afterwards Janet gave the newlyweds
a small feast in her own hall in the West Wing.

It was a small celebration, but a merry one, and it
ended in great hilarity with the putting to bed of the
bride and the groom. Since it was winter the newlyweds'
house could not be started until spring, so they were for
the present making their home in the castle.

Janet, Marian, Jean, Fiona and Jane hustled the bride
from the hall to the nuptial chamber. There they divested
the happy girl of her wedding finery, put her into a prettily embroidered soft wool nightgown, brushed her long
hair, and helped her into the bed. They were none too
soon, for the door opened, and a laughing Charles, Ian,
and Adam pushed a grinning Hugh into the room.

"We all wish ye joy," said Janet quietly, herding the
rest of the guests out before any ribald comments could
embarrass Ruth. "Good night, my dear children."

The following morning the mothers of both the bride
and the groom paid the newlyweds an early morning visit.
Several minutes later from the bedchamber window the
bedsheet—with its bloody virgin stain—flew proudly
in the winter wind.

With the festivities of New Years, Twelfth Night, and
the wedding over, things settled down. Janet, in defiance
of her class status, had bought a large herd of sheep and
intended raising them as a cash crop.

The winter was bitterly cold, with blowing snows. Had
Lady Leslie not been popular with the peasants she might
not have obtained the best shepherds in the area to care
for her flock, but she did; and unlike others who lost

over half their new lambs, she retained three quarters of hers.

"Why," she asked Marian one sunny May morning, "do those innocent little creatures gamboling down in the meadow choose to be born during the worst of winter?"

"Because they're stupid, madame! There's no other reason for it," she snapped.

The sheep might be stupid, but the lady of Sithean was wise. Her business flourished. After shearing, the wool was washed, dried, combed and carded by the men and women in Janet's village of Crannog which had sprung up on the lake shore opposite the castle. The process was repeated to make the wool extra-fine. It was then dyed with special dyes made up by Janet herself. The formulas for these dyes were known to her alone. She was assisted by Dumb Jock, Glenkirk's former slavey, whom she had rescued. It was his job to set the dyes. Jock might be voiceless, but he was neither deaf nor unintelligent. He also had a fine sense of humor and chuckled to himself when he heard pleasing comments on the clarity of the wool's color. He wondered what people would say if they knew the dyes were set with sheep's urine.

After dying, the wool was spun and then woven by Janet's own people. There was no mill; instead each family of weavers had its own loom in a separate room off its cottage. This was done to keep the cloth from being stained by either food, smoke, or heat. The shorter bits of wool were used to make felt; the longer strands were woven into a soft, extra-fine woolen cloth which was discreetly brokered by the Kira family in Edinburgh.

The Kiras were her one link with the past. Through them her allowance from Istanbul flowed, and through them she received letters from her dearest friend, Esther Kira. These letters were the source of her greatest pleasure and her greatest pain.

Janet had been home one year when a Kira courier brought her a letter from Esther. Seated in the bay of her private anteroom, Marian and Ruth with her, she opened the large packet. She began to read aloud.

Beloved madame,
As I now judge it safe to write, I send this message to you by the hand of my nephew, Aaron. It is

carried on his person at all times, and in the event the ship shoud be attacked by any of Khair ad-Din Pasha's friendly ships, or the equally friendly ships of the Christian nations between here and Leith, he is to destroy the letter immediately. Should you be reading these words, however, then praise be to God, or Allah, or Yahweh, or whoever!

The seated women laughed, and then Janet continued.

Your son has mourned you greatly. Removing yourself from his sphere has truly made you dead to him. Khurrem has, of course, taken advantage of this. You had not been gone a week when we received word that old Shah Ismail's son, Prince Tahmasp, had broken the truce made so many years ago with Sultan Selim. The prince captured Bitlis, and his horsemen were seen at Baghdad.

Sultan Suleiman sent Ibrahim Pasha to put down this rebellion. This was done at Khurrem's suggestion. At first I did not understand the reasoning behind it, but as I have watched carefully over the months I now know with certainty that she is out to destroy Ibrahim. You were wrong, madame, to assume her only ambition lay within the harem. She would rule the empire, but not subtly as you did, but openly and boldly. With Gulbehar and Cyra Hafise gone, only Ibrahim Pasha and Prince Mustafa stand in her way, and I fear for them both. She managed to have Iskander Chelebi sent with Ibrahim Pasha to quell the rebellion.

"God in heaven," whispered Janet. "That accursed treasurer—and Ibrahim's greatest rival for Suleiman's ear!"

"Read on, madame," begged Marian.

Janet continued.

Ibrahim was ordered to press straight on to Baghdad. Instead he turned into the mountains around Lake Van near Bitlis, and resecured the frontier posts. Then he pushed his troops across the mountains towards Tabriz where Prince Tahmasp reigns.

Janet nodded approvingly. "He thinks like Selim," she said.

However, messengers returning to the sultan said that the Ibrahim had gone mad with power, and claimed he alone won the victories which the Ottoman sultan could no longer achieve. They even showed Suleiman an order signed by Ibrahim as 'Serasker Sultan.' Khurrem showed it to me, and I marveled that Ibrahim should be so bold. She is quite pleased with me, and I am in her favor. It seems to be important to her that I am her friend. I think she feels that because you and I were such confidantes, I give her a measure of respectability. Cyra Hafise may be dead for over a year, but Khurrem is still afraid of her.

The signature, by the way, was an excellent forgery. I never realized how truly talented Iskander Chelebi really was. Such reports, however false, distressed the sultan, and he left Khurrem to join Ibrahim.

Baghdad is again secure, and Iskander Chelebi, having been caught skimming off monies from the army supplies fund and dealing secretly with the Persians to defeat our sultan, has been executed. Not, however, before trying to implicate Ibrahim. He claims they were in the scheme together and also that Ibrahim bought assassins to kill Suleiman. Had Ibrahim and Suleiman not been practically raised together—. Nevertheless I fear for the vizier.

I have warned him through your daughter, his wife, but his ego will not allow him to take Khurrem seriously. This could be a tragic mistake in view of something I have heard.

The slavegirl who tends Khurrem's hair is a jewess. When I found this out, I begged Khurrem's permission to buy the girl's freedom. She allowed it on the condition that the girl personally train another slavegirl in her technique of hairdressing. Sarai, for that is the girl's name, is doing so. However, she is very grateful to me for obtaining her freedom and giving her a position in my house.

Recently she told me Khurrem has boasted openly

that the sultan is going to marry her. I have heard nothing of this though I've increased my visits to the Eski Serai. It is, of course, absurd! And now, dear lady, before I close I ask you to remember me to my good friend Marian, and her daughter, Ruth. May your God keep you all safe.

I am your faithful friend,
Esther Kira.

The three women sat silently for a few minutes. Then Janet burst into a string of oaths. When she had finished she stood up, shook her skirts, and asked, "Has the messenger from the Kiras begun his return journey yet?"

"Nay," replied a white-faced Ruth.

"He isna to leave until I have written a message which he will carry to Edinburgh for me. In fact since it is late, he is to stay the night and start out at first light. This will gie me time to compose something sensible. Go and tell him, Ruth."

"Yes, m'lady," said Ruth slipping from the room.

Janet began pacing the room. "How could a son of mine and my lord Selim's be such a soft fool? Charles only spent six years of his life in Turkey, and yet when I told him of Khurrem's treachery towards me, he said he would hae bowstringed her! He is more the Grand Turk than his father's firstborn. No Ottoman since Osman has formally married a wife. He shames the memory of all the women who hae borne Ottoman heirs, including me, Firousi, Sarina and Zuleika! I will not allow it! That she dared to even hint at such a thing! God curse the day I saw her sewing in my daughter's house and rescued her from certain obscurity!"

"There is nothing you can do, my lady. The kadin Khurrem now has the upper hand," said Marian harshly. "You are dead in Ottoman Turkey."

"Not while there is a breath in my body," said Janet fiercely. "Bring me paper and ink at once! Then leave me to write my letter. No one is to come in here until I've finished, and I call. No one! Should my lord Hay arrive you are to tell him I see no one, even him, till this is finished. If he attempts to gain entry, call out the guard!"

"Yes, madame," said Marian setting the writing case in her lady's hands.

The door closed behind her, and for several minutes Janet sat quietly gazing at the paper before her. Then she picked up the sharpened quill, and began.

My dear Esther,
Your letter has distressed me greatly as you have undoubtedly judged by the speed of my reply. I am enclosing a separate message for my son, which I ask you to read before delivering.

I set you a hard task, my friend. To obtain a totally private moment with my protocol-proud son. I am sending some small gifts peculiar to our country which you may tell him come from Lord Leslie, the Scots envoy who visited him last year. I shall, when this matter is settled, write more fully about my own life. So you and my sisters do not fret, however, I tell you that I am well, in fact, thriving.

I also have happy news. Dearest Ruth was married in early January to my own captain of the guards, and is already expecting a child to be born in mid-autumn. I close now safe in the knowledge that you will not fail me.

CH, Sultan Valideh.

Janet laid her message to Esther Kira aside, and taking up a second sheet of parchment began a second letter.

My son,
Word has reached me that Khurrem boasts openly in the harem that you will marry her. Should this be true, and I cannot believe it, I tell you that I forbid it! How dare you shame the memory of Cyra Hafise?! And that of every kadin who has borne her lord a son, including poor Gulbehar, who is mother to your own heir, Mustafa. Or is he to be set aside when you do this terrible thing? No sultan since Osman has found it necessary to formalize his relationship with a woman. Perhaps you have forgotten that in my great love for you I allowed you to keep a woman who twice tried to poison me; and then I departed from your life so there might be peace in your

house. I have given up everything for you. My name.
My final resting place beside your father. My home,
my friends, my children, my grandchildren. And my
position. I expected no reward for my great sacrifice,
but to be shamed in such a manner is more than I
can bear. If you do this foolish thing, my death will
be on your conscience.
        CH, Sultan Valideh.

Reading over the letters, Janet smiled, and sealing
first with her tugra the missive to Suleiman, she placed it
inside the message to Esther Kira, and sealed that with
the Leslie seal. Taking a third sheet of parchment, she
wrote to the head of the House of Kira in Edinburgh.

This message is to go by the absolute fastest route
possible. It is imperative it reach Istanbul quickly.
My personal thanks to Aaron Kira for his efforts on
my behalf.
        Janet Leslie.

"Marian, come to me!"
The door opened.
"Has the messenger been fed?"
"Aye, madame."
"His horse properly cared for?"
"Aye, madame."
"Bring him to me."
"At once, madame."
A few minutes later a young boy knelt before her. His
hair was black, his eyes dark and luminous.
"Your name, lad?"
"Aaron Kira, my lady."
"Ye are Esther's nephew? Yes! I see the family resem-
blance now. I dinna think ye so young. Ye hae done me
a great service, laddie, and I am going to ask ye do me
another. At first light ye will come and receive from me
an important message packet that must go back to Edinburgh. Ye must ride like the wind, Aaron Kira, for there
is no time to be lost. Ye will be told the posting places ye
may change horses at by my captain, Hugh More-Leslie."
The boy looked up at her, his eyes shining. "I will
reach Edinburgh before the wind, my lady."

She laughed. "How old are ye, Aaron Kira?"

"Fourteen, my lady."

"I thought so. Once I had four sons, and as I remember fourteen is a wonderfully confident age."

"Where are your sons now?" asked the boy.

"Two are dead, and one lives here wi' me."

"And the fourth?"

"He is very far away, laddie." She gently patted his head. "Off wi' ye, boy. If you ride for the Lady of Sithean at dawn, ye must be well rested. Be sure cook feeds ye before ye go, and gies ye something for the road. Here are some coins which will buy ye whatever else ye need."

He caught her hand, and pressing it to his forehead Eastern fashion backed from the room.

"Esther would be so proud of him, wouldn't she, Marian?"

"Aye. He's a fine lad. Och! I'm forgetting! Lord Hay is here. I've put him in the small dining room wi' some supper before him."

"Good. Go and see if he's through. Then ye may go to bed. See that the Kira boy is fed and given food for his journey in the morning. Have Hugh tell him posting stations tonight and see Aaron is brought to me at dawn."

"What have ye written to my lord Suleiman?"

"That I forbid any formality between him and Khurrem."

"Will he listen?"

"I pray to God he will!"

"I also. Good night, madame."

"Good night, Marian."

45

THE KING was coming to Sithean. He had sent word that he would return to Edinburgh from his highland progress via the Leslie lands. Anne was furious he was not staying at Glenkirk.

"Undoubtedly the countess's reputation as a hostess has been bruited about to his majesty," laughed Lord Hay.

"Possibly," said Janet, "but I rather fancy our Jamie comes to see me. He made me a very flattering offer when we met at court. A lusty cock is our wee king!"

"He's also a rapacious little bastard when it comes to money," said Colin. "His greed is unbelievable. He adds to his wealth by seizure and forfeiture of his nobles' lands. His lust for money is like his English grandfather's, Henry VII. He's already ruined the earls of Bothwell, Morton, and Crawford, as well as others I could name. The Douglases have suffered worse, though they deserve it. I pity our Jamie should war break out. He's made so many enemies among his own, that there would be none to fight for him."

"Would you, my lord?"

"Only if the country were invaded. Unlike the more prominent members of my family, I hae no wish to be involved wi' the Stewarts."

Janet smiled. "Neither do I, my love. I simply wish to live quietly in my own little world."

"If that be the case, sweetheart, ye hae best not let Jamie guess at yer wealth, or ye'll be back in yer tower at Glenkirk under the vigilant eye of my lady Anne."

"Come to bed, my lord." She shrugged her robe off and stood facing him, her lovely breasts full and pointed in the firelight.

"Jesu, if Jamie could see what I see, my head wouldna
be long on my shoulders!"

"Flatterer!" She climbed into their bed, and he joined
her. "Remind me to pick a pretty bunch of extra housemaids tomorrow so his majesty may be diverted. Hae ye
anything nice on yer estate?"

"My dear, I couldna tell ye. The one condition ye made
to becoming my mistress was that I shouldha no other
women. I value ye too highly to jeopardize our arrange-
ment."

"Why, Colly, I'm touched; however, I simply said I
didna want ye sleeping wi' another woman. Ye may look
all ye like."

His eyes twinkled. "In that case Gilbert tells me that
there are two girls, sisters I believe, who are worthy of
mention. I'll have them sent over."

James V, king of Scotland and the Isles, arrived at
Sithean on the fifteenth of November. It had been a long
and warm autumn, and the trees were still full with their
gold and scarlet leaves, a fitting frame for the small gray
stone castle, set on its green island, in the little blue loch.
The lady of Sithean greeted her liege, who was accompanied only by Lord Gordon, the earl of Huntley, and half
a dozen retainers. Noting Janet's astonishment at the small
size of his party, the king smiled and said, "I dinna wish to
impose on yer hospitality, Lady Leslie. I hae sent the better part of my people on to Huntley's castle. Damned nui-
sance, anyhow!"

Janet laughed. "My lord the king is always welcome at
Sithean with or without his retinue. Come in now, my lord,
and I shall show ye my little home."

As they entered Janet explained that the castle was built
in the shape of an H and that her son, Charles and his family lived in this, the East Wing, and she lived in the West
Wing.

"I have put ye and Lord Gordon in the West Wing, sir.
I thought perhaps the children in the East Wing would disturb yer majesty."

"How many children, madame?"

"Well, there are my grandsons—Patrick, who's almost
three, and his brother, Charles, who's a year and a half.
Then there's my nephew's son, Wee Patrick, he's the same

age as little Charles, and his baby sister, Mary, who is but five months. And my daughter-in-law is breeding again, and my younger waiting woman's just been churched of her first child, a lovely boy." She paused for breath, and the king laughed.

"Faith, madame, ye present me a most domesticated picture."

Leading him into the main anteroom in the East Wing she presented the king and Huntley to Adam, Anne, Ian, Jane, Charles, and Fiona.

"We hae," said the earl of Glenkirk, "arranged a hunt for ye tomorrow, sire. Stag!"

The young king was pleased, and his mellow mood lasted throughout the evening. Dinner was a simple family affair; tomorrow would be time enough for the neighboring gentry to descend on Sithean. Afterwards James was escorted to his apartments, and Lord Gordon to his. Janet had warned Colin to stay away during the two nights the king was at Sithean. Janet wanted no scandal in her house when the king was there.

It was therefore with some surprise that she noted her chamber door opening to admit the king. She sprang from her bed. "My liege! Is aught amiss?"

James smiled charmingly. "My bed is cold."

"But I assigned several pretty lasses to prepare yer majesty's rooms," she said severely.

"They dinna suit." His amber eyes flicked over her scantily clad body.

"I must again remind ye, my liege, that I am old enough to be yer mother."

"Yet ye lie wi' Lord Hay."

Surprised at his intelligence, she nevertheless coolly replied, "Lord Hay is my contemporary."

"Is it the same as when ye were young?"

She swallowed hard. "Aye." Then catching his thought, she bit back her laughter.

"Then God's nightgown, madame! If ye lie wi' Lord Hay, and 'tis the same as it ever was, why will ye nae lie wi' me?"

"Because, sir, I am no wanton. I dinna lie wi' boys, and when I take a lover I prefer to do my own choosing."

"I never thought ye were the wanton, my dear. Ye keep telling me ye could be my mother, yet ye are not my

mother. From the moment I first saw ye at court seven
months ago, I wished to sleep wi' ye. Why do ye think I
broke my journey at Sithean? Now, madame, I have had
enough talk, and I am cold. Get into bed!"

She dared not disobey. Blowing out the bedside candle,
the king took Janet in his arms. Stripping the sheer robe off
her, James fondled her ripe breasts. Murmuring happily,
the king buried his face in her body. She lay quietly neither
encouraging, nor discouraging him. Forcing his knee between her legs he spread them wide, and mounting the
body beneath him, he thrust up her.

She tried very hard not to respond, but her body betrayed her, and she moved smoothly under him in perfect
rhythm. Sighing contentedly he sought his release, and
finding it, he rolled off her and immediately fell asleep.
There was nothing else for her to do but fall asleep also.
When she awoke the following morning, the king was gone
from her bed.

That morning after a mass celebrating the feast of Saint
Margaret, they hunted stag in the hills around the loch.
The king behaved courteously towards her as he had pre-
viously. That night she gave a banquet for the neighboring
families of rank. Lord Hay was among them. Afterwards
there was dancing, and leading her through a figure Colin
asked, "Tonight?"

"Nay, hinny! He goes tomorrow. Tomorrow night, my
love!"

And after all was quiet that night James appeared again
in her rooms, took his pleasure, and slept. Janet didn't
know whether to be glad or sad that she had forbade Lord
Hay to visit. The following morning the king took her a
final time, and then departed.

As they stood in the main hall of the East Wing, James
smiled and said, "Lady Leslie. Ye hae given forty years of
yer life, and more, to Scotland. I canna let such devotion go
unrewarded. Sithean is far too lovely for a mere 'Sir'
Charles Leslie. I am therefore creating yer son earl of
Sithean, and ye madame," his eyes twinkled at her, "will
be known as the dowager countess of Sithean."

Kneeling, she kissed his hand. "My lord, once again ye
hae rendered me speechless."

He nodded graciously and raising her up said softly,
"Were I ten years older, the master of Grayhaven would

nae have a chance!" In a louder voice, "Farewell, madame! We hope to see ye at court again some day."

After the king had left, Janet went to her own apartments and indulged herself in a long and lovely bath in her
Turkish bathroom. Lying on the marble bathbench, the
steam hissing on the stones, she thought how fortunate it
was that she was not of childbearing age. Then she thought
of her warning to Lord Hay concerning other women. Suddenly the incongruity of the situation hit her, and she began to laugh.

Dearest Colly, she thought. I shall nae tell ye of the two
nights James Stewart spent in my bed. Not only would it
hurt ye, my love, but ye'de nae believe that despite the fact
the Stewarts have a reputation for being supurb lovers, our
Jamie performs in a rather dull and perfunctory manner.

When Lord Hay arrived that night, his mistress greeted
him affectionately.

"Were ye ten years younger, sweetheart, I might suspect
ye. What on earth did ye do to get Charles an earldom?"

"Spent forty years in a Turkish harem," she laughed.

"Witch!" He tumbled her onto the bed and kissed her
soundly.

"His majesty said that I had given forty years to my
country. I suppose he meant that had his father not sent
mine as his ambassador to San Lorenzo, I should have remained home and not been kidnapped and sold as a slave.
When ye think of it, Colly, the royal Stewarts did owe me
something."

"Were they bad, those years away, my hinny?"

"No, Colly. There wasna a bad year in all the forty, except when my husband died. And that, my love, is all I'll
say about it."

The following morning the weather turned from unusually warm, to wet and cold. Within a few days the colorful
trees were stripped bare. Janet organized an expedition of
children from the village to go nutting, for she suspected it
would be another long and cold winter. She was a good
liegelady and took care of her people. The barns at the
castle were full with provisions—wheat, rye, and oat flours;
salted and smoked meats and fish; edible roots and apples;
sugar; and dried peaches, pears, plums and raisins. Days
had been set aside in season for the village women to make
their preserves, comfits, cordials and soaps. Those who

went without did so due to their own laziness. No one, however, on Sithean lands would go hungry. The food would be given as needed monthly. Milk was given daily, and each family owned several chickens thanks to their lady's generosity.

The countess of Glenkirk remonstrated with her husband's sister, the dowager countess of Sithean, for what she called "foolish wastefulness." Janet laughed to herself. Anne was like so many of the old nobles. She did not understand that well-fed, decently housed, and clothed peasants worked better than half-starved, half-frozen wretches. Hunger and cold bred despair, rebellion, and physical weakness that was called laziness by both the church and the rich. Janet had no patience with this kind of attitude but kept silent and went her own way. If her family grew rich, it was because of her clever management and her policy of putting out her own effort as example to the peasants, a lesson she had learned from the Ottoman.

At New Year's, Lord Hay presented his mistress with a heavy gold ring set with rubies and a golden brown velvet cloak lined in dark brown sable. On Candlemas he became a grandfather for the first time when his eldest son's wife bore a son to be called James. On March sixth Janet became a grandmother for the twelfth time when Fiona presented Charles with a third son, Andrew.

In mid-spring word came at last from Istanbul. Young Aaron Kira had personally taken Janet's message, going a shorter, albeit more dangerous way. Normally one would sail from Leith down into the English Channel, across the Bay of Biscay, through the straits of Gibraltar into the Mediterranean. The ship would then sail through the Mediterranean, the Aegean, the Dardanelles, the Sea of Marmora, and into the Bosporus to Istanbul.

Instead this brave and resourceful youth had shipped out on a Kira-owned vessel for the Baltic port of Hamburg. In Hamburg he had bought a smaller boat and recruited some half a dozen young and adventurous Germanic Kira cousins to help him. They had sailed along the Baltic coast to the mouth of the Vistula River and then up the Vistula to its headwaters. Here he left five of the boys and the boat awaiting his return, taking only one cousin, Moishe. Buying horses in a nearby Cossack village, the boys rode to

Gran. They were now safe in Suleiman's empire, and here the Kiras had a network of posting houses to supply horses to their messengers. Within a few short weeks Aaron Kira and his wide-eyed cousin arrived safely in Istanbul.

Esther was astounded to see her nephew so soon, but when she read Janet's message she understood. Enlisting the aid of Janet's dearest friend, Firousi, she waited until she knew—thanks to her own spies—that Khurrem Kadin would be unavailable to Suleiman. The sultan was then invited to his aunt's for a family evening, to see his half-sister and their children. Unsuspecting he went and after a time was discreetly hustled into a private room by Firousi. There he found Esther Kira who made him obeisance, and then without speaking a word handed him the letter. He broke the seal, little knowing that Esther, at his mother's command, had already read the letter, and resealed it. She watched as his face went from white to red, then white again.

"I must destroy the letter when you are sure you're through, my lord sultan."

"Why?"

"Because the sultan valideh Cyra Hafise is dead, my lord."

"Do you know what is in this letter, Esther?"

"Yes, my lord Suleiman. Your mother wrote me, also."

"I have already married Khurrem."

"I know, my lord."

He didn't seem surprised. Esther Kira, like his mother, had her ways of knowing things. "What shall I do, Esther? If mother heard rumors that I might marry Khurrem what will happen when she knows I have?"

"You married Khurrem in secret, my lord. Divorce her the same way."

"Two months ago I stood before an old mufti and wed with her. The old man died shortly afterwards. There are no witnesses to our marriage. I cannot divorce her without a witness."

"I will be your witness, my lord. If I stand behind a curtain she need not know who it is; yet I can write your mother with truth."

"Khurrem will be so angry with me, Esther. She has nagged and nagged at me for months to marry her."

"Of course she will be angry, my lord. You should not have given in to her. If she complains, you must remember you are sultan! Besides, would you raise her above your mother?"

Several days later Sultan Suleiman, known in the Christian West as "the Magnificent," stood in a hidden kiosk deep within the gardens of the Eski Serai and said to his wife of just two months, "I divorce thee. I divorce thee. I divorce thee."

For a moment she stared horrified at him, then laughed. "My lord, you must not frighten me again that way."

"It is no game, Khurrem. I have divorced you."

"You cannot without a witness!" she gasped.

"There was one. Behind the tapestry, now gone through the door back there. If need be, this witness can be brought forth."

"Why, my lord? Why? I thought you loved me!"

"I do, my dove, but I cannot raise you above my mother, the late valideh."

"Sultan Selim never loved your mother as you love me! He could not have! He had four kadins, and god knows how many other concubines."

"My father held my mother above all women, and not simply because she gave him four sons. Zuleika gave him as many. He recognized her greatness as I did. I married you to stop your nagging. I divorce you because I have come to my senses. If you speak one more word to me on the subject, woman, I will have you sewn into a sack and dropped into the sea! Get down on your knees and thank Allah that I have made you my second kadin!"

Suleiman then stormed from the kiosk leaving a very frightened Khurrem. He was usually so manageable. The only time he ever showed any spunk towards her had been after his mother, Allah curse her, had spoken with him. Now the old bitch reached out from the grave to her! Perhaps Suleiman had some spine after all. Khurrem shrugged her shoulders. You could live with a man for years and not really know him. Oh well, she would simply be more careful in the future. Besides, Suleiman had been kind enough to divorce her privately. The rumors were thick that they had married. She had seen to that. Who need ever know that they were not married? The witness, whoever it was, would say nothing unless called upon by the sultan. She was safe, and no one would ever know the truth.

That very day Aaron Kira and his cousin, Moishe, began their return journey to the headwaters of the Vistula, to Hamburg, to Scotland, to Sithean.

46

The year 1536 was an eventful one for Janet.

On April 5th, Ruth was delivered of her second son, Hugh. Marian was ecstatic. "I never thought to see one grandchild, let alone two," she chortled.

Three months later, Lady Leslie received tragic news. It was brought to her by David Kira, Esther's brother who had helped Janet's son, Charles, to flee Ottoman Turkey many years ago. From the moment he entered her presence, she knew the news was bad. Her heart began to pound violently. She attempted to observe the polite amenities, but seeing her white face David Kira spoke out.

"Not the sultan, my lady. It is Ibrahim."

Visibly relieved, she asked, "Dead?"

"Yes."

"How?"

"They say the sultan ordered it."

"Never! Never! He has always been too soft to take a life—especially of one whom he loves."

"It is publicly said he ordered it. It must be said to save the dignity of the throne. The truth is too terrible. The sultan had been ill with a bad cold. He had asked Ibrahim, as he often did, to join him for supper. Afterwards Ibrahim slept in the anteroom outside the sultan's bedchamber, as he had done many times. Khurrem joined her lord that night and according to my information drugged him so that he slept heavily. She then took Sultan Suleiman's seal ring with his personal tugra and filling in the name of Ibrahim Pasha on an execution order, signed it with the seal. Sending it to the executioners she returned to her own apartments. The next morning the grand vizier's body was found thrown outside the doors of the Divan. He must have put up a terrible struggle, for the sultan's anteroom was covered in blood."

Janet's face was like stone. Finally she spoke. "My daughter and her children?"

"Safe, and they will continue to be so. My informant overheard the sultan warn the second kadin that he could follow in the footsteps of his grandfather, Sultan Bajazet, if she so much as glances in the direction of Nilufer Sultan, or her children."

Janet smiled grimly, remembering how Selim's father had strangled his second kadin, Besma, after she attempted the murder of Selim's four kadins and their children. She looked up at David Kira. Her eyes were green-gold ice.

"Can Khurrem be poisoned?"

"Impossible, madame. She touches nothing, not even a sweetmeat unless someone else tastes it first. She keeps a special guard of both black and white eunuchs about her and rarely leaves the palace. It's impossible to assassinate her."

"Jesu! Jesu! My lord's aunt warned me that I clung in my heart to my Western Christian ethics. I should have killed Khurrem when I had the chance, instead of leaving her to destroy the empire and my son. Only Mustafa stands between her and her goal. David! Esther is to warn my my oldest grandson! He is to be protected at all costs. The thought of Khurrem's spoiled, weak oldest son following Suleiman is too horrifying. Esther is also to tell my son, Suleiman, for I dinna trust myself to write him again, that should anything else of this nature happen, I shall return from the dead claiming that Khurrem faked my death and had me imprisoned. There are more who would rejoice to see Cyra Hafise alive than the Khurrem imagines."

David Kira did his duty. For the time being the world heard no more scandal from the Ottoman Empire, and Janet was able to once again settle into her new life.

In October, Adam's fifth grandchild, Ian and Jane's second son, James, was born. Janet's woolen business thrived. At Christmas Gilbert Hay was finally married to Alice Gordon.

In May of 1538 the King James took a second wife, a wealthy and noble French widow, Marie of Guise-Lorraine. All Scotland rejoiced, for his first wife had died two years earlier, after a marriage of only six months.

Ruth's first daughter was born several days after the wedding. She was baptized Marie, but called Molly. Gilbert Hay's wife produced young Gilbert, nine months and three days to her marriage day. Charles' and Fiona's fourth son, David, arrived November first. Proud of her sons, Fiona nevertheless wished for a daughter.

"Like you," she smiled at her mother-in-law, "another Janet."

The dowager countess of Sithean laughed. She was flattered, pleased, and secretly feeling very smug because of her latest letter from Esther Kira. Suleiman's fleet under Khair ad-Din had scored a great victory at Prevesa. The Holy Roman Emperor, Charles; the doge of Venice, and the pope himself had thrown their combined fleets at Suleiman—and lost! Venice was destroyed as a sea power and ended up paying the Turks for the privilege of being beaten by them. It cost three hundred thousand gold ducats. The old doge died of shame and grief. Despite the propaganda hurriedly manufactured by Christian Europe, the plain truth was that from the Straits of Gibraltar in the West, to Famagusta in the East, the Mediterranean was an Ottoman lake.

"How can you be so pleased?" asked Maria.

"Why should I care what happens to the Germans and the Italians?" snapped Janet. "You know what they did in Tunis. The good Christian knights were so kind to the populace of the city that mothers with infants and children in their arms threw themselves from the walls of the town rather than submit to further savagery!"

The following year, 1539, there was some small rebellion in the north of Scotland initiated by a chieftain on the Isle of Skye. It broke the peace that had been kept for years in the highlands. None of this affected the peoples of Sithean and Glenkirk, however, who seemed to be living in an almost perfect, bucolic existence. There was no war, and those families not caught up in the royal circle and its court politics, managed to live fairly sane lives.

Ian Leslie's third son, Donald, was born and Gilbert Hay's wife produced a second son, Francis, and Queen Marie bore Scotland another James. In 1540 James Hay's wife bore another son, Ewan; Ruth had her second daughter, Flora; and Fiona got her daughter at long last—duly baptized Janet Mary after her grandmother, but called

Heather because of the heathery blue color of her eyes.

Several weeks after her longed-for daughter's birth, Fiona contracted milk fever. A doctor was sent for from Edinburgh. Too many children in too few years was his verdict. He could do nothing, and a few days later, Fiona died.

Janet couldn't believe it. Sweet Fiona who had been more a daughter to her than her own daughter.

Charles Leslie was devastated. He and his wife had known each other since childhood, but had been married less than nine years. He could not imagine life without his Fiona, and he had to be physically restrained from harming his aunt, the countess of Glenkirk, who briskly told him, a week after the funeral, that the best thing for him to do would be remarry at once. His children needed a mother, she said. With his title and the money coming to him one day from his mother, he could probably get himself a passable heiress. Charles damned her and her passable heiress to hell and stormed out of the castle.

"For God's sake, Anne!" Janet exclaimed. "Fiona's scarce been buried a week! In time the pain will recede and possibly Charles will remarry, but now we must give him time to purge his grief."

"He'd best do it quick! Those four unruly boys of his need discipline. Fiona was much too soft. And what of the new baby? What kind of female will she grow up to be in this masculine household without the example of a good woman?"

Janet raised an eyebrow. "And what am I, dear sister?"

"You can't mean you intend to raise those children yourself?"

"Until Charles remarries, why not?"

"Why not? Why not? You're an old woman, that's why not! You'll be sixty at the end of this year!"

"I am younger at fifty-nine, my dear, than you are at fifty-two! What is age, Anne? It is but the passing of time. It is how you feel, and I feel magnificent!"

Anne Leslie threw up her hands in exasperation and stamped back to her own home. Janet Leslie's mocking laughter followed her.

Janet was feeling far from brave. Dear God help me, she prayed to herself. To have this responsibility now. I have spent my life in service to others raising five children

of my own, running various palaces, and finally for a time
a government. These last few years I have been free for
the first time in my life; and, oh, dear God, how I have enjoyed it! However, she knew that there was no one else,
and she could not disappoint either her grieving son or her
grandchildren.

They were so young to be motherless, but at least Patrick who was eight, little Charles who had just celebrated
his seventh year, and Andrew who was five, would have
memories of their lovely mother. David at eighteen months
and baby Heather would not. It was sad.

Lord Hay, quietly coming in, put a reassuring arm about
her. "Ye'll manage, sweetheart."

"Ah, Colly! I must be getting old." A tear slid down her
cheek.

"You?" He laughed. "Never, my darling! If ye live to be
a hundred, ye'll nae be old! Never!" Folding her in his
arms the big, bluff earl, his dark hair finally showing silver
gray, comforted her. "Yer deep in a fit of the glooms,
hinny. Do ye think I don't know how ye loved Fiona?" He
stroked her lovely hair. "It will pass. It will pass. Right
now the important thing is to help the children. How confused they must be wi'out Fiona."

Safe in her lover's arms Janet cried for the first time
since Fiona's death. Great wracking sobs shook her body,
and the sound of her weeping filled the chamber. Her grief
gradually eased, and she buried her swollen face in Lord
Hay's chest.

"I must look a sight," she murmured.

"I have never seen ye look lovelier, my dear," he said
raising her face up. "Marry me, Jan"

"Really, Colly! I am in mourning."

"I dinna believe it!" he returned.

"What?"

"Do ye realize this is the first time in seven years ye
haven't given me an outright No?"

She gave a watery chuckle. "It's my weakened condition."

"Never, madame! I will wager ye have never been in a
weakened condition."

The outburst had done her good. Leaving her son,
Charles, to his grief, she began to reorganize the household
and the children. One thing she refused to give up, how-

ever, was her privacy. She did not move into the East Wing
of the castle, but the doors between the two wings were
now always open.

Each of the younger children had a nursemaid
of its own and lived in the communal nursery. Patrick and
little Charles had been given at age six their own quarters
and a tutor to oversee them. The older boys took their main
meal at mid-day with their grandmother, and when he was
there, their father.

The earl of Sithean, was, however, rarely at home now.
He had gone to court and offered his services to the king.
At the moment those services consisted of merely being
charming, witty, and gay. Charles complied with good
will. Anything to forget Fiona and the four sons who only
reminded him of her. He refused to acknowledge his
daughter. After all, had she not been responsible for her
mother's death? Once he brought home a Lady Diana
Fergusson.

"Do ye intend to marry her?" asked Janet.

"Of course not," he replied carelessly. "She's my latest
leman."

"Then take your high-bred whore and leave my house,"
she commanded. "Because you're hurt, I'll not allow you
to hurt the children. They're just beginning to recover."

He drew himself up proudly, and for the barest moment
she was reminded of Selim. "I remind you, madame, that I
am the earl of Sithean."

"True," she agreed, "but Sithean belongs to me,
Charles. And I might remind you that you are the earl of
Sithean because of me. Don't you ever wonder how you
came by yer title?"

"The king said ye gave forty years of yer life for Scotland."

"My God, Charles! The king couldn't care less that I
spent forty years out of Scotland. What mattered to Jamie
was that he spent two nights in my bed! I did not solicit his
attention, of course. I simply cooperated rather than cry
rape when he entered my bed." She laughed at the look on
his face. "Take Lady Fergusson back to Edinburgh,
Charles. I dinna care who ye sleep with, my son, but if ye
must bring yer whore home, do bring one who's not so
obvious."

Charles laughed in spite of himself. "By God, mother!

There's no one like you! Shall I take yer love to the king?"

"No, but take my prayers to him and his queen. To lose one child is terrible, but to have lost both their little princes —ah well, they're both young. There'll be plenty of time for other children. Be grateful for yer own, Charles. What has happened has happened. Dinna hold Heather and the boys responsible. Fiona wanted them, especially yer daughter who looks just like her."

Charles returned to court, and through him the dowager countess of Sithean heard all the news that led her to believe a war would soon touch Scotland. However, before the year's end another personal tragedy had touched the Leslies. Anne, countess of Glenkirk, took a chill in a September rain and died suddenly. Janet and Anne had certainly never been friends, but her sister-in-law's sudden death forced her to face the possibility of her own demise.

In 1542 there were religious rumblings throughout Scotland. A passion for reformation was sweeping the land. King James had declared for Rome and the "auld alliance" with the French. Henry of England, however, had boldly gained independence of the papacy and eagerly sought an understanding with his nephew of Scotland. They had planned a meeting at York, and Henry, arriving at the appointed time was furious to find that his nephew would not be there after all. The Scots privy council had refused to let their king join his uncle because of rumors of a possible abduction. Actually the queen, and the churchmen on James' council were fearful that Henry would convince his nephew to follow his example regarding Rome. It would have been better if the queen and the nervous priests had remembered that England was closer than Rome.

Henry was feeling particularly mean as the New Year began. His fifth queen, Catherine Howard, the "Rose without a thorn," had been proven an adulteress, and been beheaded on Tower Green. Lonely, ill, and disillusioned, Henry sought solace in a war. Once winter loosed its hold, the northern levies were called up, and under the leadership of Sir Robert Bowes, crossed over the border into Teviotdale. They were roundly defeated by Lord Gordon, Jamie's faithful earl of Huntley.

Next into the fray jumped the duke of Norfolk, anxious to get back on Henry's good side since both his nieces, Anne Boleyn, and Catherine Howard, had the unpleasant distinction of being the only two of Henry's queens to be beheaded. He was more successful putting Roxburgh, Kelso, and some smaller towns to the torch. Henry then pulled out the old English chestnut of suzerainty over Scotland, and James was forced to fight.

James mustered a force, kissed his again-pregnant queen good-bye, and marched off. He got as far as Fala Moor, and there his nobles refused to go any further. Without them he had no army, and they would not, they said, spill Scots blood for France, which was what it all boiled down to in the end. They disbanded, but three weeks later on November twenty-first James marched out of Edinburgh at the head of ten thousand men recruited with the help of Cardinal Beaton, and the earl of Moray—the other James Stewart.

With the king, and leading a combined force of men, rode Charles, his uncle Adam, his cousins, Ian and Hugh. Their neighbors, James and Gilbert Hay, rode with them. The master of Grayhaven had been ill, and left behind at Sithean. Colin had angrily protested, but Janet, having a premonition, drugged his wine, and he slept for two days.

It was for naught. Awaking early on the morning of the twenty-third of November, Colin Hay crept softly from Janet's bed, dressed himself warmly, slipped into the stables, saddled his horse, and left Sithean to join the others.

He reached the battlefield in time to help Red Hugh, and what remained of the Leslie-Hay contingent collect the bodies of their dead. Both families had escaped the tragedy of Flodden, but they did not escape Solway Moss. Among the dead were Adam Leslie, earl of Glenkirk. His son and heir, Ian. His nephew, Charles Leslie, the Earl of Sithean. James Hay, heir to Grayhaven. His brother, Gilbert. And close to two hundred young men and boys from the three estates. The remaining men were able, by commandeering wagons, to transport the bodies back to Glenkirk, Sithean and Grayhaven.

Epilogue—August 1566

PATRICK LESLIE, fourth earl of Glenkirk, came in from the sunny warmth of a summer's afternoon and descended to the cool, damp burial vault of the Leslies, located behind and below the altar in the family chapel. A dozen vigil lamps glowed softly.

Sitting quietly on the marble bench that had been placed for prayer and meditation, he gazed at the plaques that marked each tomb. All the plaques but one were marked simply with the occupant's name and birth and death dates.

There was his great-grandfather Patrick, the first earl, for whom he was named. He had died peacefully in his bed at the age of eighty. The earl could barely remember him —a tall, grizzled old man with thick white hair and a deep voice. Near him rested his wife, Agnes Cummings.

His grandfather Adam, his father, Ian, and his great-aunt Janet's son Charles, all of whom had died at the battle of Solway Moss in 1542, were next. Each lay beside his wife. His grandmother Anne MacDonald and the tiny tomb of her oldest son, who had died at the age of three. Fiona Abernethy, Charles's wife, dead in childbed of her fifth child. The earl's own mother, Jane Dundas, who upon hearing the news from Solway Moss fell dead in the courtyard of the castle, leaving five orphaned children.

Along with Charles's children, they had been raised by their great-aunt Janet Leslie. His heart swelled with love at the memory of her. She had been sixty-two then—a venerable age—but it hadn't stopped her. Shouting down some distant cousins who had appeared in an attempt to take over both sets of children and the Leslie goods and chattels, she had taken immediate charge.

Stunned at the loss of both his parents, the nine-year-old earl had wanted to cry. Softly but sternly, she had warned

him that a peer of the realm, no matter how young, did not
weep publicly. Later that night he had privately sobbed
his heart out in her loving arms.

She and she alone had been responsible for the happiness of them all. His sisters and his female cousins had all
been married to fine, loving, wealthy men. His brothers
and his male Leslie cousins, Aunt Janet's grandchildren,
had settled down with good livings.

The one memory that would remain with him as long as
he lived was the fact that she had never seemed to grow
old. For as long as he could remember, her hair had been
a soft peach color, and her wonderful eyes a green-gold.
He knew from a portrait of her that hung in the Great Hall,
painted when she had been betrothed at the age of thirteen, that her hair had once been the same red-gold as his.

"Bless you, Cyra," he was startled to hear his voice say.
Then he laughed. No one had heard him; and even if they
had, they would not have understood that Patrick, fourth
earl of Glenkirk, knew the wonderful secret of his aunt's
past.

Slowly he withdrew the letter from his doublet—a letter
from Esther Kira to his great-aunt. Their letters had obviously crossed in passage—his to Esther, telling her of
Cyra's death, and Esther's to Cyra, telling of the death of
Sultan Suleiman on April 14, 1566.

In the years to come, those who read her epitaph, "Born
a Scot, she died a Scot," would think her a poor, sad spin-
ster. They could never even begin to imagine those fantastic years between her birth and her death. As the irony
struck him, his laughter echoed strangely in the silent burial vault.

Wiping his eyes on his sleeve, he moved toward the
doorway. "Godspeed, Cyra," he said, and, ascending the
steps, Patrick Leslie walked back through the chapel and
out into the bright August afternoon.